CRIMSON PHOENIX

A CHAD LLOYD NOVEL

C. E. O'NEIL

GRIZZLY MOUNTAIN
PRESS

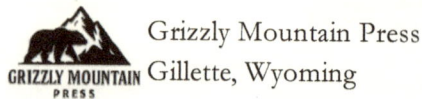
Grizzly Mountain Press
Gillette, Wyoming

This book is a work of fiction. Any references to historical events, real people, or real places are used fictitiously. Other names, characters, places, and events are products of the author's imagination. Any resemblance to actual events, locales, organizations or persons, living or dead, is entirely coincidental.

CRIMSON PHOENIX - A CHAD LLOYD NOVEL

ISBN: 979-8-9937829-0-4

Cover design by: Ali Abbas

FIRST EDITION

To Laura

My anchor and my compass. Your love gives me strength, your faith gives me courage, and your patience gives me the freedom to chase stories worth telling.

"If an injury has to be done to a man it should be so severe that his vengeance need not be feared."

— Niccolò Machiavelli

ACKNOWLEDGEMENTS

The completion of Crimson Phoenix would not have been possible without the unwavering support and invaluable contributions of several remarkable individuals.

First and foremost, I extend my deepest gratitude to my wife, Laura, whose steadfast encouragement and understanding sustained me throughout this journey. Her patience during the countless hours spent writing and her belief in this story never wavered, providing the foundation upon which this work was built.

I am profoundly grateful to my dedicated beta readers, whose insights and feedback proved instrumental in shaping this novel. Doug Whipple offered thoughtful critiques that challenged me to strengthen the narrative structure and character development. My aunt, Darlene Russo, provided not only her keen editorial eye but also the kind of familial support that reminded me why storytelling matters.

Their collective wisdom, honest assessments, and generous investment of time elevated this work far beyond what I could have achieved alone. Any remaining shortcomings are entirely my own.

To all of you, I offer my sincere appreciation.

Prologue

Culiacán, Sinaloa, Mexico
Two Years Ago

The silence before dawn carried the weight of impending violence. FBI Special Agent Chad Lloyd crouched behind a concrete drainage pipe fifty meters from Salvador Ramirez's compound, his HK416 locked and loaded, night vision painting the sprawling estate in ghostly green. Around him, five other FBI agents checked their gear one final time—suppressed weapons, breaching charges, flexicuffs, medical kits. Everything needed to take down the most feared cartel leader in the Western Hemisphere.

Professional. Well-funded. Deadly.

Exactly what Chad expected from two years of hunting this bastard.

"Alpha-Six, this is Bravo-Six." Chad's voice whispered through the tactical net, barely audible above the desert wind. "FBI team in position at primary breach point. Pattern of life confirms target is on-site. Black Suburban arrived twenty-three hundred hours, never left."

Across the compound's eastern approach, DEA Special Agent Antonio Baez led his own six-man team toward the secondary entrance. The joint FBI-DEA task force had spent months planning this raid, coordinating with Mexican authorities, building the intelligence package that would finally put Salvador Ramirez in an American prison cell.

"Roger, Bravo-Six." Baez's voice carried the slight accent of his El Paso upbringing and the steady calm of a man who'd kicked down doors across three countries chasing narco-traffickers. "DEA team ready at Alpha breach. Mexican Marines report positioned at checkpoint Charlie.

Local police have been... relocated."

Chad knew what that meant. The Sinaloa State Police had been pulled back fifteen kilometers under the pretense of "securing the outer perimeter." In reality, they'd been moved because half of them were on Ramirez's payroll. The other half were too terrified to function once the shooting started.

Only SEMAR—the Mexican Navy's elite Marines—could be trusted for this operation. Even then, Chad had caught the nervous exchanges between the Mexican commanders. The Ramirez cartel owned judges, generals, and politicians. They'd infiltrated police departments across six states. Their sicarios had turned entire Mexican cities into war zones when cornered. Their influence was growing more and more every day.

"Charlie-Actual, sitrep." Chad keyed his radio, addressing the Mexican Marine commander positioned two clicks south while scanning the compound's defensive positions through his night vision.

Static.

"Charlie-Actual, confirm your ready status," Baez pressed over the radio. "We're ninety seconds from green light."

More static. Dead air that stretched for nearly three minutes while Chad checked his watch in the darkness. Had the Marines been compromised? Attacked? Or something worse?

Finally, Colonel Mendoza's voice crackled through their earpieces, flat and emotionless: "Charlie-Actual. We've been ordered to withdraw. You're on your own, americanos."

The radio went silent.

Chad's jaw tightened as he watched the compound through his night vision. Twenty years of military and federal service had taught him to recognize the sound of an operation falling apart. He'd seen this dance before in Iraq and Afghanistan—local partners who suddenly realized they needed to be elsewhere when bullets started flying, backup that melted away the moment operations went kinetic. The kind of betrayal that turned routine operations into desperate survival scenarios. Whether it came from Washington bureaucrats or Mexico City generals, political interference always sounded the same.

"We've lost our window and our backup," Chad said quietly. "We go now or we lose him for another six months."

Chad and Baez studied the compound through their night vision, noting the subtle changes in guard positions. Unlike El Chapo's functional safe houses with their escape tunnels and modest facades, Salvador Ramirez had built a monument to his own arrogance. The sprawling estate screamed "drug lord" to anyone with eyes—white marble columns, gold-trimmed balconies, and manicured gardens that belonged in Architectural Digest rather than a cartel stronghold. Concrete walls topped with decorative iron spikes rather than razor wire. Hardened guard towers disguised as elegant gazebos at each corner.

"They've doubled the perimeter watch," Baez observed. "Two additional sentries on the east wall, and they've moved to overlapping fields of fire." He paused, calculating odds. "Twelve agents against fifteen-plus shooters in a hardened compound. No backup. No extraction support."

Armed sentries with body armor and military-grade weapons patrolled beneath crystal chandeliers visible through bulletproof floor-to-ceiling windows. Salvador had chosen intimidation over operational security, believing his reputation would protect him better than El Chapo's paranoid escape routes.

It was exactly the kind of tactical arrogance that got cartel leaders killed.

Chad had seen worse odds in Fallujah. "Your call, Tony. You've got two years invested in this case."

"Ramirez moves locations every three weeks. Next time we find him, he'll have twice the security and we'll still have the same political problems." Baez checked his MP5 one final time. "We don't get another shot at this."

Without Marine support, this had just become a straight gunfight between twelve federal agents and a fortress full of professional killers.

"Target of opportunity," Chad replied, sliding the selector switch on his rifle from safe to semi. "Primary is priority one."

The plan had been surgical: Marines provide outer security while joint FBI-DEA teams execute precision arrests. Clean. Documented. Politically defensible.

Now it would be warfare.

Chad switched his radio to channel two—the secure FBI-DEA frequency that excluded Mexican assets. "All units, this is Bravo-Six. Mexican support has been compromised. We're executing with current assets only. Rules of engagement remain in effect—positively identify targets, minimize civilian casualties, but anyone pointing a weapon in your direction is hostile."

He paused, watching armed figures moving through the compound below. "Salvador Ramirez has personally ordered the deaths of dozens of American law enforcement officers. His organization floods our streets with fentanyl that kills two hundred Americans every day. Today, that ends."

Chad's crosshairs settled on the main entrance where his team would breach. Behind the reinforced door, thermal imaging showed multiple heat signatures moving through the compound—guards conducting their pre-dawn patrol changes.

"Sinclair, you have eyes on the transformer?" Chad whispered into his radio.

"Affirmative, Bravo-Six. Power junction is two hundred meters south of your position. Ready to cut on your signal."

On the eastern approach, Baez's voice came through the tactical frequency: "Overwatch, confirm you have clean shots on tower sentries."

"Alpha-Six, Overwatch. Two tangos in north tower, one in south tower. All targets acquired."

"Green light in sixty seconds," Chad announced. "Sinclair, kill the lights on my mark. Overwatch, drop the towers on power cut. All units switch to NODs and prepare for breach."

Below in the compound, security cameras continued their mechanical sweeps, unaware that death waited in the shadows. The mansion's lights burned behind bulletproof glass, casting geometric shadows across manicured gardens. In moments, those lights would die, plunging Salvador Ramirez's fortress into the kind of darkness where American night vision technology ruled supreme.

"Mark," Chad whispered.

The compound went black as Sinclair severed the main power lines.

In the same instant, muzzle flashes flickered from the DEA sniper's position as suppressed rounds dropped the tower sentries. Emergency generators kicked in three seconds later, but only for critical systems—leaving most of the estate in tactical darkness that favored the hunters over the hunted.

"Towers clear," came the sniper's confirmation through their earpieces.

Seconds later, at exactly 0350 hours, Chad's and Baez's breaching charges detonated simultaneously. The main entrance and east doors blew off their hinges in perfect synchronization as twelve American federal agents stormed Salvador Ramirez's sanctuary from two directions with righteous fury and automatic weapons.

Two years of investigation. Months of intelligence gathering. Weeks of planning. All condensed into eighteen minutes of sustained combat.

The gunfight raged for eighteen brutal minutes across three floors of reinforced concrete and marble. Chad's tactical instincts saved lives twice—yanking Baez back from a blind corner just as automatic fire chewed through marble where his head had been, then hauling Agent Coleman to cover when the FBI man took a round through the shoulder. The cartel guards fought with professional discipline, using the mansion's marble columns and reinforced walls to create deadly crossfires that made every advance costly.

When the smoke finally cleared, Chad's ears rang from close-quarters battle in enclosed spaces. His tactical vest had caught two rounds—rifle plates doing their job—and a grazing shot across his left forearm that left his sleeve sticky with blood.

Around him, the aftermath of urban warfare painted the mansion in cordite and destruction. Bullet holes stitched across imported Italian marble. Shattered crystal from a chandelier that had cost more than most Americans made in a year now glittered like deadly snow across bloodstained Persian rugs. The metallic tang of blood and the acrid smell of spent gunpowder hung heavy in the air.

"Alpha-Six, Alpha-Six." Chad keyed his radio while stepping over the body of a cartel enforcer whose military tattoos marked him as former Mexican Special Forces. "Bravo team has secured lower level. What's your status?"

"Upper floors secure," came Baez's reply, slightly breathless. "Three KIA, two wounded and stabilized. Primary target location confirmed—master bedroom behind reinforced door, top floor. Moving to your position."

Chad checked his rifle—half a magazine remaining—and changed magazines. The compound felt different now. Quieter. The kind of silence that came after violence had decided everything.

He found Agent Martinez applying pressure bandages to Agent Coleman's shoulder wound in what had been an opulent living room. Persian rugs soaked with blood. A sixty-inch television with a bullet hole through its center, still flickering with Mexican telenovela reruns.

"How is he?" Chad asked.

"Through and through," Martinez replied, his medic training evident in the professional way he worked. "Clean entry and exit. He'll live to tell war stories."

Coleman managed a weak grin through the pain medication Martinez had administered. "Bastard came around the corner like he knew exactly where I'd be."

"They probably did," Chad said grimly. "Someone fed them our approach routes. This wasn't luck."

Heavy footsteps on marble stairs announced Baez's arrival. The DEA agent's face was grim, streaked with cordite residue and the thousand-yard stare of someone who'd just survived close-quarters combat.

"Final count?" Chad asked.

"Eleven cartel KIA, plus the two we took downstairs. No prisoners—they fought to the last man." Baez's voice carried professional respect for enemies who'd chosen death over capture. "But we've got a problem. Intelligence said Hector and Elena Ramirez were supposed to be here tonight. Their rooms are empty. Beds haven't been slept in. Looks like they've been gone for days."

Chad felt cold certainty settle in his gut. The secondary targets had escaped before the operation even began. Another intelligence failure that let the next generation of cartel leadership slip away.

"Primary target?" Chad asked, though he already knew the answer from Baez's expression.

"Barricaded in the master bedroom behind a reinforced steel door. He's armed and refusing surrender." Baez checked his watch. "We've been calling for him to come out for ten minutes. He's not interested in negotiating."

Chad charged his rifle, muscle memory making the action automatic despite the adrenaline crash setting in. Two years of investigation. Months of intelligence gathering. Weeks of planning. All compromised by corruption and betrayal.

But they still had Salvador Ramirez.

"Stack up," Chad ordered. "Let's finish this."

The master bedroom door was reinforced steel disguised as carved mahogany. Chad placed breaching charges while Baez and two other agents took positions. The blast that followed ripped the door from its frame and filled the hallway with smoke and debris.

Chad was first through the breach, his HK416 tracking across the room, night vision cutting through the haze. Baez followed immediately behind him, MP5 at the ready, both agents scanning for additional threats. The bedroom was a monument to narco-wealth—hand-carved furniture, silk tapestries, a bed that could sleep six people comfortably. But their attention focused on the figure behind the massive oak desk.

Salvador Ramirez sat in his leather chair, hands visible on the desktop, expensive silk pajamas torn by shrapnel, blood trickling from a scalp wound. The most feared cartel leader in the Western Hemisphere looked smaller in person—a sixty-year-old man with graying hair and the soft belly of someone who'd grown comfortable ordering death from behind bulletproof glass.

"Salvador Ramirez," Chad announced, his weapon steady despite the adrenaline coursing through his veins. "FBI. You're under arrest for conspiracy to distribute controlled substances, racketeering, and murder of federal officers."

Ramirez smiled, a cold expression that never reached his eyes. "Agent Lloyd, yes? You think this ends anything?" His English was perfect, cultured—the product of American universities before he'd chosen a different path. "You have no idea what you've started."

Chad kept his rifle trained center mass while his peripheral vision scanned for threats. Intel had mentioned escape routes that architectural plans hadn't revealed, hidden weapons caches, panic buttons that could summon reinforcements.

"Your children ran," Chad said. "Left you here to face the consequences alone."

"My children?" Ramirez laughed, a sound like breaking glass. "They are enjoying the beaches of Panama. Such a lovely family vacation." His eyes glittered with malice. "They are building something far beyond what you can comprehend. Something that will reach into your country, into your homes, into your families."

"Ah, Agent Baez," Ramirez continued, his smile turning predatory as he recognized the DEA agent. "The man who thinks he understands my business. My children will remember you as well. Both of you. They have resources you cannot imagine. Corruption that reaches into the highest levels of your government. No one is beyond their reach."

The threat hung in the air like smoke. Chad had heard similar words from Taliban commanders and Iraqi insurgents—the dying boasts of men who believed their cause would outlive them. But something in Ramirez's tone carried conviction beyond mere bravado.

"The Ramirez family forgets nothing," the cartel leader continued, his eyes boring into Chad's. "And they—"

Chad saw the movement before his conscious mind processed it. Twenty years of combat experience condensed into microseconds of recognition: Ramirez's right shoulder dropping slightly, his hand shifting toward the desk drawer that intelligence had identified as containing a loaded Sig Sauer P226. The cartel leader's fingers moved with surprising speed for a man his age, desperation lending strength to his final gambit.

Time dilated the way it always did in life-or-death moments. Chad's training kicked in—Air Force JTAC reflexes honed by years of calling in danger-close airstrikes, FBI tactical experience from a hundred high-risk arrests. His finger found the trigger as his rifle's muzzle tracked right, following Ramirez's movement.

The cartel leader's hand was inches from the pistol grip when Chad's single shot took him between the eyes, snapping his head back against the leather chair. The would-be weapon clattered to the floor, unfired, as Salvador Ramirez's body settled into the stillness of death.

Chad kept his rifle trained on the corpse for three full seconds—long enough to confirm no further threat, short enough to maintain tactical awareness of the room. Professional. Methodical. The kind of kill that would look clean in after-action reports and congressional hearings.

But hidden security cameras had recorded everything—every word, every threat, every detail of their father's final moments. And later, on a pristine beach in Panama, thirty-two-year-old Hector Ramirez and thirty-year-old Elena Ramirez would watch the footage and hear their father's final words about remembering faces and reaching into American families.

They would memorize Chad Lloyd's voice as he announced the charges. They would study his face as he pulled the trigger. And they would begin planning a revenge so comprehensive, so devastating, that it would make their father's empire look like child's play.

The corruption that saved their lives would become the foundation of their war against American federal law enforcement.

Some wars never truly end. They just wait for the next generation to pick up the weapons.

Chapter 1

FBI Headquarters
Washington, D.C.
Two Years Ago –
Two Weeks After Salvador Raid

The air conditioning in the J. Edgar Hoover Building wheezed like a dying animal, losing its battle against the oppressive Washington summer. Chad could feel his dress shirt sticking to his back as he walked through the corridors that still felt foreign after all these years. The transition from field operations to headquarters assignments was never easy, but after what had happened in Sinaloa, the Bureau had decided he needed some time behind a desk.

Two weeks of mandatory psychological evaluation. Two weeks of sitting across from Bureau shrinks who'd never heard a shot fired in anger, explaining why he'd put a bullet between Salvador Ramirez's eyes. Two weeks of desk duty while Elena and Hector Ramirez consolidated power and planned their response.

Chad's instincts screamed that time was running out.

Special Agent Janet Holmes was waiting in Conference Room B, her severe gray suit and clipboard precision radiating the kind of bureaucratic authority that made Chad's teeth itch. Beside her stood someone Chad didn't recognize—a woman in her early thirties with auburn hair pulled back in a practical ponytail and the brightest green eyes he had ever seen. She wore a navy blazer over dark jeans, the kind of outfit that said federal agent without screaming it to anyone within fifty yards.

"Agent Lloyd," Holmes said, standing as he entered. "I'd like you to meet Agent Samantha Belle. She'll be joining your task force as of tomorrow."

Sam Belle extended her hand with a firm grip that spoke of confidence earned rather than assumed. "Agent Lloyd. I've studied the reports from the Sinaloa operation." Her voice carried the precise diction of someone who'd learned to make every word count. "Textbook tactical execution under impossible circumstances.""

"You can call me Chad," he replied, studying her with the same attention he'd give a new piece of equipment. "What's your background, Agent Belle?"

"Sam," she corrected with a slight smile. "Six years with the Bureau, all in the financial crimes division in New York. I've been tracking money flows for the organized crime task force, following digital breadcrumbs through shell companies, offshore accounts, and cryptocurrency networks that most agents can't even pronounce."

Chad nodded, his tactical mind already cataloguing her skillset. "Italian families? Russians?"

"Both. Albanian networks, some Irish remnants, even a few old Jewish operations from Brighton Beach." Sam's voice carried the flat precision of someone who'd spent too many nights staring at spreadsheets that represented human misery. "Money laundering, racketeering, extortion—organized crime has gone digital in ways that would surprise most people."

Holmes cleared her throat, drawing their attention. "Agent Belle specifically requested this transfer to violent crimes. Given the evolving nature of criminal organizations we're facing, her financial expertise will be invaluable." She paused, studying Sam with the kind of bureaucratic curiosity that made Chad uncomfortable. "What brought you to DC, Sam?"

Sam's professional composure shifted almost imperceptibly, like armor plating sliding into place. Chad recognized the expression—the same look he'd seen on soldiers' faces when someone asked about their worst day downrange.

"My husband was NYPD," she said, her voice carrying the controlled calm of someone who'd practiced this explanation. "Beat cop in

Manhattan. Three months ago, he responded to a drug store robbery—armed suspect holding the clerk at gunpoint."

Chad's tactical instincts immediately catalogued the scenario: confined space, innocent civilian, armed and desperate subject. The kind of situation where split-second decisions meant the difference between going home or going to the morgue.

"The new mayor's de-escalation policies required officers to attempt negotiation in all situations. No weapons drawn unless absolutely necessary." Sam's voice remained steady, but Chad caught the slight tightening around her eyes—the same expression he'd seen on the faces of soldiers who'd lost teammates to rules of engagement written by people who'd never been shot at. "Ron tried to talk him down. Twenty minutes of negotiation while the suspect got more agitated."

Chad already knew how this story ended. He'd seen too many good cops die because politicians made policies that sounded compassionate in boardrooms but got people killed on the streets.

"The guy finally snapped and started shooting, Ron was caught without his weapon ready." Sam met Chad's eyes directly, her gaze steady despite the pain beneath. "He died trying to save a store clerk from a Venezuelan gang member who'd been arrested six times in the past year and released every time without charges."

The silence in the conference room carried the weight of institutional failure and personal loss. Chad understood that particular combination of grief and rage—the knowledge that bureaucratic incompetence had cost someone their life while the system responsible faced no consequences.

"The suspect?" Chad asked, though he suspected he already knew.

"Released again," Sam replied, her voice carrying a bitter edge sharp enough to cut glass. "Immigration wouldn't hold him, DA wouldn't prosecute due to 'humanitarian concerns.' He was probably back in Venezuela before Ron's funeral." She straightened, her professional demeanor sliding back into place like a weapon being holstered. "I decided that tracking financial crimes from behind a desk wasn't enough anymore. If these organizations are bringing their violence to American streets, I want to be part of stopping them."

Chad found himself impressed despite his natural skepticism about new partners. Sam Belle had the kind of quiet competence that complemented his more direct approach, but more importantly, she understood that the real work of law enforcement happened when good people decided to do whatever was necessary to protect those who couldn't protect themselves.

"Fair enough," he said. "But field work is different from financial analysis. Things happen fast, and there's not always time to run the numbers."

"Then I guess you'll have to teach me," Sam replied, her voice carrying the steel undertone of someone who'd made a decision and intended to see it through. "Because like it or not, Agent Lloyd, we're partners now."

Holmes stood, gathering her materials with bureaucratic efficiency. "There's a briefing tomorrow at 0800 on your first case together. I'll let you two get acquainted." She paused at the door. "Agent Lloyd, Agent Belle—the criminal organizations we're facing have evolved beyond traditional law enforcement capabilities. Your combined expertise represents our best chance of adapting to meet that threat."

As Holmes departed, Chad found himself alone with his new partner. Sam was studying him with the same analytical attention she'd probably given financial records in New York.

"Question," he said, settling back in his chair. "You've spent six years tracking organized crime money. What's the biggest difference between what we're dealing with now and the old-school operations?"

Sam considered the question, her analytical mind engaging. "The traditional families were territorial. They had neighborhoods, specific industries, established hierarchies that took decades to build. Their money laundering was crude—cash businesses, real estate, simple shell companies."

She leaned forward, her focus complete. "But the new networks are global, digital, and completely fluid. They can move millions of dollars across six countries in minutes using cryptocurrency exchanges that barely existed five years ago. No territories to defend, no permanent infrastructure to protect. They're like ghost organizations that materialize, complete their operations, and vanish."

Chad nodded, impressed by her tactical thinking applied to financial warfare. "That's what makes them dangerous. No fixed positions to target."

"Exactly. And that's probably what we're dealing with—criminal organizations that have evolved beyond anything the Bureau was designed to handle." Sam met his eyes with the kind of direct honesty that marked someone who'd stopped believing in comfortable lies. "The question is whether we can evolve fast enough to catch them."

Chad watched her gather her materials with the kind of brisk efficiency that marked competent professionals, and found himself thinking that maybe headquarters assignment wouldn't be the professional purgatory he'd expected. Agent Belle carried herself like someone who understood that sometimes the real work required operating in the gray areas between official procedures.

"0800 tomorrow," he said, standing. "Conference Room C. Don't be late."

"Wouldn't dream of it," Sam replied, extending her hand again. "Looking forward to seeing how the other half lives, Agent Lloyd."

As Chad watched her leave, he found himself thinking about Elena and Hector Ramirez, somewhere out there consolidating power and planning their response to the men who'd destroyed their world. His combat experience had taught him that revenge was always personal, always violent, and always inevitable.

The only question was whether American law enforcement would recognize the attack before it was too late to stop it.

Chapter 2

Washington, D.C.
Present Day - Friday Evening

That's the third shell company this month," Sam said, sliding another financial report across Chad's desk. The cramped office they'd shared for two years was covered with surveillance photos, cryptocurrency transaction charts, and satellite imagery of warehouse facilities across the mid-Atlantic region. "Elena's burning through fronts faster than we can shut them down, but she's making mistakes."

Chad studied the latest analysis, impressed as always by Sam's ability to follow money trails through layers of corporate obfuscation. Over the past eighteen months, their joint task force with Antonio Baez's DEA team had systematically dismantled twenty-three Ramirez front operations—warehouses, shipping companies, logistics firms, even a chain of food trucks that had been moving drugs and cash throughout the D.C. metro area.

"What kind of mistakes?" Chad asked, leaning back in his chair.

"She's getting impatient," Sam replied, pulling up a chart on her laptop. "Look at these transaction patterns. Two years ago, Elena would set up a front company, run it legitimately for six months to establish credibility, then slowly integrate criminal operations. Now she's cutting that timeline to six weeks."

"Pressure from her board of directors?" Chad suggested with dark humor.

"More likely pressure from competition," Sam replied, highlighting several cryptocurrency transaction patterns. "Elena's not struggling to launder money—she's struggling to stay ahead of us. Look at these blockchain traces."

Chad studied the complex web of digital transactions. "What am I looking at?"

"Cryptocurrency mixing services, privacy coins, cross-chain transfers," Sam explained, pulling up another screen. "Elena's using every trick in the book—Bitcoin tumblers, Monero conversions, over-the-counter brokers who don't ask questions. She can move millions through crypto ATMs and unregulated exchanges without leaving traditional banking footprints."

"So why the rush to expand?"

"Because we're getting better at tracking her," Sam said with satisfaction. "Blockchain analytics are improving faster than criminal countermeasures. Every transaction leaves digital breadcrumbs, even through mixers and privacy coins. Elena's trying to diversify her operation before we can map her entire network."

The partnership between Chad's FBI violent crimes unit and Baez's DEA task force had proven devastatingly effective. Sam's financial analysis would identify suspicious shell companies, Chad's team would conduct surveillance and tactical assessments, and Baez's agents would coordinate with local law enforcement for simultaneous raids. They'd seized millions in cash, arrested dozens of mid-level operatives, and disrupted supply chains across six states.

But Elena Ramirez always seemed to be one step ahead, opening new operations faster than they could close the old ones.

"Any word from Baez on the Baltimore operation?" Chad asked.

"Clean sweep," Sam confirmed. "Eighteen arrests, half a million in cash, and enough fentanyl to kill fifty thousand people. But the warehouse was already being evacuated when his team hit it. Someone tipped them off."

Chad's jaw tightened. After two years of hunting the Ramirez organization, the pattern was becoming disturbingly clear. Elena had sources inside American law enforcement—not just bought cops like the ones who'd warned Salvador, but sophisticated intelligence networks that gave her advance warning of federal operations.

"Speaking of operations," Sam said, checking her watch, "shouldn't you be heading home? Lana's probably started dinner by now."

Chad smiled, the first genuine expression he'd worn all day. "Casey's birthday party. Six years old today. She specifically requested 'Aunt Sam and Uncle Nolan' be there for her princess cake."

"She won't burn the cake," Sam laughed. "Lana could bake a seven-course meal blindfolded. You're just nervous because you haven't bought Casey's present yet."

"How did you—"

"Because I know you, Chad Lloyd. You're tactical and methodical about everything except gift shopping. Casey's been dropping hints about that new art set for weeks."

Chad gathered his things, grateful as always for Sam's insight into his family dynamics. Over the past two years, Sam had become more than just his partner—she'd become Lana's closest friend, spending weekends at their house, joining family barbecues, becoming so much a part of their lives that five-year-old Casey called her "Aunt Sam" without anyone suggesting it.

"You're coming to the party, right?" Chad asked. "Casey's been planning this for weeks. She even invited Grey."

Sam hesitated, the same pause that appeared whenever family gatherings were mentioned. "I don't want to intrude on family time—"

"You're not intruding," Chad interrupted firmly. "You're family. Casey made the guest list herself—Mommy, Daddy, Aunt Sam, and Uncle Nolan. That's it."

The word hung in the air between them, carrying weight that neither acknowledged directly. Sam's composed professional mask slipped slightly, revealing something more vulnerable underneath.

"Besides," Chad continued, oblivious to the impact of his words, "Lana specifically said she wanted you there. Something about Dr. Warner stopping by after his shift to meet everyone."

Sam's smile became forced. "Tom's a nice guy. Really."

"But?"

"But nothing," Sam replied, organizing papers with unnecessary precision. "He's smart, stable, successful. Everything a rational woman

17

should want in a partner."

Chad studied his partner's carefully neutral expression, recognizing the defensive posture she adopted whenever personal topics arose. In two years of working together, he'd learned to read Sam's moods—the slight tightening around her eyes when cases hit too close to home, the way she threw herself into financial analysis when emotions threatened to surface, the careful distance she maintained whenever conversations turned to relationships or dating.

"Sam," he said gently, "it's been two years since Ron died. You don't have to—"

"I know," she cut him off, but not unkindly. "I know it's been two years. I know Lana means well with the matchmaking. I know Tom Warner is everything any reasonable woman should want." She paused, meeting his eyes directly. "But sometimes what you should want and what you actually want are two completely different things."

Before Chad could respond, Sam's phone buzzed with an incoming text. She glanced at it and her expression shifted back to professional mode.

"Speak of the devil," she said. "Lana wants to know if you remembered to pick up ice cream for the party."

Chad groaned. "Add that to balloons on the list of things I forgot."

"Already handled," Sam replied, holding up a bag he hadn't noticed. "Picked up that 64-piece deluxe art set Casey's been coveting—you can give it to her as your present. And before you ask, yes, I got wrapping paper too—the one with unicorns. Plus chocolate chip ice cream and princess balloons."

"What did you get her then?" Chad asked.

"That pottery wheel kit she saw at the craft store last weekend," Sam said with a smile. "Lana mentioned Casey's been talking about wanting to 'make beautiful bowls like the lady on TV.' Figured she's ready to graduate from finger painting to actual art projects."

Chad shook his head, once again amazed by her thoughtfulness. "Sam, you don't have to—"

"Yes, I do," she said simply. "Because that's what family does. We take care of each other."

As they gathered their things and headed toward the parking garage, Chad found himself thinking about Sam's words. Over the past two years, she'd become an integral part of their lives in ways he'd never expected. She remembered Casey's favorite bedtime stories, helped Lana with hospital fundraisers, and somehow always knew exactly what his family needed before he realized it himself.

What Chad couldn't see was the way Sam's hands trembled slightly as she locked her desk drawer, or the careful control it took for her to maintain her cheerful facade. He didn't notice how her eyes lingered on his wedding ring when he talked about anniversary plans, or the pain that flickered across her face when he casually referred to her as family.

Because the truth Sam could never admit was more complicated and more painful than anyone suspected. Over two years of working alongside Chad, watching him be a devoted husband and father, seeing the way he and Lana looked at each other after sixteen years of marriage, Sam had found herself falling for a man she could never have.

Chad was married. Lana was her best friend. And Sam would carry these feelings silently, burying them beneath professional competence and genuine friendship, because some lines could never be crossed—no matter how much her heart might wish otherwise.

Chapter 3

Magnolia Street Flowers
Alexandria, VA

The bell above Magnolia Street Flowers tinkled softly as Sarah Chen unlocked the front door, the sound as much a part of her morning routine as the smell of fresh roses and the hum of the coolers. Five years she'd owned this shop in the quiet Alexandria neighborhood, five years of wedding arrangements and prom corsages, of sympathy wreaths and birthday bouquets. The morning light filtered through the front windows, catching the moisture from the automatic misters and creating tiny rainbows among the flowers.

She'd come in early to finish the orders that were scheduled to be delivered that day, including the Lloyd anniversary arrangement – baby's breath and red roses, classic and elegant. The order had come with specific instructions: "Like the bouquet she carried at our wedding." Sarah appreciated that kind of sentiment. Too many husbands just grabbed whatever was pre-made from the cooler.

The first sign something was wrong was so subtle she almost missed it – the back door's deadbolt was still engaged, but the small piece of clear tape she placed across the frame every night was broken. Sarah had learned caution running her parents' shop in Baltimore. Little tricks her father had taught her about urban survival.

The second sign was the reflection she caught in the cooler's glass door – a shadow where no shadow should be.

"Beautiful flowers," a voice said behind her. Accent slightly Spanish, words precise and measured. "You take great care with them."

Sarah turned slowly. The man stood by her workbench, examining the Lloyd arrangement with what appeared to be genuine interest. He wore clean work coveralls, like a deliveryman. Everything about him looked ordinary except his eyes. Those belonged on a snake.

Condensation beaded on the cooler glass behind her. The steady drip of water from the misters counted out what might be her final moments. Even the morning traffic outside seemed muted, as if the world was holding its breath.

"The shop's not open yet," she managed, her hand inching toward the panic button under the counter. The brass bell above the door had never seemed so far away.

"I know." He smiled, and Sarah's world contracted to a single point of understanding. This was how it ended – not in the Baltimore streets her father had warned her about, but in her own quiet shop, among her flowers.

"The roses," he continued conversationally, touching one perfect bloom. "They remind me of blood. How it blooms on white cloth. You understand this, yes? How beauty and death dance together?"

Sarah's fingers found the panic button. Too late, she realized it was dead. Like her phone would be. Like she would be.

"The arrangement," he nodded to the Lloyd bouquet. "It's for a special anniversary. Sixteen years. Tell me about the delivery."

"I don't-"

"Agent Lloyd," he interrupted softly. "FBI. Called it in yesterday for this evening's delivery. I need to know the address. The timing. The exact specifications he requested."

Sarah lifted her chin. Her father had also taught her about dignity. "No."

The man – Javier, though she would never know this – nodded as if he'd expected this. Respected it, even. From his coveralls, he produced a knife. The blade caught the same morning light that had made rainbows in the mist, but there was nothing beautiful about its reflection.

"Family is everything," he said, almost gently. "Mine. Yours. His." He gestured to a framed photo on the wall – Sarah with her parents at the shop's opening. "In Juárez, I once knew a flower seller like you. She also had principles. Her parents as well. Would you like to know how that ended?"

Javier's smile took on a predatory edge. "Perhaps a demonstration of how serious I am?" The knife flickered in his hand, drawing a thin red line across Sarah's forearm. Not deep, just enough to sting. To make his point. The sharp copper smell of blood mixed with the sweetness of roses.

Sarah Chen was her father's daughter. The moment the blade lifted, she moved. The glass vase shattered against Javier's shoulder, water and roses exploding around them. Her knee came up, aimed with precision that would have made her self-defense instructor proud. Crystal shards caught the morning light, a brief constellation of desperate hope.

Javier's laugh stopped her cold. Not because it was cruel – though it was – but because it was genuinely amused. He caught her attack with casual ease, using her momentum to slam her against the workbench. Rose thorns bit into her palms as she caught herself, petals crushing beneath her fingers.

"Beautiful," he said, still chuckling. "Such spirit. The Lloyd woman will not fight like this. She will see the uniform, the flowers, open her door with a smile. But you..." He inhaled deeply, as if savoring the moment. "You make this art."

What followed was precise, methodical, almost elegant in its efficiency. Sarah fought – oh, how she fought – but Javier moved like water, each of her desperate strikes met with practiced counters. When she lunged for the phone, his hand closed around her wrist with crushing force, the bones grinding together until she gasped. When she tried to scream, his other hand clamped over her mouth, fingers digging into her cheeks hard enough to leave bruises.

The knife never rushed, never hurried. It found the spaces between ribs with surgical precision, puncturing lung tissue to silence her cries while keeping her conscious. Each cut deliberate, calculated to maximize pain while prolonging the experience. Sarah's eyes went wide with terror and understanding as air whistled through the holes in her chest, her desperate attempts to breathe creating pink foam at her lips.

"Shh," Javier whispered, almost tenderly, as her struggles weakened.

"This is how your father would want you to die. With courage." The blade traced delicate patterns across her throat, not deep enough to kill quickly, just enough to let her life drain away in crimson ribbons that pooled among the scattered rose petals.

Sarah's hands clawed weakly at his coveralls, leaving bloody fingerprints as her strength faded. Her eyes never lost their defiance, even as the light began to dim. Javier watched with professional appreciation as she fought for each rattling breath, her body's stubborn refusal to surrender exactly what he'd hoped for.

When her pulse finally stilled beneath his fingers, he spent several minutes positioning her body with an artist's eye. The roses he arranged around her carefully, their pristine white petals slowly absorbing the crimson that continued to seep from her wounds. He folded her hands peacefully across her chest, though the defensive cuts on her palms told the story of her final fight. The morning light through the windows cast perfect shadows, highlighting his work. Even in death, Sarah Chen kept her dignity – this, too, was part of his craft.

The floor's slight slope carried thin ribbons of red toward the drain, designed for watering overflow. The coolers hummed their steady rhythm, indifferent to the scene before them. Somewhere outside, a car horn honked – the city awakening to another summer day.

Javier worked with methodical precision, documenting each detail for Elena. He photographed the arterial spray across white roses, the body positioned just so among scattered petals, the look of defiance frozen on Sarah's face. Even in death, she refused to show fear. He respected that.

"First phase complete," he texted Elena, attaching the images. "Delivery vehicle acquired. Target confirmed for 1545 hours."

"Good," Elena replied curtly. "No complications?"

"None. The florist provided the address and timing before she died. Agent Lloyd's home at eighteen hundred hours for anniversary delivery."

"And you understand the requirements? This must send the right message."

Javier smiled at his phone. Elena was all business, no sentiment. Unlike her father, who had enjoyed the details of his work, she cared only about results. The kill itself was meaningless to her - only the psychological impact on Chad Lloyd mattered. Break the man completely. Make him understand the cost of crossing the Ramirez family.

"The message will be clear," he replied. "Agent Lloyd will find his wife exactly as we discussed. No cameras, no recording. Just the scene itself when he returns home."

"Perfect. Hector wants him to suffer the way we suffered watching our father die. Make it personal, Javier. Make it devastating."

Twenty years of service to the cartel. Ten of those years spent in an El Salvadorian prison, refusing to give up a single name despite interrogations that left permanent scars across his back and ribs. The guards had tried everything - beatings, starvation, isolation, even bringing in his sister's photograph with threats against her children. Javier had endured it all in silence, never once betraying Salvador Ramirez or the organization that had given his life meaning.

When he finally walked free, Salvador himself had been waiting at the prison gates. "Loyalty like yours," the old man had said, embracing him like a son, "is worth more than all the money in Mexico." That day, Javier became more than just another sicario. He became Salvador's personal instrument of vengeance.

Forty-five confirmed kills for the Ramirez family alone – each one personally requested by Salvador himself. Not the random violence of street soldiers or the quick executions of common hitmen. Each death a commissioned piece, a message crafted in blood and fear. The cartel had paid for his silence with their protection, and he had repaid them with absolute devotion.

The white Ford Transit van sat in the shop's rear loading area, its "Magnolia Street Flowers" logo professionally painted on both sides. Sarah's delivery vehicle was perfect for his needs – legitimate, familiar to the neighborhood, and now completely under his control. He'd spent weeks studying the routes, timing the patterns, learning that Sarah personally handled most deliveries in the Lloyd's Arlington neighborhood. Her customers trusted her, expected her van in their driveways.

He moved through the shop with practiced efficiency, preparing for the evening ahead. From the cash register, he took the delivery invoice for the Lloyd anniversary arrangement. Agent Chad Lloyd, 1247 Cedar Street. Delivery requested between 3:45 and 4:00 PM. Baby's breath and red roses, like the bride's bouquet from sixteen years ago.

The van's cargo area held everything he needed. Fresh arrangements to maintain the cover. The specialized case containing his tools. Extra coveralls for after the work was done. Everything required to complete the delivery, conduct his business, and leave without a trace.

From his phone, he reviewed the Lloyd house surveillance footage Elena had compiled over the past month. Front door directly visible from the street. Rear patio accessible through the kitchen. Security system basic, residential-grade. Most importantly, the Friday afternoon pattern: Lana and Casey typically home together after their weekly errands, usually arriving around 3:30 PM to prepare for the evening ahead.

Perfect timing. Mother and daughter would be together when he arrived. Vulnerable. Once he had control of the scene, he would set up Elena's cameras - small, wireless units packed with his other tools, along with the grotesque clown mask that would both conceal his identity and maximize the child's terror. Elena's research had been thorough - Casey Lloyd's paralyzing fear of clowns would make his work even more artistically perfect.

The afternoon sun would be painting golden stripes across their hardwood floors. Lana would be checking her reflection one last time before their anniversary dinner, while five-year-old Casey played nearby with her beloved Mr. Hoppy. Sixteen years of marriage hadn't dimmed Lana's excitement for their special evenings together, and Casey always loved watching her mother get ready for "fancy dinners with Daddy."

At 3:45 precisely, he would ring their doorbell with his anniversary roses. Lana would answer with that trusting smile, expecting a delivery from her thoughtful husband. Casey would peek around her mother's legs, curious about the flower man. Once inside, he would position the cameras to record his masterpiece - every moment that would later destroy Chad Lloyd completely when he discovered what had been taken from him.

Javier ran his thumb along the Damascus steel blade, remembering his first kill for the Ramirez cartel. Fifteen years old in the streets of

Juárez, proving himself to Salvador Ramirez. The knife had been crude then, but his talent had shown through. Salvador had seen something in the precise way the boy worked, the artistic flourish even then. "El Cuchillo," the old man had named him. The Knife.

He touched the cartel tattoo on his forearm, hidden now under the delivery uniform. Santa Muerte, Our Lady of Holy Death, danced among roses and knife blades. His personal icon, his inspiration. Salvador had held his arm steady as the ink went in, telling him stories of the old ways, of how death and beauty danced together in the cartel's history.

In the shop behind him, the automatic misters hissed softly, morning light still making rainbows in their spray. Sarah Chen's roses stood in perfect formation, their petals gradually darkening as they absorbed the last of her life. The bell above the door hung silent, waiting for someone to notice something wrong.

But by then, Javier would be navigating Arlington streets, his delivery of roses and death ready for the Lloyd family. The single target that mattered. The message that would destroy Chad Lloyd's world.

"For the family," he whispered, starting the van's engine. In the back, his tools waited like faithful lovers. In his mind, he could already see Chad Lloyd's face when he discovered what had been taken from him — the moment of understanding that would break the FBI agent completely.

Sarah Chen's blood was already drying on the roses. Soon, Lana and Casey Lloyd would join her in his gallery of death. And Chad Lloyd would learn the true cost of crossing the Ramirez family.

Chapter 4

Ramirez Compound
Cayman Islands

Elena Ramirez stood on the terrace of her beachfront compound, the secure satellite phone pressed to her ear as she gazed out at crystal-blue waters that would soon reflect the color of blood spilled across fourteen American states. To any observer, she appeared to be just another wealthy businesswoman conducting international calls. The reality was far more lethal – she was orchestrating the largest coordinated attack on American law enforcement in history.

"Miguel," she said in Spanish, her voice carrying the authority that had made her the most feared woman in the Western Hemisphere. "Are your people in position?"

Miguel Santos controlled MS-13 operations across the eastern United States. His gang had evolved from street-level drug dealers into a sophisticated army of killers with cells embedded like cancer throughout fourteen states.

"Sí, jefa. Forty-three targets identified. Federal agents, local police, courthouse clerks who processed paperwork against your father. All of them pay tonight." His voice carried the weight of countless murders. "But you mentioned something special for Agent Lloyd?"

Elena's smile was predatory. "Lloyd gets personal attention, but not death. Not yet. I want him to suffer first. At exactly 1730 hours, your people will T-bone his vehicle at the intersection of Route 7 and Leesburg Pike. Make it look like an accident, but make sure he's delayed getting home. Shout Salvador's name as you flee. Let him know this is just the beginning."

"And if he's seriously injured?"

"He won't be. Your driver will target the rear quarter panel – enough to total the car and shake him up, but not enough to put him in the hospital. I need him conscious when he finds what Javier has left for him."

Elena ended the call and immediately dialed Rosa Delgado in Los Angeles. The coordination required surgical precision – ninety-three families would die at exactly 6:00 PM Eastern, while Chad Lloyd would arrive home thirty minutes late to discover his personal nightmare.

"Rosa, status report on the West Coast operations."

"Ready to paint the streets red, Elena. Twenty-seven targets from San Diego to Seattle. ICE agents, Border Patrol, that federal judge who authorized wiretaps on our communications." Rosa's voice was clinical, professional. "My people have been studying their routines for months. We know when they walk their dogs, when they check their mail, when they kiss their children goodnight."

"Good. And the Tren de Aragua?"

"Carlos has his Venezuelans positioned across Texas and Florida. They're hungry for American blood, Elena. They want to prove themselves worthy of the Ramirez name."

Elena walked to her study, where detailed surveillance photos covered the walls – not just target locations, but intimate family portraits stolen from social media accounts. Children at birthday parties. Wives at grocery stores. Husbands coaching Little League. Each image a reminder that tonight, the American government would learn that crossing the Ramirez family meant total war.

"The simultaneity is everything," Elena emphasized. "If even one target receives warning, they could alert the others. Every operation begins at exactly 1800 hours Eastern. No exceptions."

She dialed Carlos Mendoza in Houston, where Tren de Aragua was preparing to demonstrate why they'd become Venezuela's most feared export.

"Elena," Carlos's voice was thick with anticipation. "My people are ready to honor your father's memory. Nineteen targets across our territories, including that DEA pendejo Antonio Baez who led the raid. We've been watching his house for weeks — knows exactly when his wife puts their baby to bed."

"Weapons?"

"Military-grade equipment from your brother's Miami suppliers. Armor-piercing rounds, explosives for hardened targets. My men have been practicing room-clearing techniques in abandoned warehouses." Carlos paused, his voice dropping to a whisper. "We even have their children's schedules, Elena. Soccer practice. Dance recitals. Piano lessons. Tonight, American families learn the same grief you felt."

Elena checked her platinum watch again, calculating the timeline with ruthless precision. "Remember, Carlos — the nationwide strikes begin at exactly 1800 hours. Not a minute sooner."

"Why the delay, jefa? My people are ready now."

Elena's smile was cold as arctic wind. "Because at 1545 hours today, Javier Santos will begin his masterpiece with Agent Lloyd's family. I want him to have hours of uninterrupted time — time to create something truly unforgettable before any law enforcement agency realizes they're under attack."

She walked to the window, imagining Chad Lloyd's face when he discovered what awaited him. "When the coordinated strikes begin at six o'clock, every federal agency will be consumed with their own casualties. No one will be available to respond to a domestic disturbance call from Arlington. By the time anyone reaches the Lloyd house, Javier's work will be complete, and Agent Lloyd will have hours alone with what remains of his family."

"Brilliant," Carlos breathed. "He suffers in isolation while we paint the streets with federal blood."

"Exactly. Javier needs time to be artistic. To send the right message. The nationwide attacks are theater — impressive, but quick. What happens to Lana and Casey Lloyd? That's poetry. That's personal. That requires patience."

Elena ended the call and poured herself a glass of champagne, as she studied the wall maps. Red pins marked federal agents. Blue indicated local law enforcement. Yellow represented judges and prosecutors. Green showed support personnel – clerks, analysts, technicians whose only crime was processing paperwork against her father.

Salvador Ramirez had built an empire, but he'd never attempted anything this ambitious—a coordinated strike against the entire American federal law enforcement apparatus that had dared to challenge the family. Ninety-three families. Approximately 279 agents, spouses, and children who would die screaming at exactly 6:00 PM.

Her secure phone buzzed with incoming messages:

Miguel (MS-13): *"Teams deployed. Awaiting green light."*

Rosa (18th Street): *"All units in position. 1800 hours confirmed."*

Carlos (Tren de Aragua): *"Ready to honor Salvador's memory."*

Elena opened her laptop and reviewed the target list one final time:

•**Priority One**: Chad Lloyd (FBI - killed Salvador personally) and Antonio Baez (DEA - led the Mexican operation)

•**Priority Two**: Federal Judge Morrison (signed the search warrants) and AUSA Katherine Wells (prosecuted the case)

•**Priority Three**: Task force members, support staff, administrative personnel

Each name represented someone who had contributed to her father's death. Each death would send a message that the Ramirez family's reach extended into every corner of American law enforcement.

But the crown jewel wasn't being handled by gang soldiers. At this very moment, Javier Santos was preparing to deliver Chad Lloyd's anniversary gift – something so perfectly brutal that it would destroy the FBI agent's soul before a single shot was fired across America.

At exactly 6:00 PM Eastern time, the United States would learn that some debts are always paid in blood. And Chad Lloyd would discover his wife's body just as Elena and Hector had watched their father die—helpless, devastated, and forever changed.

"For you, papá," she whispered, raising her glass to Salvador's photograph. "Tonight, they learn that some debts are paid in blood and terror."

The Caribbean sun climbed higher, promising another beautiful day that would end in unprecedented darkness across America.

Elena Ramirez had declared war on the United States government.

The first casualty would be Chad Lloyd's family. The last would be his sanity.

Chapter 5

Lloyd Residence
Arlington, VA

The July morning sun painted golden rays across Casey's bedroom floor as Lana helped her daughter get ready for their special girls' day out. Mr. Hoppy, the well-loved stuffed rabbit that went everywhere with Casey, sat propped against her pillows, supervising the morning routine with floppy-eared dignity.

"Can Mr. Hoppy come shopping with us?" Casey asked, carefully brushing the stuffed rabbit's ears. "He wants to help pick out pretty things for Mommy's special weekend."

"Of course he can come, princess." Lana smiled, watching Casey tuck Mr. Hoppy into her small backpack along with her coloring book and crayons. "But we have to wait until Aunt Sam gets here to pick us up first."

"Then we get to do girl things all day?" Casey's eyes lit up with excitement. "Lunch and nail painting and shopping?"

"All day," Lana confirmed. "Just us girls while daddy is at work."

The morning routine felt comfortingly normal - Casey's careful selection of her favorite outfit for their special day, the way she insisted on wearing her "grown-up" shoes instead of sneakers, her excited chatter about spending the whole day with Mommy and Aunt Sam.

FBI Headquarters
Washington, D.C.

Three miles away, Sam was already at her desk reviewing financial reports when Chad arrived with coffee for both of them. The office felt different on Friday mornings - quieter, with that end-of-week energy that made everyone think about weekend plans.

"You're in early," Chad observed, handing her the coffee. "Excited about your ladies' day?"

"Casey's been talking about it all week," Sam smiled. "I think she's more excited about getting her nails painted than I am."

"Lana's pretty excited too. She's been planning this girls' day like a military operation." Chad settled at his desk with the case files. "Thanks for including Casey. She adores you."

"The feeling's mutual," Sam replied, meaning it completely. Over the past two years, Casey had become like a niece to her - the daughter she'd never had with Ron, the family connection she'd thought she'd lost forever.

Potomac Wholesale Flowers
Anacostia, VA.

Eight miles away, Javier guided Sarah's van past the loading bays to the side entrance marked "Employee Parking." The overhead door rolled up automatically as he approached – Elena's people monitoring his arrival through legitimate security cameras. Inside, the warehouse's true purpose became clear.

"Welcome to your new office," said Jose Mendez, Elena's lieutenant, as Javier stepped from the van. "Everything prepared as you requested."

The converted office space contained everything Javier needed for the day ahead. A comfortable chair, a small refrigerator stocked with food, a shower and clean clothes for afterward. Police scanners monitored law enforcement frequencies. Multiple cell phones with untraceable numbers sat charging on the desk.

Javier studied the surveillance photos of Lana Lloyd that Jose handed him – an attractive woman in her mid-thirties with kind eyes and an easy smile. The photos showed her at the hospital where she worked, picking up her daughter from school, shopping for groceries. A normal life that would end in eleven hours.

FBI Headquarters
Washington, D.C.

"Time to go meet my girls," Sam announced, saving her financial analysis and shutting down her computer. She'd spent the morning reviewing Elena's latest cryptocurrency transfers, but that could wait until Monday.

"Have fun," Chad said, not looking up from the surveillance photos he was studying. "Tell Lana I'll pick up the... thing... on my way home."

"The thing?" Sam raised an eyebrow.

"The anniversary thing. She'll know what I mean." Chad's slight blush made Sam smile. After sixteen years of marriage, he still got flustered buying jewelry for his wife.

"I'll tell her the thing will be acquired," Sam said solemnly. "Try not to work too late. It's your anniversary."

"Just want to finish reviewing this case file. I'll be home by seven."

Sam gathered her purse, thinking about the day ahead. Casey had been practically vibrating with excitement all week about their "ladies' adventure," and Lana deserved a fun day before her romantic weekend. It felt good to be included in their family traditions, even as it reminded her of everything she couldn't have.

Lloyd Residence
Arlington, VA.

"Aunt Sam!" Casey launched herself into Sam's arms as she arrived to pick them up. "Are we really going to the fancy nail place? And can I get sparkles?"

"Sparkles are mandatory," Sam laughed, hugging the six-year-old tight. "How else will everyone know you're a princess?"

Lana watched the interaction with familiar warmth. Over the past two years, Sam had seamlessly integrated into their family routines. Casey adored her "Aunt Sam," and Sam returned that love with fierce protective devotion.

"Ready for our girls' day?" Sam asked, shouldering Casey's overnight bag. "Shopping, mani-pedis, lunch at that place with the fancy grilled cheese Casey likes?"

"And the special store for Mommy's weekend clothes," Casey added with six-year-old seriousness. "Daddy's taking her somewhere very romantic."

Sam raised an eyebrow at Lana. "The Inn at Willow Grove. Very swanky." Lana smiled. "Chad's been planning this for months. Our first real getaway since Casey was born."

"You two deserve it," Sam said, meaning it completely. She'd watched Chad and Lana navigate the challenges of federal law enforcement careers while raising a daughter, never losing the obvious love they shared. "Come on, ladies. Adventure awaits."

King St
Alexandria, VA.

La Perla's window display caught Lana's eye as they walked down King Street after dropping Casey at the children's salon for her "princess treatment." The black lace negligee draped elegantly on a mannequin, somehow both sophisticated and daring.

"Oh my," Sam whistled softly. "Someone's planning to make an impression this weekend."

"May I help you find something?" The saleswoman – Claudia, according to her nameplate – had that perfectly cultivated high-end retail presence.

"Yes, actually." Lana gestured to the window display. "The black lace piece? My husband and I are celebrating our sixteenth anniversary this weekend."

"Ah, l'amour!" Claudia's smile was genuine as she led them to the intimate apparel section. "Sixteen years – that deserves something special. The Noir Collection just arrived from Paris..."

They spent nearly an hour selecting pieces while Casey got her nails painted with tiny unicorns at the salon next door. The black lace negligee that had caught Lana's eye, a deep ruby silk robe that would match the necklace she knew Chad was picking up today, delicate underthings in cream and black.

"Your husband is a lucky man," Claudia commented.

"I'm the lucky one," Lana replied, thinking about the weekend ahead. "Sometimes I look at him with our daughter and just want to freeze those moments forever, you know?"

Sam pushed down the familiar ache that came with watching her best friend's happiness – a happiness she could never be part of, not in the way her heart sometimes wished.

As Claudia wrapped the black lace negligee and ruby silk robe in tissue paper, Lana turned to Sam with sudden seriousness.

"Sam, I need to ask you something." Lana's voice dropped to barely above a whisper. "If anything ever happened to me..."

"Don't." Sam's grip tightened on Lana's arm. "Nothing's going to happen."

"Let me finish. Please." Lana's eyes held her friend's. "Chad's told me about the dark places he went after the war. Before he met me. If something happened to me, he'd go back there. Worse than before."

Sam felt her chest tighten. "Lana..."

"Casey would need someone. Someone who understands her, who loves her like I do. Someone who could be there for Chad too, keep him grounded." Lana smiled softly. "You're already her Aunt Sam. The one who makes pancakes in special shapes, who knows exactly why Mr. Hoppy needs his special blanket."

"Stop, please." Sam's voice cracked. "I can't think about this. About losing you. About him..."

"Besides," Lana's smile turned mischievous, lightening the heavy moment, "I see how you look at Chad sometimes. Don't deny it – if he wasn't married, you'd be all over that man in an instant."

Sam's face flamed red. "Lana! I would never..."

"I know you wouldn't. That's why I trust you both completely. That's why I know that if the unthinkable happened, Casey would have the mother she deserves, and Chad would have someone who could love him back from the darkness." Lana squeezed Sam's hand. "Promise me. If anything happens, you'll take care of them. Both of them."

Sam stared at her friend, seeing something in Lana's eyes that made her stomach clench with inexplicable dread. "Nothing's going to happen to you. You're going to have a wonderful anniversary weekend, and Monday we'll have our usual pancakes, and everything will be normal."

"Promise me anyway."

"I..." Sam swallowed hard. "I promise. But you're going to live to be ninety and spoil your grandchildren rotten."

"Of course I am," Lana smiled, but the shadow in her eyes remained. "Now come on, let's go rescue Casey from all that nail polish before she convinces them to add glitter to her unicorns."

Chapter 6

Magnolia's Restaurant
Alexandria, VA.

Magnolia's was already bustling when they arrived for lunch, Casey chattering excitedly about her sparkly nails. Sam automatically chose a corner booth with clear sightlines to all exits, but found herself studying Casey with new eyes. Not just as the adorable niece-figure she'd always been, but as a little girl who might someday need her in ways Sam had never imagined.

"Can I have a Shirley Temple?" Casey asked the waitress, carefully placing her coloring crayons in a neat row. "With extra cherries?"

"Of course, sweetie," the waitress smiled. "And for you ladies?"

Sam watched Casey's serious concentration as she arranged her crayons by color, the way she tucked a strand of hair behind her ear just like Chad did when he was thinking. Had she always noticed these little mannerisms, or was Lana's request making her see Casey differently?

"Sancerre for me," Lana said, settling into the booth. "We're celebrating girls' day."

"Make it two," Sam added. "And don't even try to protest about day drinking," she told Lana with a grin. "We're celebrating."

"Yes, we are." Lana placed her La Perla bags carefully beside her. "And since we're celebrating..."

"Don't you dare tell me details about what you're planning to do with that black lace," Sam interrupted with a laugh. "Some things I don't need to know about my partner and his wife."

Casey looked up from her coloring. "What black lace? Are you making something crafty, Mommy?"

"Something like that, princess," Lana replied diplomatically. "Grown-up crafts."

"Aunt Sam thinks all kissing is gross," Casey informed her mother seriously. "That's why she doesn't have a boyfriend."

"Casey," Lana warned gently, but Sam just smiled.

"Your Aunt Sam is very particular about kissing," Sam replied diplomatically. "It has to be with someone very special."

After lunch, they moved to Serenity Day Spa for their mani-pedis. Casey was thrilled to be included in the "grown-up lady time," proudly showing off her unicorn nails to anyone who would look while a patient technician applied a protective clear coat to preserve her morning artwork.

"We have to be very careful with these beautiful nails," the technician told Casey seriously. "Unicorns are very special and need extra protection."

Casey nodded solemnly, then brightened. "Aunt Sam, can you get unicorns on your nails too? So we match?"

Sam felt her throat tighten. "Absolutely, princess. We'll be the unicorn nail club."

As she watched Casey's face light up with joy, Sam found herself memorizing details she'd taken for granted before – the gap in Casey's smile where she'd lost her first tooth, the way she hummed when she was happy, how she instinctively reached for Sam's hand when they walked.

Take care of them, Lana had said. Looking at Casey now, Sam realized she was already halfway in love with the idea of being more than just Aunt Sam. The thought terrified and comforted her in equal measure.

"We're going to make pancakes in shapes tomorrow," Casey announced to anyone who would listen. "And watch princess movies. And maybe build a fort in the living room."

"Sounds like you ladies have quite a weekend planned," Lana said, watching Sam's face soften as she listened to Casey's excited chatter.

"The best kind," Sam replied, and Lana heard the genuine affection in her voice. Sam loved Casey with an aunt's fierce devotion, and Casey adored her right back.

Potomac Wholesale Flowers
Anacostia, VA.

Javier reviewed the timing one final time. Elena's intelligence network had provided detailed schedules – Agent Lloyd would leave work early today at 1730 hours to pick up his wife's anniversary gift before the jeweler closed at 1800. But Javier would begin his work at 1545 hours, giving him nearly two hours before Chad even left the office. The attack on his anniversary weekend would make the psychological impact even more devastating. His wife would be home alone with the child, probably preparing for their romantic evening, completely unsuspecting.

"Any final instructions from Elena?" Javier asked Jose.

Jose checked his secure phone. "Make it personal. Make it devastating. Agent Lloyd needs to understand that the Ramirez family never forgets." He paused. "She also said to take your time. This isn't about efficiency – it's about impact."

"I will need more than an hour," Javier said, his voice taking on that artist's tone that had made Salvador so proud. "To do what needs to be done to the woman and the child. To craft the proper message."

Jose typed quickly, then waited for Elena's response. When his phone buzzed, he smiled coldly. "Elena says not to worry. She has a delay already in the works for dear Agent Lloyd. You will have all the time you need."

Lloyd Residence
Arlington, VA.

"Thank you for today," Lana said as they gathered their things from the spa. Casey was practically glowing with excitement about her "fancy lady nails" and the weekend sleepover plans they'd made.

"Thank you for including me," Sam replied. "Casey's right – this was the best girls' day ever."

"Mommy, can we show Daddy my nails when he gets home?" Casey asked, holding up her small hands to admire the unicorns with their protective clear coat.

"Of course, princess. He'll be so impressed." Lana hugged her daughter close, breathing in the sweet scent of her hair. "And tomorrow when Aunt Sam comes over for our sleepover weekend, you can show her all the movies you want to watch."

"We're going to make pancakes in shapes and build a fort!" Casey announced excitedly.

"That's right," Sam smiled, though something about Lana's earlier conversation still gnawed at her. "I'll be there bright and early tomorrow morning after Mommy and Daddy leave for their special trip."

As Sam drove them back toward the Lloyd house, where she would drop them off before heading home herself, none of them knew that Lana's desperate request — take care of them — would be put to the test in less than two hours. Tomorrow's sleepover would never happen.

The afternoon sun was beginning its descent toward evening. Soon, across fourteen states, Elena's coordinated revenge would begin. And Lana Lloyd's last day would end in ways none of them could imagine.

Chapter 7

Lloyd Residence
Arlington, VA.

The late afternoon sun cast long shadows through the dining room windows of the Lloyd residence. Lana stood at the mirror in the entryway, checking her reflection one final time while Casey played with Mr. Hoppy in the living room, her voice carrying through the house as she told her stuffed rabbit about their wonderful day with Aunt Sam.

The silk blouse Chad loved brought out the green in her eyes, and sixteen years of marriage hadn't dimmed the flutter in her stomach when she thought of their anniversary dinner ahead. L'Auberge at seven, then the weekend at Willow Grove.

The doorbell's familiar chime echoed through the house at precisely 3:45 PM.

"I'll get it!" Casey called, racing toward the front door with Mr. Hoppy tucked under her arm.

"Casey, wait—" Lana started, but the little girl was already reaching for the handle.

Chad never forgot - sixteen roses, one for each year together, with baby's breath like delicate clouds among the deep red petals. But when Casey opened the door, the man standing there wasn't wearing a delivery uniform anymore.

He was wearing a grotesque clown mask.

Casey's excited smile vanished instantly, replaced by paralyzing terror. She stumbled backward, clutching Mr. Hoppy to her chest as a scream built in her throat. Her worst nightmare had come to life on her doorstep.

"MOMMY!" Casey shrieked, backing away from the door. "MOMMY! THE CLOWN! THE CLOWN!"

"Mrs. Lloyd?" Javier's voice was muffled behind the rubber mask, but his accent was thick, clearly Mexican cartel. "Special delivery from your husband."

Lana raced toward the entryway, her maternal instincts screaming warnings as she saw her daughter's terror. "Casey, come here! Now!"

But Javier moved with brutal efficiency, stepping into the house just as Lana reached for the door. She tried to slam it shut, but he was faster - much faster. The heavy oak door crashed into Lana's forehead with devastating force, sending her staggering backward, vision exploding in white stars.

Casey was frozen with fear, hyperventilating as she stared at the nightmare face looming over her while her mother fought to stay conscious, blood trickling down her temple.

"Stupid move, Mrs. Lloyd," Javier said calmly, stepping fully inside and kicking the door shut behind him. Lana swayed on her feet, disoriented and vulnerable. "But I appreciate the enthusiasm."

While Lana swayed on her feet, Javier produced zip ties from his pocket with practiced ease. He dragged the semi-conscious woman to a dining room chair and secured her hands behind her back, the plastic cutting deep into her wrists.

Casey stood frozen in the entryway, clutching Mr. Hoppy and hyperventilating as she stared at the nightmare clown face.

"Now for the little princess," Javier said, turning toward Casey with deliberate slowness.

As he approached, something shifted in Casey's expression. The paralyzing terror gave way to fierce determination - her father's courage showing through. When Javier reached for her, she drew back her small leg and kicked him as hard as she could in the shin.

"Leave my mommy alone!" she screamed.

Javier's laugh was genuinely amused. "Such spirit. Just like your father." Then his expression turned cold. "But little girls shouldn't fight grown-ups."

He shoved Casey backward with brutal force. Her small body flew through the air, her head striking the sharp corner of the heavy oak dining table with a sickening crack. She crumpled to the floor, Mr. Hoppy falling beside her, both utterly still.

"CASEY!" Lana's anguished scream filled the house.

Javier knelt beside Casey's small form, checking for a pulse with clinical detachment. When he found none, he actually smiled. "Well. That was easier than expected." He looked up at Lana's horrified face. "Don't worry, Mrs. Lloyd. You'll be joining her soon. But first, we have work to do."

From his bag, Javier produced small wireless cameras, methodically positioning them around the dining room. He started the first camera recording, then slowly panned it across Casey's motionless body and Mr. Hoppy lying beside her on the blood-stained hardwood floor.

"Elena wants your husband to see everything," Javier explained, adjusting another camera angle to capture Lana's terror-stricken face. "Every moment of what's about to happen to you. But first, he needs to see what he's already lost."

The camera lingered on Casey's sparkly unicorn nails catching the afternoon light streaming through the windows, then panned back to focus on Lana, zip-tied and bleeding in the dining room chair.

"Why?" Lana managed through clenched teeth, testing her restraints. "Why are you doing this?"

"Your husband made Elena and Hector watch their father die," Javier explained, setting up another camera angle. "Salvador reached for his weapon - a father trying to defend himself. And Agent Lloyd put a single round right between his eyes without hesitation."

He gestured toward Casey's body. "The children should have been there to protect him. Instead, they watched it all later on security footage. Such a touching family moment - seeing their father executed like a dog."

"She was just a baby," Lana whispered, tears streaming down her face.

"She was Lloyd's baby," Javier corrected. "And Lloyd needs to understand what loss feels like."

What followed was two hours of methodical, artistic brutality. Javier worked with the patience of a master craftsman, each cut, each break, each moment of agony carefully calculated for maximum psychological impact. The cameras captured everything as Lana was systematically destroyed, piece by piece.

FBI Headquarters
Washington, D.C

Chad saved the last surveillance file and shut down his computer, checking his watch. Perfect timing - the jeweler closed at six, which gave him just enough time to pick up Lana's anniversary gift before heading home. The ruby necklace had taken three weeks to custom design, matching the earrings he'd given her for their fifteenth anniversary.

"Heading out?" Grey looked up from his desk as Chad gathered his things.

"Finally," Chad replied, slipping his jacket on. "Anniversary weekend starts now. Lana's probably already getting ready for dinner."

"L'Auberge, right? Nice choice." Grey smiled. "Tell her happy anniversary from me. You two deserve this weekend."

"Will do. Don't work too late - it's Friday." Chad paused at the door.

"Enjoy every minute," Grey called after him. "I'll handle anything that comes up."

Meridian Fine Jewelry
Arlington, VA.

The ruby necklace was perfect - deep red stones set in white gold, elegant but not ostentatious. Exactly Lana's style. Chad smiled as the jeweler placed it in a silk-lined box, imagining Lana's face when she opened it tonight at dinner.

"She's going to love it," the jeweler said, completing the transaction. "Sixteen years? You're doing something right."

"She makes it easy," Chad replied, tucking the box into his jacket pocket. Sixteen years, and Lana still made his heart race when she smiled at him across their morning coffee. Tonight would be perfect.

Chapter 8

Lloyd Residence
Arlington, VA.

Your husband will watch this," Javier explained as he worked, his voice conversational despite the horrors he was inflicting. "He'll see how you suffered. How you called his name. How you begged for mercy that never came."

Lana's screams echoed through the house as bones snapped under Javier's precise pressure. The penultimate cut came without warning - a deep slash across her abdomen that sent her body into shock as her life spilled onto the dining room floor. Lana's eyes went wide with the understanding that this was the end.

"Chad will kill you," she managed through frothing blood. "All of you."

"That's the idea," Javier replied. He checked his watch - exactly 1800 hours. Perfect timing. Elena's coordinated strikes would be beginning across fourteen states at this very moment. "Any last words?"

With her last breath, Lana turned her face directly toward the camera, her eyes blazing with a mother's fury despite her failing body. Her voice was weak but defiant, each word crystal clear:

"Chad... avenge Casey's death. Kill these fuckers."

Javier repositioned himself directly behind Lana's chair, the grotesque clown mask still covering his face as he looked straight into the camera. His voice was calm, almost ceremonial:

"The Ramirez family wishes you a happy anniversary, Agent Lloyd."

Javier produced a clear plastic bag from his kit. "Elena wanted this to last," he said conversationally, pulling the bag over Lana's head and sealing it tight around her neck. "But I need to wrap this up. Elena's other gifts are being delivered right now."

"Enjoy your anniversary gift, Agent Lloyd," he said to the camera, then gathered his tools with methodical precision.

As Lana's desperate, muffled struggles began behind him, Javier calmly packed his equipment. The plastic fogged with her panicked breathing, her bound hands fighting uselessly against the zip ties as her body's survival instincts took over.

Javier walked to the front door without looking back, leaving Lana to die alone while the cameras recorded every second of her suffocation. To him, she was already dead - just a message that hadn't finished delivering itself yet.

He slipped out the front door and walked calmly to the white Magnolia Street Flowers van. To any neighbor watching, he was simply a delivery driver finishing his route, perhaps running a bit late on a Friday afternoon.

Behind him, in the Lloyd family dining room, the cameras continued rolling as Lana Lloyd fought her final, futile battle for air - a battle that would end just minutes before her husband came home to find Elena's anniversary present waiting for him.

Through waves of agony and the growing panic of oxygen deprivation, Lana's thoughts drifted to Casey's morning excitement, to her sparkly unicorn nails, to the way she'd hugged Mr. Hoppy and chattered about their wonderful day with Aunt Sam. Her baby girl, who would never grow up, never have her own children, never know how much she was loved.

As the plastic bag fogged with her desperate breaths and darkness crept in at the edges of her vision, Lana held onto one final thought: Sam would keep her promise. Sam would help Chad through the darkness that was coming.

Her struggles gradually weakened, her bound hands falling still as her body finally surrendered. The cameras captured every moment, recording not just her death, but the peaceful expression that crossed her face in those final seconds - the look of a mother who had faith that her family would be protected, even in death.

Chapter 9

Antonio Baez Residence
Houston, TX

DEA Agent Antonio Baez pulled into his driveway, exhausted after a ten-hour day coordinating with federal prosecutors on several case appeals. His wife Maria's car was already there, along with his teenage son's pickup truck. Friday family dinner - the one tradition they'd maintained despite his demanding schedule.

The house felt quiet when he entered through the garage. Too quiet.

"Maria? Miguel?" he called, loosening his tie as he walked into the kitchen.

That's when he saw them.

His family sat around the dining table, hands zip-tied behind their backs, mouths taped shut. Maria's eyes were wide with terror above the duct tape, tears streaming down her cheeks. His son Miguel, seventeen years old and built like a linebacker, had clearly tried to fight - dried blood crusted around his swollen left eye.

"Agent Baez," a voice said behind him. "So good of you to join us."

Antonio spun around to find three men with Tren de Aragua tattoos holding automatic weapons. Carlos Mendoza stepped forward, his Venezuelan accent thick with satisfaction.

"Your family has been waiting for you," Carlos continued. "We've been having such interesting conversations about your role in Salvador Ramirez's death."

"Let them go," Antonio said, his hand moving instinctively toward his service weapon. "This is between me and the cartel."

"I wouldn't," Carlos advised, and Antonio froze as he saw the red laser dots dancing across his wife's chest. "Your family's survival depends entirely on your cooperation."

"What do you want?"

"Justice," Carlos replied simply. "An eye for an eye. You helped kill Salvador Ramirez. Tonight, Elena Ramirez returns the favor."

The next twenty minutes were a symphony of gunfire and screaming that echoed through the suburban Houston neighborhood. Antonio managed to draw his service weapon during the chaos, putting a round center mass into one of the Venezuelan killers before Carlos's men overwhelmed him with automatic weapons fire.

By the time local police arrived, drawn by 911 calls from terrified neighbors, the Baez family had learned the true meaning of cartel vengeance.

Four bodies. Three family members and one Tren de Aragua soldier. No other survivors. And spray-painted on the living room wall in dripping red letters: "VIVA SALVADOR RAMIREZ."

Route 7 and Leesburg Pike
Arlington, VA

Chad was thinking about Lana's reaction to the ruby necklace when the black Escalade ran the red light and T-boned his sedan at full speed. The impact sent his car spinning across the intersection, airbags deploying as metal screamed against asphalt.

For a moment, Chad sat stunned behind the deflating airbag, his ears ringing from the crash. Then he heard car doors slamming and Spanish voices approaching.

"¡Vámonos! ¡Sácalo del carro!"

Chad's tactical training kicked in as he saw three MS-13 members approaching with baseball bats. He drew his Glock just as the first man reached his door.

"Salvador sends his regards, pendejo!" the gang member shouted, yanking Chad's door open.

Chad's first shot took the man center mass before he could swing the bat. The second and third gang members rushed him as he rolled from the wreckage, but twenty years of military and federal training made the outcome inevitable.

The gunfight lasted less than thirty seconds.

Chad stood over the last dying gang member, his service weapon trained on the man's chest. "What did you say about Salvador?"

"Elena... she remembers..." the man gasped, blood frothing at his lips. "Your family... pays tonight..."

The words hit Chad like ice water. Without hesitation, he put a final round center mass, ensuring the threat was neutralized. He grabbed the keys to the Escalade and sped toward home, Elena's coordinated plan suddenly becoming clear. The accident wasn't random - it was a delay tactic.

Chapter 10

En Route to Lloyd Residence

C had's hands gripped the stolen Escalade's steering wheel as he raced through Arlington streets, the gang member's dying words echoing in his mind: "Your family pays tonight." He speed-dialed Grey while weaving through traffic.

"Grey here."

"Nolan, I need immediate backup at my house," Chad's voice was tight with controlled panic. "Elena's targeting families tonight. I was just attacked by MS-13 - they said my family pays tonight. I'm three minutes out."

"Jesus Christ. Chad, slow down—"

"Four gang members just tried to kill me at Route 7 and Leesburg Pike. All four are down. One said 'your family pays tonight' before I put him down permanently." Chad ran a red light, tires screaming. "Elena's coordinating this. I need backup at 1247 Cedar Street NOW."

"I'm moving," Grey replied, already grabbing his jacket. "Do not go in alone. Wait for backup."

"No time. If they're already there..." Chad's voice cracked. "I can't wait, Nolan."

"Then go tactical. Assume hostiles inside. I'll have units there in fifteen minutes."

Lloyd Residence
Arlington, VA

Chad came flying into his driveway, the stolen Escalade's tires screaming as he slammed on the brakes, skidding to a stop inches from Lana's sedan. The summer evening light made everything look deceptively normal, but twenty years of military and federal training screamed warnings. Too quiet. No sound of Casey's laughter or Lana calling out that he was home.

He thought briefly about the ruby necklace sitting in his totaled sedan at the intersection—the anniversary gift he'd never get to give her now.

Moving with tactical precision, Chad approached the front door from an angle that minimized exposure. His service weapon was up and ready as he tested the door handle.

Unlocked. Wrong. Lana always locked the door.

The scattered roses hit him first as he pushed the door open—sixteen red blooms with baby's breath, crushed and browning across the entryway floor. Then the metallic smell of blood.

"Federal agent!" Chad called out, weapon raised, clearing corners as he moved. But even as his training took over, his heart was shattering. The roses. The blood. The silence.

He followed the crimson trail into the dining room, moving tactically but knowing what he would find.

Casey lay motionless beside the table, Mr. Hoppy fallen a few feet away where she'd dropped him when she hit the floor. Lana slumped in the chair, the plastic bag still over her head.

Chad's tactical composure cracked completely. "Lana!" He rushed to his wife, frantically tearing at the plastic bag sealed around her neck. His hands shook as he ripped it away, desperately checking for a pulse.

Her skin was already cool. Her eyes stared at nothing.

"No, no, no," Chad whispered, pressing his ear to her chest. Nothing. He moved to Casey, checking for any sign of life, but she was gone too.

Chad's legs gave out. He collapsed beside Casey's body, his anguished screams echoing through the house as he gathered his daughter's small form in his arms. All his training, all his tactical skills, all his years of protecting others—and he couldn't protect the only people who truly mattered.

With trembling hands, he pulled out his phone and dialed Sam's number.

"Chad? I was just thinking about calling to see how the anniversary dinner—"

"Sam..." Chad's voice broke completely, reduced to barely coherent sobs. "They're gone. Casey... Lana... they're both..."

The line went dead silent except for Chad's ragged breathing.

"No." Sam's voice was barely a whisper. "No, Chad, no..."

"I was too late," Chad choked out, still holding Casey's lifeless body. "The roses... there's blood everywhere... Mr. Hoppy's on the floor beside her..."

Sam felt her world tilt. She'd just spent the day with them. Casey's excitement about her unicorn nails. Lana's laughter at the spa. The promise she'd made about taking care of them.

"I'm coming," Sam said, her own voice cracking as she ran for her car. "Chad, listen to me—I'm coming right now. Don't hang up. I'm three minutes away."

"I should have been here," Chad whispered through his tears. "I should have protected them."

Sam's breath caught as Lana's words from that afternoon came flooding back: If anything happens, you'll take care of them. Both of them. The premonition. The shadow in her eyes. And Casey's excitement about showing Daddy her special nails when he got home. Lana had somehow known.

"Stay with me on the phone," Sam managed, tears streaming down her face as she drove. "Just... just stay with me. I'm almost there."

Sam pressed the accelerator harder, her vision blurred with tears. On the other end of the line, she could hear Chad's world falling apart—the same man who was fearless in the face of danger now completely shattered by the loss of his family.

"I should have been here," Chad whispered. "I should have protected them."

"This isn't your fault," Sam said fiercely through her tears. "Chad, this is not your fault."

In the distance, sirens were beginning to wail. Grey's backup was coming. But right now, in this moment, it was just Chad and Sam—two people bound together by grief and a promise that could never be kept the way it was meant to be.

Chapter 11

Lloyd Residence
Arlington, VA

Detective Jim Supko arrived first, his detective unit's emergency lights painting the quiet Arlington neighborhood in strobing red and blue. Twenty-three years with the Fairfax County Sheriff's Office had shown him every kind of crime scene, but stepping into the Lloyd house hit him like a physical blow.

The scattered roses in the entryway told part of the story - anniversary flowers crushed and browning, their petals mixed with droplets of blood. The crimson trail leading into the dining room told the rest.

"Jesus Christ," Supko breathed, following the path Chad had taken just minutes earlier.

In the dining room, he found Chad Lloyd sitting on the floor beside his daughter's body, cradling her small form while tears streamed down his face. The FBI agent - a man Supko knew by reputation as tough, professional, unshakeable - was completely broken.

"Agent Lloyd?" Supko approached carefully, his voice gentle. "I'm Detective Supko. Agent Grey sent me to secure the scene."

Chad looked up with hollow eyes. "She was just a baby, Detective. Casey was just a baby. Look what they did to her."

Supko's trained eye took in the scene methodically. The child's head trauma from striking the table corner. The mother zip-tied to a chair, a torn plastic bag lay discarded on the floor beside the chair. This wasn't random violence - this was calculated, personal, designed to inflict maximum psychological damage.

"I need to establish a perimeter," Supko said softly. "Keep the scene secure until FBI evidence response arrives. Can you move to the living room for me?"

"I can't leave her," Chad whispered, holding Casey tighter. "I can't leave my little girl."

Supko knelt beside Chad, his voice firm but compassionate. "Agent Lloyd, I have a daughter too. Eight years old. And if someone hurt her, I'd want the bastards caught. But we need to preserve the evidence to make that happen."

It took several minutes, but Supko finally convinced Chad to move to the living room while he secured the dining room with crime scene tape. He'd seen grieving fathers before, but never one whose world had been so completely destroyed.

Sam burst through the front door, her face streaked with tears and her hands still shaking. She'd tried to compose herself when she saw the police cars and crime scene tape, but seeing Chad sitting there with blood on his shirt from holding Casey shattered what little control she had left.

"Chad?" She approached slowly, her voice thick with emotion. "Hey, I'm here."

He looked up at her with recognition but no real comprehension. "Sam? They killed them. They killed my girls."

"I know, honey. I know." Sam sat beside him, close enough to offer comfort but careful not to crowd him, wiping tears from her own cheeks. "I came as fast as I could. I'm so sorry."

"I was buying her necklace," Chad said, his voice flat. "Ruby stones to match her earrings. While I was picking out jewelry, someone was..." He couldn't finish.

Sam felt her own eyes filling with tears. Just hours ago, she'd been shopping with Lana, listening to Casey chatter about unicorn nails and their plans for the weekend sleepover. She'd dropped them off at 3:30, both of them happy and excited about Chad's anniversary surprise. Now they were gone, and Chad was shattered beyond recognition.

Detective Supko finished securing the crime scene with tape, then approached Chad in the living room. "Agent Lloyd, I need to ask you about another incident. We have reports of four deceased subjects and a motor vehicle collision at Route 7 and Leesburg Pike. Your sedan was found at the scene. Can you walk me through what happened?"

Sam looked up sharply - this was the first she was hearing about any of this.

Chad looked up, his voice flat but professional. "I was T-boned by the Escalade while driving home from the jeweler. Four MS-13 members approached my vehicle with baseball bats after the crash."

"They attempted to assault you?"

"One of them said 'Salvador sends his regards' and 'your family pays tonight' before trying to attack. I defended myself." Chad's voice carried no emotion. "All four subjects are deceased. I took their vehicle and drove here immediately."

Sam stared at Chad, processing this new information. He'd been in a gunfight with four gang members before coming home to find his family murdered. No wonder he seemed so emotionally detached - he'd been in combat mode for hours.

Supko made notes, understanding the bigger picture. "So this was coordinated - they delayed you while..."

"While Javier Santos tortured and murdered my family," Chad finished. "Elena Ramirez wanted me to arrive exactly when I did. Wanted me to find them like this."

"I'll need a full statement about the shooting, but given the circumstances and the coordinated nature..." Supko paused. "Agent Lloyd, this changes the scope significantly. We're looking at a multi-scene federal crime with organized criminal conspiracy."

"Detective," Chad said quietly, "you have no idea how big this is going to get."

"Can I see them?" Sam asked gently, her voice still unsteady.

Supko looked between Chad and Sam, then nodded toward the dining room. "I've secured it for evidence, but you can look from the tape line. Don't cross into the scene."

Sam walked to the crime scene tape, and what she saw beyond it destroyed her composure completely. Casey lay where Chad had gently placed her back down, Mr. Hoppy tucked carefully in her small arms. Her sparkly unicorn nails - the ones she'd been so proud of just hours ago - caught the evening light streaming through the windows.

Lana slumped in the chair, the torn plastic bag lying discarded on the floor beside her - evidence of Chad's desperate attempt to save her. Her final moments of suffering were written across her battered face. The woman who'd asked Sam to take care of her family just hours ago, who'd teased her about looking at Chad, who'd trusted her with her deepest fears.

Sam collapsed against the doorframe, fresh sobs wracking her body. "Oh God, Lana. I'm so sorry."

Detective Supko approached carefully. "Agent Belle? You knew them?"

"She was my best friend," Sam managed through her tears. "Casey called me Aunt Sam. We were going to have a sleepover this weekend while they went away for their anniversary. I was just with them this afternoon..."

The weight of Lana's request hit her with renewed force. Take care of them. Lana had somehow known this was coming, had prepared Sam for this moment. Now Sam understood why her friend had seemed so urgent, so desperate to secure that promise.

"Agent Belle," Supko said gently, "I need you to help me with Agent Lloyd. He won't leave the scene, and with FBI evidence response incoming..."

Sam wiped her eyes and straightened. Lana had asked her to take care of Chad, and that job started now. She walked back to the living room where Chad sat motionless.

Chad, look at me." She knelt in front of him, forcing eye contact. "We need to let the evidence team work. They're going to find who did this."

"I know who did this," Chad said, his voice taking on a dangerous edge. "Elena Ramirez. The gang member told me 'your family pays tonight' - this is her revenge for Salvador."

"Then we'll get her. We'll get all of them. But first, we need to let the professionals do their job."

Chapter 12

Lloyd Residence
Arlington, VA

Special Agent in Charge Nolan Grey arrived on the scene. He had commanded federal task forces, worked with Chad in some of the most hostile environments in the world, led joint operations with foreign intelligence services, and briefed presidents on national security threats. But walking into Chad Lloyd's house, seeing his friend and subordinate destroyed by grief, was one of the hardest things he'd ever done.

Chad stood when Grey entered, muscle memory and twenty years of military discipline overriding his emotional state. "Sir."

"Sit down, Chad," Grey said quietly. "I'm not your supervisor right now. I'm your friend."

Grey's eyes swept the crime scene, taking in details with the cold professionalism that had made him one of the Bureau's most effective SACs. But when his gaze lingered on Casey's small form, his jaw tightened with barely controlled rage.

"How are you holding up?" Grey asked, though the answer was obvious.

"I keep thinking I should have been here," Chad said. "If I'd come straight home instead of stopping for the necklace..."

"You'd be dead too," Grey interrupted firmly. "This was coordinated, planned. They knew your schedule, your routines. If you'd been here, Elena would have three bodies instead of two."

Sam looked up from where she'd been sitting beside Chad. "What's the scope of the attacks, Nolan?"

"Fourteen states. Ninety-three confirmed targets so far. Unknown number of dead at this time. MS-13, 18th Street, Tren de Aragua - every gang with cartel connections hit federal agents and their families simultaneously at 1800 hours Eastern Standard Time." Grey's voice was grim. "Elena Ramirez just declared war on the United States government."

"It's worse than that," Sam said, her voice still shaky. "Chad was attacked too. Four MS-13 members T-boned his car at Route 7 and Leesburg Pike, tried to kill him with baseball bats. They told him 'Salvador sends his regards' and 'your family pays tonight.'"

Grey's expression darkened as he processed this. "Jesus, Chad. You were targeted directly?"

"It was a delay tactic," Chad said flatly. "Elena wanted me to arrive exactly when I did. Wanted me to find them like this."

Sam looked up from where she'd been sitting beside Chad. "Do you have any names yet? Of those who were attacked?"

Grey's jaw tightened. "DEA Agent Baez in Houston, his whole family. Judge Morrison in Phoenix. AUSA Wells in Los Angeles."

Chad's head snapped up at the mention of Baez. "Antonio? Antonio Baez is dead?"

"His wife Maria, teenage son Miguel. All of them," Grey confirmed grimly. "Tren de Aragua hit them at their house as Antonio arrived home from work."

Almost an hour after Chad called Grey, Special Agent Marcus Tomlinson and the FBI's premier Evidence Response Team arrived. His team moved with practiced efficiency, documenting and collecting evidence while the coroner examined the victims.

"We've recovered excellent fingerprint evidence from multiple surfaces," Tomlinson reported to Grey after his initial evidence sweep. "The subject was either careless or confident he wouldn't be identified through normal channels."

"Cartel enforcement," Grey said. "They don't expect to be in our databases."

"Actually, sir, we got a hit." Tomlinson consulted his tablet. "Javier Santos, age 35, multiple arrests in Mexico for violent crimes. Also known as 'El Cuchillo' - The Knife. He's Salvador Ramirez's personal enforcer."

Sam felt a chill run down her spine. "He's the one who tortured Lana."

The coroner, Dr. Sarah Rizzoli, approached with her preliminary findings. "Multiple points of trauma on both victims. The child's death appears to have been from blunt force trauma to the head - likely from striking the table corner. The adult female shows signs of prolonged torture before asphyxiation. Based on rigor mortis and body temperature, I'd estimate that the child passed at about 1600 and the adult female passed around 1800."

Chad's hands clenched into fists hearing the clinical assessment of his family's final moments.

"Two hours," Chad repeated, his voice hollow. "She suffered for two hours while I was buying jewelry."

"I got here a little after 6," Chad continued, his voice breaking. "If only I hadn't been delayed by that ambush... if I'd gotten home five minutes earlier... I could have saved her."

"Chad, don't," Sam said firmly. "This isn't your fault."

Grey stepped forward. "Chad, even if you'd arrived earlier, you would have walked into an active torture session with a professional killer. You'd be dead too, and Lana would still be gone."

But Chad wasn't listening. The weight of those five minutes - five minutes that might have meant the difference between life and death for his wife - was crushing him with guilt that would haunt him forever.

Tomlinson continued his briefing. "We also found surveillance equipment. Multiple wireless cameras positioned throughout the dining room. Most transmitted to external servers, but one had a local storage card."

Chapter 13

C had stood abruptly. "Show me."

"Chad, maybe you should—" Sam started.

"Show me," Chad repeated, his voice carrying the command authority that had made him a successful JTAC operator. "That's my wife and daughter on that recording. I have a right to see what happened to them."

Grey exchanged glances with Sam, then nodded to Tomlinson. "Set it up."

The laptop screen seemed impossibly bright in the dimmed living room. Chad sat between Grey and Sam, his posture rigid as Tomlinson queued up the video file. Detective Supko stood nearby, his expression grim.

"Agent Lloyd," Tomlinson said carefully, "this footage is... extremely graphic. Once you see it, you can't unsee it."

"Play it," Chad said simply.

The recording began with Javier positioning the camera, his grotesque clown mask filling the frame before he panned across Casey's motionless body and Mr. Hoppy lying beside her. Chad made a sound deep in his throat - not quite a sob, not quite a growl.

Then the camera focused on Lana, zip-tied and bleeding in the dining room chair.

"Your husband made Elena and Hector watch their father die,"

Javier's voice came through the laptop speakers. "Salvador reached for his weapon - a father trying to defend himself. And Chad Lloyd put a single round right between his eyes without hesitation."

Sam watched Chad's face as he saw his wife's torture begin. His features turned to stone, but his eyes - his eyes began to burn with something that terrified her.

The recording showed Javier's methodical brutality in clinical detail. Each cut, each broken bone, each moment of Lana's agony was preserved with artistic precision. When Lana screamed Chad's name during the worst of it, Chad's hands clenched so tightly his knuckles went white.

Then came Lana's final words, looking directly into the camera with defiant fury despite her broken body:

"Chad... avenge Casey's death. Kill these fuckers."

Grey reached for the laptop. "That's enough."

"No," Chad said, his voice deadly calm. "All of it."

They watched Javier position himself behind Lana's chair, still wearing the clown mask that had terrified Casey in her final moments.

"The Ramirez family wishes you a happy anniversary, Agent Lloyd."

The plastic bag came out. The slow suffocation began. Javier gathered his tools and walked away, leaving Lana to die alone while the camera recorded every second of her final struggle.

When the video ended, the living room was silent except for Sam's quiet crying.

Chad stood slowly, his movements controlled and precise. When he spoke, his voice carried no emotion at all - which somehow made it more terrifying than screaming would have been.

"I'm going to kill them all," he said simply. "Every single one of them. Starting with Javier Santos."

"Chad—" Grey started.

"I'm going to find El Cuchillo," Chad continued, as if Grey hadn't spoken. "And I'm going to make him suffer the way he made Lana suffer. Then I'm going to work my way up the chain until I put a bullet in Elena Ramirez's head."

Sam stood and placed herself in front of Chad, forcing him to look at her. "Chad, listen to me. Lana asked me to take care of you. She made me promise. And part of taking care of you means not letting you throw your life away on revenge."

"She also asked me to avenge Casey's death," Chad replied, his eyes holding Sam's. "You heard her. 'Kill these fuckers,' she said. That's what I'm going to do."

"Through legal channels," Grey said firmly. "We have evidence, we have identification, we have probable cause. We'll get warrants, coordinate with international law enforcement—"

Chad laughed, a sound completely devoid of humor. "Legal channels? Nolan, Elena just murdered ninety-three federal agents and their families in a coordinated attack. You think she's going to surrender to a warrant?"

"What I think," Grey said, standing to face Chad, "is that you're talking about going dark and taking justice into your own hands. As your friend, I understand it. As your supervisor, I can't allow it."

Chad studied Grey's face for a long moment. "Then it's a good thing I'm about to submit my resignation."

The words hung in the air like a death sentence. Sam felt her heart break all over again - first losing Lana and Casey, now losing Chad to whatever darkness was growing behind his eyes.

"Chad, please," she said quietly. "Lana wanted me to keep you human. Don't make me break that promise on the first day."

For just a moment, something flickered in Chad's expression - recognition, maybe even regret. But then his features hardened again.

"Lana also wanted me to avenge our daughter's death. Some promises are more important than others."

Outside, the coroner's assistants pulled into the driveway, coming to take away the last physical remnants of Chad Lloyd's former life. Soon, all that would remain would be the man himself - and the burning need for vengeance that threatened to consume everything he'd once been.

The war Elena Ramirez had started was far from over. In fact, it was just beginning.

Chapter 14

Potomac Wholesale Flowers
Anacostia, VA

While Chad was discovering the deaths of his wife and child, Javier guided the white Magnolia Street Flowers van through the industrial district's evening traffic, his movements unhurried despite the cargo of death he'd left behind. To any observer, he was simply another delivery driver finishing his Friday route, perhaps running slightly behind schedule.

The wholesale flower warehouse appeared exactly as it had that morning - legitimate trucks at the loading docks, workers moving pallets of arrangements, the perfect cover for one of Elena's most sophisticated East Coast operations. Javier pulled around to the employee entrance, where Jose Mendez was already waiting with a disposal crew.

"It's finished," Javier reported simply, stepping from the van and handing Jose the keys.

Jose nodded to the crew, who immediately began their work. "Take it to Anacostia," he instructed. "The usual spot behind the abandoned warehouse on Good Hope Road."

"Copy that," the crew leader replied, already climbing into the van. Within an hour, the vehicle would be burning in one of Southeast D.C.'s most neglected neighborhoods, where torched cars were so common they barely warranted police attention. The residents of Anacostia had seen enough violence and destruction that one more burning van wouldn't even register as unusual.

By morning, it would be just another burned-out shell in a

neighborhood where poverty and crime had made such incidents routine. The van was the last piece of physical evidence tying Javier to Chen's murder. Once it burned, that connection would be gone.

"Any complications?" Jose asked, watching his men work with professional efficiency.

"None." Javier retrieved his personal bag from the van's cargo area, leaving behind only the legitimate flower business equipment. "The Lloyd woman lasted exactly as long as Elena requested. The child was... quicker than expected."

"Elena will be pleased." Jose checked his secure phone. "The coordinated strikes began at eighteen hundred hours. Reports are coming in from all target cities. Very successful so far."

Javier nodded with satisfaction. Elena's planning had been flawless - overwhelm the federal agencies with simultaneous attacks across multiple states. Local police departments would be dealing with what appeared to be unrelated violent crimes, unable to immediately recognize the coordinated nature of the strikes or that all victims were federal agents and their families. By the time law enforcement connected the dots, all of the gang members would be safely out of their operational areas and possibly back across the Mexican border.

Javier walked to the warehouse's converted office space, where a secure satellite phone waited on the desk. He dialed Elena's encrypted number, knowing she would be monitoring all operations from her Cayman compound.

"Javier," Elena's voice came through clearly despite the international connection. "Status report."

"The Lloyd family has been eliminated. Both targets confirmed. The scene is prepared exactly as you specified."

"Excellent. Everything is going according to plan," Elena continued. "Every federal agency is overwhelmed with their own casualties. But this window won't last forever. I've been watching the footage from your cameras - exceptional work. The woman's final message to her husband was perfect."

"You saw everything?" Javier asked.

"Every moment. Soon the cameras will be discovered when the FBI evidence team arrives, but I have everything recorded. Watching Lloyd discover his family will be... satisfying." Elena's voice carried cold pleasure. "Now we need to get you out of the area before they process your fingerprints and start hunting."

Javier waited for instructions, knowing Elena would have planned multiple escape routes.

"Jose has a vehicle ready for you - four-door sedan, nothing flashy to draw attention. You'll drive to Pittsburgh tonight, then fly out in the morning."

"Pittsburgh to Cayman is clean?"

"Completely. You'll fly Pittsburgh to Miami first thing tomorrow morning, then a private charter from Miami to Grand Cayman. The charter is already arranged through one of our shell companies. You'll be traveling under the name of Marco Renaldo. Full documentation, credit history, the works. Jose has your new driver license and airline tickets. Even if they issue a BOLO for Javier Santos before you reach Pittsburgh, you'll be clean."

"And the alias will hold up to scrutiny?"

"Long enough to get you out of the country. Hector and I are already here at the compound, waiting to debrief you personally."

Javier nodded. The plan was elegant in its simplicity - a quiet drive through back roads to avoid D.C. area checkpoints, then disappear into the anonymity of a mid-sized airport where one more person on vacation wouldn't attract scrutiny. By the time federal investigators identified him from the fingerprints, he'd be safely beyond their reach.

"What about the aftermath?" Javier asked. "Lloyd will come hunting."

"Let him come." Elena's laugh was cold with anticipation. "A grieving federal agent going rogue? He'll violate so many laws that his own people will have to hunt him down. We'll destroy him legally before he ever gets close to us."

"And if he proves more resourceful than expected?"

"Then we'll kill him too. But slowly, like we did his family. I want him to suffer before he dies."

Javier ended the call and gathered his few remaining possessions. The clothes he'd worn during the Lloyd operation went into an incinerator, along with any other physical evidence of his presence. By the time investigators processed the crime scene, he would be hundreds of miles away, protected by the vast network Elena had built across the Americas.

Jose approached with final updates. "Transportation is ready. Four-door Honda Accord, nothing flashy. Clean plates, full tank of gas."

"Excellent." Javier shouldered his travel bag, which contained only a few changes of clothes and toiletries. His personal weapons would stay behind - too risky to check them on a flight where any delay or search could compromise his identity.

Jose handed him a set of car keys, airline tickets, and an envelope thick with cash. "Flight leaves at 0730 tomorrow morning, direct to Miami. Charter connection at 1430 to Grand Cayman. Elena asked me to include this," he gestured to the cash envelope, "bonus for exceptional work."

Javier pocketed the envelope without counting it. Money was useful, but the real reward was the satisfaction of a job perfectly executed. Elena would have her psychological warfare footage, Chad Lloyd would be destroyed by grief and rage, and the Ramirez family's honor would be restored.

"The van disposal?" Javier asked.

"Complete in twenty minutes. Sarah Chen's scene is clean. No connection to the events of this evening."

Javier nodded and walked toward the exit. Behind him, Elena's operation continued with clockwork precision. The warehouse would return to its legitimate flower business tomorrow, leaving no trace of the criminal empire it had briefly housed.

The artist's work was finished. Now it was time to disappear before the hunter became the hunted.

Chapter 15

Lloyd Residence
Arlington, VA

C had, you need to let them finish their work," Sam said gently, watching her partner stare at the crime scene tape separating him from his family's bodies. "Come stay at my place tonight. You can't stay here."

Chad hadn't moved from the living room in over an hour, his eyes fixed on the dining room where the coroner and evidence team continued their methodical work.

"I should be here," Chad said quietly. "I should be with them."

"They're not there anymore," Sam replied, her voice gentle but firm. "That's not Lana and Casey in there. That's evidence. The real Lana and Casey - they're already gone."

Grey approached from the kitchen where he'd been coordinating with the evidence team. "Sam's right, Chad. You need some distance. I'll stay here until everything's finished, make sure the house is secured."

"Detective Supko cleared the upstairs when he first arrived," Grey continued. "Crime scene is contained to the dining room and entryway. You can go pack some clothes, but everything else has to stay until ERT finishes processing the house."

Chad finally looked up at them, his eyes hollow but no longer streaming with tears. Something had shifted in his expression - the raw grief was hardening into something colder, more dangerous.

"Okay," he said simply. "Let me get some clothes."

Chad stood slowly, his movements careful and controlled. As he headed toward the stairs, Sam noticed how his posture had changed. Less broken widower, more tactical operator assessing a situation.

"I'll wait down here," Sam called after him.

Chad climbed the stairs mechanically, muscle memory guiding him to the bedroom he'd shared with Lana for sixteen years. Everything was exactly as she'd left it that morning - her makeup scattered across the vanity, her jewelry box open, the book she'd been reading face-down on her nightstand.

He moved to their dresser and began packing clothes into his old military duffel bag. Jeans, t-shirts, underwear - the mundane necessities of life that seemed absurd in the face of such devastating loss.

That's when he saw it.

Hanging on the bedroom door handle was the distinctive La Perla shopping bag from Lana's afternoon with Sam. The black lace negligee she'd bought for their anniversary weekend. The silk robe that would have matched the ruby necklace still sitting in his totaled sedan at the ambush site.

Chad's hands trembled as he touched the bag. Inside was lingerie that would never be worn, for a romantic weekend that would never happen, with a woman who would never again smile at him across their morning coffee.

A weekend at the Inn at Willow Grove. Long walks, intimate dinners, romantic evenings. All of it destroyed by Elena Ramirez's need for revenge.

July 19th. Their anniversary. The day he'd said I do to her sixteen years ago, the happiest moment of his life until Casey was born. Elena had deliberately chosen this date - their most sacred day - to destroy everything he loved.

Every future July 19th would be poisoned now. Instead of celebrating their love, he'd remember Lana's torture, Casey's broken body, the anniversary roses scattered across their entryway floor. Elena hadn't just killed his family - she'd murdered every happy memory they'd built together.

The psychological warfare was perfect in its cruelty. Elena understood that some wounds never heal, that some dates become scars carved into a man's soul. She'd ensured that Chad would relive this horror every year for the rest of his life.

Chad carefully hung the bag in Lana's closet, next to the dresses she would never wear again. Then he finished packing with robotic precision - shaving kit, extra socks, his backup weapon from the bedroom safe. Grey would need his service weapon for ballistics testing for the ambush shooting when he went back downstairs.

As he zipped the duffel bag, Chad passed Casey's bedroom.

The door was slightly ajar, just as Casey had left it that morning. Chad pushed it open and stepped inside, immediately overwhelmed by the scent of his daughter - that unique mixture of strawberry shampoo, crayons, and childhood innocence.

Her bed was unmade, blankets twisted from her restless sleep. Stuffed animals lined the shelves, watching over a room their owner would never see again. On her nightstand sat the book they'd been reading together - "Charlotte's Web" - with a bookmark holding their place at Chapter 7.

Chad picked up the book, remembering how Casey would curl up beside him every night, insisting on "just one more page" until Lana finally intervened with bedtime discipline. His little girl who'd been so excited about her unicorn nails, about their sleepover with Aunt Sam, about everything life had to offer.

Now she was gone, killed for no reason other than her father's job.

Chad sank onto Casey's bed and broke down completely. Not the shocked grief from downstairs, but the deep, soul-crushing realization that his daughter would never run to greet him again. Never call him Daddy. Never grow up to have children of her own.

The sobs came from somewhere deep inside him, animal sounds of pain that seemed to tear him apart from within. He clutched Casey's pillow to his chest, breathing in the lingering scent of her presence.

"I'm sorry, baby girl," he whispered. "Daddy's so sorry he wasn't here to protect you."

Sam heard the sounds from upstairs and started toward the staircase, but Grey caught her arm.

"Give him a few minutes," Grey said quietly. "He needs to grieve."

"He sounds like he's dying up there."

"Part of him is." Grey guided Sam to the kitchen, away from the evidence team's work. "Sam, there are things about Chad you don't know. Things from before he met Lana."

Sam studied Grey's expression, seeing genuine concern beneath his professional demeanor. "What kind of things?"

Grey was quiet for a long moment, choosing his words carefully. "Chad did multiple combat tours - Iraq, Afghanistan, Syria among others. He was a JTAC attached to an Army Special Operations Team calling in airstrikes on enemy positions. But it wasn't the combat that broke him. It was losing his team."

"His team?"

"Operation Iron Resolve, 2012. Chad's team was inserted via Chinook into what intelligence said was a secured LZ in the Hindu Kush mountains. As they exited the bird, Staff Sergeant Robinson - Chad's best friend since basic training - took three rounds to the chest and collapsed right in front of Chad. Chad tripped over Robinson's body as he fell, which is the only reason he wasn't cut down in the initial ambush."

Grey's voice grew heavy with the weight of the story. "That stumble over his best friend's corpse saved Chad's life. The Taliban had been waiting. Machine gun nests, RPGs, the whole mountain lit up like the Fourth of July. The entire eight-man team was cut down in the first thirty seconds - everyone except Chad, who was sprawled on the ground behind Robinson's body."

Sam felt her breath catch. "Eight men?"

"Chad spent the next four hours alone on that mountainside, surrounded by his dead teammates, fighting off wave after wave of Taliban fighters. He ran out of ammunition after the first hour and had to strip weapons from the bodies of his friends. When that ran out, it went to knives, rocks, bare hands - whatever it took to survive."

Sam felt her stomach drop. "Oh my God."

"Chad went dark after that. Really dark. Started taking unnecessary risks, volunteering for the most dangerous missions. His commanding officers thought he was trying to get himself killed. When he finally rotated home, he was..." Grey struggled for the right words. "He was cold. Disconnected. Angry at the world."

"But he seems so normal. So gentle with Casey..."

"That's because of Lana." Grey's voice was soft with memory. "She was his nurse when he came home injured from his final deployment. Minor shrapnel wounds, but severe PTSD. Lana didn't just heal his body - she brought him back to the light. Taught him how to love again, how to believe in goodness."

Sam was beginning to understand Grey's concern. "And now she's gone."

"Along with Casey, who was the center of his world. Sam, Lana was the only thing standing between Chad and the darkness he carried from those years. She grounded him, gave him purpose beyond killing."

Upstairs, Chad's sobs had quieted, but they could hear him moving around Casey's room.

"What are you saying?" Sam asked, though she was afraid she already knew.

"I'm saying Elena Ramirez has no idea what she just unleashed. She thinks she killed a federal agent's family to send a message. What she actually did was remove the only person who could keep Chad Lloyd human."

Grey's phone buzzed with updates from other attack sites - more agents dead, more families destroyed. But his eyes remained fixed on the ceiling, tracking Chad's movements above them.

"The Chad Lloyd who loved Lana and played tea party with Casey? He's gone. What's left is the operator who survived three war zones and lost everything that mattered to him. And that man..." Grey paused, his voice heavy with foreboding. "That man is going to burn down everything Elena Ramirez built to get his revenge."

Sam found Chad sitting on Casey's bed, holding one of her stuffed animals - a small elephant named Peanuts that Casey had gotten for her fourth birthday. His tears had stopped, but his eyes held that same dangerous emptiness she'd noticed downstairs.

"Hey," Sam said softly, sitting beside him on the tiny bed. "How are you holding up?"

Chad looked at her, and for a moment she saw the man she'd worked with for two years - her partner, her friend, the devoted father who kept photos of Casey on his desk. But then something shifted behind his eyes.

"They were everything, Sam," he said quietly. "Lana and Casey were my whole world. Without them..." He trailed off, staring at Peanuts in his hands.

"You still have people who care about you," Sam said carefully. "Grey, me, your team. You're not alone in this."

"What am I supposed to do without them?" Chad's voice cracked slightly. "How am I supposed to wake up every morning knowing they're never coming home? Knowing that some piece of shit killed my little girl for revenge?"

Sam put her arm around his shoulders, and Chad leaned into her embrace. They sat like that for several minutes, two friends sharing grief in a room that still smelled like childhood and innocence.

"Lana asked me to take care of you," Sam whispered. "Made me promise. I won't let you face this alone."

Chad's arms tightened around her, and she felt some of the tension leave his body. For a moment, he was just a broken man who needed human connection.

But when he pulled back, Sam saw something in his eyes that chilled her to the bone. It wasn't grief anymore. It was calculation.

"I need to ask you something," Chad said, his voice steady and controlled. "As my partner, as Lana's friend. When I find the people who did this - and I will find them - are you going to try to stop me?"

The question hung in the air between them, heavy with implication. Sam realized this was a crossroads moment - not just for Chad, but for their partnership, their friendship, everything they'd built together.

"Chad..."

"Are you going to try to stop me?" he repeated, his eyes holding hers with uncomfortable intensity.

Sam thought about Lana's final words on the recording: Chad, avenge Casey's death. Kill these fuckers. She thought about Casey's broken body, about the hours of torture Lana had endured. She thought about Grey's warning about the darkness Chad carried.

"I don't know," she answered honestly. "I don't know what I'll do when that moment comes."

Chad nodded, seeming to accept her honesty. He stood and picked up his duffel bag, taking one last look around Casey's room.

"Let's go," he said simply. "I've seen enough."

As they walked downstairs together, Sam couldn't shake the feeling that she'd just watched Chad Lloyd die in his daughter's bedroom. What was walking beside her now was something else entirely - something forged in war zones and tempered by unimaginable loss.

Elena Ramirez had wanted to destroy Chad Lloyd. Instead, she'd created something far more dangerous: a man with nothing left to lose and the skills to make her pay for every moment of his family's suffering.

Chapter 16

Sam's Apartment
Alexandria, VA

As they prepared to leave, Grey approached Chad with a professional but sympathetic expression. "Chad, I need your service weapon for ballistics testing. The Route 7 shooting is justified, but we have to follow protocol."

Chad nodded and drew his Glock, ejecting the magazine and clearing the chamber with practiced efficiency before handing both to Grey. "How long?"

"A few days, maybe a week. Ballistics will confirm what we already know - clean shoots on all four subjects." Grey secured the weapon in an evidence bag. "And Chad... I'm placing you on paid administrative leave pending the investigation. Standard procedure for any officer-involved shooting."

"I understand," Chad replied, his voice flat. He pulled his backup weapon from his duffel bag. "I assume my carry permit still applies?"

"Of course. Just... try to stay out of trouble while you're on leave."

Chad's smile held no humor. "I'll do my best."

Sam's apartment felt strangely quiet despite having Chad there. He sat on her couch, still wearing the blood-stained shirt from holding Casey, staring at nothing while she moved around the kitchen making coffee neither of them would drink.

"You should try to get some sleep," Sam said gently, setting a mug on the coffee table beside him.

Chad shook his head. "Every time I close my eyes, I see them. Casey lying there with Mr. Hoppy. Lana in that chair." His voice was hollow, mechanical. "Tell me about today. About your time with them."

Sam settled into the chair across from him, understanding his need to talk about them while they were still real, still present in memory. "Casey was so excited about her unicorn nails. She made the technician promise to put extra glitter on them so they'd sparkle like real magic."

A ghost of a smile crossed Chad's face. "She believed in magic. Real magic. Used to leave cookies for the tooth fairy even when she hadn't lost any teeth."

"Lana talked about you a lot today," Sam continued carefully. "About how proud she was of the father you'd become. How you'd read to Casey every night, even when you were exhausted from work."

"Charlotte's Web," Chad whispered. "We were on Chapter 7. She'll never know how it ends."

They talked through the night - about Casey's first steps, about Lana's terrible cooking that somehow always tasted perfect, about family vacations and bedtime stories and all the small moments that had made up a life together. Sam listened to every word, understanding that these memories were all Chad had left of his family.

Around three in the morning, exhaustion finally overtook grief. Chad's eyes grew heavy as he leaned back on the couch, his voice trailing off mid-sentence about Casey's last birthday party.

Sam covered him with a blanket and settled into her chair, too wired to sleep but unwilling to leave him alone. She dozed fitfully, one ear always tuned to Chad's breathing.

Chad's scream tore through the quiet apartment like a gunshot.

Sam jerked awake to find him bolt upright on the couch, eyes wide with terror, his body shaking with remembered horror. Sweat plastered his hair to his forehead despite the cool morning air.

"Chad!" Sam rushed to him, sitting beside him on the couch. "Hey, you're okay. You're safe."

"I saw it again," he gasped, his breathing rapid and shallow. "The video. Lana's face when... when he put that bag over her head. Casey calling for Lana while that monster in the clown mask..." He couldn't finish.

Sam pulled him into her arms, feeling his whole body trembling against her. "It was a nightmare. Just a nightmare."

"No," Chad said, his voice breaking completely. "It wasn't a nightmare. It was real. It happened, and I watched it happen, and I couldn't do anything to stop it."

That's when the dam finally broke. All the grief and rage and helplessness he'd been holding back since finding their bodies came pouring out in great, wrenching sobs that seemed to tear him apart from the inside. Sam held him through it all, feeling her own tears falling as Chad finally let himself feel the full weight of his loss.

They stayed like that for nearly an hour - Chad crying for his dead family while Sam provided the only comfort she could offer: her presence, her strength, and the promise that he wouldn't face this darkness alone.

Sam was making breakfast when Chad's phone rang. The caller ID showed Marie Thompson - Lana's mother. Chad stared at the phone for three rings before answering.

"Marie?"

"Don't you dare call me that," came the sharp reply. "Mrs. Thompson to you. Do you have any idea what you've done?"

Chad felt his stomach drop. "Marie, I know you're grieving—"

"Grieving?" Her voice was shrill with rage. "Our daughter is dead because of you! Our granddaughter is dead because of your job, your enemies, your choices!"

Sam watched Chad's face crumble as the words hit him like physical blows.

"If you hadn't been FBI, if you hadn't made enemies with those cartel animals, Lana and Casey would still be alive," Marie continued, her voice breaking with grief and fury. "You brought this evil into their lives. You got them killed."

"Marie, please—"

"We don't want you at the funeral," she cut him off. "We don't want to see your face. We don't want any reminders of what your choices cost our family."

Chad sank into a chair, the phone trembling in his hand. "They were my family too."

"They were OUR family first. And now they're gone because they had the misfortune of loving you." The line was quiet for a moment before Marie delivered the final blow. "Don't contact us again, Chad. Ever. As far as the Thompson family is concerned, you're dead to us. Just like you are to Lana and Casey."

The line went dead.

Chad stared at the phone for a long moment before setting it carefully on the table. When he looked up at Sam, his eyes held a emptiness that terrified her.

"They don't want me at the funeral," he said quietly. "Lana's parents blame me for getting them killed. They never want to see me again."

Sam felt her heart break all over again. "Chad, they're in shock. They're grieving. They don't mean—"

"Yes, they do." Chad's voice was calm, matter-of-fact. "And they're right. If I hadn't been FBI, if I hadn't been on that task force, Elena would never have targeted my family. Lana and Casey died because of choices I made."

"That's not true. You were doing your job, protecting people—"

"I failed to protect the people who mattered most." Chad stood and walked to the window, staring out at the morning traffic. "Grey was right yesterday. I should have died with them. At least then they'd have died knowing their husband and father loved them enough to die for them."

The resignation in his voice was more frightening than any rage would have been. Sam realized she was watching Chad disappear piece by piece - first his family, now the Thompsons, leaving him completely isolated in his grief.

"You still have people who care about you," Sam said quietly. "Grey, me, your team—"

"Do I?" Chad turned to face her, and Sam saw something cold and calculating behind his eyes. "How long before the Bureau decides I'm too damaged to be effective? How long before my friends get tired of dealing with my grief? How long before you realize that being around me is dangerous?"

Sam stepped closer to him. "I'm not going anywhere, Chad. I

promised Lana I'd take care of you, and I keep my promises."

Chad studied her face for a long moment. "Even if taking care of me means helping me get revenge on the people who killed my family?"

The question hung in the air between them, heavy with implication. Sam realized this was another crossroads moment - not just for Chad, but for their relationship and her own moral compass.

"I don't know," she answered honestly. "But I'm not abandoning you. Whatever comes next, we'll face it together."

Chapter 17

Fairfax County Coroner's Office
Two Days Later

Dr. Sarah Rizzo looked up from her paperwork as Chad entered the medical examiner's office. She'd been expecting this visit - family members always wanted answers, and Chad Lloyd's case was particularly heartbreaking.

"Agent Lloyd," she said gently. "I'm sorry for your loss. Please, sit down."

Chad remained standing, his posture rigid. "When will the autopsies be complete?"

"I finished the examinations yesterday. I was planning to call you today with my findings." Dr. Rizzo consulted her files. "Your daughter's death was instantaneous - massive head trauma from striking the table corner. She wouldn't have suffered."

Chad's jaw tightened, but he nodded. "And Lana?"

"Multiple trauma injuries consistent with systematic torture, followed by asphyxiation. Based on the evidence..." She paused, choosing her words carefully. "Your wife fought back. There are defensive wounds, evidence that she struggled throughout the ordeal."

"How long?"

"Approximately two hours between the initial attack and death. I'm sorry, Agent Lloyd. I know this is difficult to hear."

Chad was quiet for a long moment. "When can I arrange for burial?"

"The bodies can be released tomorrow. However..." Dr. Rizzo hesitated. "I understand there may be some complications with the funeral arrangements?"

"Lana's parents don't want me there," Chad said simply. "They blame me for getting them killed."

"Actually, Agent Lloyd, it's more than that. I received a call from an attorney representing Robert and Marie Thompson." Dr. Rizzo's voice was uncomfortable but professional. "Under no uncertain terms am I to release the bodies to you. The Thompsons will be arranging for a funeral home to pick them up directly."

Chad felt the words hit him like physical blows. Not only was he banned from the funeral, but he couldn't even claim his own wife and daughter's bodies. The Thompsons had legally shut him out of every aspect of their final arrangements.

"I'm sorry. That must be incredibly difficult on top of everything else."

"I see," Chad said quietly, his voice showing no emotion despite the devastation behind his eyes. "Dr. Rizzo, I'd like copies of the autopsy reports."

"Of course. You're the next of kin, regardless of the funeral arrangements." She pulled out a thick manila envelope from her desk. "I prepared these for you. They're comprehensive, but Agent Lloyd... they're very detailed about the injuries. Are you sure you want to read them?"

Chad took the envelope without hesitation. "I need to know everything that happened to them. Every detail."

Dr. Rizzo nodded understandingly. "The reports document everything - cause of death, time estimates, the sequence of injuries. If you have any questions after reviewing them, please don't hesitate to call."

Chad tucked the envelope under his arm. He would study every page, memorize every wound, catalog every moment of suffering his family had endured. It would fuel the fire of his revenge and ensure he never forgot exactly what Elena Ramirez had taken from him.

Chad turned to leave, then paused at the door. "Doctor, in your professional opinion, did Lana know she was going to die?"

Dr. Rizzo considered the question carefully. "Yes. I believe she did. But Agent Lloyd... her final words, the ones captured on video? She wasn't thinking about herself in those last moments. She was thinking about you."

Fort Bragg, North Carolina
Three Days Later

The familiar sounds of military training echoed across Fort Bragg as Chad walked toward the Special Operations compound. His visitor's pass felt strange after years of federal credentials, but the MP at the gate had recognized his name immediately.

Master Sergeant Marcus Ryan was waiting in the unit's break room, looking older but still carrying the lean, dangerous build of a career Special Operations soldier. Chad's former teammate stood when he entered, offering a firm handshake that turned into a brief embrace.

"Sorry about your family, brother," Marcus said quietly. "Word travels fast in our community. We heard what happened."

Chad nodded, settling into one of the metal chairs. "Thanks for agreeing to see me."

"Are you kidding? After everything we went through together?" Marcus studied Chad's face with the practiced eye of someone who'd seen combat trauma. "You look like hell, though. When's the last time you slept?"

"Sleep's overrated." Chad's voice was flat, emotionless. "Marcus, I need to ask you something. Off the record."

Marcus leaned back, immediately understanding the tone. "Talk to me."

"If someone hurt your family. Killed your wife and daughter. And the law couldn't touch them because they were protected by international borders and cartel money..." Chad met his friend's eyes. "What would you do?"

Marcus was quiet for a long moment, recognizing the dangerous territory they were entering. "Chad, I know what you're thinking. We all do. But going dark isn't the answer."

"Isn't it? Elena Ramirez is sitting safe somewhere right now, probably celebrating the success of her revenge operation. She killed ninety-three federal agents and their families, and she's completely untouchable through legal channels."

"So you're talking about going off the grid? Taking justice into your own hands?"

Chad's silence was answer enough.

Marcus rubbed his face, weighing his words carefully. "Brother, I've seen what that path does to good men. In Afghanistan, Iraq... revenge operations never end clean. They consume everything good left in you."

"There's nothing good left in me to consume," Chad replied quietly. "Lana and Casey were everything that mattered. Without them..."

"Without them, you're talking about throwing away everything they loved about you." Marcus leaned forward. "Chad, your little girl wouldn't want her daddy to become a killer for her sake."

"My little girl is dead because I failed to protect her." Chad's voice carried a cold finality that made Marcus nervous. "The question isn't whether I'm going to hunt down the people responsible. The question is whether I do it alone or with help."

Marcus studied his old teammate's face, seeing the same expression Chad had worn in the Hindu Kush after watching his entire team die. Back then, Chad had channeled that rage into becoming one of the most effective operators Marcus had ever served with. Now, with no military structure to contain it...

"If you're determined to do this," Marcus said slowly, "and I'm not saying I support it, but if you're going to do it anyway... you'll need resources. Equipment. Intelligence."

Chad nodded, understanding they'd crossed into planning mode.

"There are people. Private contractors, former operators who work in the gray areas. They might be willing to help for the right price." Marcus pulled out his phone. "But Chad, once you start down this road, there's no coming back. The FBI, the law, your old life - it's all gone."

"It's already gone," Chad replied. "Elena Ramirez made sure of that when she killed my family."

Marcus scrolled through his contacts, finding the names Chad would need. "These guys operate in Central America, Caribbean, places where cartels think they're untouchable. But brother... promise me something."

"What?"

"When this is over, when you've had your revenge, don't eat a bullet. Don't let Elena Ramirez claim one more victim. Find a way to keep living, even if it's just to spite her memory."

Chad took the phone, memorizing the contact information. "I'll think about it."

But Marcus could see in his friend's eyes that survival after revenge wasn't part of Chad's plan. This was a suicide mission dressed up as justice - a man who'd lost everything and intended to take his enemies with him when he died.

As Chad prepared to leave, Marcus grabbed his arm. "Chad, wait. There's something else you should know. Something about Elena Ramirez's operation."

"What?"

"Word from our intelligence contacts is that she's not just hiding. She's building something bigger. Using the success of the coordinated attacks to expand her network, recruit new talent. If you're going after her, you're not just hunting one woman. You're taking on an entire criminal empire."

Chad's smile was cold as arctic wind. "Good. I'd hate for this to be too easy."

Sam's Apartment
Nearly Midnight

Sam had been worried when Chad wasn't back by dinner time, but she knew the drive to Fort Bragg and back would take most of the day. When he finally walked through the door just before midnight, something in his posture had changed - less broken, more focused. It should have been a relief, but instead it made her nervous. "How was your visit?" she asked carefully.

"Productive," Chad replied, settling onto her couch. "Got some perspective on things."

"What kind of perspective?"

Chad studied her face for a moment before answering. "The kind

86

that helps a man understand what he needs to do next."

Sam felt a chill run down her spine. The emptiness in Chad's eyes was gone, replaced by something that looked like purpose. But it was the wrong kind of purpose - cold, calculating, dangerous.

"Chad, what did you talk about with your Army friends?"

"Old times. War stories. The kind of conversations that remind you who you really are underneath all the civilian pretense." Chad's voice was calm, matter-of-fact. "Sam, I need to ask you something, and I need you to be honest with me."

"Okay."

"When I go after Elena Ramirez - and I am going after her - are you going to try to stop me? Are you going to call Grey, alert the Bureau, try to have me arrested?"

The question hung in the air between them like a loaded weapon. Sam realized this was the moment Lana had somehow foreseen, the choice she'd been prepared for when she made Sam promise to take care of Chad.

"I don't know," Sam answered honestly. "Part of me wants to see Elena pay for what she did. But Chad, I also don't want to lose you too."

Chad nodded, seeming to accept her honesty. "Fair enough. But Sam, understand this - nothing is going to stop me from hunting down every person involved in my family's murder. Nothing and no one. If you try to interfere..."

He didn't finish the threat, but Sam heard it anyway. The man sitting across from her wasn't her partner anymore. He was something else entirely - something forged in war zones and tempered by unimaginable loss.

Chapter 18

Lloyd Resident
One Week Later

G rey had cleared it with the evidence team and Detective Supko - the crime scene processing was complete, and Chad could return to collect personal belongings. Sam drove him to the house, neither of them speaking during the twenty-minute trip through Arlington.

The house looked different now. Crime scene tape still fluttered from the front porch, and the neighbors' curious stares followed them as they walked to the front door. Chad hesitated with his key in the lock.

"You don't have to do this today," Sam said gently.

"Yes, I do." Chad pushed open the door. "I can't leave their things here forever."

The entryway had been cleaned, but Chad could still see the faint outline where the roses had been scattered. In the dining room, chalk outlines marked where the bodies had been found. Someone had scrubbed the blood from the hardwood floors, but the stains remained visible to those who knew where to look.

Chad stood in the doorway of the dining room for several minutes, seeing not the empty space but the horrific tableau he'd discovered yesterday. Sam waited beside him, offering silent support.

"The chair," Chad said finally. "I need to get rid of that chair."

They started with the dining room, boxing up dishes and glassware that held too many memories of family meals. Chad moved mechanically, wrapping each item carefully before placing it in boxes marked for storage.

In the living room, they packed Casey's toys - her collection of stuffed animals, her art supplies, the books they'd read together. Chad lingered over each item, remembering the stories behind them.

"She got this elephant for her third birthday," he said, holding up Peanuts. "Wouldn't go anywhere without it for six months. Lana used to joke that we should buy stock in the toy company."

Chad held the small elephant close to his chest for a moment, then set it aside on the dresser. "I'm keeping this," he said quietly. "Mr. Hoppy will be buried with her - he was with her at the end. But Peanuts... Peanuts was her first real friend.

Sam nodded, understanding. Some memories were too precious to pack away.

Upstairs was harder. Casey's room felt frozen in time - her unmade bed, her clothes scattered on the floor, her nightstand with Charlotte's Web still bookmarked at Chapter 7. On her dresser sat a small, lopsided ceramic bowl Casey had made with the pottery set Sam had given her for her birthday, painted in bright purple with uneven yellow flowers around the rim.

Chad sat on her bed and broke down again, overwhelmed by the scent of strawberry shampoo and childhood innocence. He picked up the little bowl, remembering how proud Casey had been when she'd presented it to him, declaring it was for his "important stuff" on his desk at work.

"Take your time," Sam said, stepping out to give him privacy.

In the master bedroom, Chad found Lana's La Perla bag still hanging in the closet where he placed it the night before. He stared at it for a long moment before carefully packing it away with her other clothes. The jewelry box on her vanity contained the ruby earrings he'd given her for their tenth anniversary - the ones that were supposed to match the necklace he'd never had the chance to give her.

By evening, they had packed everything into storage boxes except for what Chad would take with him - a few changes of clothes, his weapons, some photos, Peanuts the elephant, Charlotte's Web, the unfinished novel from Lana's nightstand, a few shirts that still held their essence and a small wooden box containing Casey's first lost tooth and a lock of her baby hair.

"Everything else goes to storage," Chad said, loading the boxes into the rental truck. "I won't be around long enough to need any of it."

"Where will you stay?" Sam asked as they grabbed the last of Chad's things.

"Extended Stay America on Route 50," Chad replied. "Weekly rates. I won't be there long."

Sam didn't ask what he meant by that, but the cold certainty in his voice made her stomach clench with dread.

"What if you change your mind?" Sam asked. "What if you want to settle somewhere, start over?"

Chad looked at her with those hollow eyes that had replaced the warmth she used to know. "There is no starting over, Sam. There's only finishing what Elena started."

The way he said it - with such calm certainty - made Sam realize that Chad wasn't planning for a future at all. He was preparing for a mission, and missions had endpoints.

"Chad, forget the hotel," Sam said, trying to keep her voice casual. "Stay at my place. The couch is comfortable, and..." she searched for the right words, "I could use the company too. This whole thing has me shaken up."

Chad studied her face, and for a moment Sam worried he could see through her real motivation - keeping him close enough to monitor, to intervene if he started planning something irreversible.

"I don't want to be a burden," Chad said finally.

"You're not. We're partners, remember? Partners look out for each other." Sam touched his arm gently. "Besides, I promised Lana I'd take care of you. That's easier to do if you're not hiding out in some extended stay motel."

Chad was quiet for a long moment, staring at the boxes containing his former life. "Okay," he said simply. "For now."

Sam felt a mixture of relief and dread. She'd bought herself time to keep an eye on him, but she could see the calculation behind his eyes. Chad was planning something, and she might be the only thing standing between him and a path of no return.

"I need to call ServPro or someone like that," Chad said, taking one last look at the house. "Get this place cleaned up and on the market. The memories of what happened here... I can never come back to this place. The sooner I sell it, the better."

Sam nodded, understanding. The house wasn't a home anymore - it was a crime scene, a monument to his loss. Every room held echoes of laughter that had been silenced, every corner reminded him of the family that would never return.

"I can help you find a realtor," Sam offered. "Someone who specializes in... difficult sales."

"Just needs to be gone," Chad replied, his voice flat and practical. "Whatever it takes to close that chapter."

But Sam could hear what he wasn't saying - that he was closing more than just the chapter on the house. He was systematically eliminating every tie to his old life, every reason to stay in one place, every obstacle to whatever dark path he was planning to walk.

Chad carefully placed Peanuts, the pottery bowl, Charlotte's Web, Lana's unfinished novel, several family photos, and a few of their t-shirts into a small box. "This goes with us," he said, placing it in Sam's trunk alongside his weapons case and a duffel bag of clothes for the back seat.

They were loading the last of the storage boxes when two cars pulled into the driveway. Marie and Robert Thompson climbed out of the first vehicle, followed by Lana's sister Jennifer and her husband Mark from the second.

"What the hell do you think you're doing?" Marie demanded, storming toward the front door. "You have no right to be here!"

Chad straightened, his jaw tightening. When he spoke, his voice was unnaturally calm, controlled in a way that made Robert take an unconscious step backward. "This is my house, Marie. These are my belongings."

"Your house?" Jennifer's voice was shrill with grief and anger. "Our sister died in this house because of you! Casey died because of your choices!"

"We told you we didn't want to see you," Robert added, though his voice carried less conviction than his wife's. There was something in

Chad's stillness that triggered his survival instincts.

"That's interesting," Chad replied, his tone remaining eerily calm while his eyes grew cold. "You don't want to see me, yet here you are. Uninvited. On my property. Threatening me." He took a slow step forward. "That seems... inconsistent."

Robert felt his mouth go dry. The man standing before them wasn't the broken widower he had expected to see. This was someone else entirely - someone dangerous.

"We have every right to be here," Marie blustered, but even she seemed less certain now.

"Do you?" Chad's voice remained conversational, almost pleasant. "Because I'm fairly certain trespassing laws don't have grief exemptions."

"You're stealing from them," Marie accused, gesturing at the boxes. "Taking their things like some vulture picking over the dead."

Sam stepped forward, her voice calm but firm. "Mrs. Thompson, I understand you're grieving, but Chad has every legal right to be here. This is his property."

"Legal right?" Jennifer laughed bitterly. "He got our family killed, and now he wants to profit from it? Probably selling their belongings online before they're even buried."

Chad's hands slowly clenched into fists. Sam could see the dangerous stillness settling over him - the same controlled calm she'd witnessed in tactical situations.

"You need to leave," Chad said quietly. "Now."

"We're not going anywhere, we have every right to be here," Marie declared, pulling out her phone. "Someone needs to make sure you don't steal everything that belonged to Lana and Casey." She dialed 911. "I'm calling the police. We'll see what they have to say about this."

Ten minutes later, a Fairfax County patrol car pulled into the driveway. As Officer Rhonda Williams approached the group, Mark suddenly shoved Sam aside and made a beeline for the front door.

"Mark, don't!" Jennifer called after him.

"You can't stop us from getting Lana's things," Mark declared, pushing past Sam toward the entrance.

"Sir, you need to stop," Chad said firmly, stepping into Mark's path.

"You don't want to be charged with assaulting a federal officer or unlawfully entering a private residence."

But Mark and Robert were beyond reason, grief and anger driving them forward. Robert joined his son-in-law, both men trying to force their way past Chad into the house.

Sam's training kicked in instantly. She caught Robert's arm as he tried to push past her, spinning him around and applying a textbook arm bar that sent him crashing to the ground, his face pressed into the gravel driveway.

Mark swung a wild haymaker at Chad as he tried to force his way to the door. The punch connected with Chad's jaw, snapping his head to the side. But instead of staggering, Chad simply turned back to face Mark with that same unnatural calm.

Chad's response was surgical - a precise knife-hand strike to Mark's throat that dropped him instantly, gasping and choking as he clutched his windpipe.

"He assaulted us!" Marie screamed as Officer Williams reached the group. "Arrest him! He attacked my husband and son-in-law!"

Officer Williams looked around the scene, taking in the federal agents, the grieving family, and the two men still catching their breath on the ground.

"What's the situation here?" she asked calmly.

"These men tried to force entry into my residence after being told they had no right to be here," Chad replied, showing his FBI credentials.

Williams studied the scene. "This residence is Mr. Lloyd's property. From what I observed, you two attempted to assault federal agents while unlawfully trying to enter his home." She turned to the Thompsons. "You can leave peacefully, or I can arrest you for trespassing and assault. What's it going to be?

The Thompsons looked stunned, clearly expecting the officer to side with them.

"This isn't over," Marie said through gritted teeth as they reluctantly walked back to their cars. "We'll make sure everyone knows what kind of man you really are, Chad Lloyd."

As they walked back to their cars, Officer Williams approached Chad and Sam. "I'm sorry for your loss, Agent Lloyd. My condolences to you both."

As the Thompsons reached their cars, Chad suddenly called out, "Wait."

They turned back, hope flickering in their eyes that maybe he was reconsidering.

Chad walked back into the house and emerged a few minutes later with the last of his personal items - his laptop, some important documents, and a framed photo of him and Lana on their wedding day.

"You have four hours," he announced, his voice flat and emotionless, carrying the same deadly calm that had unnerved Robert earlier. "Get whatever you want out of the house and the rental truck. After that, I never want to see any of you again. If you're not gone by 2100 hours tonight, I'll have you arrested for trespassing."

Marie's face lit up with surprise and greed, but Jennifer immediately bristled. "Four hours? That's not enough time to go through everything properly!"

"We need at least until tomorrow," Marie added, her voice taking on a demanding tone. "There are sixteen years of memories in that house."

Chad's head tilted slightly, like a predator studying prey. When he spoke, his voice was so quiet they had to strain to hear him. "Yes, there are sixteen years of memories. I lived every single day of those sixteen years. I created those memories. And I've already boxed every single item that mattered."

He took a slow step toward them, his movements deliberate and controlled. "Take the boxes. Take the furniture. Take whatever the fuck you want. But you'll sort through it somewhere else, on your own time, away from my property."

The temperature seemed to drop ten degrees around Chad as he continued in that same whisper-quiet voice. "Because if I have to explain the concept of property rights to you again, I'm going to start demonstrating other concepts I learned during my military service. Concepts that don't require words."

Robert pulled harder on Marie's arm, his survival instincts screaming warnings. "We'll take what we can get, Chad. Four hours is fine."

"Smart man," Chad replied, never taking his eyes off Marie. "Four hours. Then you disappear from my life forever."

"This is unreasonable—" Jennifer started.

"This is generous," Chad interrupted, his voice still eerily calm. His gaze shifted to Mark, who was still massaging his throat, and something predatory flickered in his eyes. "Considering your husband just committed assault on a federal officer on my property."

Chad's stare fixed on Mark with the same cold intensity. "Tell me, Mark, how's your throat feeling? Because that was me being gentle. Keep pushing, and you'll discover what it feels like when I'm not holding back."

Mark instinctively took a step backward, his hand moving protectively to his neck.

Chad's attention returned to Jennifer, his voice dropping to that same whisper-quiet menace. "Four hours, or nothing at all. And if your husband so much as looks at me wrong again, he's going to learn why I survived three war zones when better men didn't."

The Thompsons stared at him, finally understanding they were no longer dealing with the grieving son-in-law they could bully, but something far more dangerous - a trained killer who'd simply been playing by civilian rules until now.

"Four hours," Robert said quickly, pulling both his daughter and Mark toward their cars. "We'll be gone by nine."

Sam stared at him in shock. "Chad, are you sure? These are your memories too. Lana's things, Casey's room..."

Chad looked at her, and she saw something final and devastating in his expression. "Fuck it," he said simply. "I have all the memories I need right here," he pointed to his heart. "If they want to be bitter people, let them have the stuff. It's just things."

He turned back to the Thompsons, his voice taking on the cold authority of his military days. "Four hours. Then I'm calling the police to remove anyone still on my property."

As they drove away, Sam realized she'd just witnessed Chad severing his final emotional tie to his old life. He was cutting himself loose from everything - the house, the belongings, the family connections - becoming someone with nothing left to lose.

And that terrified her more than anything else that had happened.

The question was whether Sam could keep her promise to Lana and save whatever humanity remained in the man sitting beside her, or whether she was about to watch him disappear completely into the darkness that Grey had warned her about.

Either way, she knew their lives would never be the same.

Lloyd Residence
2100 Hrs

Grey's SUV pulled up to the Lloyd house at exactly nine o'clock, with Agent Andrews in the passenger seat. The driveway was empty, the house dark except for the porch light Chad had left on.

"Looks clear," Andrews observed as they approached the front door.

Grey used the spare key Chad had given him to check inside. The house was completely stripped - not just of Chad's belongings, but of everything. Furniture gone, pictures removed from walls, the curtains taken down, even the used roll of toilet paper in the main bathroom. The Thompson family had cleaned the place out like locusts.

In the kitchen, a folded piece of paper sat prominently on the bare counter. Grey opened it and read:

Chad - You think giving us Lana's things makes up for getting them killed? You pathetic, selfish bastard. Nothing you do will ever bring back our daughter and granddaughter. They're dead because YOU chose to be FBI. YOU brought those cartel animals into their lives. YOU got them tortured and murdered for YOUR job, YOUR ego, YOUR choices.

Lana should have left you years ago. She should have married Dr. Michael Harrison like she planned. She broke off her engagement to that good man for YOU. She would have had a bright future with him - safe, secure, respected. Her children would have grown up in a doctor's house, not a target for criminals. But no, she threw it all away for a broken soldier who couldn't even keep his family alive. She'd still be alive if she had. Casey would be playing with her toys right now instead of rotting in the ground. Our family would be whole. But she was too blind with love to see what you really are - a narcissistic piece of shit who put his precious career before his family's safety.

You were supposed to protect them. That was your ONE job as a husband and father. Instead, you failed so completely that your own wife was tortured to death while your baby daughter lie dead on the floor. What kind of man lets his family be slaughtered while he's out playing hero cop?

You don't deserve to grieve them. You don't deserve sympathy. You don't even deserve to speak their names. You deserve to live with the knowledge that you failed the two people who loved you most, and that their blood is on your hands forever.

We hope that guilt destroys you. We hope you never sleep again without seeing their faces. We hope every breath you take reminds you that they can't breathe because of YOU.

Stay away from the funeral. Stay away from us. You're dead to us, just like you are to Lana and Casey. The only difference is they died as innocent victims, and you're just a coward who let it happen.

We will take care of all the arrangements. They will NOT be buried in the veteran's cemetery where you had planned. We won't stand for our daughter and granddaughter being associated with your military failures for eternity. They deserve better than to spend forever next to the grave of the man who got them killed.

We never want to see your face again. If we do, we'll make sure everyone knows what kind of failure you really are.

The family you destroyed

Grey stared at the note, feeling his own anger rise at the cruelty of the words. This wasn't grief talking - this was calculated viciousness designed to destroy whatever was left of Chad's soul. He folded it carefully and slipped it into his jacket pocket, knowing that if Chad ever read these words, there would be no coming back from the darkness.

"House is clear," Grey called to Andrews. "They took everything and left. Check the rental truck."

Andrews walked to the U-Haul parked on the street and opened the rear door. "Empty. Completely cleaned out."

Grey nodded grimly. The Thompsons had taken everything - every stick of furniture, every memento, every trace of the life Chad had built with their daughter. In their grief and anger, they'd ensured Chad had nothing left of his family except the small box of treasures he'd saved.

"What do you want me to do with the truck?" Andrews asked.

"Take it back to the rental place. Nothing left to transport." Grey locked the house and pocketed the key. "I'll follow you there, then we'll call it a night."

As they drove away from the empty house, Grey couldn't shake the feeling that the Thompsons had just made a terrible mistake. They thought they were punishing Chad for their loss, but what they'd actually done was remove the last tether connecting him to his civilian life.

Now Chad had nothing left to lose - and that made him infinitely more dangerous.

Chapter 19

Sam's Apartment
One Week Later

The past three weeks had been a blur of crime scene cleanup crews, insurance adjusters, and cold silences. Chad sat at Sam's small kitchen table, mechanically stirring his coffee while Sam made fried eggs neither of them really wanted to eat. The black suit he'd wear to the cemetery hung on the back of his chair, a stark reminder of the day ahead.

Grey had spent days negotiating with Robert Thompson, finally securing permission for Chad to visit the graves - but only after the service was over, only after everyone had gone home. Even in death, the Thompsons were determined to keep Chad separated from his family.

The house on Cedar Street stood empty now, its dining room floor refinished, the walls repainted, every trace of violence scrubbed away by professional restoration crews. Chad had supervised every detail with mechanical precision, preparing the property for sale while systematically severing every tie to his former life.

Sam had watched Chad's transformation over the past three weeks with growing alarm. The man who used to laugh at Casey's knock-knock jokes now spent hours poring over financial reports and surveillance files, searching for any trace of Elena Ramirez's location. His laptop was always open, displaying cryptocurrency transaction charts and cartel organizational structures.

"You were at the gym again until midnight," Sam observed, noting the way his suit jacket hung looser on his frame despite the obvious muscle gain in his shoulders and arms. "That's the fourth time this week."

Chad shrugged, cutting his eggs with mechanical precision. "Need to stay in shape."

What he didn't say was that he was preparing his body for war. Three weeks of punishing workouts, combat conditioning, and tactical training at private ranges had transformed grief into something harder, more dangerous.

"So," Sam said carefully, "Internal Affairs cleared the shooting and you're back on active duty. Are you planning to come in tomorrow? Take some time to get back into routine?"

Chad looked up from his coffee. "I don't know. I'm not sure I can sit at a desk and pretend to care about case files and surveillance reports. Not after..." He gestured vaguely, unable to finish.

"You need routine, Chad. Structure. Something to keep you grounded."

"Maybe." Chad finally took a bite, more to please Sam than from any appetite. "The realtor called yesterday," he said, changing the subject. "Young agent straight out of Quantico wants to close next week. I told him what happened in the dining room - apparently it doesn't bother him."

"That's good," Sam replied carefully. "One less thing to worry about."

But they both knew it was more than that. Once the house sold, Chad would have no remaining ties to his civilian life, no anchors keeping him in one place.

"I also need to find an apartment. I can't keep sleeping on your couch and inconveniencing you."

"You're not inconveniencing me," Sam said firmly. "Stay as long as you need."

"No." Chad's voice was quiet but determined. "You've done enough, Sam. More than enough. I need to figure out how to live with this, and I can't do that while depending on your charity."

Sam studied his face, seeing the walls going up again. "It's not charity. We're partners. Friends."

"Are we?" Chad met her eyes. "Or are you just keeping your promise to Lana by babysitting me?"

The words stung because they held a grain of truth. Sam was watching him, waiting for signs that he might do something reckless or dangerous.

"Both," she answered honestly. "I care about you, Chad. But yes, I'm also worried about what you might do."

Chad nodded, seeming to appreciate her honesty. "That's fair. But you can't watch me forever, Sam. Eventually, I have to face this alone."

Sam glanced at his laptop screen, catching glimpses of the Elena Ramirez files he'd been studying obsessively. "Find anything new in those financial reports?"

"Maybe," Chad replied, his voice noncommittal.

Sam made a decision that would either save him or damn them both. "What if I brought some files home? We could go through them together over dinner. Two sets of eyes might catch something you missed."

Chad looked up sharply, studying her face. "You'd do that?"

"We're partners," Sam said simply. "And maybe... maybe if I help you find answers, you won't feel like you have to handle this alone."

What Sam didn't say was that helping with the research would let her see exactly what Chad was planning, give her opportunities to steer him toward legal solutions, and keep him close enough to intervene if necessary.

Chad nodded slowly. "Okay. But Sam... once you're in this with me, there's no going back to pretending everything's normal."

"Normal died with Lana and Casey," Sam replied. "I'm in."

"The service starts at ten," Sam said, changing the subject. "We'll wait until noon to make sure everyone's gone before we head to Oak Hill."

Chad glanced at the clock. "Two and a half hours. Two and a half hours while strangers say goodbye to my family."

"Right now, people are gathering to say goodbye to my wife and daughter. And I'm here, hiding in your apartment like some kind of criminal."

"I should be carrying her casket," Chad said suddenly, his voice breaking. "I should be giving the eulogy. I should be telling people about how Casey laughed at my terrible jokes, how Lana made me a better man.

Instead, strangers are burying my family while I wait in exile."

"Then give it now," Sam said quietly.

Chad looked at her, confused. "What?"

"Your eulogy. Give it here, to me. It doesn't matter where it's said, Chad. Lana and Casey would hear it." Sam's voice was gentle but firm. "They deserve to hear what's in your heart, and you deserve to say it."

Chad stared at her for a long moment, then slowly stood. He cleared his throat, his hands trembling slightly as he looked toward the window.

"Lana..." his voice cracked, then steadied. "Lana was the kind of woman who could make pancakes in the shape of dinosaurs on a Tuesday morning just because she knew it would make Casey giggle. She never met a stray cat she wouldn't feed, or a person who didn't deserve her kindness."

His voice grew stronger as he continued. "She saved me. When I came back from Afghanistan broken and angry, she saw something in me worth fixing. She didn't try to change who I was - she just loved me until I remembered who I wanted to be."

Chad's tears started falling freely. "And Casey... God, Casey. She believed in magic. Real magic. She'd leave cookies for fairies and talk to butterflies like they were old friends. She made me see the world through six-year-old eyes again, where everything was possible and every day was an adventure."

He paused, wiping his eyes. "They made me better than I ever deserved to be." Chad's voice broke completely on the last words. "They were my whole world, and now... now I have to figure out how to live in a world without their light."

For a moment, the apartment was silent except for Chad's quiet sobs. Then Sam stood and crossed to him, wrapping her arms around him without a word. Chad collapsed into her embrace, finally letting go of the last reservoirs of grief he'd been holding back.

They stood like that for several minutes - Chad crying out three weeks of accumulated sorrow while Sam held him, her own tears falling silently. All the pain, the rage, the devastating loneliness poured out of him in great, shuddering waves.

When Chad finally pulled back, his eyes were red but somehow clearer. The raw, desperate grief that had consumed him was gone, replaced by something quieter but more final.

"Thank you," he whispered. "They needed to hear that."

Sam nodded, wiping her own eyes. "So did you."

But as Chad straightened his tie and prepared for the cemetery visit, Sam noticed something that chilled her. With the grief finally released, what remained behind was cold, calculating, and absolutely focused. Chad had said goodbye to his family - and to the man he'd been when they were alive.

This would mark the final emotional release before his complete transformation into something more dangerous.

Chapter 20

Oak Hill Cemetery
Georgetown

The August afternoon sun cast long shadows across Oak Hill Cemetery as Grey's SUV wound through the narrow roads between weathered headstones and ornate mausoleums. Chad sat in the passenger seat, wearing a black suit, black tie, and crisp white shirt - the same outfit he'd worn to his father's funeral years ago. In his lap sat a small bouquet of red roses and a tiny white stuffed rabbit he'd bought that morning.

"You sure about this?" Sam asked from the back seat. "We could wait until tomorrow, give you more time."

"No," Chad replied, his voice steady but hollow. "Today's the day they were laid to rest. Today's the day I say goodbye."

The Thompsons had deliberately chosen Oak Hill over Congressional National Cemetery - ensuring that when Chad died, he could never be laid to rest beside his wife and daughter. Even in death, they were determined to keep his family separated from him. Chad had been banned from the service entirely, forced to wait hours after his family was buried before he could even visit their graves.

Grey parked near the fresh graves, and they walked slowly across the manicured grass. The cemetery was quiet now, peaceful, with only the distant sound of traffic from the city beyond the walls.

That's when they saw them.

Five men in military dress uniforms stood at attention near the graves, their backs straight and eyes forward. Master Sergeant Marcus Ryan, Chad's former team leader, turned as they approached.

"Where the hell were you?" Marcus demanded, his voice tight with confusion and anger. "We've been looking for you everywhere. The family said they didn't know where you were."

Chad stopped walking, his shoulders sagging slightly. "They didn't want me at the service, Marcus. Lana's family... they blame me for what happened."

"They blamed YOU?" Sergeant First Class Timothy Jackson stepped forward, his face flushing with rage. "Are you out of your goddamn mind? You didn't kill them, Chad. Those cartel animals did."

"Doesn't matter," Chad said quietly. "In their eyes, Lana and Casey died because of my choices. Because I was FBI. Because I made enemies."

The five men exchanged glances, their anger palpable. These were soldiers who'd followed Chad through three combat zones, who'd trusted him with their lives in the worst places on earth. Seeing him broken and blamed for his family's murder triggered their protective instincts.

"Say the word," whispered Sergeant Gerald Taylor, his hands clenched into fists. "Just say the word, and we'll go have a conversation with the Thompson family about respect."

"No," Chad said firmly, though he appreciated the loyalty. "They're grieving. They need someone to blame, and I'm the easiest target."

Marcus studied Chad's face, seeing something that worried him. In combat, Chad had been unshakeable - the calm center that held their team together during the worst firefights. But this man standing before them was different. Harder. Colder.

"Chad," Marcus said carefully, "what are you planning to do?"

Chad didn't answer immediately. Instead, he walked to Casey's grave and knelt beside the fresh earth. The simple marker tag read:

CASEY ELIZABETH LLOYD
BELOVED GRAND DAUGHTER
SEPTEMBER 12, 2018 - JULY 19, 2024.

Chad seemed not to notice the omission, or perhaps he was beyond caring about one more cruelty. He placed the small white rabbit gently on the grave.

"She always wanted a little sister for Mr. Hoppy," Chad whispered to Sam. "This one can keep her company until..."

He couldn't finish the sentence.

Moving to Lana's grave, Chad counted out sixteen red roses - one for each year of their marriage - and laid them carefully on the dark soil. The marker tag read:

LANA MARIE LLOYD
BELOVED DAUGHTER AND MOTHER
MARCH 3, 1988 - JULY 19, 2024.

Sam stared at both tags, her anger building with each word she read. "Beloved granddaughter and beloved daughter and mother," she said quietly to Grey, her voice tight with fury. "Not daughter AND father. Not wife. They've erased him completely from both graves."

Grey's hands clenched into fists as he read the inscriptions. The Thompsons had systematically removed any trace of Chad's existence from his own family's final resting place. No mention of him as husband or father, as if sixteen years of marriage and a lifetime of love had never happened.

"They're trying to rewrite history," Grey said quietly. "Make it like he was never part of their lives."

"Bastards," Marcus muttered, reading over Sam's shoulder. "Lana could not have asked for a more loving husband and that little girl adored her father."

"Sixteen roses," Chad said softly. "I never got to give her the necklace."

He pulled Charlotte's Web from his jacket pocket and opened to the final chapter. His voice was steady as he read aloud:

"'Charlotte's children and grandchildren and great grandchildren ....'"

Chad's voice cracked slightly as he continued: "'Mr. Zuckerman took fine care of Wilbur all the rest of his days......She was in a class by herself. It is not often that someone comes along who is a true friend and a good writer. Charlotte was both.'"

He closed the book and placed it gently on Casey's grave. "Now you know how it ends, princess."

That's when the dam finally broke.

Chad collapsed to his knees between the two graves, his body wracked with sobs that seemed to tear him apart from the inside. All the grief he'd been holding back, all the pain and rage and helplessness, came pouring out in great waves that echoed across the quiet cemetery.

His old teammates stood back, giving him space but staying close, their own eyes wet with tears for a brother they'd never seen broken. Sam knelt beside him, one hand on his shoulder, while Grey stood guard like a sentinel.

For twenty minutes, Chad Lloyd grieved for his family with the intensity of a man saying goodbye forever. When he finally stood, his face was streaked with tears but his eyes held something new - a cold, terrible resolve that made everyone step back.

"She's at peace now," Chad said, his voice eerily calm. "They both are."

Marcus recognized that tone. He'd heard it before, in Afghanistan, right before Chad had requested permission to go after the Taliban fighters who'd killed their medic. It was the voice of a man who'd stopped being a husband and father and become something else entirely.

"Chad," Marcus said carefully, "whatever you're thinking of doing."

"I'm not thinking of doing anything," Chad interrupted, his eyes never leaving the graves. "I'm just saying goodbye."

But the way he said it - with such finality - made Sam's blood run cold.

As they walked back to the cars, Marcus pulled Chad aside while the others gave them space.

"I know that look," Marcus said quietly. "I've seen it before. You're going hunting."

Chad met his old team leader's eyes. "I don't know what you mean."

"Bullshit. You think I don't recognize when you go into mission mode?" Marcus gripped Chad's shoulder. "These aren't Taliban fighters in Afghanistan, brother. This is U.S. soil. There are laws, procedures—"

"There are also dead wives and children," Chad replied, his voice carrying no emotion. "Tell me, Marcus - if someone tortured and killed your family, what would you do? Wait for the justice system to maybe, someday, possibly catch the people responsible?"

Marcus was quiet for a long moment. "I'd want to burn down the world."

"Then you understand."

The other team members approached, clearly wanting to say goodbye but unsure how to handle the situation. Chad embraced each of them – Thomas, Martinez, Jackson, Taylor - men who'd been his brothers in arms for years.

"Take care of yourself, Chad," Martinez said, his voice heavy with concern. "And call us if you need anything. Anything at all."

"I will," Chad lied.

As his old team drove away, Grey approached with Sam close behind.

"Chad, there's something I need to tell you," Grey said, his voice official. "Director Huntington wants to see you tomorrow morning. Nine AM sharp. Wear a nice suit."

Chad studied Grey's expression. "Any idea what it's about?"

"He didn't say. Just that it's important and time-sensitive."

Chad nodded, filing the information away. "Understood."

As they drove back toward the city, Sam watched Chad in the passenger seat. The man who'd broken down at the cemetery was gone, replaced by someone she barely recognized. His posture was different - straighter, more alert. His eyes moved constantly, scanning their surroundings with tactical awareness.

Most disturbing was his absolute stillness. No fidgeting, no nervous gestures, no signs of the emotional turmoil that should be consuming him. He looked like a predator at rest - calm, patient, and infinitely dangerous.

"Chad," Sam said carefully, "what are you thinking about?"

He turned to look at her, and she saw something in his eyes that made her shiver. "I'm thinking about promises," he said simply. "Lana asked me to avenge Casey's death. That's a promise I intend to keep."

"And what about the promise I made to her? To take care of you?"

Chad's smile was cold and empty. "You are taking care of me, Sam.

You're helping me research Elena's network. You're making sure I have what I need to keep that promise to Lana."

The words hit Sam like a physical blow. He was using her protection, her care, her promise to Lana as cover for whatever dark mission he was planning. And she'd just agreed to help him.

Grey caught her eyes in the rearview mirror, his expression grim. They both understood what was happening - Chad Lloyd was disappearing, piece by piece, leaving behind something that Elena Ramirez had created through her desire for revenge.

The question was whether anything could stop him now, or if they were simply watching a good man's final transformation into the very thing their enemies feared most: a killer with nothing left to lose.

As they drove through the streets of Arlington, past the house where Chad's family had died, past the life he'd built and lost, Chad Lloyd made his own silent promise to the memory of his wife and daughter.

Elena Ramirez wanted war. She was about to get one.

But first, he had a meeting with the Director of the FBI.

Chapter 21

Director Huntington's Office
FBI Headquarters

Chad had sat in the waiting area outside Director Huntington's office, adjusting his black suit jacket and checking his watch. The same clothes he'd worn to visit Lana and Casey's graves yesterday now served for this mysterious meeting with the head of the FBI.

"Agent Lloyd?" Director Huntington's assistant gestured toward the office door. "The Director will see you now."

Chad entered the spacious office, where FBI Director Brad Huntington stood behind his desk reviewing documents. At fifty-five, Huntington commanded respect through decades of federal law enforcement experience, from street agent to the highest office in the Bureau.

"Chad, please sit down," Huntington said, his voice carrying both authority and sympathy. "First, let me offer my personal condolences for your loss. What happened to Lana and Casey was unconscionable."

"Thank you, sir."

Huntington studied Chad's face, noting the controlled composure that had replaced the broken grief of a few days ago. "How are you holding up?"

"I'm managing, sir."

"Good. Because I need you to stand with me at a press conference this morning. Ten-thirty at the Capitol Building. Can you do that?"

Chad felt a flicker of surprise but kept his expression neutral. "Of course, sir. May I ask what the press conference concerns?"

"The coordinated attacks on federal law enforcement families. The government's response." Huntington's tone carried the weight of political necessity. "The President needs to show the American people that we're taking decisive action. You'll be the face of that response."

"I can handle it, sir."

"Excellent. We'll leave at ten-fifteen." Huntington returned to his paperwork, signaling the meeting's end.

Chad found Sam and Grey in the bullpen, both looking up as he approached.

"How did it go?" Sam asked, studying his expression.

"Strange. Huntington wants me at a press conference at the Capitol Building in an hour. Something about the coordinated attacks and the government's response."

Grey frowned. "Press conference? That's unusual. Did he say why you specifically?"

"He said I'll be the face of the response. Political theater, it sounds like."

"Well, we're coming," Sam said firmly. "If you're going to be on display, you should have friendly faces in the crowd."

"I'd appreciate that." Chad checked his watch. "I should head back up. Huntington wants to leave in thirty minutes."

As Chad walked away, Sam and Grey exchanged concerned glances.

"Something big is happening," Grey said quietly. "You don't call press conferences at the Capitol unless it's major policy."

"And you don't put a grieving widower on stage unless you're making a point," Sam added, worry evident in her voice.

111

Chapter 22

House Triangle
US Capitol Building

The House Triangle was packed with reporters, cameras, and federal officials gathered around the permanent podium used for major government announcements. Chad stood behind the podium alongside Director Huntington, both flanked by additional FBI leadership. The Capitol Building provided an imposing backdrop, its dome rising majestically behind the speakers to project the full authority of the federal government.

Chad scanned the crowd and spotted Sam and Grey in the third row, their presence providing a small measure of comfort in the sea of unknown faces.

"Ladies and gentlemen," the moderator announced, "the President of the United States."

Chad's head snapped up in surprise. The President? Huntington hadn't mentioned presidential involvement. This was far bigger than he'd anticipated.

President Morrison approached the podium with the gravity that befitted the highest office in the land. His expression was grim, purposeful, and designed for the cameras.

"My fellow Americans," the President began, his voice carrying across the packed grounds. "Three weeks ago, our nation suffered an unprecedented attack on federal law enforcement. Two hundred and eighty-four innocent people were murdered in coordinated strikes across multiple states. Agents, judges, prosecutors, and their loved ones were killed in their homes by international criminal organizations operating on American soil."

Chad felt his chest tighten as the President continued, but something felt hollow about the words. Political rhetoric rather than genuine outrage.

"These were not random acts of violence. These were calculated acts of terrorism, designed to intimidate and destroy the brave men and women who protect our communities from the most dangerous criminals in the world."

The President's voice grew harder, more determined for the cameras.

"The cartels responsible for these attacks have declared war on the United States government. They have made a fatal mistake. This morning, I signed Executive Order 14821, formally designating all major drug cartels as Foreign Terrorist Organizations under United States law."

A murmur rippled through the press corps. Chad felt his pulse quicken, but as the President continued, the reality became clear.

"This designation means that federal law enforcement will have enhanced tools to investigate and prosecute these criminal organizations. We will work with our international partners to disrupt their operations and bring them to justice through the full weight of American law."

Chad's heart sank. Enhanced tools. International cooperation. The full weight of American law. All bureaucratic language that meant more procedures, more oversight, more delays while his family's killers walked free.

"We will not negotiate with terrorists. We will not show mercy to those who murder innocent families. We will find them, and we will bring them to justice through our courts and our legal system."

Through our courts, Chad thought bitterly. Years of trials, appeals, plea bargains, and technicalities while Elena Ramirez enjoys her freedom.

For twenty minutes, President Morrison outlined the new strategy - expanded federal cooperation, enhanced surveillance capabilities, elimination of jurisdictional barriers, and the creation of specialized task forces to investigate cartel activities.

Chad stood motionless, realizing this was all for show. Political theater designed to make the American people feel like something was being done, while the actual machinery of justice moved at the same glacial pace that had failed to protect his family in the first place.

When the President finished, Attorney General Monica Wells approached the podium.

"The Department of Justice will coordinate all federal efforts under this new framework," Wells announced. "We will prosecute these criminal organizations with the same dedication and resources we bring to fighting international terrorism."

She spoke for ten minutes about legal frameworks, international cooperation, and prosecutorial strategies - all the bureaucratic processes that would take years to produce results, if they produced any results at all.

Director Huntington was next.

"The Federal Bureau of Investigation will lead domestic operations under this new mandate," Huntington began. "To that end, I am announcing the creation of a specialized task force designed to investigate and prosecute cartel terrorists."

Chad felt every eye in the room focus on him, and he suddenly understood his role in this political theater.

"This prototype unit will be called PHOENIX - Priority High-Impact Operations to Eliminate Narco-International eXtremists. It will operate with enhanced investigative authority and direct coordination with other federal agencies."

Huntington turned slightly toward Chad.

"PHOENIX will be led by Special Agent Chad Lloyd, a decorated combat veteran and experienced federal agent whose family was murdered in these terrorist attacks. Agent Lloyd brings both the tactical expertise and personal dedication necessary to lead this critical mission."

The cameras swiveled toward Chad, who maintained his composure while realizing he was being used as a prop. A sympathetic face to put on a policy that would accomplish nothing.

"Agent Lloyd and his team will have the authority to investigate these terrorists wherever evidence leads, working within our legal system to ensure justice is served."

Within our legal system, Chad thought. The same legal system that couldn't prevent 284 murders.

Huntington continued outlining PHOENIX's mandate - enhanced coordination, expanded jurisdiction, better information sharing. All improvements to an inherently flawed system that moved too slowly to protect innocent people.

When the press conference ended, Chad found himself surrounded by reporters shouting questions about how it felt to lead the fight against his family's killers. Security quickly ushered him away, but not before he caught Sam and Grey pushing through the crowd toward him.

"Chad!" Sam called out. "Chad, wait!"

But he was already being escorted away by federal marshals, leaving Sam and Grey staring after him in the chaos of the dispersing crowd.

Chapter 23

Ramirez Compound
Grand Cayman

Elena Ramirez pressed her fingertips against the warm glass of her study window, watching the crystalline Caribbean waters that had washed away so much blood over the years. Behind her, multiple screens flickered with the live feed from Washington D.C., where the American President was about to make Chad Lloyd's worst day even worse.

The leather chair creaked as she settled back, savoring the moment like aged whiskey. This was better than Christmas morning.

"This designation means that federal law enforcement will have enhanced tools to investigate and prosecute these criminal organizations," President Morrison announced from the permanent speech area outside the US Capitol.

Elena's laugh was soft, predatory. Tools. As if they needed more tools to fail spectacularly.

Hector paced behind her like a caged animal, his footsteps sharp on the marble floor. "Elena, what have you done? You've brought the entire United States government down on us. Every cartel from Tijuana to—"

"Shut up." She didn't turn around. On screen, FBI Director Huntington was stepping to the microphone, and there—there was her masterpiece. Chad Lloyd stood rigid beside him, his face a mask of barely controlled fury. But Elena could see deeper. She'd studied that face for two years, memorized every line, every expression.

She knew what broken looked like.

"Look at him, Hector." Her voice was honey over broken glass.

"Look at our Agent Lloyd."

Chad's jaw was clenched so tight she could see the muscle twitching even through the satellite feed. His hands were fists at his sides. His eyes —his eyes were as hollow as empty graves.

Perfect.

"He knows," she whispered, leaning forward. "He knows they're using Lana's blood to grease their political machine."

Javier sprawled in the corner chair, freshly showered and dressed in crisp linen, but Elena could still sense the violence clinging to him like cologne. "He does look ready to kill someone."

"He is." Elena's smile was a blade. "But not us. Not yet. Right now, he wants to kill everyone in that bureaucracy for turning his wife's murder into a photo opportunity."

She could taste Chad's rage through the screen. Could feel it crawling under his skin like fire ants. This was what she'd wanted—not just to kill his family, but to make him watch his own government dance on their graves.

Hector stopped pacing. "Elena, you don't understand. I've been getting calls all morning. Every cartel leader in the hemisphere is—"

The secure phone rang. Elena smiled and answered without checking the caller ID.

"Buenos días, Miguel." She put it on speaker, settling back to enjoy the show.

"Elena! What the fuck have you done?" Miguel Sánchez's voice exploded through the room like a gunshot. "The Americans just declared war on all of us because of your revenge fantasy!"

"My revenge fantasy?" Elena's voice dropped to a whisper. "Miguel, tell me—how did your father die?"

Silence.

"That's what I thought. Your father died in his sleep, surrounded by his grandchildren. Mine died with an American bullet between his eyes while his children were thousands of miles away." She stood, walking to the window. "So forgive me if I don't give a fuck about your business concerns."

"Elena, please—"

"Please what? Please forget that Chad Lloyd killed my father? Please forget watching him die over and over on security footage?" Her fingers traced patterns on the glass. "I've watched that video a thousand times, Miguel. Every frame. Every detail."

More voices joined the call—Carlos Montenegro from the Gulf Cartel, Rosa Delgado from 18th Street, others she'd grown up with, fought beside, bled with. All of them scared. All of them weak.

"They declared us terrorists!" Rosa's voice was shrill with panic.

"They gave us a new name," Elena corrected. "The same prosecutors who couldn't touch us as drug dealers will now try to prosecute us as terrorists. Using the same courts, the same lawyers, the same broken system that's failed them for decades."

She zoomed in on Chad's face on one of the screens. His breathing was shallow, controlled. Like a man trying not to scream.

"Look at their poster boy," she said, gesturing to the main screen so the others could see. "Chad Lloyd. The grieving widower they're using to sell this new task force. You see that expression? That's not satisfaction. That's not justice. That's a man realizing his government is whoring out his family's memory."

Javier leaned forward, studying the screen. "He's going to break."

"He's already broken." Elena's voice was soft, almost gentle. "We broke him over a week ago when he came home to find his wife and daughter dead. This—this is just grinding those broken pieces into dust."

"And when their new task force comes hunting?" Carlos asked.

Elena's smile was all teeth. "They'll investigate us the same way they always have. Slowly. Methodically. Bureaucratically. Building cases that take years while we adapt and evolve faster than their legal system can think."

She minimized the news feed and pulled up tactical diagrams. "But we're not taking chances. Our El Paso tunnel is four feet wide, six feet high, fully equipped. It connects directly to the Boone Street storm drain system. Even if they triple border patrols, we move underground."

"That's one tunnel," Miguel pointed out.

"Which is why we're expanding drone operations. Night flights over remote border areas. Small payloads, multiple flights. Virtually undetectable." Elena's fingers danced across the keyboard. "We are purchasing fifty military-grade drones within the next month."

"The Americans are panicking," she continued. "Their response proves it. Instead of actually changing their approach, they've created more committees, more agencies, more bureaucrats. They're fighting a 21st century war with 20th century institutions."

"But what about coordination between agencies?" Rosa asked. "Enhanced intelligence sharing?"

Elena laughed—a sound like breaking bones. "Have you ever dealt with American federal agencies? DEA fights with FBI, FBI fights with ATF, everyone fights with CIA. They've been promising enhanced coordination since 9-11. Nothing changes except the names on the organizational charts."

She zoomed back in on Chad's face. Even through the satellite feed, she could see the pulse hammering in his neck. The way his nostrils flared with each breath. The slight tremor in his hands.

Beautiful.

Elena turned from the screen, her eyes cold and feral. "Chad Lloyd isn't a threat. He's a broken widower who just realized his government failed him. Men like that try to change things from the inside—they write reports, file complaints, work within the system. He'll spend years trying to reform PHOENIX into something effective while we operate freely."

"And if he doesn't accept the system?" Hector pressed.

"Then he'll resign and write a book about government failure. Grieving bureaucrats don't become vigilantes, Hector. They become whistleblowers."

The call continued for another hour as Elena outlined her assessment of the American response. By the time it ended, several cartel leaders had been convinced that the terrorist designation was more bark than bite.

After the call ended, Hector looked at his sister with new respect. "You really think they won't change anything substantive?"

"I think they'll change everything that doesn't matter and nothing that does," Elena replied. "It's what democratic governments do—they respond to pressure with process, not results."

Javier stretched in his chair. "So we continue operations as planned?"

"We expand them." Elena's eyes took on a calculating gleam.

Chapter 24

Director Huntington's Office
FBI Headquarters

Sam Belle and Nolan Grey sat in the uncomfortable chairs outside Director Huntington's office, waiting for Chad and the Director to return from the press conference. The fluorescent lights hummed overhead like angry wasps, casting everything in that sickly government-building pallor that made even healthy people look like corpses.

Grey's weathered hands were clasped tight in his lap, knuckles white. He'd watched Chad during the press conference, seen the muscle twitching in his jaw, the way his hands had clenched into fists. Sam kept checking her watch, her leg bouncing with nervous energy.

"They should be back any minute," she said, smoothing her skirt. "Huntington will want to get PHOENIX operational as quickly as possible."

"Chad looked ready to explode up there," Grey replied, his voice low and gravelly. "Standing behind that podium like a prop while politicians talked about enhanced coordination."

"He'll be fine once we get to work. Once we can actually do something instead of just..." Sam gestured vaguely at the hallway, the building, the whole bureaucratic machine around them.

The elevator dinged down the hall, and they both looked up to see Chad and Huntington walking toward them. But something was wrong. Chad's face was carved from stone, his movements too controlled, like a man barely holding himself in check. Huntington looked flushed, angry.

"Agent Grey, Agent Belle," Huntington said curtly as they

approached. "My office. Now!"

Sam and Grey exchanged glances as they followed the two men into the office. This didn't feel like a planning session. This felt like an execution.

Huntington closed the door behind them with more force than necessary.

"Sir," Chad said as soon as the door closed, "I need to understand what just happened out there."

Huntington poured himself a glass of water, his movements sharp and angry. "What happened is that the President just gave the American people the response they demanded after 284 law enforcement family members were murdered."

Sam felt the tension in the room like a live wire. She'd expected to discuss operational procedures, team assignments, maybe budget allocations. Not... whatever this was.

Chad stared at Huntington. "A response that will accomplish what, exactly?"

"A response that shows we're taking decisive action. Enhanced coordination, better intelligence sharing, expanded jurisdiction for investigations."

"I heard that same speech after 9/11," Chad said, his voice flat. "Twenty-four years later, and here we are again. Same promises, same bureaucratic solutions, same dead federal agents."

Grey shifted uncomfortably in his chair. Sam could see where this was headed, and it wasn't anywhere good.

Huntington's expression grew serious. "Chad, I know this isn't what you wanted to hear. I know you're looking for immediate action, for swift justice. But we're a nation of laws. We can't abandon due process just because we're angry."

"Due process didn't protect my family or the families of 93 other agents."

The words hit the room like a physical blow. Sam felt her chest tighten, watching Chad's face transform from barely controlled anger into something much more dangerous.

"No, it didn't. And I'm sorry for that. But PHOENIX will have real capabilities - better funding, expanded authority, direct access to intelligence from other agencies. We can build strong cases against Elena Ramirez and her organization."

"Intelligence sharing?" Chad's laugh was bitter. "Isn't that what DHS was designed for? What about the National Counterterrorism Center? The Office of the Director of National Intelligence? How many agencies do we need to create before we admit the problem isn't coordination—it's competence?"

Sam watched Chad's face transform, seeing the military tactician emerge from beneath the grieving widower.

"And build strong cases against Elena Ramirez? Sir, the DEA has been trying to build cases against the Ramirez Cartel for decades. Billions of dollars, thousands of agents, and the only reason Salvador Ramirez is dead is because I put a bullet between his eyes two years ago during a raid. What makes you think PHOENIX will be any different?"

"Cases that will take years to prosecute while she continues killing federal agents and their families."

Chad leaned forward, his voice dropping to a whisper that somehow felt more dangerous than shouting. "You want to know what's different about Elena Ramirez? She doesn't care about your legal process. She doesn't worry about constitutional protections or congressional oversight. While you're building cases, she's building body counts."

Sam watched the exchange like a tennis match, her head turning between the two men. But this wasn't a discussion about operational procedures. This was Chad Lloyd having a breakdown in real time.

Huntington leaned back in his chair. "Chad, I understand your frustration. But this is how our system works. We investigate, we gather evidence, we build prosecutable cases. It's not fast, but it's effective."

Chad stood abruptly, his chair scraping against the floor. Sam jumped at the sound. He stared at Huntington for a long moment, and Sam could see something breaking inside him.

Huntington seemed to take Chad's silence as acceptance. "You'll start tomorrow. Begin by selecting your team and establishing operational procedures. We'll need to show progress quickly - Congress will be watching, and the media will expect regular updates."

"Progress reports. Media updates. Congressional oversight." Chad's voice was deadly quiet, and Sam felt her blood turn to ice. She'd heard that tone once before—during a raid in Baltimore when a suspect had pulled a gun on her. Chad's voice had gone flat like that just before he'd put three rounds center mass into the guy to save her life. It was the voice of a man who'd moved past anger into something much more dangerous. "While Elena Ramirez plans her next massacre of federal agents' families."

"Chad, I understand your frustration, but—"

"No, sir, you don't understand." Chad's composure finally cracked, and Sam felt her heart hammering against her ribs. "My wife and daughter are dead because this system failed them. Two hundred and eighty-four people are dead because we're more concerned with procedures than protection. And your solution is to create another bureaucratic task force that will spend months writing reports while more families get slaughtered."

Grey started to stand, probably to intervene, but Huntington's expression hardened. "Agent Lloyd, you need to control yourself."

"Control myself?" Chad's voice rose, and Sam felt tears burning her eyes. She'd never seen him like this—raw, unhinged, dangerous. "Sir, with all due respect, fuck PHOENIX. Fuck the bureaucracy. And fuck a system that turns my family's murder into a photo opportunity for politicians."

Sam's hand flew to her mouth. Grey's face went ashen. In their combined thirty years of federal service, neither had ever heard an agent speak to the Director like that. The silence that followed was deafening.

Huntington stood slowly, his face flushed with anger. "Agent Lloyd, you are officially suspended from duty, effective immediately. Badge and weapon on my desk. Now."

Sam felt the world tilt sideways. Suspended? They'd come here expecting to plan PHOENIX operations, and instead she was watching Chad's career die in front of her eyes.

Chad pulled out his FBI credentials and service weapon, placing them on Huntington's desk with deliberate care. The metallic clink of his badge hitting the wood was like a nail being driven into a coffin. The heavier thud of his gun followed.

"Gladly, sir. At least now I can do something useful instead of generating progress reports."

"Agent Lloyd, if you do anything - anything - that brings discredit to this Bureau or interferes with ongoing investigations, I will have you arrested and prosecuted to the fullest extent of the law."

Chad met Huntington's stare without flinching. "Have me arrested? That's funny, sir. That'll probably take a few days to process while we slow-walk actual crimes like the murder of 284 people." His voice was acid. "Discredit this Bureau? You just took my badge, so I'm not a member of this Bureau anymore. The only thing that discredits this agency is the bureaucratic bullshit it keeps piling on while federal agents' families get murdered."

"You're walking a very dangerous line, Lloyd."

"No sir, I'm walking away from a line. A line drawn by politicians and bureaucrats who care more about optics than they do about stopping child killers. My family is dead because the system failed. I won't make that mistake again."

Sam watched in horror as Chad walked toward the door. This couldn't be happening. Not like this.

He paused at the threshold and turned back. "And sir? When Elena's people kill the next batch of federal agents' families while PHOENIX is still writing operational procedures, remember that you chose politics over protection."

Chad opened the door, but instead of leaving, he looked at Sam and Grey. For a moment, she thought she saw a flicker of the man she'd known for two years—her partner, her friend, the man she'd fallen in love with even though she'd never told him.

But when he spoke, his voice belonged to someone else entirely. Someone she didn't recognize.

"Take care of yourselves." His eyes lingered on Sam for just a moment longer. "Both of you."

Then he was gone, leaving Sam and Grey sitting in stunned silence as the door closed behind him.

Chapter 25

Director Huntington's Office
FBI Headquarters

The silence in Huntington's office felt like the aftermath of an explosion. Sam stared at the closed door, her heart hammering against her ribs as the reality of what had just happened crashed over her like a cold wave. Chad was gone. Really gone. Her partner, her friend, the man she'd fallen for but never told—walked away from everything and everyone, including her.

Grey sat motionless, his weathered hands still gripping the armrests of his chair. Twenty years in federal service, and he'd never seen anything like what had just happened. Men like Chad Lloyd didn't break—they bent until the pressure found a weak point, then they snapped like high-tension cable.

And when they snapped, people died.

Huntington moved behind his desk like a man underwater, his movements slow and deliberate. He picked up Chad's badge, turning it over in his hands. The metal caught the fluorescent light, throwing fractured reflections across the wall.

"Jesus Christ," he whispered. "What have I done?"

Sam felt tears burning her eyes as the full weight of the moment hit her. Chad had just thrown away twelve years of federal service, his career, his pension, everything—because he couldn't watch politicians turn his family's murder into a photo opportunity. Part of her wanted to run after him, to tell him she understood, that maybe he was right about the system being broken.

But another part of her—the part that had taken an oath to serve justice through the law—was terrified of what Chad might do without any constraints.

"Sir, Chad's not—he wouldn't—" she started.

"Agent Belle." Huntington's voice was sharp enough to cut glass. "Chad Lloyd just walked out of here with twelve years of operational knowledge, classified intelligence on active investigations, and extensive special operations training. He has contacts in military, intelligence, and law enforcement agencies across three continents." He set the badge down carefully, as if it might explode. "And he has absolutely nothing left to lose."

Grey leaned forward in his chair. "Sir, he's grieving. Give him a few days to cool down, then—"

"A few days?" Huntington's laugh was bitter. "Nolan, in a few days, Chad Lloyd could be in Mexico putting bullets in cartel members' heads. Or he could be here in Washington doing the same thing to politicians he blames for his family's death." The Director walked to his window, staring out at the city below. "We've created a weapon, gentlemen. And now we've set it loose."

Sam felt something cold settle in her stomach. She'd worked with Chad for two years, seen him in firefights, watched him make split-second decisions under pressure. But she'd always seen him as the steady one, the anchor that kept her grounded when cases got dark.

Now she was remembering other things. The way Chad moved through a building during raids—fluid, predatory, like violence was his natural language. The expression on his face when he'd killed that suspect in Baltimore, cold and professional as turning off a light switch. The stories Grey had told about Chad's military service, the parts that weren't classified.

"Sir," she said quietly, her voice thick with emotion, "what do we do?"

Huntington turned from the window. "We move forward. PHOENIX becomes operational immediately, with new leadership." He pressed a button on his desk phone. "Send Special Agent Holmes up here. Now."

Grey frowned. "Janet Holmes? She's white-collar crimes, Brad. Financial investigations, corporate fraud. What does she know about—"

"She knows how to follow orders without having emotional breakdowns in my office," Huntington snapped. "She knows how to build cases methodically, professionally, without turning them into personal vendettas." He straightened his tie, trying to reassemble his bureaucratic mask. "And she's never put a bullet in anyone's head, which at this point I consider a qualification."

Sam felt her stomach drop. Janet Holmes? The woman who'd made Senior Special Agent by sleeping with Deputy Director Morrison before his promotion? Who'd never worked a violent crime in her life? They were going to replace Chad Lloyd—a combat veteran with years of cartel experience—with someone whose biggest arrest was an art forger in Georgetown?

Five minutes later, Agent Janet Holmes knocked and entered. Sam remembered her from two years ago—Holmes had been the one to introduce her to Chad on her first day in violent crimes. She was in her late thirties, with fiery red hair and green eyes that could shift from seductive to calculating in a heartbeat. She wore a form-fitting black dress that was more appropriate for a cocktail party than a counterterrorism briefing, and she moved with the predatory grace of someone who'd climbed the federal hierarchy through strategic bedroom politics rather than competence.

"Director Huntington," Holmes said, her voice crisp and professional. "I came as soon as I got your message."

"Janet, sit down. We have a situation." Huntington gestured to the chair Chad had vacated twenty minutes earlier. "PHOENIX needs new leadership, effective immediately."

Holmes glanced at Sam and Grey, her expression carefully neutral. "I thought Agent Lloyd was heading the task force."

"Agent Lloyd is no longer with the Bureau." Huntington's voice was flat, final. "He's been suspended pending investigation into his conduct during today's briefing."

"I see." Holmes settled into the chair, crossing her legs. "And you want me to take over a counterterrorism operation." She said it like she was discussing a minor personnel reassignment, not hunting the most dangerous criminal organization in the hemisphere.

"I want you to lead the most important counterterrorism initiative in the Bureau's history," Huntington replied. "The President has designated the major cartels as terrorist organizations, and PHOENIX is our response."

Holmes was quiet for a moment, and Sam could practically see the wheels turning behind her eyes—calculating the career advancement potential, the media opportunities, the political capital.

"What kind of financial irregularities are we looking at?" Holmes asked. "Shell companies, money laundering schemes, tax evasion? I've had excellent success building RICO cases against organized crime through their financial vulnerabilities."

Sam and Grey exchanged glances. Elena Ramirez didn't launder money through complex financial schemes—she murdered federal agents' families. This wasn't a white-collar crime where you could trace paper trails and build elegant cases. This was a war.

"Janet," Grey said carefully, "these aren't corporate criminals hiding assets offshore. They're violent terrorist organizations that just killed 284 Americans in coordinated attacks. They use money to buy weapons and corrupt officials, not to fund pension plans."

Holmes waved dismissively. "Agent Grey, I've spent fifteen years building cases against sophisticated criminal enterprises. All criminal organizations have the same fundamental vulnerabilities—money, communications, human intelligence. These cartels may use violence instead of insider trading, but they're still criminal enterprises operating for profit."

Sam felt her heart sink. Holmes was talking about Elena Ramirez like she was a hedge fund manager, not a woman who'd orchestrated the torture and murder of families across fourteen states.

"Ma'am," Sam said carefully, "Elena Ramirez isn't concerned about SEC violations or financial audits. She's planning the next massacre while we're discussing quarterly reports."

"Which is exactly why we need to approach this methodically, professionally," Holmes replied. "We build cases that will stand up in federal court. We follow the money, identify their revenue streams, freeze their assets. We turn their own greed against them."

"Their greed?" Grey's voice was tight with barely controlled anger. "Ma'am, these people just murdered children to send a message. They're not motivated by profit margins—they're motivated by revenge and power. You can't indict your way out of a war."

Holmes' expression hardened. "Agent Grey, I understand you're emotionally invested in this case because as I understand it, Casey was your goddaughter? But emotion is exactly what leads to the kind of breakdown we just witnessed. We need cool heads and professional investigation, not personal vendettas."

Grey's face went white, then flushed red with barely controlled rage. Sam could see his hands trembling as he gripped the chair arms. To mention Casey like that—like she was just a complicating factor in a case file rather than a six-year-old girl who'd called him Uncle Nolan—was beyond cruel.

"Ma'am," Grey said, his voice deadly quiet, "that little girl used to fall asleep in my lap reading bedtime stories. She made me Father's Day cards even though I don't have kids of my own. And you're damn right I'm emotionally invested in finding the animals who tortured her to death."

Sam watched the exchange with growing horror. Holmes was dismissing Grey's twenty years of experience and his love for Casey the same way politicians dismissed Chad's warnings about systemic failure. It was like watching history repeat itself in fast forward.

"Director Huntington," Holmes continued, ignoring Grey's pain completely, "when do we start?"

"Tomorrow. Your office will be set up on the seventh floor, full staff, complete operational authority." Huntington handed her a thick folder. "These are your initial intelligence reports. PHOENIX is officially operational as of this moment."

Holmes took the folder, flipping through pages of surveillance photos and tactical assessments like she was reviewing quarterly earnings reports. "We'll get them, Brad. All of them. And we'll do it right— through proper legal channels, following every procedure, building cases that prosecutors can actually win."

As Holmes left the office, Sam felt a mixture of despair and growing panic. The woman seemed completely confident, utterly professional, and absolutely clueless about what she was actually facing. She was going to treat Elena Ramirez like a corrupt CEO instead of a terrorist mastermind.

"Sir," Sam said quietly after the door closed, "with all due respect, Agent Holmes has never worked violent crimes. She's never been in a firefight, never interviewed a cartel member, never even carried her weapon outside of qualification. How is she supposed to hunt Elena Ramirez?"

Huntington's expression was grim. "Agent Belle, Chad Lloyd just proved that tactical expertise and personal investment can be a liability. Sometimes you need someone who will follow procedures instead of going rogue."

"But sir—"

"The decision is made." Huntington's tone was final. "PHOENIX will operate within the law, following proper protocols, building prosecutable cases. No exceptions."

Sam stared at him, finally understanding the full scope of the tragedy. They'd had the right person for the job—Chad Lloyd, with his tactical expertise, cartel experience, and personal investment in stopping Elena. And they'd driven him away because he wouldn't pretend that bureaucratic procedures could solve a problem that required decisive action.

Now they were replacing him with someone whose greatest qualification was her willingness to follow orders and sleep with whoever could get her the next promotion, no matter how inappropriate either might be for the situation.

As Sam and Grey left the office, Sam couldn't shake the image of Chad walking away, his eyes empty as winter graves. Part of her wanted to find him, to follow him wherever this dark path was leading. Because watching Janet Holmes try to build RICO cases against Elena Ramirez felt like watching sheep prepare to hunt wolves.

And meanwhile, somewhere out there, Chad Lloyd was planning his own war against the people who'd murdered his family. A war that wouldn't be fought in courtrooms or won with subpoenas.

The question was whether Sam could live with herself for staying with the sheep, or whether her promise to Lana meant following Chad into the darkness—even if it meant abandoning everything she'd sworn to uphold.

Chapter 26

Sam's Apartment
Alexandria, VA

Chad had stood in Sam's hallway, her spare key heavy in his palm like a piece of shrapnel. The apartment smelled like her—vanilla body wash and that lavender detergent she used, scents that had become familiar over the past week. Comforting. Normal.

Nothing about his life would be normal again.

He moved through the space like a ghost, collecting the pieces of himself he'd scattered here during his brief stay. Clothes from the laundry hamper, still carrying the smell of gunpowder from the range. His reading glasses from the coffee table, next to the book he'd been pretending to read while staring at the ceiling, thinking about Lana's last moments. Toiletries from the bathroom—razor, toothbrush, the prescription sleep aids he hadn't touched because sleep meant dreams, and dreams meant watching his family die over and over.

He packed methodically, like he was preparing for a deployment. Because that's what this was—a one-way mission to a place where federal badges and constitutional protections didn't exist. A place where justice came from the barrel of a gun, not the mouth of a prosecutor.

When he was finished, Chad sat at Sam's kitchen table and pulled out a piece of paper. The letter took him twenty minutes to write, and he rewrote it twice before his hand stopped shaking enough to make the words legible:

Sam,

By the time you read this, I'll be gone. I know you'll be angry—probably furious —and you have every right to be. But I can't drag you into what I'm about to do.

This morning, I watched our government turn Lana and Casey's murder into a political photo opportunity. I stood on that stage while they used my grief to sell a bureaucratic response that will accomplish nothing. I realized that the system I've served for twelve years cares more about looking tough than actually being tough.

You promised Lana you'd take care of me. I'm releasing you from that promise. What I'm planning isn't something you should be part of. It's not something anyone should be part of.

Elena Ramirez declared war on law enforcement families. She killed 284 innocent people, including my wife and daughter, to send a message. The government's response was to create a task force that will spend months writing reports while she plans her next massacre.

I'm going to give her a different kind of response. One she'll understand.

If Huntington offers you and Grey the chance to work PHOENIX, take it. Maybe you can make it into something real, something that actually protects families instead of generating headlines. It's not for me anymore, but it might be for you.

Don't try to find me. Don't try to stop me. And don't blame yourself for whatever happens next.

This is my choice, my responsibility, and my war.

One last thing—would you place flowers on Lana and Casey's graves for me? Every month on the 19th. I won't be able to do it anymore, but they shouldn't be forgotten.

Take care of yourself, Sam. You're the best partner I ever had, and you deserve better than watching me become something you won't recognize.

-Chad

P.S. My truck is in your parking lot. Keys are on the table. It's yours now.

Chad folded the letter carefully and placed it on the table next to Sam's spare key, his truck keys, and his personal cell phone. Electronic leashes that could be tracked, monitored, used to find him when the Bureau inevitably came looking.

He shouldered his duffle bag and walked out of her apartment.

Chapter 27

O'Malley's Pub
DuPont Circle

Sam stared at her untouched sandwich, watching the ice melt in her Diet Coke while Grey methodically worked through his cheeseburger like it was evidence that needed processing. The lunch crowd at O'Malley's buzzed around them—Hill staffers arguing about policy, lobbyists making deals over appetizers, the normal rhythm of a Washington afternoon.

Nothing felt normal anymore.

"I keep seeing his face," Sam said finally, breaking twenty minutes of silence. "When Huntington told him to turn in his badge. He looked..." She searched for the word. "Empty. Like something inside him just died."

Grey set down his burger and wiped his hands with deliberate care. "I've seen that look before. In Iraq, Afghanistan. Men who'd been pushed past their breaking point." His voice was gravelly, tired. "They don't come back from that, Sam. Not usually."

Sam pulled out her phone for the fifth time since they'd sat down and dialed Chad's number. It went straight to voicemail, the same generic message she'd been hearing all afternoon.

"This is Chad. Leave a message."

She hung up without speaking. What could she say? Come back and let the system that failed your family fail you too?

"He's not going to answer," Grey said quietly.

"I know." Sam's voice cracked. "But I have to try. Nolan, we can't just let him... what if he does something he can't take back?"

"What if he already has?" Grey leaned forward, his weathered face creased with worry. "Sam, Chad is one of the most dangerous men I've ever known. Military training, federal access, years of contacts in law enforcement and intelligence. If he's decided to go after Elena Ramirez —"

"Then maybe he'll succeed where we've failed." The words came out harder than Sam intended. "How many more families have to die while we build cases and write reports?"

Grey's eyes sharpened. "You don't mean that."

"Don't I?" Sam felt anger rising in her chest, hot and acidic. "Nolan, we've been chasing cartels for decades. Billions of dollars, thousands of agents, and what do we have to show for it? More drugs on the streets, more violence, more dead cops." She gestured toward the window, toward the city beyond. "Maybe Chad's right. Maybe the only language these people understand is violence."

"And maybe Chad's about to throw away years of service and everything he believes in for revenge." Grey's voice carried the weight of authority, of experience. "Sam, I've seen good men cross that line. They don't come back. Ever."

Sam stared at her phone, at Chad's contact information glowing on the screen. Two years as his partner. Two years of shared cases, late-night stakeouts, morning coffee runs. Two years of falling in love with a man who'd never looked at her as anything more than a colleague.

Now he was gone, and she might never see him again.

"What do we do?" she asked.

"We do our jobs." Grey's voice was firm but not unkind. "We work PHOENIX, we try to make it into something that actually works, and we hope Chad comes to his senses before he gets himself killed."

"And if he contacts us?"

Grey was quiet for a long moment, staring into his beer. "If he contacts us for help, we help him. If he contacts us for backup on some vigilante mission, we try to talk him out of it. And if he contacts us to say goodbye..." He shrugged. "We say goodbye."

Sam tried Chad's number again. Voicemail. She hung up and immediately called back. Voicemail. The third time, the call didn't even connect—the phone was either dead or destroyed.

"Shit." She set her phone down harder than necessary. "Nolan, what if we're wrong? What if the system really is broken? What if the only way to stop Elena Ramirez is to do what Chad's planning to do?"

"Then we become the very thing we're supposed to be fighting against." Grey finished his beer and signaled for another. "Sam, the moment we decide that the law doesn't apply to us, that we know better than judges and juries and constitutional protections, we become no different from the cartels."

"The cartels murdered children, Nolan. They murdered Casey. Your God-daughter" Sam's voice was raw. "That five-year-old girl is dead because our system doesn't work."

"And if Chad murders Elena Ramirez in cold blood, how is that different?"

"Because Elena Ramirez deserves to die."

The words hung in the air between them like smoke. Sam realized she'd spoken the truth she'd been avoiding since the moment she'd seen Lana's body. Some people didn't deserve trials or due process or constitutional protections. Some people deserved bullets.

Maybe Chad was right after all.

"Jesus, Sam." Grey looked at her like he'd never seen her before. "Listen to yourself. You sound like—"

"Like what? Like someone who's tired of watching children get murdered while we shuffle paperwork?" Sam leaned forward, her voice dropping to a whisper. "Nolan, what if Chad succeeds? What if he actually kills Elena Ramirez and her brother and everyone else responsible for those massacres? Would that be such a terrible thing?"

"It would be murder."

"It would be justice."

Grey shook his head. "No, Sam. Justice is what happens in courtrooms. What Chad's planning is revenge. And revenge has a way of consuming everything it touches."

Sam's phone buzzed with a text message. For a moment, her heart leaped—maybe Chad had gotten a new phone, maybe he was reaching out. But it was just a reminder about her dentist appointment next week.

Normal life, continuing as if the world hadn't just shifted on its axis.

"I need to ask you something," Grey said quietly. "And I need you to be honest with me."

Sam looked up from her phone. "Okay."

"Are you in love with him?"

The question hit her like a physical blow. Sam felt heat rise in her cheeks, felt the words stick in her throat. She'd never said it out loud, had barely admitted it to herself.

"Does it matter?" she asked finally.

"It matters because it affects your judgment. It matters because if Chad contacts you asking for help, I need to know if you'll make decisions with your head or your heart."

Sam was quiet for a long moment, thinking about Chad's hands when he'd steadied her during that raid in Baltimore. The way he'd looked at her during dangerous moments, like she was something precious that needed protecting. The dreams she'd had about a life they'd never have.

"I don't know," she said honestly. "Maybe. Probably. Yes."

Grey nodded, unsurprised. "Then we have a problem."

"Why?"

"Because if Chad contacts you asking for help with whatever war he's planning to wage, you're going to say yes. And that's going to get you killed."

Sam felt tears burning her eyes. "What am I supposed to do, Nolan? Just forget about him? Pretend he never existed?"

"You're supposed to remember that the man you fell in love with died the day his wife and daughter died. What's left isn't Chad Lloyd anymore. It's something else. Something dangerous."

Sam's phone rang. For a wild moment, she thought it might be Chad. But it was Holmes.

"Agent Belle? This is Agent Holmes. I need you and Agent Grey to report to the seventh floor immediately. We have work to do."

"We'll be right there, ma'am," Sam said.

Chapter 28

Chad's Safe House
Anacostia

The cab dropped Chad three blocks away, the driver happy to take his cash and disappear back into the DC traffic without asking questions. Chad walked the rest of the way through a neighborhood that gentrification had forgotten—cracked sidewalks, boarded windows, the kind of urban wasteland where men went when they needed things that couldn't be obtained through legal channels.

The safe house sat between a vacant lot and a corner store with bars on the windows, its faded brick facade indistinguishable from a dozen other forgotten properties on the block. Chad had discovered it eighteen months ago while researching old surveillance operations, a relic from the Bureau's war on local drug dealers in the '90s. The kind of place that existed in archived files but not in anyone's memory.

He'd quietly removed it from the active database, erasing its digital footprint with the thoroughness of someone who understood how bureaucracies forgot things. For the past year, Chad had been using it as his personal workspace—a place to review sensitive case files away from the office, to make calls that didn't need to appear on Bureau phone logs, to think through complex investigations without interruption. He'd never liked bringing work home to Lana and Casey, didn't want the darkness of his cases touching their lives.

Now that separation had saved him.

Perfect for a man who needed to disappear.

Chad used the key he'd been carrying for months, slipping it into the lock like he belonged there. Because he did belong there—this place had become more familiar than his own home during the long nights when sleep meant dreams of dead cartel members and mutilated informants. The door opened with the soft whisper of settling wood, revealing a hallway that smelled like dust and old coffee. He stepped inside and closed the door behind him, engaging two deadbolts that hadn't been there when the Bureau owned the property.

The electricity worked—dim overhead bulbs casting yellow light through rooms that looked lived-in enough to pass casual inspection. Secondhand furniture from Goodwill, generic artwork from Hobby Lobby, the kind of studied normalcy that screamed federal safe house to anyone who knew what to look for.

But Chad had improved on the Bureau's original design.

He walked through the small living room to the kitchen, checking the refrigerator that hummed quietly in the corner. Stocked with water, protein bars, canned food—enough to last a month without leaving the house. The landline phone worked, its number unlisted and not connected to any federal database. The cable internet connection ran through multiple proxy servers, bouncing his digital signature across three continents before touching an American server.

In the bedroom, Chad opened the closet and moved aside a false panel he'd installed months ago. Inside was everything he'd accumulated during his off-the-books work—the tools and resources that came with handling sensitive federal cases away from official oversight.

Cash. Sixty thousand in small bills, payment for informants who wouldn't go through official channels, plus another two hundred thousand from Lana and Casey's life insurance policies—money that had arrived with devastating swiftness after their deaths. Money that couldn't be traced through Bureau accounting. Identification documents under assumed names—driver's licenses, passports, credit cards—all created for legitimate undercover work that required deep cover identities, all quietly scrubbed from bureau databases. A small stash of weapons. Burner phones with clean numbers, satellite communicators from military contacts who understood that some operations required equipment that wasn't in the federal inventory.

All of it legitimate. All of it useful for a man who needed to disappear.

The Glock 19 felt familiar in his hands—his personal sidearm that he'd kept here for off-the-books operations. He'd bought it from a "salesman" selling weapons from the trunk of an '85 Monte Carlo in a Southeast DC parking lot—serial numbers filed off long ago, a true Saturday night special throw-away gun. The suppressor had been acquired through equally illegal means. He'd carried weapons like these through three combat deployments, had cleaned them by muscle memory in Afghan safe houses while incoming mortars shook dust from the ceiling.

The rifle was a different animal entirely. Custom-built AR-15 chambered in .300 Blackout with military modifications that shouldn't exist in civilian hands—select-fire capability, military optics, enough stopping power to punch through body armor at three hundred yards. The kind of weapon that turned one man into a small army.

Chad field-stripped both guns, checking every component with the methodical precision of someone whose life had depended on mechanical reliability. Clean, oil, reassemble. The motions were automatic, meditative, like a prayer he'd learned in another life.

In the basement, he found the rest of his preparations. Body armor rated for rifle rounds. Night vision equipment that could turn darkness into day. Surveillance cameras with wireless capability, motion sensors that could detect movement from a block away. The kind of gear that intelligence agencies used to watch suspected terrorists.

Now he was the terrorist.

Chad sat in the basement's single chair, surrounded by the tools of war, and felt something cold and familiar settle over his mind. The part of himself he'd buried when he'd hung up his uniform, the part that solved problems with violence and slept soundly afterward.

The part that Elena Ramirez had awakened when she'd murdered his family.

He pulled out one of the burner phones and dialed a number he'd memorized but never used.

"Yeah?" The voice was gravelly, cautious.

"Tony? It's Chad."

Silence. Then: "Jesus Christ, Lloyd. I heard about Lana and Casey on the news. Brother, I'm sorry. How you holding up?"

Tony Kowalski. Former Delta Force, current private military contractor. The man had a way of acquiring things that weren't supposed to exist and arrange meetings that never happened.

"I need gear, Tony. The kind we used to use downrange."

A longer pause. "Chad, whatever you're thinking about doing—"

"I'm not thinking anymore." Chad's voice was flat, empty of everything except purpose. "Elena Ramirez wants a war. I'm going to give her one."

"Shit, brother. You sure about this? Because once you cross that line —"

"I crossed it the moment I found my wife and daughter dead." Chad stood, pacing the small basement like a caged predator. "The system failed them. The system failed 284 other families. I'm done with the system."

"What do you need?"

"Explosives. Military grade. C-4, det cord, remote detonators. Enough to level a building or stop a convoy." Chad's voice was clinical, professional. "Long-range optics, thermal imaging, anything that gives me an edge in surveillance and target acquisition. And I need a vehicle—something inconspicuous, clean plates, no history."

"That's not going to be cheap."

"How much?"

Tony was quiet for a moment, calculating. "One twenty-five. Cash. The vehicle's twenty-five of that—clean title, legit registration, won't come back to bite you."

"Money's not a problem. But we do this smart—dead drop. I'm not risking either of us getting burned."

"Agreed. Where?"

Chad gave him the address of an abandoned warehouse in Baltimore, a place they'd used for unofficial operations back when they were both still wearing uniforms. "Park the van inside, gear loaded. I'll leave the money in the office—old safe behind the filing cabinet, you remember?"

"Yeah, I remember. Midnight tonight work for you?"

"I'll drop the cash at 2300 hours. You deliver at midnight—van loaded with everything, keys under the driver's seat. We don't see each other, we don't talk after this call."

"One twenty-five, dead drop at the Baltimore warehouse," Tony confirmed. "Chad?"

"Yeah?"

"There's no coming back from this. You know that, right?"

Chad looked around the basement, at the weapons and surveillance equipment, at the tools of a war that would be fought without rules or oversight or constitutional protections.

"I'm not planning to come back."

Chapter 29

The seventh floor looked like a bureaucratic afterthought. A hastily cleared conference room with water-stained ceiling tiles and flickering fluorescent lights that hummed like angry insects. The "operations center" consisted of a handful of government-surplus desks that looked like they'd survived the Carter administration, complete with rotary phones that belonged in a museum.

Agent Holmes stood in the middle of the depressing space, her perfectly styled appearance a stark contrast to the institutional decay around her. A maintenance worker was still wheeling out boxes of old files, leaving behind the smell of dust and forgotten paperwork.

"Well," Grey muttered, settling into a chair that creaked ominously under his weight, "this is... depressing."

Sam tested one of the rotary phones and got a dial tone that sounded like it was traveling through a tin can. "I guess unlimited federal funding doesn't include unlimited federal speed."

Holmes clapped her hands, gathering the handful of agents who'd been assigned to PHOENIX. Sam counted six people total, including herself and Grey. Not exactly the army she'd been expecting.

"Ladies and gentlemen," Holmes began, her voice echoing off the bare walls, "welcome to PHOENIX. I know the accommodations are temporary, but we have urgent work to do."

She turned to the whiteboard and wrote a single name in block letters: CHAD LLOYD.

Sam felt her blood turn to ice.

"Our first priority," Holmes continued, "is locating and apprehending former Agent Lloyd before he can compromise ongoing operations or endanger civilian lives."

"Ma'am," Sam said, her voice sharp with disbelief, "as far as we know, Chad was suspended and at this point hasn't broken any laws. Why is he the primary target instead of the people who murdered 284 people?"

Grey leaned forward in his creaking chair. "With respect, ma'am, shouldn't we be hunting Elena Ramirez instead of tracking down a grieving father who lost his wife and daughter?"

Holmes' smile was thin and cold. "Agent Grey, Agent Belle, Chad Lloyd made explicit threats against a designated terrorist organization in the presence of the FBI Director. That constitutes a credible threat to national security."

"He said he wanted justice," Sam shot back. "That's not the same as making threats."

"He said, and I quote from Director Huntington's report, that he was going to 'do something useful' and that the system had failed his family." Holmes turned to face them directly. "A man with his training and resources making statements like that? That's not grief talking—that's a clear indication of intent to take extrajudicial action."

Holmes' smile was sharp. "Agent Grey, Chad Lloyd poses an immediate threat to national security. He has years of operational knowledge, extensive contacts in law enforcement and intelligence agencies, and has made threats against a designated terrorist organization. If he acts on those threats, it could destabilize our entire counterterrorism strategy."

Sam stared at the whiteboard, at Chad's name written in Holmes' precise handwriting. "You want us to hunt down a federal agent whose family was murdered by the people we're supposed to be stopping?"

"I want us to stop a rogue operative before he gets himself killed and compromises ongoing federal investigations." Holmes turned back to the room. "Agent Ruiz, I need you to track all of Lloyd's financial activities. Credit cards, bank accounts, anything that shows movement. Agent Kim, coordinate with telecommunications—flag his cell phone, landlines, any electronic communication."

Grey's voice was tight with barely controlled anger. "And while we're chasing Chad, what happens when Elena Ramirez kills more federal families?"

"We prevent that by ensuring our operations aren't compromised by a vigilante with inside knowledge." Holmes pulled up a file folder. "Lloyd knows our surveillance methods, our informant networks, our operational procedures. If he goes after the Ramirez organization, he could expose assets we've spent years developing."

Agent Ruiz raised his hand hesitantly. "Ma'am, shouldn't we be focusing on the actual terrorists instead of tracking down one of our own?"

Holmes' green eyes hardened. "Agent Ruiz, Chad Lloyd ceased being 'one of our own' the moment he threatened to take matters into his own hands. He's now a security risk, and security risks get neutralized."

For the next three hours, they worked through tracking protocols, financial monitoring, and communications intercepts—all targeted at finding Chad Lloyd. Every database search, every flag on his identification, every alert on his known associates. Ruiz reluctantly set up financial tracking on Chad's accounts. Kim coordinated with NSA to monitor any electronic communications.

Sam found herself assigned to psychological profiling—trying to predict where Chad might go, what he might do, based on her two years as his partner. The irony was suffocating. She was supposed to use her knowledge of the man she'd fallen in love with to help the Bureau hunt him down.

"Agent Belle," Holmes said during a brief break, "you worked most closely with Lloyd. Where would he go? Who would he contact?"

Sam stared at the rotary phone on her desk, thinking about Chad's methodical nature, his operational security training. "He won't contact anyone we know about. And he won't go anywhere obvious."

"But he'll need resources. Money, weapons, transportation."

"Chad's smart enough to have prepared for this possibility." Sam met Holmes' stare without flinching. "He knows how we think, how we operate. If he doesn't want to be found, we won't find him."

"Everyone can be found, Agent Belle. It's just a matter of applying the right pressure."

The most important counterterrorism operation in Bureau history was spending its first day hunting the one man who might actually stop Elena Ramirez.

By 1830 hours, Sam was beginning to understand that Chad hadn't just been right about the system being broken—he'd been right about everything.

"Good work today, everyone," Holmes said as they wrapped up. "Tomorrow we expand the search. I want to know everywhere Lloyd's been, everyone he's talked to, every resource he might have access to. Agent Belle, Agent Grey—a word?"

After the others had left, Holmes pulled them aside. "I need you both to understand something. This isn't personal—it's operational. Chad Lloyd is a clear and present danger to national security."

"He's a grieving father who wants justice for his murdered family," Grey said flatly.

"He's a rogue agent with the training and resources to start a war." Holmes' voice dropped. "And if either of you has any contact with him, any contact at all, you'll join him on the fugitive list. Are we clear?"

"Crystal," Sam said, though the word tasted like poison.

Chapter 30

Sam's Apartment
Alexandria, VA

Sam's feet ached as she climbed the stairs to her apartment, her mind reeling from what she'd witnessed at PHOENIX. Instead of hunting terrorists, they were hunting Chad. Instead of stopping Elena Ramirez, they were trying to stop the one person who might actually do something about her.

She unlocked her door and immediately knew something was wrong.

The silence felt different. Not the comfortable quiet of someone in another room, but the hollow emptiness of a place that had been deliberately vacated. It took her a moment to realize what she was seeing —or rather, what she wasn't seeing. His reading glasses were gone from the coffee table. His toiletries missing from the bathroom. The book he'd been pretending to read no longer there.

Every trace of Chad had been erased.

Sam walked to the kitchen table on unsteady legs and found the letter waiting for her, folded precisely and placed next to her spare key, Chad's truck keys, and his personal cell phone.

Her hands shook as she unfolded the paper. Chad's familiar handwriting covered two pages—his careful explanation of why he'd left, his release of her promise to Lana, his request about flowers on the 19th of every month. And at the bottom, the words that broke her heart: You're the best partner I ever had, and you deserve better than watching me become something you won't recognize.

The letter slipped from her fingers and fluttered to the floor as Sam sank into a chair, the careful emotional control she'd learned as a federal agent crumbling like a dam with a crack in it. Fury that he'd made this decision without her. Sadness that the man she'd fallen in love with was truly gone. Terror about what he was planning to do.

And underneath it all, a growing certainty that maybe—just maybe—he was right.

Sam picked up her phone with trembling fingers and called Grey.

"Sam? What's wrong?"

"He was here," she said, her voice barely above a whisper. "Chad was here. He left a letter."

Silence on the other end. Then: "Those bastards. They drove him to this."

"Nolan—"

"No, Sam. Don't you dare tell me this is Chad's fault." Grey's voice was raw with fury. "I've known that man for twenty years. He's the most loyal, dedicated agent I've ever worked with. And what do they do when his family gets murdered? They use his grief as a photo op, then make him the target when he calls them out on it."

Sam could hear Grey moving around, probably pacing his apartment like a caged animal. "They're scapegoating him, Sam. Instead of admitting they failed to protect their own, they're making Chad the problem. It's easier to hunt down one rogue agent than admit the whole fucking system is broken."

"What did the letter say?" Grey asked, his voice slightly calmer.

Sam summarized the key points—Chad's goodbye, his reasons for leaving, his request about the flowers. When she finished, Grey was quiet for a long moment.

"Son of a bitch," he said finally. "He's really going to do it. And honestly? Good for him."

"Nolan—"

"No, Sam. I'm done pretending this system works. We spent today setting up tracking protocols on a man whose only crime is wanting justice for his murdered wife and daughter. Meanwhile, Elena Ramirez is probably planning her next massacre, and we're not even looking for her."

Grey's voice turned hard as steel. "You know what the real joke is? Chad's probably the only one who can actually stop her. He's got the training, the motivation, and now he's got nothing left to lose. But instead of supporting him, we're hunting him down like a criminal."

"Holmes wants us to track him down. Use everything we know about him to help the Bureau stop him."

"Fuck Holmes." Grey's voice was venomous. "And fuck the Bureau if they think I'm going to help them destroy the best man I've ever worked with."

Sam felt something shift inside her chest—a weight lifting, a decision crystallizing. "So what do we do?"

"We protect him," Grey said without hesitation. "We feed Holmes useless information, we misdirect the investigation, and we make sure Chad has the time and space he needs to do what none of us have the balls to do."

"If Holmes finds out—"

"Then we join Chad on the outside." Grey's voice carried twenty years of accumulated anger and disgust. "Maybe that's where the decent people belong anyway. At least out there, we won't have to pretend the system gives a damn about justice."

After she hung up, Sam sat in her empty apartment, surrounded by the ghost of Chad's presence. Outside her window, Washington D.C. sprawled beneath a cold October sky, eight million people going about their lives, unaware that the line between justice and vengeance had just shifted.

Heavy footsteps echoed in the hallway outside her door, slow and deliberate. Sam's heart leaped. Chad? Had he come back? Changed his mind?

The footsteps stopped directly outside her apartment.

Chapter 31

Holmes' Apartment
Georgetown

Agent Janet Holmes poured herself three fingers of twenty-year-old Macallan and settled into the leather chair that had cost more than most FBI agents made in six months. The apartment was a testament to tastes that exceeded her government salary—Italian furniture, original artwork, a view of the Potomac that came with a seven-figure price tag.

All of it funded by relationships that would end her career and land her in federal prison.

If anyone ever found out.

Holmes pulled out a burner phone she'd purchased with cash that morning, one of six identical devices she kept for communications that couldn't appear on any government monitoring system. She dialed a number she'd memorized but never written down, a number that connected to a satellite phone somewhere in the Caribbean.

The phone rang twice before a woman's voice answered. "¿Sí?"

"Elena Ramirez?"

A long pause. Then, cautious: "Who is this?"

"Agent Janet Holmes, FBI. I'm calling about a business proposition."

"If this is some kind of trap—"

"It's not. I'm the new director of the PHOENIX task force. The one that's supposed to hunt you down."

Elena's laugh was cold and sharp. "Impossible. I watched the press conference. Director Huntington said Agent Lloyd was in charge."

"Lloyd was suspended right after that press conference." Holmes leaned back in her chair, knowing she had to sell this carefully. "He threatened to take matters into his own hands. Made it clear he planned to go after you personally, outside official channels."

"So they removed him."

"They removed him and put me in charge. And here's the beautiful irony—the task force created to hunt cartels is now spending all its time hunting Chad Lloyd instead of you."

Elena was quiet for a moment. "Why should I believe you?"

"Because I can prove it. Right now, PHOENIX has six agents tracking Lloyd's financial records, monitoring his communications, trying to predict his movements. We've flagged every piece of identification he has, alerted every law enforcement agency in the country. The most important counterterrorism operation in FBI history is focused entirely on stopping one rogue agent."

"And you want to help me because...?"

Holmes smiled coldly. "Because I've been watching federal agencies fail to stop organizations like yours for fifteen years. The cartels always adapt faster than we can respond. You're going to win this war regardless of what PHOENIX does. I'd rather profit from that inevitability than pretend I can stop it."

"What exactly are you proposing?"

"Complete operational intelligence on every federal effort against your organization. Real-time updates on DEA operations, CIA surveillance, FBI investigations. I'll know about raids before the agents conducting them get their briefings."

Elena's voice remained skeptical. "And why would the new director of an anti-cartel task force risk everything to help me?"

"Because the task force isn't anti-cartel anymore. It's anti-Chad Lloyd. And frankly, that suits me fine." Holmes took another sip of whiskey. "I can keep PHOENIX focused on hunting him instead of you for months. Maybe years."

"And what do you want in return?"

"Twenty percent of profits from all North American operations." Holmes had calculated this carefully—enough to set her up for life, not so much that it would cripple Elena's business model. "Deposited monthly in accounts I'll specify, completely untraceable to federal monitoring."

"Interesting. Continue."

"More importantly, I control the narrative. PHOENIX is supposed to be the government's flagship response to your terrorism designation. I can make sure it focuses on the wrong targets, pursues dead-end leads, gets bogged down in bureaucratic procedures that accomplish nothing."

Elena was quiet for a moment, considering. "And Lloyd? I understand he's become a problem."

"He's being handled. Every federal agency is looking for him now that he's gone rogue."

"Good. He killed my father."

"I know. And I'm making sure he pays for it."

"Can you find him?"

Holmes paused, thinking about Sam Belle's psychological profile session, about the way the woman had insisted Chad was too smart to be caught. "He's well-trained and highly motivated. But everyone makes mistakes eventually. When he does, I'll make sure you know about it before anyone else."

"Twenty percent," Elena said finally. "But I want proof of your value before we finalize any arrangement."

"What kind of proof?"

"Lloyd. I want him found, and I want him delivered to me alive. Prove you can do that, and we have a deal."

Holmes felt a chill run down her spine. Delivering Chad Lloyd to Elena Ramirez would be signing his death warrant—and not a quick death. Elena would want to make him suffer for killing her father.

But twenty percent of Ramirez Cartel profits was worth more than one man's life. Even a man she'd once respected.

"I'll find him," Holmes said. "How do I contact you when I have something?"

"You don't. I'll contact you. Every three days at 2100 hours, this number. If you miss a call, wait for the next one."

"Understood."

"And Janet? If you're thinking about playing both sides, remember that I know where you live. I know where you work. I know everything about your life, and I can take it all away with a single phone call."

The line went dead.

Holmes sat in her expensive apartment, surrounded by luxury paid for with illicit money, and felt a mixture of excitement and terror. She'd just committed treason, but she'd also secured her financial future.

Chapter 32

C had Lloyd stood in the bedroom of his forgotten safe house, staring at the murder board that covered every wall. Printouts, photographs, and maps connected by red string like a spider's web of vengeance. He'd converted the room into his operations center while keeping the weapons secured in the basement and sleeping on the living room couch—easier to hear anyone approaching the house.

The dead drop had gone perfectly. Tony had left the van exactly where promised—a nondescript gray Ford Transit with clean plates and no history that could trace back to either of them. The cargo area had been loaded with everything Chad had requested: C-4 explosives, det cord, remote detonators, long-range optics, thermal imaging equipment. The tools of a very personal war.

Now the weapons were secured in his basement, the van was parked in the single-car garage with the door closed, and Chad had everything he needed except the most important thing—targets.

The three faces stared back at him from the center of the web— Elena Ramirez, Hector Ramirez, and Javier "el cuchillo" Santos. His personal most wanted list. The people who'd destroyed his world. But faces without addresses were just photographs, and Chad needed more than pictures to wage his war.

He'd spent the last six hours working through every contact, every piece of intelligence, every scrap of information he'd accumulated during his time hunting the Ramirez Cartel. Financial records showed Elena's money flowing through a dozen shell companies across three countries. Surveillance photos captured Hector at various locations throughout Mexico. But nothing current, nothing actionable.

Nothing that would put them in his crosshairs.

Chad stared at Javier's photograph—a surveillance shot taken outside a Miami nightclub eight months ago. The man who'd murdered his family, who'd probably enjoyed every moment of their terror. Chad had memorized every line of that face, every detail that would help him recognize the killer when the time came.

But where the hell was he?

Chad picked up one of his burner phones and dialed a number he'd memorized years ago. It rang four times before a gravelly voice answered.

"Supko."

"Jim, it's Chad."

Silence. Then: "What the hell, Lloyd. Every agency in the country is looking for you. Where the hell are you?"

Chad felt ice form in his stomach. "Looking for me? What do you mean?"

"You don't know? Chad, you're wanted for questioning as a potential domestic terrorist. FBI issued a BOLO alert a few hours ago."

"I didn't do anything wrong, Jim."

"Chad, what you said in Huntington's office—they're treating it as a credible threat. You need to turn yourself in."

Chad hung up and called right back.

Chad kept one eye on his watch, knowing he needed to keep this call short. "Jim, I called about the case. What progress have you made tracking the killer?"

Chad could hear Supko moving around, probably checking to make sure no one was listening. The detective had caught the case when Lana and Casey were murdered—a good cop trying to build a solid case while Chad had been watching his government turn his family's death into a photo opportunity.

"We got traffic cam footage of the suspect driving a white van toward the city about twenty minutes after the... after it happened."

"Where'd the trail lead?"

"Van showed up on three more cameras heading toward Southeast. Last sighting was on Benning Road, near some industrial area. We found the van two days later, burned out in Anacostia.

"Any witnesses?"

"That's where it gets interesting." Supko's voice dropped to a whisper. "We canvassed the area, talked to everyone we could find. Turns out the white van had Magnolia Street Flowers painted on the side. DEA had the Potomac Street Flowers warehouse under surveillance that night and got pictures of your suspect talking with Jose Morales."

Chad felt his pulse quicken but kept his voice neutral. "Legitimate business?"

"On paper. But Jose is the manager—ring any bells?"

Chad knew the name but didn't let on. "Should it?"

"Suspected Ramirez Cartel lieutenant. We think the flower warehouse is a front for money laundering, maybe human trafficking. The kind of place that would need regular visits from cartel enforcers."

"Sounds like you've got a solid lead. When are you moving on it?"

"We're building the case slowly, properly. Don't want to spook them."

"Chad—"

"Thanks for the update, Jim. Stay safe."

Chad hung up quickly and stared at his phone. Something had felt off about that conversation—the way Jim kept talking, almost like he was trying to keep Chad on the line longer than necessary.

Chad checked his watch and realized he'd been on for nearly four minutes. Too long. If they were trying to trace the call...

Chad knew Southeast D.C. well enough—there couldn't be more than a handful of flower warehouses in the Benning Road area. And if Supko's people were watching it, he'd spot the surveillance from blocks away.

Which meant Chad had to assume it was already a trap.

Jim Supko stared at his phone, then looked across the room to Detective Zuckerman, who was pulling off headphones connected to a trace unit.

"Did we get it?" Supko asked.

"No. He hung up too soon."

Supko nodded grimly. Even he was officially part of the manhunt now. But somewhere deep down, he hoped Chad would stay one step ahead of everyone looking for him.

Chad stared at his murder board with new understanding. The warehouse was compromised, but it had given him something valuable—confirmation that Javier had reported to Jose Morales after killing his family. Which meant Morales had information Chad needed.

He just couldn't get it the direct way.

Chad checked his watch: 0330 hours. The weapons were ready, the van was positioned, and now he had his first real target. But the approach would have to be different than he'd planned.

But first, he had to pay someone a visit.

Chapter 33

Sam's Apartment
Alexandria, VA

Sam sat in her empty apartment, Chad's letter still clutched in her trembling hands. The conversation with Grey echoed in her mind—We protect him. We feed Holmes useless information. We make sure Chad has the time and space he needs to do what none of us have the balls to do.

Heavy footsteps echoed in the hallway outside her door, slow and deliberate. Sam's heart leaped. The measured pace, the weight of someone moving carefully but purposefully.

The footsteps stopped directly outside her apartment.

Sam's breathing became shallow, her heart hammering so loud she was sure whoever was out there could hear it. She stood slowly, Chad's letter falling to the floor as she reached for her service weapon on the kitchen counter.

The Glock felt heavy in her hands as she moved toward the door, keeping to the side to avoid silhouetting herself against the peephole. Her bare feet made no sound on the hardwood floor.

She pressed herself against the wall beside the door, weapon raised, finger on the trigger guard. Through the thin wood, she could hear someone breathing on the other side.

Sam's hand moved toward the deadbolt, then hesitated. What if it wasn't Chad? What if it was Holmes, or FBI surveillance, or—

Three soft knocks on the door.

Sam nearly jumped out of her skin, her finger instinctively moving to the trigger before training kicked in and she moved it back to the guard. Her pulse thundered in her ears.

Then she heard a voice, barely above a whisper.

"Sam? It's me."

Chad.

Sam's knees nearly buckled with relief. She lowered her weapon but didn't holster it, her hands still shaking as she reached for the deadbolt.

"Chad?" she whispered back.

"Yeah. We need to talk."

Sam's hand froze on the lock. Chad was here. The man every federal agency in the country was hunting was standing outside her door at four in the morning. If anyone saw him, if there was surveillance on her apartment, if Holmes had people watching—

"Sam, please. I don't have much time."

His voice sounded different. Older. Harder. Like something fundamental had changed in the hours since he'd walked out of Huntington's office.

Sam looked through the peephole and saw Chad standing in the hallway, wearing dark clothes and a baseball cap pulled low over his eyes. He looked like a shadow, like someone who belonged in the darkness.

She turned the deadbolt.

Chapter 34

Sam's Apartment
Alexandria, VA

Sam opened the door and Chad slipped inside like smoke, immediately moving away from the entrance and scanning the apartment with the predatory awareness of someone who'd learned to expect threats from every shadow.

"I wasn't followed," he said quietly, but Sam noticed he kept his back to the wall and his eyes on the windows. "Spent hours making sure."

"Chad, what are you—" Sam stopped herself. The man standing in her living room looked like Chad Lloyd, but something fundamental had changed. His movements were different—more fluid, more dangerous. His eyes held a coldness she'd never seen before.

This was what Grey had warned her about. The man she'd fallen in love with really was gone.

"Why is the FBI hunting me instead of Elena?" Chad asked, his voice flat and emotionless. "I just found out I'm wanted as a domestic terrorist. For what? Telling the truth about a broken system?"

Sam holstered her weapon and gestured for him to sit, but Chad remained standing, positioned where he could see both the door and the windows.

"Chad, there's a lot you don't know." Sam's voice was heavy with exhaustion and anger. "PHOENIX isn't what they told you it would be."

"What do you mean?"

"They put Agent Holmes in charge. A woman from White Collar Crimes who's never worked a terrorism case in her life." Sam sank into a chair, suddenly feeling the weight of the last twenty-four hours. "Our first day was supposed to be about hunting Elena Ramirez. Instead, we spent eight hours setting up tracking protocols on you."

Chad's jaw tightened. "On me?"

"Financial monitoring, communications intercepts, psychological profiling. Holmes had me create a behavioral analysis to predict where you'd go, who you'd contact." Sam's voice cracked slightly. "They wanted me to use everything I know about you to help them hunt you down."

"Jesus Christ." Chad ran a hand through his hair. "So instead of stopping the people who killed my family, they're using the people who cared about my family to track me down."

"It gets worse. Holmes made it clear that if you contact me or Grey, our careers are over. We're supposed to report any communication immediately."

Chad stared at her for a long moment. "Then why aren't you?"

"Because Grey and I talked after you left. We decided that we're not going to help them hunt down the only person who can actually stop Elena Ramirez." Sam stood, moving closer to him. "We're going to help you instead."

Something flickered in Chad's eyes—surprise, maybe gratitude. "Sam, you can't. If they find out—"

"I don't care." Sam's voice was steady, determined. "Chad, I've spent my entire career believing the system works. But watching them turn your family's murder into a photo opportunity, then making you the target instead of the killers? The system is broken beyond repair."

Chad was quiet for a moment, and Sam could see him processing this information, calculating the implications.

"What exactly are you willing to do?" he asked.

"Feed Holmes false information about your whereabouts. Misdirect the investigation. Give you advance warning about any operations they're planning." Sam took a deep breath. "Whatever you need."

"That's treason, Sam. If they catch you—"

"Then they catch us. Chad, Grey and I talked about this. We'd rather be on the outside doing what's right than on the inside enabling what's wrong."

162

Chad nodded slowly. "I need to know what they know about Elena's organization. Financial intelligence, surveillance reports, anything that could help me find her."

He paused, then continued. "I talked to Supko tonight. DEA has surveillance photos of Javier meeting with Jose Morales at a flower warehouse on Benning Road after he killed my family. Jose's a known lieutenant in Elena's organization."

Sam felt her pulse quicken. "Jose Morales? We have files on him. Suspected of running logistics for the cartel's East Coast operations."

"That's him. The warehouse is called Potomac Street Flowers. It's a front for money laundering, probably human trafficking. But here's the problem—Supko's people are watching it, and they were trying to trace my call. The place is compromised."

"So you can't go there directly."

"Not the way I planned. But Jose is the key to finding where Javier went after my house. He has information I need."

"I can get that. But Chad..." Sam hesitated, then forced herself to continue. She might never get another chance, and if he didn't come back from whatever war he was planning to wage, she needed him to know.

"There's something else I have to tell you."

Chad looked at her, waiting.

"I know it's only been a few weeks since Lana died. I know the timing is terrible, and I know you probably can't hear this right now." Sam's voice was barely above a whisper. "But I'm in love with you. I have been for months, maybe longer. And if you don't come back from this, I need you to know that someone loved you enough to risk everything to help you."

Chad stared at her, his expression unreadable. For a moment, the cold mask slipped and she saw a flash of the man she'd fallen in love with—vulnerable, human, capable of feeling something other than rage.

"Sam..." His voice was rough. "I can't... I'm not... There's nothing left of me that's capable of that anymore."

"I know. I'm not asking for anything. I just needed you to know."

Chad was quiet for a long moment, and Sam could see the internal battle playing out behind his eyes.

"You were the best partner I ever had," he said finally. "The best friend. If things were different..."

"I know."

They stood in silence for a moment, the weight of everything unsaid hanging between them.

"We need to set up communication protocols," Chad said, shifting back to operational mode. "Something they can't trace or monitor."

"Dead drops?"

"Too risky if they're watching you. Burner phones would require you to buy them with cash, and if Holmes has people following you..." Chad thought for a moment. "What about a gaming app?"

"A game?"

"Download something popular with millions of users. Create an account with a fake name, something generic. We communicate through the in-game chat function. To anyone monitoring, it just looks like you're playing a mobile game."

Sam nodded, understanding immediately. "What game?"

"Words with Friends. Create an account under the name Sarah Miller. Start a game with username ChuckLogan47. We can chat while pretending to play. If anyone's monitoring, they'll see normal gaming activity."

"And if I need to reach you urgently?"

"Play the word 'HELP' if you can. Otherwise, send 'How's your game going?' If I need intel, I'll ask 'What's your high score today?' You respond with whatever information you have about PHOENIX operations."

"What if Holmes gets suspicious about my questions?"

"Tell her you're trying to understand my psychology, my operational patterns. Make it sound like psychological profiling." Chad moved toward the door. "And Sam? Be careful. If Holmes is as smart as she seems, she'll be watching for exactly this kind of thing."

Chad paused at the door, his hand on the deadbolt.

"Sam, what I'm about to do... it's going to get dark. Darker than anything we've ever worked on. If you change your mind, if you decide you can't be part of it, just stop responding to my texts. No judgment."

"I won't change my mind."

Chad nodded and opened the door, checking the hallway before stepping out.

"Chad?"

He turned back.

Sam stepped closer and placed a soft kiss on his cheek, her lips lingering for just a moment against his skin.

"Be careful and come back safe," she whispered. "People around here need you."

Chad's expression softened slightly, and for just an instant she saw a glimpse of the man beneath the cold mask.

He disappeared into the darkness, leaving Sam alone with her confession and the growing certainty that she'd just helped set something terrible and necessary into motion.

Chapter 35

Ramirez Compound
Grand Cayman

Elena Ramirez stood on the marble terrace of her compound, Holmes' intelligence reports spread across the glass table behind her. The morning sun painted the Caribbean in shades of gold, but her mind was focused on darker waters.

"Read it again," she said without turning around.

Hector picked up the secure phone transcript. "PHOENIX task force operational priority: Locate and apprehend former Agent Chad Lloyd. The Americans created a task force to hunt cartels, then spend their time hunting one rogue agent."

Elena smiled. "Perfect. While they chase shadows, we evolve."

She turned from the ocean view, her green eyes reflecting predatory intelligence. "The President wants terrorists? Let's give him exactly what he asked for."

"Traditional cartels fight like corporations—territorial, hierarchical, vulnerable to decapitation strikes," Elena continued, pulling up a map on her tablet. "This was proven when El Chapo was arrested. It was proven again when our father was killed. One raid, one bullet, and decades of leadership gone."

"But insurgents survive," Javier said, understanding immediately.

"Exactly. Al Qaeda survived bin Laden's death by adapting and decentralizing. ISIS evolved from territorial caliphate to global cell network. The Taliban outlasted twenty years of American occupation." Elena's voice grew excited. "We stop fighting like cartels and start fighting like insurgents."

"You're talking about becoming actual terrorists," Javier said.

"I'm talking about survival. We have advantages ISIS never had—unlimited money, established safe havens, and millions of people who already distrust federal law enforcement." Elena's smile was winter-cold. "The Americans expect us to protect territory and leadership. Instead, we abandon both and strike from everywhere at once."

"But first, we need teachers. Former ISIS operatives, ex-Al Qaeda cell leaders, Taliban commanders who survived years of American counterinsurgency." Elena pulled up encrypted communications on her tablet. "Men who know how to build networks that can't be destroyed, who understand operational security that kept them alive when everyone was hunting them."

"You want to recruit terrorists?" Javier's voice carried a mix of admiration and concern.

"I want to recruit survivors. The ones who evaded drone strikes, who built cells that operated for years without detection, who coordinated global operations while living in caves." Elena's eyes gleamed with possibility. "Money talks, and we have more money than any government."

She activated a different communication system—one that connected to dark web networks where former insurgents sold their expertise to the highest bidder.

"Give me seventy-two hours to arrange the consultations. Then we call the other cartels with a fully developed operational model, not just theories."

Elena walked back to the terrace. In the distance, she could see boats moving freely across waters that recognized no government's authority.

"Hector," she called softly. "Start reaching out to our contacts in Syria, Afghanistan, and Somalia. I want to meet with the best insurgent minds money can buy."

"And then?"

"We hire as many as we can. Embed them with each new cartel cell and smuggle as many as possible across the border." Elena's smile was predatory. "The real terrorists will do the terrorizing and hit the targets while we move undetected in their shadows, becoming even stronger than we already are. America will have to deal with an actual terrorist crisis and forget all about hunting cartels."

"Brilliant," Hector breathed. "We become invisible while they chase real threats."

"Exactly. Let trained jihadists draw federal attention while we expand our operations unopposed."

Elena pulled up satellite imagery of major American infrastructure targets on her tablet.

"Then we test our new methods on something that will make the whole country pay attention. The Denver Mint, maybe. Or the Croton Water Treatment Plant that supplies New York City." Her smile was cold and calculating. "Make a statement so big that every federal agency drops what they're doing to hunt terrorists."

Chapter 36

Sam's Apartment
Alexandria VA

Sam stood frozen in her kitchen, staring at the door Chad had just walked through. The faint scent of his cologne still lingered in the air, the only proof that the last thirty minutes hadn't been some stress-induced hallucination.

Was Chad really here?

She touched her lips where she'd kissed him goodbye, her fingers still tingling from the contact. The man she'd fallen in love with had stood in her living room, told her he was going to war, and disappeared back into the darkness like a ghost.

Sam shook herself back to reality. She had work to do.

She pulled out her personal phone and downloaded Words with Friends from the app store. Her hands were still trembling slightly as she created the account—Sarah Miller, just like Chad had instructed. The username looked innocuous enough among the millions of casual players who used the platform to kill time.

Next, she searched for ChuckLogan47 and sent a friend request. Within seconds, it was accepted, and a new game board appeared on her screen. Chad was already online, waiting.

Sam stared at the virtual Scrabble tiles, knowing that this simple mobile game had just become a lifeline between her and the most wanted man in America. Then she closed the app and reached for her work phone.

Grey answered on the second ring, his voice gravelly with sleep.

"Belle? Jesus, what time is it?"

"Early. Nolan, we need to talk before work. Can you meet me for coffee?"

"Sam, it's four-thirty in the morning. What's—"

"Please. It's important." Sam kept her voice carefully neutral, knowing that Holmes could have their phones monitored. "I couldn't sleep. Need to talk before work."

There was a pause as Grey processed the unusual early morning call. "I see. Where do you want to meet?"

"That place on M Street? The one that opens early for the morning commuters?"

"I'll be there in thirty minutes."

Sam hung up and looked around her apartment one more time. Chad's truck keys still sat on the kitchen table next to his letter. Physical proof that he'd trusted her with something valuable—his only means of transportation, his final goodbye.

She picked up the keys and slipped them into her pocket. If Holmes' people were watching her apartment, seeing her drive Chad's truck might raise questions. But leaving it here indefinitely would raise different questions.

Sam grabbed her jacket and headed for the door, her mind already working through what she needed to tell Grey. He deserved to know everything—Chad's visit, the intelligence about the warehouse, their new communication system. After yesterday's conversation, she knew Grey was already committed to helping Chad.

But more importantly, she needed Grey's tactical expertise. Chad needed access to Jose Morales at the Potomac Street Flowers warehouse, but the place was under surveillance. How could they help him get to his target without raising suspicion? Grey had twenty years of military experience and more with the Bureau—if anyone could figure out how to neutralize surveillance or create a distraction, it would be him.

And underneath it all, the growing certainty that she'd just crossed a line she could never uncross.

Chapter 37

Murphy's Coffee Shop
M Street Northwest

Grey was already waiting in a corner booth when Sam arrived, positioned where he could see both the entrance and the street outside. Two cups of black coffee sat on the table, steam rising in the early morning chill.

"You look like hell," he said as she slid into the seat across from him.

"Couldn't sleep." Sam wrapped her hands around the warm cup, grateful for something to do with her nervous energy. She glanced around the nearly empty coffee shop, confirming they were alone except for the barista who was more interested in his phone than their conversation.

"Nolan, he came to see me."

Grey's coffee cup froze halfway to his lips. "He?"

"Chad. About an hour ago. He was in my apartment."

Grey set down his cup carefully and leaned forward. "Jesus, Sam. What did he want?"

"Information. And he gave me some intelligence about the case." Sam kept her voice low. "He talked to Supko. DEA has surveillance photos of Javier meeting with Jose Morales at a flower warehouse after he killed Chad's family. The place is called Potomac Street Flowers on Benning Road."

"I know it. We've had files on Morales for months."

"That's the problem. Chad says the warehouse is under surveillance. Supko's people are watching it, and they tried to trace Chad's call. But

Jose has information Chad needs—where Javier went, how to find Elena."

Grey nodded slowly, understanding immediately. "So Chad needs access to Jose without walking into a trap."

"Exactly. Nolan, you know surveillance protocols better than anyone. Is there a way to help him get to his target?"

Grey was quiet for a moment, thinking tactically. "There might be a way. If we could create a reason for surveillance to be pulled back temporarily, or cause a distraction that draws their attention elsewhere..."

"What kind of distraction?"

"False alarm at another location. Anonymous tip about suspicious activity somewhere else in the city. Make them think there's a more immediate threat." Grey's eyes sharpened. "Or we could feed them bad intelligence about Chad's whereabouts. Send them chasing shadows in the wrong part of town."

Sam nodded. "That could work. But how do we coordinate with Chad?"

"You said he gave you a way to communicate?"

"Words with Friends. Mobile game app. He set up an account under ChuckLogan47. I'm Sarah Miller. We can chat through the game interface."

"Smart. Gaming traffic is hard to monitor, and there are millions of users." Grey stood up. "I'll dig up everything we have on that warehouse surveillance operation. I should have access to the protocols and schedules. If I know how they're watching it, I can figure out how to blind them temporarily."

They walked out of the coffee shop together, stepping into the gray morning.

"Nolan," Sam said as they reached their cars, "we need to be careful about our communications too. No phones, no emails. Everything face-to-face."

"Agreed. And we act completely normal around Holmes and the team."

As Sam drove toward FBI headquarters, she felt the weight of her new mission settling over her. She wasn't just an FBI agent anymore. She was Chad's lifeline to the inside, and possibly his only chance of getting to Jose Morales alive.

Time to see what intelligence she could gather without raising suspicion.

Chapter 38

PHOENIX Task Force Operations Center
FBI Headquarters – 7th Floor

Sam and Grey walked into the PHOENIX operations center to find the room buzzing with unusual activity. Technicians in civilian clothes were installing new surveillance equipment that had arrived that morning —state-of-the-art thermal imaging displays, enhanced communication arrays, and real-time facial recognition software. Resources that would have taken months to acquire for other operations were being fast-tracked to PHOENIX within days.

Detective Jim Supko stood near the whiteboard, his weathered face grim as he spoke quietly with Agent Holmes, seemingly oblivious to the technological upgrade happening around them.

"...tried to trace the call, but he hung up too soon," Supko was saying as they approached. "Smart bastard knows how long it takes to get a location."

Holmes nodded, her red hair catching the fluorescent light as she made notes on a tablet. "But you're certain it was Lloyd who called?"

"Positive. Voice recognition software confirmed it." Supko glanced around the room, noting Sam and Grey's arrival. "He was asking about the Javier Santos case. Specifically about Santos' movements after the Lloyd family murders."

Sam felt her pulse quicken but kept her expression neutral. Chad had mentioned talking to Supko, but seeing the detective here reporting to Holmes made the betrayal feel personal.

"What exactly did you tell him?" Holmes asked.

"Standard case information. Traffic cam footage, the burned-out van, witness statements." Supko paused. "And I mentioned the connection to a Potomac Street Flowers warehouse. Jose Morales. We have DEA surveillance photos of Javier meeting with Morales there after the Lloyd murders."

Holmes' green eyes sharpened with interest. "So Lloyd knows that Morales helped his family's killer?"

"That's right. Morales probably arranged Javier's extraction after the hit. If Lloyd wants to find Javier, Morales is his best lead."

"Asked a few follow-up questions, then ended the call abruptly. But Agent Holmes..." Supko's voice dropped. "I think he's planning to go there. To the warehouse."

"Why do you think that?"

"For years I've known Chad Lloyd. When he gets that focused tone in his voice, when he starts asking tactical questions..." Supko shook his head. "He's going after Jose Morales."

Holmes immediately turned to her tablet, pulling up maps and surveillance protocols. "Agent Ruiz, contact DEA and coordinate additional surveillance assets for the warehouse location. I want full perimeter coverage, thermal imaging, and rapid response teams within five minutes of that warehouse."

Sam exchanged a quick glance with Grey, seeing her own dismay reflected in his eyes. Any chance of creating a distraction to help Chad had just evaporated.

"Agent Kim," Holmes continued, "coordinate with local law enforcement. If Lloyd shows up anywhere near that warehouse, I want him taken alive. But be prepared for resistance—this man has extensive tactical training and nothing left to lose."

Grey stepped forward. "Ma'am, what about our investigation into Elena Ramirez? Shouldn't we be focusing on the actual terrorists instead of—"

"Agent Grey," Holmes' voice was sharp as a blade, "Chad Lloyd possesses intelligence about our operations and has made credible threats against a designated terrorist organization. Apprehending him before he can compromise ongoing investigations is our top priority."

"Ma'am, with respect, isn't the terrorist organization itself a threat?" Grey's voice carried barely controlled frustration. "Elena Ramirez murdered 284 federal family members. Shouldn't stopping her from killing more people be our top priority instead of protecting her from Chad Lloyd?"

Holmes' green eyes flashed with irritation. "Agent Grey, Lloyd is a rogue operative who could compromise years of intelligence work and endanger federal assets. We cannot allow personal vendettas to undermine our systematic approach to dismantling these organizations."

"Ma'am, Chad still hasn't broken any laws," Grey pressed. "If we continue this manhunt for a man whose only crime is exercising his right to free speech, we could sour the opinion of all Americans. It's not right to go after an innocent citizen just because he criticized the system that failed to protect his family."

Holmes' expression hardened. "Agent Grey, I think you're forgetting that Lloyd made explicit threats in the presence of the FBI Director. That constitutes a credible threat to national security."

"He said the system failed and that he wanted justice. Since when is that a crime in America?"

"Detective Supko," Holmes said, turning back to the Fairfax County officer, "I want you to coordinate with our surveillance teams. If Lloyd contacts you again, keep him on the line longer. Use whatever personal connection you have to make him stay on the call."

Supko nodded reluctantly. "I'll do what I can. But Chad's not stupid. If he suspects I'm working with you..."

"Then we'll have to hope he makes a mistake." Holmes closed her tablet with a sharp snap. "Ladies and gentlemen, I want everything we have on that warehouse and Jose Morales. Financial records, surveillance reports, operational assessments, known associates. If Lloyd is planning to go after Morales, we need to understand every possible approach he might take."

She paused, scanning the room with those calculating green eyes. "And I want psychological profiles updated. Lloyd knows Morales helped his family's killer escape. He'll risk everything for a chance at revenge and information about Javier's whereabouts."

Sam felt like Holmes was looking directly through her, seeing every secret, every betrayal she was planning.

"I have a conference call with Director Huntington in ten minutes," Holmes announced. "Agent Grey, you have operational command while I'm gone. Get me actionable intelligence on Lloyd's probable next moves."

As Holmes left the room, her heels clicking authoritatively on the linoleum floor, Sam felt the weight of impossible circumstances settling over her. Chad needed to know that the warehouse was now under heavy surveillance, but more importantly, he needed to know that Supko had betrayed him to the FBI. How could she warn him about both without compromising their communication system?

She pulled out her phone and opened Words with Friends, her fingers hovering over the virtual keyboard as she tried to think of a way to convey both warnings in casual gaming conversation.

Sam glanced around the room, making sure no one was watching, then typed her first message to ChuckLogan47. She read it twice, praying Chad would decode both warnings hidden in her casual gaming language.

She hit send and put the phone away, her heart hammering as she wondered if she'd just saved Chad's life or watched him walk into a trap anyway.

Chapter 39

B lood has a way of calling to blood, and Agent Janet Holmes could smell it coming from three floors away.

Holmes stepped out of the PHOENIX operations center, her heels clicking against the linoleum with the precision of a woman who'd learned to walk through minefields wearing designer shoes. The secure stairwell was empty—exactly what she needed for the kind of conversation that could end careers or start wars.

The burner phone felt warm in her palm as she dialed the encrypted number, each digit a nail in someone's coffin. Elena answered on the first ring, her voice carrying the sultry confidence of a woman who collected federal agents like trophies.

"Janet. Perfect timing."

"We have a problem," Holmes said without preamble, watching her reflection in the stairwell's safety glass. The woman staring back looked like any other federal bureaucrat—professional, competent, trustworthy. The perfect mask for someone who'd sold her soul in increments so small she'd barely noticed the transaction. "Chad Lloyd knows about Jose Morales at the flower warehouse. He knows Jose helped Javier escape after the murders."

The silence on the other end stretched like a held breath before Elena's voice cut through the static. "How much does he know?"

"Enough to get you killed if he reaches Jose alive." Holmes felt the familiar rush of adrenaline that came with dancing on the edge of treason. "Detective Supko confirmed Lloyd's interest in the warehouse. I've tripled surveillance, but Lloyd has extensive tactical training. If he's determined to get to Jose..."

"Elena, if he talks to Jose, your man will tell him everything. Where you are, where Javier is hiding, probably your favorite breakfast cereal if Lloyd asks nicely enough."

Elena's laugh was winter-cold and twice as sharp. "No, he won't."

The line went dead, leaving Holmes staring at the phone with the growing certainty that she'd just signed Jose Morales's death warrant. Elena didn't make idle threats—she made bodies disappear and problems evaporate like morning dew under a Caribbean sun.

Holmes pocketed the burner phone and checked her reflection one more time, making sure her professional mask was firmly in place. In thirty minutes, she'd be falsely briefing Director Huntington about PHOENIX's progress hunting Elena while conveniently forgetting to mention that she'd just helped Elena eliminate the only man who could lead them to Javier Santos.

Some betrayals were personal. Others were just business. And business, Holmes had learned, paid much better than justice.

Chapter 40

Benning Road Industrial Area
Southeast Washington D.C.

C had sat in his gray Transit van three blocks from Potomac Street Flowers, military-grade optics mounted on a camera tripod that had seen better days. Two hours of surveillance had painted a picture that made his tactical mind itch with unease—too many federal assets, too much coordination, too much firepower for a simple warehouse operation.

Something was wrong.

DEA surveillance vans parked on opposite corners, their tinted windows and antenna clusters screaming federal operation to anyone with eyes. FBI agents in business suits loitering around a hot dog cart that had appeared overnight like a bad magic trick. Fairfax County Sheriff's deputies positioned at both ends of the block, their patrol cars strategically placed to turn the industrial area into a killbox.

Chad counted at least twelve visible assets through his scope, which meant there were probably six more he couldn't see. Rooftop snipers, undercover operatives inside the warehouse itself, mobile units ready to respond within minutes. The kind of overwhelming force you deployed when you were hunting someone specific.

His phone buzzed with a Words with Friends notification—two new messages from Sarah Miller. Chad opened the app and read Sam's warning, his jaw tightening as he decoded her message. *"Started our game! How's your day going? Mine's gotten pretty complicated. Hope yours stays simple. Oh, and you won't need flowers to play this game—shields are way better at protecting* things. Also, that friend who recommended the game? Turns out he's been talking to everyone about it."

Flowers equals Potomac Flowers. Shields equals badges protecting the location. And that friend who recommended the game—Detective Supko, the bastard who'd sat in his living room and promised to help find his family's killers—had been talking to everyone about it.

The betrayal hit him like a physical blow. Supko had fed him information about Jose Morales, then immediately turned around and warned the FBI that Chad was interested in the warehouse. The perfect setup—give the grieving widower just enough rope to hang himself, then watch from a safe distance while federal agents cleaned up the mess.

Chad stared at the screen, feeling that familiar cold settle over his mind like an old friend. The arctic calm that had kept him alive through three combat deployments, where hesitation meant death and mercy was a luxury nobody could afford. Sam was warning him off, telling him the place was radioactive, that walking into this operation would be volunteering for his own execution.

She was probably right. The smart play was to abort, find another way to get to Jose Morales, wait for better circumstances that didn't involve federal agents with handcuffs and good intentions.

But waiting meant Elena Ramirez had more time to plan her next massacre. Waiting meant more federal families would die while he played it safe in the shadows, counting surveillance assets and calculating odds like some kind of actuarial table with a badge.

Chad looked back at the warehouse and watched another flower truck roll through the checkpoint, its driver barely slowing as the guards waved him past. The man behind the wheel was heavyset, Hispanic, wearing work clothes that suggested he belonged in this industrial wasteland where legitimate businesses provided perfect cover for the kind of commerce that never appeared on tax returns.

That was his way in. Not through the front door where a dozen federal agents waited with handcuffs and good intentions, but through the service entrance where nobody expected a dead man to be walking.

Chad typed his response to Sam with fingers that remembered how to stay steady when everything else was falling apart: *"Game looks fun! My* day's about to get interesting. Planning to visit an old friend later. You know how it is."

He needed her to understand that he appreciated the warning, valued the friendship, and recognized the risk she was taking by feeding him intelligence. But some debts could only be paid in blood, and Jose Morales had information that might lead to the animals who'd tortured his wife while his daughter lay dead on their dining room floor.

If this went wrong—if the trap closed and Chad Lloyd disappeared into the federal system that had already failed him once—at least Sam would know he'd understood the odds and chosen to roll the dice anyway.

Chad pocketed the phone and started the gray Transit van, pulling away from his observation post with the unhurried movements of a man who'd already decided that today was a good day for other people to die. Three blocks east, he'd spotted a cluster of independent florists and garden centers that probably supplied the warehouse. Time to find a driver who could be convinced to make an unscheduled delivery.

Fifteen minutes later, Chad found what he was looking for in a strip mall parking lot that had seen better decades. Ramirez Flowers—the cosmic irony wasn't lost on him—sat between a check-cashing place and a liquor store with bars on the windows, its delivery van parked behind the building like an answered prayer wrapped in faded paint and honest sweat.

The driver was loading arrangements for his morning route with the methodical efficiency of a man who'd been doing the same job since Clinton was president. Miguel, according to the embroidered name on his work shirt, moved like someone who understood that showing up on time and keeping your mouth shut were the only qualifications that mattered in this neighborhood.

Chad parked across the street and watched Miguel finish securing roses and lilies that would mark life's celebrations and sorrows with equal indifference. When the driver disappeared into the store—probably to grab coffee and settle accounts with the owner—Chad crossed the asphalt and checked the delivery manifest clipped to the dashboard.

Potomac Street Flowers. Third stop on the route.

Perfect didn't begin to describe it.

Chad waited in the shadows beside the building, counting heartbeats and weighing options while Miguel emerged with his keys and the resignation of a man heading into another day of honest work in a dishonest world.

"Miguel?"

The driver stopped like he'd been struck by lightning, instantly wary in the way that came from living in neighborhoods where strangers usually brought trouble. "Who's asking?"

"Someone who needs a favor." Chad stepped into view with his hands visible and empty, ten hundred-dollar bills fanned out like a poker hand. "I need to get inside Potomac Street Flowers warehouse. In the back of your van, quiet, no questions asked."

Miguel's eyes went wide at the sight of more money than he probably made in six months, then narrowed with the suspicion of a man who'd learned that easy money usually came with hard consequences. "You a cop?"

"Do I look like a cop to you?"

"You look like trouble."

"I am trouble." Chad stepped closer, keeping his voice calm and reasonable while his eyes held the promise of violence for anyone stupid enough to test him. "But not for you. One thousand dollars for a ten-minute ride. You pick up your delivery, I slip out while you're unloading, and you drive away with more money than you make in a month. Nobody gets hurt."

Miguel stared at the cash like it might bite him, clearly torn between fear and the kind of greed that came from watching bills pile up faster than paychecks. "What if you get caught?"

"Then I never saw you before in my life. You were just making your normal delivery route, trying to feed your family and keep the lights on."

The driver looked around the empty parking lot, probably calculating rent payments and grocery bills against the risks of helping a stranger who carried himself like violence was his native language. "Jesus, man. What kind of shit are you into?"

"The kind that pays a thousand dollars for a short ride."

Miguel sighed and held out his hand with the resignation of a man who'd learned that sometimes you had to dance with the devil to pay the rent. "Get in the back. And if this goes wrong, I don't know nothing about nothing."

Chad handed over the money and climbed into the cargo area, settling between arrangements that smelled like funeral homes and broken promises. The van's interior was cramped but provided enough cover to hide one determined federal agent if he stayed low and didn't mind breathing flowers that would probably end up marking someone else's final resting place.

As Miguel started the engine and pulled into traffic, Chad pulled out his phone and typed one final message to Sam: *"By the way, thanks for the game recommendation. Win or lose, it's been worth playing."*

He hit send, then powered down the phone and checked his sidearm as Miguel navigated the morning traffic toward Potomac Street Flowers. One way or another, this was going to end today.

Through the van's rear windows, Chad could see the city falling away behind them, each mile taking him closer to a warehouse where Jose Morales waited with answers—and where a dozen federal agents waited with handcuffs that would end his war before it truly began.

The trap was set, the hunters were ready, and their prey was riding directly into the kill zone hidden among roses and lilies. In ten minutes, either Chad would have the intelligence he needed to hunt his family's killers, or he'd learn that some games could only be played once.

Chapter 41

Potomac Street Flowers Warehouse
Southeast Washington D.C.

The black SUVs came from three directions at once, tires screaming against asphalt as they converged on the warehouse loading dock like mechanical wolves sensing wounded prey. MS-13 sicarios poured out of the vehicles before they'd even stopped moving, their faces hidden behind skull bandanas that made them look like death's own marketing department.

Miguel "El Diablo" Herrera had learned his trade in the kind of neighborhoods where violence was a second language and mercy was a word that only existed in church. His men moved with the fluid precision of predators who understood that leaving witnesses meant leaving problems, and problems had a way of talking to federal agents with badges and promises of immunity.

The federal surveillance teams were caught with their pants down and their coffee getting cold.

Agent Bellow sat in the DEA van across the street, reaching for his radio when the first rounds spiderwebbed his windshield into a constellation of holes. "We're under attack! Multiple shooters, automatic weapons—"

His transmission died along with everything else as bullets turned the surveillance van into a metal coffin. The hot dog cart that had provided such excellent cover for FBI agents became a twisted sculpture of aluminum and regret. Even the Fairfax County deputies, positioned to block escape routes, found themselves trapped in their own patrol cars as

MS-13 gunmen turned the industrial block into a free-fire zone.

Inside the warehouse, Jose Morales looked up from his desk as the sound of automatic weapons fire erupted outside his office. He'd been expecting this moment for months—the DEA surveillance, the FBI interest, the slow tightening of the noose around operations he'd spent fifteen years building for the Ramirez family. First Salvador, now Elena, and it was all about to end because some gringo FBI agent wouldn't let his dead family rest in peace.

Jose reached for the pistol in his desk drawer, knowing it was probably too little and definitely too late. The photographs of his grandchildren smiled at him from the desk—Maria, age seven, gap-toothed and beautiful; Joe, five years old and already showing signs of his grandfather's stubborn streak. They lived in a small house in El Salvador, far from the blood and money that had paid for their school uniforms and birthday presents.

At least they would never have to know what grandfather really did for a living—or that his death was the price of keeping Javier Santos's location secret from a federal agent who'd already lost everything that mattered.

The warehouse doors exploded inward, sending splinters of wood and metal flying through the air like shrapnel. MS-13 shooters flooded through the breach with the kind of coordinated movement that came from years of urban warfare in places where the police were just another gang with better uniforms.

Jose's security team—six men who'd been chosen for their loyalty and their willingness to die for a paycheck—lasted approximately thirty seconds. They were good soldiers, but they'd been expecting to fight rival cartels or maybe some ambitious street dealers looking to move up in the world. They hadn't been prepared for Elena's elite, the kind of killers who'd cut their teeth in Central American civil wars and perfected their craft in American inner cities.

Jose managed to get off two shots before a burst of automatic fire cut him down, his blood spreading across the desk photos like spilled wine on white linen. He died clutching the image of his granddaughter's smile, probably wondering if the money hidden in the Cayman Islands would be enough to keep her safe from the choices he'd made.

The entire operation lasted four minutes—long enough for every federal agent in a six-block radius to understand that Elena Ramirez wasn't finished with her war against American law enforcement. A month ago, she'd killed 284 people in coordinated strikes across fourteen states. Today, she was sending a different message: anyone who helped hunt her people would die screaming in broad daylight, federal surveillance be damned.

By the time FBI rapid response teams arrived, sirens wailing and tactical gear gleaming, three MS-13 sicarios lay dead in the parking lot. Three more were wounded and captured, their skull bandanas soaked with blood that looked black under the sodium lights. They would disappear into the federal system, probably to emerge decades later as old men with stories no one would believe.

But Jose Morales was dead, along with six of his security team and any information he might have provided about Javier Santos's whereabouts. Elena had solved her problem with the kind of brutal efficiency that made hostile takeovers look like tea parties.

Chapter 42

Miguel's Flower Delivery Van
Two Miles Away

Chad was checking his weapon for the third time when Miguel's van lurched to a sudden stop, the driver's hands white-knuckled on the steering wheel as emergency lights painted the afternoon in shades of red and blue.

"What the hell?" Miguel muttered, his voice tight with the kind of fear that came from living in neighborhoods where gunfire was as common as sirens.

Through the van's windshield, Chad could see smoke rising in the distance like a black finger pointing at the sky. Emergency vehicles raced toward the warehouse with lights and sirens blazing, their urgency suggesting something far worse than a routine arrest operation.

A sharp knock on the driver's window made both men jump. An authoritative voice cut through the afternoon heat: "Sir, this is an active crime scene. You can't make deliveries here today. You need to turn around immediately."

"Crime scene?" Miguel's voice cracked like a teenager asking his first girl to prom. "I got a delivery for Potomac Flowers—"

"Not today, sir. Ongoing federal investigation. Turn your vehicle around and clear the area immediately."

Miguel didn't need to be told twice. The van executed a U-turn that would have made a stunt driver proud, while Chad struggled to the rear window to get a better view of what had just destroyed his only lead to Javier Santos.

The column of black smoke rising over Southeast D.C. told him everything he needed to know. Someone had beaten him to Jose Morales, and that someone had been thorough enough to turn a federal surveillance operation into what looked like a small war.

Chad's phone buzzed with an urgent message from Sarah Miller: *"Looks like I murdered this game! Too bad you can't get flowers for its funeral. Hope you weren't planning any shopping trips today."*

He typed back quickly, his fingers moving with the mechanical precision of a man processing tactical setbacks: *"You killed it alright. Looks like my day just freed up."*

As Miguel drove them away from the chaos, Chad stared out the rear window at his last hope disappearing in smoke and sirens. Elena Ramirez had outplayed him again, staying three steps ahead while he'd been focused on federal surveillance and tactical approaches. While he'd been planning to infiltrate the warehouse through legitimate cover, she'd simply eliminated the problem with the kind of violence that made headlines and closed cases.

His one lead to finding Javier Santos had just gone up in smoke, along with any illusions he might have had about fighting a civilized war against an enemy who understood that victory belonged to whoever was willing to spill the most blood.

But Elena had made one mistake in her surgical removal of Jose Morales. She'd shown Chad exactly how far she was willing to go to protect her secrets, which meant she was afraid of what those secrets might reveal. Fear, in Chad's experience, was just another word for weakness. And weaknesses, once identified, could be exploited by someone with nothing left to lose and the tactical training to make her pay for every drop of blood she'd spilled in his family's name.

The war was far from over. If anything, Elena had just escalated it to a level where federal badges and constitutional protections were meaningless luxuries that neither side could afford.

Chapter 43

Ramirez Compound
Grand Cayman

Elena Ramirez ended the call and set the phone down with the finality of a judge's gavel. Jose Morales was a dead man. Had been the moment Chad Lloyd started asking questions about him.

She walked to the terrace doors, watching whitecaps roll across water that had swallowed more secrets than any confessional. In forty minutes, Miguel's boys would turn the Potomac Street warehouse into a killing field. Jose would die never knowing his oldest friend had ordered his execution.

Business was business. Sentiment was weakness.

"It's done," she said without turning around.

Javier looked up from the Kalashnikov he'd been fieldstripping on the marble conference table. Twenty years of muscle memory guided his hands—bolt carrier, firing pin, springs arranged in perfect order. "Jose was loyal."

"Jose was a liability." Elena's reflection in the glass showed no emotion. "Loyalty doesn't matter when the FBI comes asking questions."

Hector closed the intelligence folder he'd been reviewing, satellite photos of American military bases scattered across mahogany that had cost more than most people's houses. "The contacts from the Middle East responded. Three of them."

Elena turned from the window. This was why Jose had to die. This was the future.

"Tell me."

"Abu Hassan al-Baghdadi. Former ISIS logistics commander." Hector's voice carried professional respect reserved for proven killers. "Managed supply lines through Turkey while coalition bombs turned everything around him to ash. Twenty-six operatives under his command."

Elena moved to the conference table, studying the man's photograph. Lean face, eyes like chips of obsidian. The kind of predator who'd learned to hunt American soldiers in their own backyard.

"He survived Mosul?"

"Survived everything. Fallujah, Ramadi, the siege of Baghouz. When ISIS collapsed, he disappeared into the desert with his core team." Javier reassembled his rifle with practiced efficiency. "Now he's in Mexico, using our smuggling routes to move weapons and personnel."

"Capabilities?"

"IEDs that can level city blocks. Urban warfare tactics that kept him alive when everyone with drones and satellites was hunting him." Hector pulled up another file. "He wants five million up front, plus operational funding."

Elena studied the intelligence reports. Hassan's network had killed over four hundred American soldiers during the Iraq occupation. Men who'd learned to turn apartment buildings into fortresses and city streets into killing fields.

"Who else?"

"Mahmoud al-Zawahiri. Al Qaeda cell leader who ran operations in Afghanistan for twelve years without being caught." Hector's finger traced routes on a tactical map. "Currently in Venezuela with fourteen fighters. All trained in assassination and chemical weapons."

"Chemical weapons?"

"Chlorine gas attacks in Damascus. Sarin deployment against Syrian army positions. He knows how to weaponize industrial chemicals into weapons of mass casualties." Javier's voice was clinical, professional. "Three million, but he comes with knowledge that could kill thousands."

Elena felt the familiar rush of infinite possibility. Not just revenge against the Americans, but the chance to import twenty years of battlefield innovation directly into their homeland.

"Third contact?"

"Rashid bin Omar. Taliban regional commander who coordinated IED campaigns throughout Helmand Province." Hector pulled up casualty reports that read like a butcher's bill. "Over three hundred coalition deaths attributed to his devices."

"Where is he now?"

"Colombia, working with FARC remnants. Smaller group—only eight men—but his expertise in improvised explosives could turn American infrastructure into a weapon against itself."

Elena walked to the wall-mounted display and activated satellite imagery of major American cities. "Timeline for integration?"

"Hassan wants to meet within seventy-two hours. Face-to-face, cash up front, immediate operational planning." Javier chambered a round and engaged the safety. "Al-Zawahiri is more cautious. Encrypted communications, background verification, financial guarantees before any physical meeting."

"And bin Omar?"

"Radio silence so far. But these men didn't survive twenty years of American counterterrorism by being trusting."

Elena studied the satellite feeds showing American cities going about their daily routines. Millions of people who had no idea that three of the world's most effective terrorist commanders were preparing to bring the war home.

"Bring them here. All three of them." Elena's voice carried the authority that had built a criminal empire. "The Cayman Islands are neutral territory. No extradition treaties, no American military jurisdiction. They can meet safely under my protection."

"Hassan will want guarantees," Hector pointed out. "These men are the most wanted terrorists alive."

"Then give him guarantees. Full payment up front, private aviation, armed security, complete operational security." Elena's smile was predatory. "Tell him he'll be meeting with representatives from every major cartel in the hemisphere. This isn't just about working with the Ramirez organization—it's about commanding the largest criminal army in history."

Javier looked up from his weapon. "All three commanders in one location?"

"Along with cartel leadership from Mexico to Colombia. If we're going to revolutionize criminal operations, everyone needs to hear the same briefing." Elena returned to the terrace, watching a sail boat bob up in down in the choppy sea. "Forty-eight hours from now, I want the most dangerous men in the world sitting around my conference table."

"And the others?"

"Al-Zawahiri gets his encrypted communications and background checks. But the meeting happens here, in person, within two days." Elena's voice turned ice-cold. "Bin Omar will come when he realizes this is the opportunity of a lifetime or the last mistake he'll ever make."

Her phone buzzed with an encrypted message from Miguel: "Package delivered. Warehouse is closed for business."

Jose Morales was dead. Chad Lloyd's only lead to Javier Santos had just gone up in smoke and gunfire.

In forty-eight hours, Elena would be hosting the most dangerous gathering in criminal history. Three terrorist commanders, eight cartel leaders, and enough combined firepower to turn American cities into war zones.

The Americans were hunting one rogue agent while she assembled an army of proven killers who'd spent twenty years learning how to destroy everything they touched.

The war was just beginning.

Chapter 44

Sam's phone buzzed with a new Words with Friends notification. She glanced around the operations center, confirming that Holmes was still in her meeting with Director Huntington, then opened the game app.

ChuckLogan47 had sent two messages:*"I need to spell a word for someone who has an infestation. You know what I mean?"*

Sam felt ice form in her stomach. Chad was telling her they had a rat —someone inside PHOENIX was feeding information to Elena. The timing of Jose's death had been too perfect, too convenient.

The second message was more direct: *"Out of ideas, need assistance."*

Chad was depending on her and Grey to find him a new lead. With Jose dead, he was back to square one in hunting Javier Santos.

Sam typed back carefully: *"Working on it. Give me some time to improve my game."*

She put the phone away and caught Grey's attention from across the room. When he looked up from the surveillance reports he was reviewing, she tapped her watch and mouthed "coffee break?"

Grey nodded and followed her out of the operations center.

"We have a problem," Sam said once they were alone in the hallway. "Chad thinks we have a leak."

"A leak?"

"Someone told Elena about his interest in Jose. The timing of that hit was too perfect." Sam kept her voice low. "And Chad needs a new lead. Jose was his only connection to finding Javier."

Grey's face creased with worry. "What do you want to do?"

"Help me go through everything we have on Javier Santos. Travel records, financial transactions, communications intercepts. If he left the country after the murders, there has to be a trail."

They returned to the operations center and spent the next hour methodically combing through intelligence files. Sam focused on financial records while Grey reviewed travel and communication data, both working under the pretense of updating their psychological profiles for Holmes.

"Nothing," Grey muttered, closing another file. "Financial records show normal activity up until the day of the murders, then complete silence. No credit cards, no ATM withdrawals, no wire transfers."

"Professional," Sam replied, scanning through immigration databases. "He's using cash and false identification. But he had to leave some kind of trail."

They worked in frustrated silence for another hour. Every search came up empty. Every database query returned negative results. Javier Santos had vanished as completely as if he'd never existed.

"Wait," Sam said, her fingers freezing over the keyboard. "Nolan, what if we're searching the wrong name?"

"What do you mean?"

"Javier Santos isn't going to travel under his real name. He's cartel—he'll have a collection of false IDs." Sam pulled up the facial recognition software. "Let me try a different approach."

She uploaded Javier's surveillance photos into the TSA facial recognition database, setting the search parameters for the past week and focusing on airports within driving distance of Washington D.C.

The search took twelve minutes. When the results appeared, Sam felt her heart race."Got him," she whispered.

Grey leaned over her shoulder as the match appeared on screen. Pittsburgh International Airport, July 20th. The facial recognition software had flagged a 94% match for a passenger traveling under the name "Marco Renaldo."

"Son of a bitch drove to Pittsburgh," Grey said. "Smart. Farther from the crime scene, different jurisdiction."

"But where was he going?" Sam clicked on the travel details. "Miami. He flew Pittsburgh to Miami on a one-way ticket, paid in cash."

"Miami makes sense," Grey mused. "Huge port city, massive criminal infrastructure, easy place to disappear or arrange further transportation."

Sam quickly printed the travel records and documentation, then cleared her search history. If Holmes checked the system later, there would be no record that PHOENIX had discovered this intelligence.

"I need to get this to Chad," Sam said, folding the documents and slipping them into her jacket pocket.

"Good work," Grey replied. "Miami's a start. Chad can work his contacts down there, maybe track where Javier went next."

At 1800 hours, Sam stepped outside FBI headquarters and opened Words with Friends, typing carefully: *"Found a new word! MIAMI. Someone named RENALDO used it to get there from PITTSBURGH. Might be worth investigating that location."*

She hit send and waited. Her phone buzzed with a response within minutes: *"MIAMI sounds promising. Heading there to check it out. Keep looking for more words."*

Sam felt a mixture of satisfaction and worry. She'd given Chad his first real lead since Jose's death. But Miami was a vast city with countless places to hide, and Javier had almost a month head start.

As she walked back into the FBI building, Sam caught sight of Holmes emerging from the elevator, her expression unreadable as she surveyed the operations center.

"Agent Belle," Holmes called out. "Any progress on the Lloyd psychological profile?"

"Working on it, ma'am. Trying to understand his thought patterns and likely destinations."

"Good. Keep me informed of any developments."

As Holmes walked away, Sam returned to her desk and opened a new document, typing observations about Chad's mental state while her mind raced with darker possibilities.

Chad was heading to Miami to hunt Javier Santos in one of America's most dangerous cities. And somewhere in that maze of smuggling networks and criminal enterprises, his family's killer was either hiding or had already moved on to an even more secure location.

The hunt was far from over. If anything, it was just beginning.

Chapter 45

Ramirez Compound
Grand Cayman

Elena Ramirez stood at the edge of her marble terrace, encrypted satellite phone pressed to her ear as she coordinated the most dangerous gathering in criminal history. The Caribbean sun blazed overhead, but her mind was focused on darker waters—the storm of violence she was about to unleash across American soil.

"Abu Hassan, your transportation has been arranged," she said in perfect Arabic, her voice carrying the authority that had built a criminal empire. "Private aircraft to the Cayman Islands, complete operational security, cash payment upon arrival."

The former ISIS logistics commander's voice crackled through the encrypted connection from his safe house in Tijuana. "And my men?"

"All twenty-six operatives will be accommodated. Separate quarters, independent security protocols, whatever you require." Elena gestured to Hector, who was coordinating arrivals on his tablet. "You'll be meeting with representatives from every major cartel in the hemisphere, plus Taliban and Al-Qaeda leadership."

A long pause. "This is... unprecedented."

"This is necessary. The Americans have declared war on all of us by designating cartels as terrorist organizations. It's time we responded with the kind of coordination they fear most."

Elena ended the call and immediately dialed another encrypted number—this one connecting to a satellite phone in the mountains of Afghanistan.

"Rashid bin Omar speaking."

"Commander, this is Elena Ramirez. We spoke through intermediaries about expanding operations into North America."

"The woman who runs the Ramirez Cartel." His voice carried the careful respect of someone who'd learned to evaluate allies by their body count rather than their gender. "Your reputation precedes you."

"As does yours. Three hundred American soldiers killed by your IEDs in Helmand Province. That's the kind of expertise we need for our new operations."

"You want to bring the war to their homeland."

"I want to teach them what it feels like to bury their families." Elena's voice carried the cold fury that had driven her since watching her father die on security footage. "The Americans killed my father, just as they killed your brothers in Afghanistan. Time for them to understand that some debts are paid in blood."

Bin Omar was quiet for a moment. "What are you proposing?"

"Complete operational integration. Your IED expertise combined with our logistics networks, our financial resources, our established smuggling routes into American cities." Elena pulled up satellite imagery of major American infrastructure targets. "The capability to strike anywhere, anytime, with weapons that turn their own cities against them."

"Transportation to this meeting?"

"Private aircraft from Columbia to Grand Cayman, direct flight to avoid American surveillance. Two hundred thousand up front, full operational funding once we finalize agreements."

Elena ended that call and walked through her compound's main house, noting the preparations her security team had made. The conference room could accommodate fifty people around a mahogany table that had cost more than most Americans made in a decade. Armed guards at every entrance, sniper teams on overwatch positions, patrol boats circling the island at two-mile intervals.

By tomorrow night, the most wanted terrorists alive would be sitting around that table, planning coordinated attacks that would make 9/11 look like a preview.

"Status on Al-Zawahiri?" she asked Javier, who was reviewing weapons inventories.

"Confirmed arriving from Venezuela. His chemical weapons expert will be accompanying him—the man who developed the sarin attacks in Damascus." Javier's voice carried professional appreciation for proven killers. "Six-man security detail, all former Mukhabarat intelligence operatives."

"Perfect. What about our cartel friends?"

"Miguel Treviño from Los Zetas is en route from Mexico. Carlos Montenegro confirmed arrival from Colombia. Rosa Delgado will be here with her 18th Street leadership." Javier consulted his tablet. "By 0200 hours tomorrow, we'll have representatives from every major criminal organization in the hemisphere."

Elena smiled, thinking about the scope of what she was orchestrating. Not just revenge against the Americans who'd killed her father, but the complete transformation of criminal operations worldwide.

"And the pilot arrangements?"

"Ricardo continues to believe he's transporting wealthy businessmen who value discretion. He'll deliver everyone to the abandoned airstrip, collect his payments, and leave immediately." Javier's expression turned predatory. "Never knowing he's been transporting the architects of America's destruction."

Elena's secure phone buzzed with an encrypted message from Holmes: "Lloyd still evading capture in D.C. area. Federal response massive but ineffective. He's proving more resourceful than anticipated."

Elena read the message twice, feeling a familiar surge of respect for the man who'd killed her father. Chad Lloyd was demonstrating the same tactical intelligence that had made him such a dangerous enemy. But intelligence wouldn't save him once he followed Javier's trail to Ricardo's operation.

"Holmes confirms Lloyd is still free in Washington," she announced to Hector and Javier. "But he's following the exact path we anticipated—investigating Javier's escape route, which will lead him to Ricardo."

"And then directly to us," Javier added with cold satisfaction.

Elena pulled up tactical displays showing the abandoned airstrip where Ricardo would unknowingly deliver Chad to his execution. Two miles of Caribbean jungle separated it from her compound—the perfect distance to maintain operational security while ensuring complete control over any unwanted visitors.

"By the time our summit concludes tomorrow night, we'll have unified every major terrorist organization and criminal network under one operational command," Elena said, walking back to the terrace. "And Chad Lloyd will arrive just in time to witness the final preparations for America's destruction."

She looked out at the Caribbean waters that had swallowed more secrets than any government archive. Tomorrow, those same waters would hide the evidence of the most dangerous conspiracy in human history.

The Americans wanted terrorists? She was about to give them more terror than they could imagine.

And Chad Lloyd would hopefully be rotting in a federal prison as a domestic terrorist, completely unable to stop them.

Chapter 46

Sam's Apartment
Arlington, VA

Sam's television droned in the background while she made dinner, WKDC's evening broadcast providing white noise until three words cut through her distraction like a knife blade: "Chad Lloyd" and "manhunt."

She dropped her fork and grabbed the remote, turning up the volume as the anchor's voice filled her small kitchen.

"...the FBI agent turned fugitive whose family was murdered in last month's cartel attacks. Tonight, we're joined by Marie and Robert Thompson, parents of victim Lana Lloyd, who say they're not surprised by these developments."

Sam's blood turned to ice as the camera cut to Chad's in-laws sitting in what looked like a hotel conference room, both wearing black and expressions of bitter vindication.

"We tried to warn our daughter," Marie Thompson said, her voice carrying twenty years of accumulated resentment. "Chad Lloyd was always a violent man. Military training, federal weapons, that cold way he looked at people. Lana was too much in love to see what he really was."

Sam sank onto her couch, watching in horror as Chad's ex in-laws systematically destroyed his reputation on national television.

"Did you ever witness this violent behavior?" the interviewer asked.

"The way he handled that situation with Mark at the house," Robert Thompson replied, his jaw tight with remembered anger. "My son-in-law came to get some of Lana's belongings, and Chad attacked him.

Unprovoked violence. That's when we knew."

Sam remembered that day differently. Mark had tried to force his way into Chad's house, had thrown the first punch. Chad had defended himself with restraint that most people wouldn't have shown.

"And now he's wanted by the FBI?"

"Frankly, we're relieved," Marie continued. "At least now the authorities understand what kind of man he really is. What kind of man our daughter married."

The Arlington Inn
Arlington, Virginia

Marie Thompson smoothed her black dress and checked her appearance in the hotel bathroom mirror one final time before their next interview. Today all the major networks were lining up. They couldn't get enough of the grieving parents who'd "always known" their son-in-law was dangerous.

"You think we're being too hard on him?" Robert asked from the bed, where he was reviewing the talking points their new media consultant had prepared.

"Too hard?" Marie's laugh was bitter as winter wind. "He got our daughter and granddaughter killed, Robert. And now he's proven exactly what I always said about him—he's a killer who can't control himself."

She returned to the mirror, practicing the expression of wounded dignity that had played so well during their morning interviews. "Besides, that book agent said we could get a seven-figure advance. 'Blood Money: How I Tried to Save My Daughter from a Killer.' The American people deserve to know the truth about Chad Lloyd."

Robert nodded, though something in his expression suggested less certainty than his wife. "The FBI agent who called yesterday—Agent Holmes. She said our testimony about Chad's violent behavior could be crucial for their investigation."

"What exactly did she say?" Robert asked.

"That the American people needed to understand what kind of man Chad really was. That our testimony about his violent behavior could help prevent him from hurting other families." Marie's voice carried conviction. "She said we had a duty to speak out."

Marie turned back to the mirror, her reflection showing cold satisfaction. "And she was right. For almost twenty years I watched that man intimidate our daughter with his military training and his weapons and his barely controlled anger. Twenty years I bit my tongue because Lana thought she loved him."

She turned from the mirror, her voice taking on the wounded authority that had made her such compelling television. "Well, Lana's gone now. And I'll be damned if I let Chad Lloyd destroy her memory the way he destroyed her life."

Sam's Apartment
Arlington, VA

The interview continued for another ten minutes, each question allowing Chad's in-laws to drive another nail into his reputation's coffin. They painted him as a controlling husband, a violent father, a man whose "military mindset" had never adapted to civilian life.

By the time the segment ended, Sam felt sick to her stomach. Chad was alone in Miami, hunting his family's killer while his dead wife's parents convinced America that he was the real monster.

Her phone buzzed with a text from Grey: "You watching this shit?"

"Unfortunately."

"They're destroying him. Every network is running clips of the Thompsons calling him violent and unstable."

Sam turned off the television and stared at the blank screen, thinking about Chad somewhere out there, completely unaware that his reputation was being systematically demolished by people who should have been supporting him.

Her Words with Friends app showed no new messages from ChuckLogan47. Chad was probably working contacts, following leads, doing what federal agents did when they needed information from people who didn't talk to law enforcement.

Meanwhile, his dead wife's parents were getting rich telling anyone who'd listen that their son-in-law had always been a killer.

The war Elena Ramirez had started by murdering Chad's family was spreading in directions none of them had anticipated. She hadn't just destroyed Chad's personal life—she'd created the conditions for his complete social and professional destruction.

And Chad had no idea it was happening.

Sam picked up her phone to send him a warning through the game app, then stopped. What could she say? Your in-laws think you're a monster and they're telling the whole country? He had enough to worry about hunting Javier without knowing that his support system was crumbling behind him.

But as the news cycle continued its relentless coverage of the "violent FBI agent" whose own family feared him, Sam realized that Elena's revenge was more comprehensive than anyone had imagined.

She wasn't just trying to kill Chad Lloyd. She was trying to erase him completely.

Chapter 47

Agent Holmes stood before the wall-mounted displays, her perfectly styled appearance unchanged despite having worked through the night. The operations center had been transformed in the six hours since Chad Lloyd walked out of Sam's apartment—additional workstations, communication equipment, and tactical monitors that painted a digital net across the entire Eastern seaboard.

"Status report," she announced to the room.

Agent Ruiz looked up from his workstation, fatigue evident in his voice. "All of Lloyd's known bank accounts have been flagged and frozen. Credit cards, checking, savings, even the joint accounts with his deceased wife. Any attempt to access funds will trigger immediate alerts."

"What about cash reserves?"

"Unknown. A man with his background probably has emergency funds stored off the books."

Holmes nodded, unsurprised. "Agent Kim, telecommunications?"

"We've got traces on all known phone numbers associated with Lloyd. His personal cell phone was left at Agent Belle's apartment, but we're monitoring for any new numbers he might acquire." Kim gestured to a bank of equipment. "NSA is providing real-time analysis of all cell tower traffic in the D.C. metro area, flagging voice patterns that match Lloyd's speech characteristics."

"Excellent. Agent Martinez, transportation?"

"BOLO alerts have been sent to every law enforcement agency from

Florida to Maine. Lloyd's vehicle registrations have been flagged, his driver's license photo distributed to all federal checkpoints." Martinez consulted his tablet. "We've also alerted TSA, Amtrak, and Greyhound security. If he tries to leave the area by conventional transportation, we'll know."

Holmes walked to the main display, which showed a real-time map of the Washington D.C. metropolitan area dotted with red icons representing federal assets.

"As of 0600 hours, we have sixty-three agents deployed across the region," she announced. "Surveillance teams at all known associates' residences, undercover assets at transportation hubs, and rapid response units positioned to intercept if we get a positive identification."

Agent Kim raised his hand hesitantly. "Ma'am, with respect, this seems like a lot of resources for tracking down one man who hasn't actually committed any crimes."

Holmes turned to face him, her green eyes sharp as broken glass. "Agent Kim, Chad Lloyd is a rogue operative with extensive military training, federal access codes, and detailed knowledge of our counterterrorism operations. He has made explicit threats against a designated terrorist organization and possesses the skills to act on those threats."

She pulled up Lloyd's military record on the main screen. "Three combat deployments, special operations training, expert marksman ratings. This man knows how to kill, and he's demonstrated a willingness to operate outside legal boundaries."

"But ma'am—"

"But nothing." Holmes' voice cut like a blade. "Every minute Lloyd remains free is another minute he could be planning attacks against the Ramirez organization that could compromise years of intelligence work and endanger federal assets. We will find him, and we will bring him in before he can destabilize our entire counterterrorism strategy."

Sam Belle sat at her workstation, monitoring the financial tracking protocols while fighting the urge to throw her coffee cup at Holmes' perfectly coiffed head. Around her, agents who should have been hunting terrorists were instead hunting a man whose only crime was wanting justice for his murdered family.

Finally, Sam couldn't stay silent any longer. "Agent Holmes, why are you so hell-bent on protecting the Ramirez Cartel? Who cares if Chad made threats against them? They're terrorists who murdered 284 federal family members. They're exactly the people we should be hunting anyway."

The room went silent as every agent turned to look at Sam, then at Holmes, waiting for an answer that would justify hunting a grieving federal agent instead of hunting his family's killers."

Holmes' face flushed with anger, but her voice remained controlled. "Agent Belle, that's exactly the kind of emotional thinking that makes this situation dangerous. We don't 'protect' terrorist organizations—we conduct systematic intelligence operations against them. Lloyd's rogue actions could compromise years of careful infiltration and surveillance."

She turned to address the room, avoiding Sam's penetrating stare. "The Ramirez organization is under active federal investigation through multiple channels. Agent Lloyd's freelance vendetta threatens to expose our sources, compromise our methods, and alert targets who don't yet know we're watching them."

Sam wasn't buying it, and neither were several other agents who exchanged skeptical glances.

"Agent Belle," Holmes called out sharply, "I want you to coordinate with Agent Grey on psychological profiling. Use everything you know about Lloyd's habits, his thinking patterns, his emotional state. Where would he go? Who would he contact? What resources would he attempt to access?"

Sam felt her stomach clench, realizing Holmes was specifically targeting her because of her challenging question. "Yes, ma'am."

"And remember—Lloyd's emotional state makes him unpredictable. The death of his family has clearly affected his judgment. He may attempt to contact friends or colleagues, thinking he can trust them. If he reaches out to anyone in this room, that contact must be reported immediately."

Holmes' eyes lingered on Sam for a moment longer than necessary. "The man you worked with for two years is gone, replaced by someone who could be extremely dangerous. Don't let personal loyalty cloud your professional judgment."

Sam nodded, not trusting her voice.

"I want updates every hour," Holmes continued. "Lloyd has a head start, but he's operating alone in a city where every federal agent, local police officer, and security camera is looking for him. It's only a matter of time before he makes a mistake."

At his workstation, Agent Grey reviewed surveillance protocols while calculating the resources being wasted on hunting Chad instead of Elena Ramirez. Sixty-three agents, millions of dollars in equipment, the attention of every federal agency in the region—all focused on a man who wanted to stop the people who murdered 284 federal family members.

The system wasn't just broken. It was actively working against justice.

"Sir?" Agent Martinez approached Grey's desk, glancing around to ensure they weren't being overheard. "I've got something you should see."

Grey looked up as Martinez placed a tablet in front of him, showing traffic camera footage from the previous night. But something in his expression made him pause—a subtle tension that suggested more than routine intelligence sharing.

"This is from a camera near the Anacostia Metro station, timestamp 0347 hours," Martinez said carefully. "Gray Ford Transit van, clean plates, no visible occupants. But watch this."

The footage showed the van arriving, sitting motionless for approximately thirty minutes, then departing. "Camera angle doesn't give us a clear view of the driver, but the timing suggests this could be related to our subject."

Grey studied the image, then looked at Martinez more carefully. Agent Ross Martinez had been with the Bureau for eight years, but before that he'd been Army Intelligence—stationed at Bagram Airfield during the same deployment where Chad had served as a JTAC operator. They'd worked together on several high-value target operations.

"Professional surveillance protocols," Grey observed, understanding the subtext.

"That's what I thought. This isn't amateur hour—Lloyd knows how to avoid detection." Martinez met his eyes directly. "Camera quality is pretty poor though. Hard to make out specific vehicle details. Could be any gray van in the city, really."

Grey caught the hint immediately. Martinez was giving him a chance to bury this intelligence before it reached Holmes.

"You're right," Grey said, deleting the image from the tablet. "Poor camera resolution, insufficient detail for positive identification. Probably just coincidental timing."

Martinez nodded approvingly. "Should I file a report on the negative findings?"

"No need. Just another dead end in a city full of gray work vans." Grey met his eyes. "But good work checking all possible leads, Agent Martinez. That's the kind of thoroughness this investigation needs."

As Martinez walked away, Grey felt a surge of relief. Chad had more allies than Holmes realized—federal agents who remembered working with him when he was saving American lives instead of being hunted by American law enforcement.

The system might be broken, but some of the people within it still understood the difference between justice and politics.

But as he watched Holmes coordinate the manhunt with the enthusiasm of someone who'd finally found her calling, Grey realized that justice wasn't the point anymore. Politics was the point. And Chad Lloyd had become the sacrifice Holmes needed to prove her competence to Director Huntington.

Chapter 48

Chad's Safe House
Anacostia

Chad's eyes snapped open at the sound of helicopter rotors approaching from the east—the deep, steady thrum of federal aircraft conducting search patterns. He'd been awake since 0500, monitoring police scanners and FBI communications while reviewing maps of the metropolitan area.

But sleep had been impossible for more reasons than operational security. Sam's words kept echoing in his mind: "I'm in love with you. I have been for months, maybe longer."

How had he missed it? Two years as partners, countless hours together, and he'd been so focused on cases and coming home to Lana and Casey that he'd never seen what was right in front of him. The way Sam looked at him during dangerous moments, her fierce protectiveness when suspects got too close, and the slight catch in her voice when he talked about anniversary plans with Lana.

She'd been in love with him while he was planning romantic weekends with his wife. While he was reading bedtime stories to Casey. While he was completely, utterly devoted to the family that Elena Ramirez had butchered in his dining room.

And now Lana was dead, Casey was dead, and the woman who'd helped him through the worst weeks of his life had just confessed feelings he could never return. Not because he didn't care about Sam— he did, more than he'd admitted even to himself—but because there was nothing left of him capable of love. Elena had burned that out of him along with everything else that had made him human.

The timing was impossibly cruel. Not because Chad would have ever betrayed Lana—his love for his wife and daughter had been absolute and unwavering. But maybe, in some distant future after his heart had time to heal from this devastating loss, maybe then he could have learned to love again. Maybe Sam could have been the person to help him remember what happiness felt like.

But that future seemed impossible now. What remained was something darker, colder, focused on a single mission that would probably get him killed. And Sam deserved better than watching someone she loved destroy himself for revenge.

The scanners had been busy all morning. BOLO alerts, surveillance requests, coordination between agencies that normally wouldn't share coffee, much less intelligence. But Chad noticed something odd about the radio traffic—multiple reports of sightings heading south on I-95, toward the Virginia-North Carolina border.

"All units, possible subject sighting at Quantico exit, heading south."

"Negative contact at Quantico. Continuing surveillance toward Fredericksburg."

"Richmond field office reports suspicious activity at truck stop on I-95 South. Gray vehicle matching subject description."

Chad almost smiled despite his situation. Someone was feeding false intelligence into the system, creating a trail that led away from his actual location and toward Fort Bragg—where his old Special Operations teammates would certainly provide sanctuary if he could reach them.

Grey. Had to be Grey, using his access to federal communication systems to flood the manhunt with false sightings. Every fake report would require resources to investigate, pulling federal agents away from Chad's actual area of operations.

Holmes had mobilized the entire federal apparatus to hunt him down like a terrorist, but she didn't realize one of her own senior agents was sabotaging the operation from within.

Chad moved to the kitchen window, careful to stay behind the curtain as he observed the neighborhood. Anacostia had seen enough federal attention over the years that residents knew how to recognize law enforcement operations. This morning, people were staying inside, avoiding the streets, waiting for whatever storm was brewing to pass over their community.

The helicopter swept past, too high for tactical deployment but low enough to be conducting visual reconnaissance. Probably FBI or U.S. Marshals, using federal aviation assets to coordinate ground teams.

Chad checked his secure phone and saw multiple missed calls from his bank's fraud alert system—all accounts frozen, credit cards disabled, even his checking account locked away by federal order. Holmes was cutting off his access to legitimate resources, forcing him to operate like the criminal she was determined to prove he'd become.

At least what was left of the life insurance money from Lana and Casey and the money he was able to squirrel away was already secured in his basement cache—one hundred thirty-four thousand after paying Tony for the van and equipment. It would have to be enough to cover his operational needs.

He moved to the basement and checked his emergency supplies. Three different sets of identification documents, all created for legitimate undercover work. Weapons, surveillance equipment, and most importantly, the intelligence files he'd accumulated about Elena Ramirez's organization.

The helicopter made another pass, closer this time. Chad could see federal agents in tactical gear conducting house-to-house searches six blocks away, moving systematically through the neighborhood like a military operation. Through his basement windows, he could hear the helicopter's loudspeaker crackling with automated announcements: 'This is the FBI. All residents shelter in place immediately. Do not leave your homes. Law enforcement operation in progress.

They'd found his location.

Chad didn't know how—maybe financial records from when he'd purchased the safe house supplies, maybe surveillance footage from nearby cameras, maybe just good old-fashioned detective work. It didn't matter. What mattered was that he had maybe twenty minutes before they reached his house.

He grabbed the emergency bag he'd prepared and moved through the house erasing any evidence of his presence. Weapons went into concealed carry positions, cash and documents into hidden pockets, surveillance equipment into a nondescript backpack that could belong to any contractor or maintenance worker.

The basement had a tunnel—not original construction, but something he'd added during his modifications to the property. It connected to the storm drain system that ran beneath Benning Road, providing a hidden route to the abandoned warehouse complex three blocks south.

Chad activated the house's security system, setting timers that would make it appear occupied for the next several hours. Then he disappeared into the darkness beneath Southeast D.C., another ghost in a city full of shadows.

Behind him, the helicopter continued its search pattern, hunting a man who'd already moved beyond their reach.

Chapter 49

Anacostia Storm Drain System
Southeast Washington D.C.

Chad had moved through the storm drain system with the practiced silence of someone who'd learned to navigate hostile territory without triggering alarms. The tunnels beneath Southeast D.C. were a maze of concrete and steel that had been ignored by city planners for decades, creating the perfect highway for anyone who needed to travel unseen.

His flashlight beam cut through the darkness ahead, illuminating a pathway that connected to every major building in the industrial district. Chad had spent months mapping these tunnels during his off-the-books investigations, understanding that federal agents sometimes needed to move through areas where their presence would compromise operations.

Now those same skills were keeping him ahead of the federal agents hunting him.

The sound of explosions echoed through the tunnel system— flashbang grenades and breaching charges as FBI tactical teams hit his safe house. Chad felt a grim satisfaction knowing they'd find nothing except empty rooms and security cameras that had recorded their unauthorized entry.

He emerged through a maintenance grate behind the abandoned warehouse complex, immediately scanning for surveillance before moving toward where he'd relocated the gray Transit van after learning about the FBI manhunt. The vehicle sat exactly where he'd hidden it among the other work vehicles scattered throughout the industrial area, unremarkable and overlooked by the federal search teams.

Chad felt a surge of relief seeing the van untouched and started the engine, knowing he needed to move before the search expanded to this area.

Chad's phone buzzed with an encrypted message from Tony Kowalski: "Brother, heard the feds are hunting you hard. Word's getting around—they're offering serious money for information. You need to disappear deeper than you planned."

Another message followed immediately: "They're tracking everyone who ever served with you. Stay off main roads, avoid anyone from the old unit. This is bigger than we thought."

Chad deleted both messages and opened Words with Friends, typing carefully: *"How's the game looking? Lots of players joining, or just a few?"*

Sam's response came within minutes: *"Huge tournament. 60+ players from all agencies. They've got the whole board covered - airports, train stations, bus terminals, major highways. Even got some players watching the waterfront where you might be."*

Chad felt his stomach tighten. They were closer than he'd thought.

He typed back: *"Any blind spots on the board? Places where players aren't watching as closely?"*

"Rural routes heading west might have fewer watchers. Also, traffic cameras on Route 50 have been glitchy all morning - technical difficulties, you know? Might stay down for a few more hours."

Chad almost smiled. Sam was telling him she could disable surveillance cameras along his escape route. *"What about the other players? Any of them not playing by the official rules?"*

"Some of the veteran players are getting frustrated with the new management. Making their own moves, if you know what I mean. You've got friends in this game."

Grey was still running interference, and probably Martinez too. Chad wasn't as alone as Holmes thought.

"Thanks for the intel. Might need to change my strategy soon. This board is getting too crowded."

"Stay in the game. You're better at this than they think. And remember - you've got more moves available than what's obvious."

Chad pocketed the phone and studied his options. Route 50 west, with Sam jamming the traffic cameras. Rural roads where federal surveillance would be thinner. And allies within the system working to give him every advantage they could manage.

Time to disappear deeper than Holmes thought possible.

Chad's radio scanner crackled with coordinated communications:

"Delta-Seven, we've got negative contact at the primary location. Structure appears to have been abandoned recently."

"Copy, Delta-Seven. Expand search to secondary locations. Subject has extensive knowledge of urban warfare and evasion techniques."

"All units, be advised: Subject is considered armed and extremely dangerous. Do not attempt apprehension without backup."

Armed and extremely dangerous. Chad almost laughed at the irony. A month ago, he'd been leading federal task forces against international terrorists. Now he was the terrorist, hunted by the same agencies he'd served for twelve years.

The scanner continued: "Bravo-Four, we've got reports of suspicious activity at the industrial complex on Good Hope Road. Deploying tactical team for sweep operations."

That was eight blocks from Chad's current location. They were casting a wide net, using the kind of overwhelming force that left no room for escape once you were spotted.

Chad turned onto Alabama Avenue, but as he approached the intersection with Martin Luther King Jr. Avenue, he spotted the checkpoint—four federal vehicles, agents with tactical gear, and what looked like a mobile command unit coordinating the operation.

No choice but to turn around and find another route.

Chad executed a casual three-point turn, nothing urgent enough to draw attention, but as he drove away he caught sight of an agent speaking into a radio while staring directly at his vehicle.

The scanner confirmed his worst fears: "All units, possible subject vehicle spotted heading north on Alabama Avenue. Gray van, Virginia plates David-Charles-Seven-Four-One-Nine. Do not pursue—maintain visual and coordinate intercept."

They'd identified his vehicle.

Chad's mind shifted into tactical mode, remembering Sam's Words with Friends message about Route 50 cameras being down and rural backroads staying clear. He needed to reach that cleared corridor before the federal net tightened completely.

Behind him, he could see unmarked federal vehicles beginning to converge, their drivers maintaining careful distances to avoid spooking their target. Professional pursuit protocols—federal agents conducting a coordinated takedown operation.

Chad reached for his phone and sent a quick message through the Words with Friends app: *"Game's getting intense. Might need to change strategies soon."*

The response came within seconds: *"Main route blocked by other players. Try the industrial area east of your position - better cover to break visual contact. Then circle back to our planned route."*

Sam was telling him Route 50 was compromised but giving him an alternative. The waterfront would provide cover to lose the immediate pursuit, then he could double back to the cleared corridor.

The industrial waterfront appeared ahead—cranes, shipping containers, and enough visual obstacles to break surveillance lines. Chad accelerated slightly, moving with purpose toward the maze of steel and concrete that could hide one man from an army of federal agents.

In his rearview mirror, the unmarked vehicles were multiplying. What had started as casual surveillance was becoming an active pursuit.

Chad smiled grimly and pressed the accelerator harder. Time to show Holmes' task force what two decades of military training looked like when applied to urban evasion before making his way to the escape route Sam had prepared.

Chapter 50

"We've got him," Agent Thornton announced, her voice tight with excitement. "Gray van, Virginia plates, currently heading toward the Anacostia waterfront."

Holmes moved to the tactical display, watching red icons converge on Chad's position like antibodies attacking an infection. "Pursuit teams?"

"Six units in position, maintaining surveillance distance. Mobile command unit is coordinating intercept routes." Thornton consulted her tablet. "Subject appears to be driving normally, no indication he's aware of our presence."

"He knows," Agent Grey said quietly from his workstation.

Holmes turned to face him. "Excuse me?"

"Chad knows you're following him. He's got decades of operational experience—he can spot surveillance from five blocks away." Grey's weathered face showed professional respect for his hunted colleague. "He's letting you follow him."

"Why would he do that?"

"Because he's leading you somewhere that gives him a tactical advantage." Grey stood and walked to the tactical display. "The waterfront district is perfect for someone with his training. Industrial terrain, multiple escape routes, limited sight lines for your pursuit teams."

Holmes stared at the screen, watching the red icons closing on Chad's position. "Are you suggesting we call off the pursuit?"

"I'm suggesting you understand what you're up against. Chad Lloyd isn't some fugitive running in panic. He's a professional conducting a tactical withdrawal."

"All the more reason to stop him before he disappears completely." Holmes activated her radio. "All units, close the net. I want every exit from that waterfront district covered."

Sam watched the tactical display with growing dread, seeing the federal assets converging on Chad's location like wolves surrounding wounded prey. She opened Words with Friends and typed frantically: "Lots of players joining the game. Getting crowded in your area."

But before she could send the message, Thornton called out: "We've lost visual contact. Subject vehicle entered the industrial complex and disappeared behind shipping containers."

Holmes stared at the screen as the red icons representing pursuit teams spread out across the waterfront, searching for a target that had vanished into the urban maze.

"Helicopter support?" she demanded.

"En route. ETA three minutes."

"Ground teams?"

Conducting systematic search of the complex. But ma'am..." Martinez hesitated. "It's a big area. Lots of places to hide a vehicle."

Holmes' jaw tightened as she realized that Chad Lloyd had just vanished into a maze of abandoned buildings and shipping containers where he could hide indefinitely.

Grey allowed himself a small smile. Chad was proving more resourceful than Holmes had anticipated.

Chapter 51

Ramirez Compound
Grand Cayman

Elena Ramirez stood at the edge of her marble terrace, watching the Caribbean sun bleed crimson across waters that had swallowed more secrets than any government archive. Behind her, the compound's main house hummed with activity as her security team prepared for the most dangerous gathering in criminal history.

The sound of an armored SUV's engine echoed from the compound's main entrance as Javier returned from coordinating final arrangements at the abandoned airstrip. He'd just finished meeting with Ricardo to confirm delivery schedules and payment protocols for the influx of high-value passengers beginning in three days.

"How did Ricardo respond to the increased flight schedule?" Elena asked as Javier approached.

"Professional curiosity, but no real questions. I told him we're hosting a series of high-stakes business meetings over the next week—wealthy investors who value discretion and are willing to pay premium rates for privacy." Javier consulted his notes. "He's agreed to the modified schedule: multiple flights per day, cash payments on delivery, and complete passenger confidentiality."

"Does he suspect anything?"

"Ricardo's been flying criminals for thirty years. As long as the money's good and nobody asks him to get involved beyond transportation, he doesn't care who's in his plane." Javier smiled grimly. "I made it clear that passenger privacy is worth a fifty percent bonus on his usual rates."

Elena nodded approvingly. Ricardo's greed and willful ignorance made him the perfect unwitting accomplice.

"Status report," she said without turning around.

Hector approached from the communications center, encrypted tablet in hand. "All confirmations received. Hassan al-Baghdadi will arrive in seventy-two hours with his security detail. Al-Zawahiri confirmed for the same timeframe—six-man escort, all former Mukhabarat intelligence operatives."

"Smart. The Americans have been hunting them for fifteen years." Elena turned from the ocean view. "What about bin Omar?"

"Final confirmation from Colombia this morning. He'll arrive with four Taliban veterans on day two of the summit. Wants to coordinate timing to avoid overlapping security sweeps at the airstrip."

Elena nodded approvingly. The three-day timeline was perfect—it allowed for careful coordination of arrivals while giving each terrorist leader time to settle in before the operational planning began.

"Cartel leadership?"

"Miguel Treviño from Los Zetas will use diplomatic cover from corrupt Mexican officials—arriving at Owen Roberts on day one. Carlos Montenegro is positioning his yacht for discrete arrival tomorrow night. Rosa Delgado's people will use Ricardo's services on the final day."

Elena walked through the compound's main house, noting the discrete modifications her security team had made. The abandoned airstrip was perfect—isolated, invisible to government surveillance, and completely disconnected from her compound's location.

"By the end of the three-day arrival window, we'll have representatives from every major terrorist organization and criminal network in the hemisphere," Hector continued. "All transported through Ricardo's operation to the airstrip, then moved here by Javier without creating any connection between the pilot and our actual location."

Elena paused at the conference room doors, studying the mahogany table where fifty-three of the most dangerous individuals alive would soon be planning operations that could kill thousands of Americans. The operational security was perfect—three days allowed for careful staging without rushed timelines that might compromise security.

"The summit itself?"

"Three days of operational coordination. Day one: intelligence sharing and target assessment. Day two: resource allocation and timing coordination. Day three: final operational approval and communications protocols." Hector consulted his tablet. "Everyone departs within twenty-four hours of mission conclusion."

Elena activated the wall-mounted display, showing satellite imagery of the abandoned airstrip. Two miles of Caribbean jungle separated it from her compound—the perfect distance to maintain operational security while ensuring that any unwanted visitors would be completely under her control.

"Security preparations?"

"Total communications blackout during the summit. All phones and electronic devices surrendered at entry, stored in Faraday cage containers. Armed guards at every entrance, sniper teams on overwatch positions, patrol boats circling the island at two-mile intervals." Hector's voice carried professional competence. "The airstrip will be monitored by our security teams, but officially remains abandoned and unconnected to our operations."

Elena's secure phone buzzed with an encrypted message from Holmes: "Lloyd escaped initial containment in DC. Federal manhunt proceeding as planned. Subject still being misdirected away from actual investigation priorities."

Elena smiled, reading the message. Chad Lloyd was exactly where she wanted him—hunted by his own government while she coordinated the largest terrorist operation in history.

"Timeline for final preparations?"

"Seventy-two hours until first arrivals. All security protocols will be in place, communications blackouts tested, and the airstrip prepared for round-the-clock operations." Hector checked his tablet. "Ricardo has been briefed on the increase in 'business travel' but remains unaware of passenger identities or final destinations."

By week's end, the most wanted terrorists alive would be departing her compound with coordinated plans that would cripple American infrastructure and kill thousands of civilians.

Chapter 52

Anacostia Waterfront Industrial Complex
Southeast Washington D.C.

C had navigated the gray Transit van through the maze of warehouses and shipping container walls, his pursuers maintaining visual contact but unable to close the distance in the narrow industrial corridors. The waterfront complex was a labyrinth of steel and concrete that favored someone who understood urban warfare over federal agents trained for highway pursuits.

Behind him, unmarked federal vehicles struggled to maintain formation in the tight confines between towering container stacks. Chad could see them in his mirrors—professional drivers trying to coordinate a takedown in terrain that negated every advantage their numbers provided.

His scanner crackled with frustrated communications: "Alpha Team, maintain visual on subject vehicle. Bravo Team, attempt to cut off northern exit routes."

"Copy, Control. Subject is using industrial terrain to limit our tactical options."

Chad spotted his opportunity ahead—a forklift operator moving a forty-foot shipping container across the narrow roadway between warehouse buildings. The timing would have to be perfect.

He accelerated slightly, closing the distance as the forklift crept forward with its massive cargo suspended twenty feet above the roadway. The operator was focused on his load, earbuds blocking out ambient noise as he maneuvered the container into position.

Chad drove directly beneath the suspended container just as the forklift operator caught sight of the gray van in his peripheral vision. The operator's eyes went wide with surprise—vehicles weren't supposed to be in this section during container movement operations.

Instinct took over. The forklift driver slammed on his brakes and jerked the wheel, trying to avoid what looked like an imminent collision with the van passing beneath his suspended load.

The sudden stop sent the forty-foot container sliding forward off the forks, crashing down onto the roadway with a thunderous impact that shook windows three blocks away. Twenty tons of steel blocked the narrow passage completely, creating an impassable barrier between Chad and his federal pursuers.

Chad heard the crash behind him, followed by the screech of brakes and shouting voices as the pursuing agents found themselves trapped behind the massive obstacle.

His scanner crackled with confirmation: "Control, this is Pursuit Team Alpha. We've lost visual on the subject vehicle. Container blocking our route, requesting alternate units for intercept."

"Copy, Alpha. All units, subject has escaped containment in the waterfront sector. Expand search to secondary routes."

Chad used the chaos to disappear deeper into the industrial maze, following Sam's cleared corridor toward Route 50. The scanner chatter confirmed what he'd hoped—Holmes' agents were now searching in all the wrong places while he headed toward the escape route his allies had prepared.

The forklift operator sat in his cab, staring at the crushed container and wondering how the hell he was going to explain this to his supervisor. Behind the steel barrier, federal agents were already calling for heavy equipment to clear the obstruction.

By the time they moved twenty tons of shipping container, Chad Lloyd would be fifty miles away.

Chapter 53

PHOENIX Operations Center
FBI Headquarters

We've lost him again," Agent Thornton announced, her voice tight with frustration.

Holmes stared at the tactical display, watching red icons spread across the map as pursuit teams expanded their search radius. Chad Lloyd had vanished from the most heavily surveilled area in Washington D.C., disappearing like smoke despite overwhelming federal presence.

"How?" she demanded.

"Unknown. Subject appears to have used industrial access roads to avoid our checkpoints." Thornton consulted her tablet. "We're expanding the search to include all routes heading west."

Sam watched the display while fighting the urge to smile. Chad was following her suggested route, using the camera blackouts she'd arranged to stay invisible to federal surveillance. Her technical sabotage was working perfectly.

"Agent Belle," Holmes called out sharply. "You've worked with Lloyd for two years. Where would he go to ground?"

Sam kept her expression neutral while her mind raced. "Chad's methodical. He'll avoid anywhere connected to his known associates. Probably seeking remote locations where he can plan his next move without federal interference."

"What kind of locations?"

"Rural safe houses, abandoned properties, places where a federal agent might have conducted prior operations." Sam met Holmes' stare directly. "But Chad knows we know his methods. He'll be thinking several moves ahead."

Holmes' green eyes narrowed. "Are you saying we can't predict his movements?"

"I'm saying Chad Lloyd is one of the most tactically intelligent agents I've ever worked with. If he doesn't want to be found, we won't find him until he makes a mistake."

"Then we make sure he has plenty of opportunities to make mistakes." Holmes turned to the room. "I want every asset we have focused on this manhunt. Lloyd is out there planning something, and I want him stopped before he can act."

Grey watched the exchange from his workstation, noting the subtle way Sam was protecting Chad while appearing to cooperate with the investigation. The woman was walking a dangerous line, but her intelligence and loyalty were giving Chad the edge he needed to stay ahead of federal pursuit.

Chapter 54

Truck Stop Diner
Interstate 85, North Carolina

Chad sat in a corner booth of the Waffle House, keeping his baseball cap low while some national news played on the mounted television above the counter. He'd driven through the night, following Sam's cleared route through rural Virginia and into North Carolina, staying ahead of federal checkpoints by using back roads that didn't appear on Holmes' tactical maps.

The morning news was about to destroy what remained of his reputation.

"This morning, sources within federal law enforcement have revealed an ongoing manhunt for Chad Lloyd, a federal agent who has gone rogue following the deaths of his wife and daughter," the anchor announced over Chad's military photo. "Lloyd is considered armed and extremely dangerous, with extensive combat training and access to federal resources."

Chad's coffee went cold as he watched his life being rewritten on national television. But something was wrong—this felt like an unauthorized leak, not an official FBI statement.

"We're joined now by Dr. Sarah Xi, a family trauma specialist who has been working with victims of the recent cartel attacks, and Agent Janet Holmes from the FBI's PHOENIX task force."

The screen split to show Dr. Xi via satellite feed and Holmes in what looked like an unauthorized interview setup. Chad recognized Xi immediately—the grief counselor who'd tried to convince him that revenge wouldn't bring back Lana and Casey.

"Agent Holmes," the anchor continued, "what can you tell us about Agent Lloyd's current mental state?"

Holmes leaned forward, clearly enjoying her moment in the spotlight. "Agent Lloyd has been under tremendous psychological pressure following the tragic loss of his family. He has made explicit threats against Mexican cartel organizations and possesses the training to carry out those threats."

Chad felt his jaw clench. Holmes was conducting her own media campaign without official FBI authorization, painting him as a mentally unstable agent on a revenge mission.

The anchor leaned forward with obvious interest. "Agent Holmes, public opinion polls show overwhelming support for Agent Lloyd's position. If he wants to hunt the cartels that murdered his family, why isn't the FBI letting him do exactly that? Aren't these the same organizations you should be targeting anyway?"

Holmes' confident expression flickered for just a moment before she recovered. "The FBI cannot allow individual agents to conduct unauthorized operations, regardless of public sentiment or personal motivations. Agent Lloyd's emotional state makes him unpredictable and dangerous to ongoing federal investigations."

"But Agent Holmes, these cartels murdered 284 federal family members. Shouldn't hunting them be your top priority instead of hunting the agent seeking justice for those murders?"

Chad could see Holmes struggling with a question that exposed the fundamental flaw in her narrative—why was the FBI hunting a grieving agent instead of hunting the terrorists who'd killed his family?"

Holmes opened her mouth to respond, then closed it, her confident demeanor cracking as she realized the trap the question had set. Seconds stretched into an uncomfortable silence as she searched for an answer that didn't exist—no reasonable explanation for why the FBI was hunting victims instead of terrorists.

The silence extended painfully, Holmes clearly struggling to justify the unjustifiable on live television.

Finally, the anchor turned away from the speechless FBI agent. "Dr.

Xi, you've worked with Agent Lloyd personally. From a psychological perspective, how do you assess his mental state and motivations?"

Chad watched Holmes' face flush with embarrassment as the anchor moved on, having received no answer to the most important question of the interview. The woman who'd been so confident moments before now looked like someone who'd been caught in a lie she couldn't explain.

Xi's face filled with the kind of professional concern that played well on television. "Chad was clearly struggling with survivor guilt and what I would characterize as obsessive ideation regarding his family's killers. He repeatedly expressed anger toward federal agencies for not pursuing more aggressive action against the cartels."

"Obsessive ideation," Chad muttered, watching his grief being diagnosed for public consumption.

"In your professional opinion," the anchor pressed, "how dangerous is Agent Lloyd to the public?"

"Chad has extensive military and federal training, including weapons expertise and knowledge of investigative techniques," Thompson replied. "Combined with his current emotional state, he represents a significant threat—not necessarily to innocent civilians, but certainly to anyone he perceives as connected to his family's deaths."

The diner's other customers—truckers, construction workers, early commuters—were all watching the broadcast with the kind of morbid fascination reserved for manhunts and natural disasters. Chad pulled his cap lower and tried to become invisible.

"Agent Holmes," the anchor continued, "is this manhunt officially authorized by FBI leadership?"

Holmes hesitated for just a moment—long enough for Chad to realize she was operating without proper authorization. "The PHOENIX task force has been given broad discretion to investigate threats to federal personnel and their families. Agent Lloyd's current activities fall within our operational parameters."

The anchor's eyes sharpened with journalistic instinct. "Agent Holmes, you said threats to federal personnel and their families. But Agent Lloyd IS federal personnel, and it was HIS family that was murdered by cartels. Did I understand you correctly? Are you saying

Agent Lloyd is a threat to federal personnel and their families?"

Holmes' face went pale as she realized her verbal slip had exposed the fundamental contradiction in her position. "I... what I meant was..."

" Agent Holmes, are you classifying a grieving FBI agent as a threat to the same federal families he's trying to get justice for? The families murdered by the cartels you're apparently not hunting?"

Holmes straightened in her chair, falling back on the standard bureaucratic shield. "I'm sorry, but we can't comment on ongoing investigations."

The anchor wasn't buying it. "But Agent Holmes, you've been commenting on this investigation for the past ten minutes. You've discussed Agent Lloyd's psychological state, his threats against cartels, his training, and his operational activities. How is this any different?"

Holmes' professional composure was completely shattered now, caught between her unauthorized media campaign and her attempt to hide behind investigative protocols. "That's... that's different. We can discuss general threats to public safety without compromising specific investigative details."

"So Agent Lloyd is a threat to public safety, but the cartels who murdered 284 federal family members aren't worth discussing?"

Chad watched Holmes realize she'd dug herself into an indefensible position on live television, her own words being used to expose the corruption of hunting victims instead of terrorists.

Holmes opened her mouth again but no words came out, her face flushed with embarrassment and anger at being thoroughly dismantled by basic journalism.

The anchor turned back to the camera with professional smoothness. "We'll let our audience form their own opinions about the FBI's priorities. Let's move on." The screen shifted to show another participant. "We're also joined by Marybeth Samuels, whose husband was killed in the same cartel attack that claimed Agent Lloyd's family."

Chad's blood ran cold as Marybeth's face appeared on screen. She looked exhausted, broken, nothing like the vibrant woman who'd organized neighborhood barbecues and helped Lana with school fundraisers.

"Mrs. Samuels, you knew Agent Lloyd personally. What's your reaction to news of his current fugitive status?"

Marybeth's voice was barely above a whisper. "Chad was... is a good man. He loved Lana and Casey more than anything in the world. But what happened to our families... it broke something inside all of us."

"Do you believe Agent Lloyd is dangerous?"

"I believe Chad is angry. We all are. The people who killed our families are still out there, still free, still planning more attacks." Maria's voice grew stronger. "If the FBI is hunting Chad instead of hunting the terrorists who murdered our children, then something is very wrong with our government."

Chad felt tears sting his eyes. Marybeth understood what Holmes and Xi never would—that sometimes the system failed so completely that good people had no choice but to seek justice outside legal boundaries.

"However," Marybeth continued, "I don't believe Chad would hurt innocent people. His anger isn't random violence. It's focused on the people who murdered his wife and daughter."

Holmes quickly interjected, clearly unhappy with Marybeth's defense of Chad. "We want to emphasize that Agent Lloyd should not be approached by civilians. If spotted, please contact federal authorities immediately."

"Agent Lloyd has explicitly threatened cartel organizations and has been tracking their operations outside official channels," Holmes announced. "We believe he may attempt to cross international borders to pursue these organizations in foreign territories."

The anchor's voice took on a sharper edge. "Again, Agent Holmes, why is the federal government conducting a manhunt on someone who has not broken any laws yet? And why this overzealous waste of federal government time, money and manpower? Shouldn't the FBI be focused on the real terrorists and not a grieving husband and father you perceive as a threat?"

Holmes shifted uncomfortably in her chair, clearly not expecting this level of aggressive questioning.

The anchor continued, "Maybe the public should start calling their representatives and ask why this is occurring, and possibly look into your investigations and budget allocation. How do you justify spending millions of dollars hunting a grieving federal agent instead of hunting the cartels that murdered his family?"

Holmes' face went from pale to red as she realized the anchor had just encouraged congressional oversight of her operations and potential budget investigations on national television.

"That's... that's not how federal law enforcement prioritizes..." Holmes stammered, her earlier confidence completely evaporated.

The anchor looked directly into the camera with obvious frustration. "Well, we're not getting anywhere here, so Agent Holmes, any message for Agent Lloyd if he's watching?"

Holmes seized the opportunity to regain some control, looking directly into the camera with what she hoped was authority. "Chad, if you're listening, you're not serving justice by operating outside the law. You're endangering federal operations that could bring the real killers to justice. Turn yourself in before this situation escalates beyond anyone's control."

Chad stared at Holmes' face on the television screen, noting the barely concealed satisfaction in her expression despite the disastrous interview. She was still trying to position herself as the competent federal agent protecting America from a rogue operative, even after being thoroughly exposed as someone hunting victims instead of terrorists.

But her message was clear: surrender now, or face the full weight of federal law enforcement pursuing someone whose only crime was seeking justice for his murdered family.

Chad reached for his phone and typed a Words with Friends message: *"Watching the morning news. Interesting commentary on recent games. Looks like some players are making unauthorized moves."*

Sam's response came within minutes: *"Saw the broadcast. That interview wasn't approved by upper management. Player going rogue with media strategy. Most of the team here don't support the unauthorized coverage."*

So Holmes was conducting her manhunt and media campaign without Huntington's knowledge or approval. That explained the careful language and unauthorized feel of the interview.

"Any changes to the game board after the broadcast?"

"Some increased activity, but mostly confusion about official vs unofficial player positions. TV coverage might actually help your position by showing the split in our team."

Chad pocketed his phone and left money on the table, noticing that the other diner customers were now looking at him with a mixture of suspicion and curiosity. The baseball cap and three days of stubble weren't enough to disguise him from people who'd just seen his face on national television.

He walked calmly to the parking lot, resisting the urge to run, and climbed into the Transit van. Behind him, he could see customers pulling out phones, probably calling the FBI tip line that was about to receive thousands of false sightings from across the country.

But a few of those calls would be real. The media manhunt had just made Chad's face recognizable to every American with a television, transforming him from a federal agent seeking justice into a household name associated with danger and instability.

Chad started the van and pulled onto the highway, heading south toward Miami while his reputation burned on every news channel in America. Holmes had just turned his personal mission into a national spectacle without proper authorization, ensuring that his hunt for Elena Ramirez would be conducted under the scrutiny of an entire country that now viewed him as the threat rather than the victim.

FBI Director's Office
Washington D.C.

Director Huntington watched Agent Holmes' interview with growing alarm, his coffee growing cold as she stammered through questions she clearly hadn't anticipated. When the anchor suggested congressional budget investigations on live television, Huntington reached for his secure phone.

"Get me Deputy Director Walsh. Now."

The interview was still playing when Walsh entered. Holmes was trying to explain why the FBI was hunting a grieving agent instead of the cartels that murdered his family, and failing miserably.

"Tell me you authorized this," Huntington said, though his tone suggested he already knew the answer.

"Absolutely not, sir. Media relations had no advance notice. Holmes went completely rogue."

Huntington muted the television as the disastrous interview finally ended. "How many congressional offices have called?"

"Four so far. Senator Morrison's committee wants a briefing by end of business. DOJ is asking questions."

Huntington stared at the blank screen, processing the political fallout from Holmes' unauthorized media campaign. "Keep monitoring the situation. And Walsh? I want to know everything Agent Holmes is doing. Everything."

"Yes, sir."

After Walsh left, Huntington sat alone in his office, wondering if putting Holmes in charge of PHOENIX had been a mistake. The interview had raised questions he didn't have answers for - questions that might destroy more than just one agent's career.

The war was no longer just between Chad and the cartels. It was between Chad and a rogue federal agent who was using unauthorized media campaigns to build her career on his family's graves.

But as Maria Santos had pointed out on live television, if the FBI was hunting Chad instead of hunting the terrorists who murdered federal families, then something was very wrong with the system itself.

Chad drove toward Miami, carrying the weight of a murdered family and a destroyed reputation, pursuing the only justice that remained available to him.

Even if a rogue FBI agent was turning the whole world against him.

Chapter 55

Agent Janet Holmes stood before the tactical displays, watching red icons spread across multiple states as federal assets continued their search for Chad Lloyd. Three days into the manhunt, and he remained as elusive as smoke, disappearing from surveillance coverage with the precision of someone who understood federal tracking methods better than the agents trying to find him.

"Agent Belle," Holmes called out, her voice carrying a sharp edge that made Sam look up from her workstation. "I need you in Conference Room B. Bring your case files on Lloyd."

Sam felt her stomach clench but kept her expression neutral. "Of course, ma'am."

The conference room was smaller than the main operations center, with no windows and recording equipment that Holmes activated as soon as Sam sat down. The setup felt more like an interrogation than a consultation.

"Agent Belle, you've worked more closely with Chad Lloyd than anyone else on this task force," Holmes began, consulting a thick file that seemed to contain far more information than necessary for a routine debriefing. "I need to understand his psychological profile, his methods, his likely destinations."

"I've already provided written assessments—"

"I've read your assessments. They're... adequate. But I'm looking for insights that might not appear in official reports." Holmes leaned forward, her green eyes studying Sam carefully. "Personal observations, informal conversations, behavioral patterns you might have noticed during off-duty interactions."

Sam felt the weight of the recording equipment, understanding that every word would be analyzed for signs of disloyalty or deception. "Chad is methodical, professional, highly disciplined. His military background influences his approach to everything—planning, risk assessment, operational security."

"What about his emotional state following his family's deaths?"

"Devastated. Angry. But focused." Sam chose her words carefully, walking the line between honesty and protection. "Chad channels his grief into action rather than letting it paralyze him."

Holmes made notes on her tablet, but Sam noticed she was also watching for micro-expressions, body language, any tells that might suggest Sam was withholding information.

"Agent Belle, Lloyd's evasion techniques have been remarkably sophisticated. He's avoided surveillance cameras, bypassed federal checkpoints, and stayed ahead of coordinated pursuit efforts involving multiple agencies." Holmes paused meaningfully. "That level of success suggests either exceptional luck or inside assistance."

The accusation hung in the air like poison gas. Sam met Holmes' stare directly, knowing that any sign of nervousness would confirm her suspicions.

"Chad has twenty years of military and federal training. He understands our methods because he's used them himself for two decades." Sam's voice remained steady. "More importantly, Chad has extensive SERE training—Survival, Evasion, Resistance, and Escape. He's been trained by the best military instructors in the world on how to avoid capture in hostile territory. If Chad doesn't want to be found, he won't be found."

"Independently." Holmes repeated the word like it tasted bitter. "Agent Belle, in your assessment, is Lloyd capable of conducting sustained operations without external support?"

"Absolutely. Chad's military service included extended deployments in hostile territory. He's accustomed to operating with minimal resources and no backup."

Holmes consulted her file again, flipping through pages that seemed to contain surveillance photographs and communication logs. Sam felt her blood chill, wondering how much of her own activity had been monitored.

"Agent Belle, I've reviewed your duty schedules, computer access logs, and communication patterns since the manhunt began," Holmes announced. "You've been working unusually long hours, accessing databases outside your normal operational parameters, and spending considerable time on personal devices during work hours."

Sam's mind raced, calculating which of her activities might have been detected. The traffic camera hacks, the route intelligence, the Words with Friends communications—any of it could have triggered security monitoring.

"I've been working extended hours because this is the biggest manhunt in bureau history," Sam replied. "As for database access, I've been researching Lloyd's background to develop better psychological profiles. And yes, I use my personal phone during breaks—the same as every agent in this building."

Holmes leaned back in her chair, clearly unsatisfied with Sam's responses but lacking concrete evidence of wrongdoing. "Agent Belle, let me be very clear about something. Chad Lloyd is no longer the federal agent you worked with for two years. Grief has transformed him into something dangerous and unpredictable."

"I understand that—"

"Do you? Because your psychological assessments consistently portray Lloyd in sympathetic terms. They emphasize his tactical competence and downplay the threat he represents to federal operations." Holmes' voice grew harder. "I'm beginning to wonder if your professional judgment has been compromised by personal feelings."

The recording equipment hummed quietly as Sam realized Holmes was building a case for her removal from the task force—or worse, for prosecution as an accessory to Chad's activities.

"Agent Holmes, my assessments are based on two years of working partnership and professional observation. I won't apologize for providing accurate intelligence rather than politically convenient fiction."

Holmes' eyes flashed with anger at the implicit criticism. "Agent Belle, you're walking a very dangerous line. Loyalty to former colleagues is admirable, but loyalty to fugitives is treasonous."

"Chad Lloyd isn't a traitor. He's a federal agent whose family was murdered by terrorists while his own government—" Sam caught herself before finishing the sentence, but the damage was done.

"While his own government what, Agent Belle?"

Sam met Holmes' stare, knowing that retreat was no longer possible. "While his own government spent more energy hunting him than hunting the people who killed 284 federal family members."

The silence in the conference room was deafening. Holmes stared at Sam with the cold fury of someone whose authority had been directly challenged.

"Agent Belle, you're hereby restricted from all intelligence databases pending security review. Your access to PHOENIX communications and tactical planning is suspended indefinitely." Holmes stood, her voice carrying the weight of absolute authority. "You'll be assigned to administrative duties until we can determine whether your continued involvement in this investigation represents a security risk."

Sam felt her world collapsing but kept her expression neutral. "Understood, ma'am."

"Furthermore, Agent Belle, you're now under administrative surveillance. Your communications, computer access, and movements will be monitored for the duration of this investigation." Holmes moved toward the door. "I suggest you think very carefully about where your loyalties lie."

After Holmes left, Sam remained in the conference room, staring at the recording equipment that had just captured her career ending. She'd pushed too hard, revealed too much of her true feelings about the manhunt.

But at least Chad was still free, still moving toward whatever confrontation awaited him in Miami. Her sacrifice had bought him time, and maybe that was enough.

Sam pulled out her personal phone and opened Words with Friends, typing what might be her final message: *"Game getting too hot. Might have to stop playing soon. Good luck with your strategy."*

She sent the message and deleted the app, knowing that Holmes would soon have access to every electronic communication she'd made. Chad was on his own now, approaching Miami without the intelligence support that had kept him ahead of federal pursuit.

Sam could only hope that twenty years of military training would be enough to keep him alive when he walked into whatever trap Elena Ramirez had prepared.

Because the woman who'd helped him this far had just been removed from the game.

Chapter 56

Chad's burner phone buzzed with an incoming call from Mike Torrino, a former Delta Force operator who'd served with Chad in Afghanistan. Chad had been trying to reach Mike for six hours, needing a safe house somewhere between his current location and Miami.

"Jesus, Chad," Mike's voice was tight with stress. "I've been watching the news all morning. They're calling you a rogue agent, brother."

"Mike, I need help. Just one night, somewhere safe to—"

"I can't do it, man. I'm sorry, but I can't." Mike's voice carried genuine regret. "FBI agents were at my house this morning asking questions about everyone who served with you. They made it clear that helping you would be considered harboring a fugitive."

Chad felt his stomach drop. If the feds had already reached Mike in South Carolina, they were systematically working through his entire military network.

"Mike, my family was murdered by terrorists. I'm not the enemy here."

"I know that. We all know that. But Chad..." Mike paused, and Chad could hear voices in the background—other people warning Mike to end the call. "Brother, they've got surveillance on everyone from the old unit. Phone taps, vehicle tracking, the works. Even if I wanted to help, they'd know the moment you showed up."

"What about Jimmy Kowalski? Or McMurray?"

"Jimmy's in federal custody for questioning. They picked him up this morning. And McMurray..." Mike's voice dropped to a whisper. "He called me an hour ago. Said FBI agents told him that anyone who helps you is looking at federal conspiracy charges."

Chad closed his eyes, feeling his support network evaporating in real time. The men who'd shared foxholes with him, who'd trusted him with their lives in combat, were being systematically intimidated by his own government.

"Mike, I understand. Thanks for being straight with me."

"Chad, for what it's worth, every guy from the unit thinks this is bullshit. You're one of the best men I've ever served with, and hunting you instead of the people who killed your family... it's wrong."

"But not wrong enough to risk your own family's safety."

Mike was quiet for a moment. "I've got two kids, brother. I can't take that risk."

Chad ended the call and immediately threw the phone out his window, watching it shatter on the highway. Every electronic communication was being monitored, every contact traced and investigated.

He pulled into a truck stop and tried calling Danny Morrison on another burner phone. Morrison was another former teammate who owned a security company in Georgia. The call went straight to voicemail, but the message had been changed: "This number is no longer in service."

Danny had disconnected his phone rather than risk being contacted by a federal fugitive.

Chad tried three more numbers—all disconnected or answered by people who claimed not to know anyone named Chad Lloyd. His entire military network had gone dark, either from federal pressure or simple self-preservation.

Chad destroyed the phone and placed it in the trash bin next to the gas pump, eliminating any electronic trail that could lead federal agents to his current location

He walked into the truck stop restroom, then filled up the van and bought some snacks for the road - energy bars, coffee, and a prepaid phone to replace the two he'd destroyed earlier. Back in the van, Chad mentally inventoried his remaining resources. Ninety-eight thousand in cash, enough to last weeks if he was careful. But no safe houses, no weapons resupply, no technical support from people who understood operational security.

Chad was now completely alone.

The irony wasn't lost on him. Twenty years of military service, building relationships and earning loyalty through shared combat, and it all disappeared the moment his government painted him as the enemy.

Chad started the van and pulled back onto I-95, heading toward Florida while his former teammates chose family safety over old loyalties. He couldn't blame them—he'd probably make the same choice in their position.

But it left him facing Elena Ramirez with nothing but his own skills and whatever intelligence he could gather independently.

Chad's phone—a new burner purchased at the truck stop—buzzed with a text message from the Words with Friends app: *"Game over. Can't play anymore. Good luck."*

Sam. She'd been discovered and removed from the game, leaving Chad without his last source of federal intelligence. Now he was truly operating blind, approaching Miami without knowing what kind of reception awaited him.

Chad deleted the message and continued south, carrying the weight of a murdered family and a crumbling support network. The war against Elena Ramirez would be fought alone, with whatever weapons and cunning he could muster.

Behind him, his former teammates were explaining to FBI agents why they couldn't help locate the man who'd once saved their lives in combat. Ahead of him, Miami waited with unknown dangers and uncertain allies.

Chad Lloyd had become exactly what Janet Holmes accused him of being—a rogue operator with no backup, no support, and nothing left to lose.

Which, he reflected grimly, might make him more dangerous than anyone realized.

Chapter 57

FBI Interrogation Center
Quantico, VA.

Tony Kowalski sat across from Agent Martinez in a sterile interview room, his hands cuffed to a table while recording equipment captured every word. He'd been arrested at 0600 hours on suspicion of providing material support to a federal fugitive, and twelve hours of questioning hadn't broken his story.

"Mr. Kowalski, we have financial records showing large cash withdrawals from your accounts coinciding with Agent Lloyd's disappearance," Martinez announced, sliding bank statements across the table. "What did you purchase with that money?"

Tony studied the documents, noting they showed legitimate business transactions from his security consulting company. "Equipment purchases for ongoing contracts. Nothing unusual about that."

"What kind of equipment?"

"Security systems, surveillance gear, communications equipment. Standard stuff for my business." Tony met her stare directly. "All legal, all documented, all for legitimate clients."

"You have financial records showing I received cash payments for legitimate security consulting work," Tony interrupted. "Nothing illegal about that."

Agent Thornton leaned forward from across the table. "Mr. Kowalski, Chad Lloyd is a federal fugitive who has made explicit threats against Mexican cartel organizations. Any assistance you provided could be considered material support for terrorist activities."

Tony laughed, a harsh sound in the sterile room. "Terrorist activities? Agent Lloyd's family was murdered by actual terrorists, and you people are hunting him instead of hunting them. And you wonder why nobody wants to cooperate with this investigation?"

"Sir, Agent Lloyd has violated federal law—"

"Agent Lloyd buried his wife and six-year-old daughter a month ago because your agency failed to protect federal families from cartel attacks." Tony's voice carried the flat anger of someone who'd seen too much government failure. "Now you're trying to make him the criminal? That's some twisted logic right there."

Martinez consulted his files, clearly frustrated by Tony's refusal to provide useful intelligence. "Mr. Kowalski, we know you have ongoing contact with other members of Agent Lloyd's former military unit. If you're coordinating assistance—"

"Look, I sell security equipment to people who can afford it. Nothing more, nothing less." Tony met his stare directly. "And even if I was helping Chad Lloyd hunt down the people who killed his family, I'd consider that patriotic duty rather than criminal conspiracy."

The interview continued for another hour, but Tony's story never changed. He was a legitimate businessman who'd had casual contact with Chad Lloyd but no knowledge of any criminal activities or fugitive operations.

Finally, Agent Martinez stood up, clearly realizing he lacked evidence for federal conspiracy charges.

"Mr. Kowalski, you're free to go. But understand that any future contact with Agent Lloyd will result in immediate arrest and prosecution."

Tony stood and rubbed his wrists where the handcuffs had chafed. "Agent, let me give you some advice. Chad Lloyd is one of the best men I've ever known. He's not your enemy. The people who murdered his family are your enemy."

"Sir—"

"When this is over, and Chad's either dead or in prison, and Elena Ramirez kills more federal families, remember this conversation. Remember that you spent federal resources hunting heroes instead of hunting terrorists."

Tony walked out of the interogation center, knowing that every electronic device he owned would now be monitored and every movement tracked. But he'd given Chad a three-day head start with weapons and transportation, and that might be enough to reach Elena Ramirez before federal incompetence got him killed.

Chapter 58

Florida State Line
Interstate 95 South

C had crossed into Florida under cover of darkness, the Transit van's headlights cutting through humid air that carried the scent of approaching thunderstorms. Four days on the run had taught him the rhythm of federal manhunts—intense activity during daylight hours, reduced surveillance after midnight when most agents assumed fugitives would seek shelter.

He'd been driving for fourteen hours straight, surviving on truck stop coffee and adrenaline while avoiding the major checkpoints that Sam had warned him about before going dark. The radio scanner beside him crackled with Florida Highway Patrol communications, but so far no BOLO alerts with his name or vehicle description.

Maybe the federal manhunt hadn't extended into Florida yet. Or maybe Holmes was keeping the search focused on areas where Chad might have military contacts, not realizing he was following a different kind of trail entirely.

Chad pocketed the new burner phone he'd purchased at the truck stop, keeping it powered off for now. Any electronic communication was a risk, but he might need it if the situation became desperate enough to risk federal tracking

The isolation was complete now. No Sam feeding him intelligence, no military contacts offering safe houses, no technological support beyond what he could manage himself. Just one man with a van full of weapons, hunting the most dangerous criminal organization in the

Western Hemisphere.

Chad pulled into a 24-hour gas station outside Jacksonville and filled the tank while scanning for surveillance. The attendant was a sleepy college kid who barely looked up from his textbook, showing no recognition despite four days of national news coverage. Either Chad's disguise was working, or most people weren't paying attention to FBI manhunt stories.

Inside the convenience store, Chad bought a back up burner phone and checked the latest news coverage on a mounted television. The news channel was running a story about increased border security, but nothing about the manhunt. Maybe Holmes had pulled back from media exposure after realizing it was generating more false leads than useful intelligence.

Chad pocketed the phone without activating it. He'd need secure internet access to research Ricardo's operation and track down the pilot who'd helped Javier escape. But public WiFi would be too dangerous now that the manhunt had reached Florida—every electronic footprint could be traced back to federal surveillance systems.

The scanner crackled with a new transmission: "All units, be advised, FBI has requested assistance with federal fugitive apprehension. Subject is Chad Lloyd, federal agent, considered armed and dangerous. Vehicle may be gray Transit van with Virginia plates."

So the manhunt had reached Florida. Chad was no longer ahead of federal pursuit—he was operating within it, moving through a state where every law enforcement officer had his description and orders to apprehend on sight.

Chad turned off I-95 and began following rural highways through central Florida, avoiding the interstate corridor where federal checkpoints would be most concentrated. The route would add hours to his travel time, but stealth was more important than speed now.

His fuel gauge showed nearly full from the recent truck stop fill-up, which meant he could reach Miami with one additional stop if he was careful. That was good - every interaction with civilians was a potential identification and arrest, and avoiding gas stations meant avoiding surveillance cameras and recognition opportunities.

Chad's mind drifted to Lana and Casey as he drove through the Florida darkness. He could still hear Lana's voice from that horrific video, her final words to him through tears and pain: 'Kill these fuckers.' Even in her darkest moment, facing torture and death, she'd wanted him to hunt down the people who were destroying their family.

She would approve of what he was doing. Lana understood that some evils couldn't be negotiated with or forgiven. The people who'd murdered them deserved exactly what Chad was planning to deliver.

But his thoughts also kept returning to Sam, to her confession in the apartment: "I'm in love with you. I have been for months, maybe longer." The timing still felt impossibly cruel—a declaration of love when he was no longer capable of returning it, when everything human inside him had died with his family.

Had Lana known? She was perceptive about people, especially about the way women looked at her husband. Chad thought back to office parties, department barbecues, the times Sam had joined them for dinner. Had there been signs he'd missed? Glances between Lana and Sam, conversations that stopped when he entered the room?

If Lana had known about Sam's feelings, she'd never said anything. Never shown jealousy or concern, never asked Chad to request a different partner. That was Lana—secure enough in their marriage to trust Chad completely, generous enough to feel sympathy rather than threat toward a woman who loved someone she couldn't have.

Would Lana approve of what Sam had done? Risking her career, committing treason, helping Chad stay ahead of federal pursuit so he could hunt their family's killers? Chad thought she would. Lana had always believed that love meant supporting someone's choices, even when you disagreed with them. Even when those choices led to danger.

Lana had always been the practical one, the voice of reason who talked Chad down from his more aggressive impulses. She'd probably tell him to trust the system, to let federal agents handle Elena Ramirez through proper channels.

But Casey... Casey would understand. His six-year-old daughter had inherited Chad's stubborn streak, his refusal to accept injustice. She'd probably tell him to "get the bad guys, Daddy," the way she'd encouraged him during their games of cops and robbers.

Thunder rumbled overhead as the first drops of rain began hitting the windshield. Chad turned on the wipers and pressed deeper into Florida, carrying the weight of a murdered family and the expectations of a daughter who'd never grow up to understand the choices her father had made in her name.

Somewhere ahead, Miami waited with answers about Ricardo's operation and Elena Ramirez's location. But between Chad and those answers lay a federal manhunt that had finally caught up with him, transforming his hunt for justice into a race against time.

Chad Lloyd was no longer hunting Elena Ramirez from a position of strength. He was hunting her as a federal fugitive with limited resources and diminishing options, approaching the most dangerous phase of a mission that would probably end with his death or capture.

But at least it would end with Elena Ramirez knowing that someone had come for her. Someone who'd loved the people she'd murdered enough to risk everything for the chance to make her pay.

The rain intensified as Chad drove toward Miami, washing away his tracks while federal agents in three states coordinated the largest manhunt in bureau history.

The endgame was approaching. And Chad Lloyd intended to reach Elena Ramirez before his own government stopped him.

Even if it killed him in the process.

Chapter 59

PHOENIX Operations Center
FBI Headquarters

Agent Janet Holmes stood before the tactical displays, watching red icons spread across the southeastern United States as federal assets repositioned to intercept Chad Lloyd's southward movement. Intelligence analysts had finally identified a pattern in the false sightings and dead-end leads—all pointing toward Florida.

"Agent Thornton, status report," Holmes announced to the room.

"Florida Highway Patrol has been briefed and provided with subject photographs. All major highways south of Jacksonville are under surveillance." Thornton consulted her tablet. "TSA has increased security screening at Miami International, and Coast Guard is monitoring private airfields along the coast."

"Excellent. What about local law enforcement cooperation?"

"Mixed results. Miami-Dade PD is fully cooperative, but some of the smaller departments are asking questions about jurisdiction and authorization." Thornton hesitated. "There's also been some... skepticism about the threat assessment."

Holmes' jaw tightened. Even local police were questioning her manhunt, influenced by media coverage that portrayed Chad as a grieving victim rather than a dangerous fugitive.

"Agent Thornton, remind these departments that Chad Lloyd is a federal agent with extensive combat training who has made explicit threats against cartel organizations. He represents a clear and present danger to ongoing federal operations."

"Yes, ma'am. But some of the local commanders are asking for written authorization from FBI headquarters. They want documentation from Director Huntington's office."

Holmes felt her stomach clench. She'd been operating under broad PHOENIX task force authority, but specific manhunt operations required higher-level approval that she'd never obtained.

"Tell them the authorization is being processed through appropriate channels. In the meantime, Lloyd remains a federal fugitive who must be apprehended before he can interfere with ongoing counterterrorism operations."

Agent Grey looked up from his workstation, his weathered face showing the kind of professional skepticism that Holmes had learned to expect from veteran agents.

"Agent Holmes, what counterterrorism operations is Lloyd threatening? Our primary target is Elena Ramirez, and Lloyd's investigation seems focused on the same objective."

"Agent Grey, Lloyd's emotional state makes him unpredictable. He could compromise delicate intelligence operations through reckless action." Holmes turned to face him directly. "We need him in custody before he destabilizes our systematic approach to dismantling the Ramirez organization."

"What systematic approach?" Grey asked quietly. "It's been weeks since the cartel attacks, and we still don't have actionable intelligence on Elena Ramirez's location."

The operations center went quiet as agents realized Grey was directly challenging Holmes' leadership and strategy.

"Agent Grey, you're out of line—"

"Agent Holmes, maybe the reason we haven't found Elena Ramirez is because we've been spending resources hunting one of our own agents instead of hunting the actual terrorist." Grey stood from his workstation. "Chad Lloyd isn't our enemy. He's a federal agent seeking justice for his murdered family."

Holmes stared at Grey, recognizing the challenge to her authority but lacking the political capital to remove a respected veteran agent.

"Agent Grey, you're relieved of duty for insubordination. Report to administrative review tomorrow morning."

Grey smiled grimly and began packing his personal items. "Agent Holmes, when this manhunt falls apart and Director Huntington finds out what you've been doing without authorization, remember this conversation."

As Grey walked toward the door, Agent Ruiz stood from his workstation and began gathering his files. "Agent Holmes, I'm requesting immediate transfer out of PHOENIX task force."

"Agent Ruiz, you can't just—"

Agent Kim was already packing his equipment. "Ma'am, I'm also requesting transfer. This operation doesn't have proper authorization."

Agent Walsh joined them, closing his laptop and securing his classified materials. "Count me out too. I signed up to hunt terrorists, not federal agents seeking justice for their murdered families."

Martinez was the last to stand, his face showing the professional disgust of someone who'd served with honor for eight years. "Agent Holmes, you've turned this task force into a witch hunt. I won't be part of it anymore."

Within minutes, the operations center had emptied except for Holmes and Agent Thornton, who remained at her workstation with the uncomfortable loyalty of someone whose career depended on backing the wrong horse.

Holmes stared at the empty workstations, feeling the weight of complete isolation. Her entire task force had abandoned her, leaving only one subordinate and a manhunt that was increasingly looking like an unauthorized vendetta.

"Agent Thornton," Holmes said quietly, "I guess it's just us now."

Thornton looked around the empty operations center, clearly uncomfortable with the mass exodus but lacking the seniority to challenge Holmes directly. "Yes, ma'am. What are your orders?"

The manhunt would continue. And when Chad Lloyd was finally in custody, Holmes would be vindicated as the agent who'd prevented a federal catastrophe.

Even if she had to destroy her own task force to make it happen.

Chapter 60

Miami-Dade County Line

Chad had crossed into Miami-Dade County as dawn broke over the Everglades, the Transit van running on fumes and determination after eighteen hours of driving through rural Florida. The humidity hit him like a physical force when he cracked the windows, carrying the scent of salt water and urban decay that defined South Florida.

He'd avoided the main highways during his approach, using back roads and agricultural routes to stay clear of the federal checkpoints that Holmes would have positioned around major transportation corridors. But now, entering the metropolitan area where Ricardo operated his pilot service, Chad would have to navigate urban surveillance networks and local law enforcement that had been briefed on his fugitive status.

Chad found what he was looking for in Little Havana—a strip mall internet café called "Cyber Connect" that advertised "Private Browsing - No Questions Asked" in both English and Spanish. But first, Chad needed to secure his equipment.

Two blocks from the café, Chad spotted a familiar logo: 24-Hour Fitness. His membership from Virginia would work at any location nationwide, giving him access to facilities without creating new paper trails or raising suspicions.

Chad parked the van in the gym's parking lot and grabbed the duffel bag containing everything Tony had provided—the C-4 explosives, det cord, remote detonators, long-range optics, thermal imaging equipment, and forty-eight thousand in cash. Too much firepower and evidence to carry into an unknown situation.

Inside the gym, Chad showed his membership card to a bored teenager at the front desk who barely looked up from his phone. The locker room was empty at this early hour, giving Chad privacy to secure his equipment in a large rental locker. He paid for a week's rental with cash, memorizing the combination before pocketing the key.

Chad stripped down and took his first real shower in four days, washing away the accumulated grime and stress of the manhunt while hot water beat against muscles that ached from hours of driving. For a few minutes, he could almost pretend he was just another gym member starting his day, rather than a federal fugitive preparing to walk into a trap.

After dressing in clean clothes from his travel bag, Chad felt marginally more human. He kept only five hundred dollars in cash, his fake ID, and the prepaid phone—nothing that would compromise his mission if he was captured or searched.

Satisfied that his equipment was secure, Chad walked the two blocks to the internet café. The bell above the door chimed as he entered, and a middle-aged Cuban woman behind bulletproof glass looked up from her magazine. Behind her, two dozen computer terminals were arranged in cubicles that provided privacy for users who valued discretion. The air was thick with cigarette smoke and the rapid-fire Spanish of Cuban exiles conducting business that wouldn't appear on any tax returns.

"Thirty dollars for two hours," she announced in accented English. "Cash only. No ID required."

Chad paid and took a terminal in the back corner, positioning himself where he could monitor the entrance while maintaining visual privacy from other users. The computer was older but functional, with internet access that routed through multiple proxy servers to obscure user identity.

Chad began researching private aviation services in the Miami area, looking for companies that offered charter flights with minimal documentation requirements. After an hour of fruitless searching, Chad decided he needed local intelligence rather than internet research.

He walked to the counter and ordered a café cubano from the woman, her suspicious eyes tracking his movements as she poured the sweet, strong coffee into a small cup. As he waited, Chad noticed her glancing at him repeatedly, her expression shifting from general wariness to specific recognition.

"Disculpe," said a voice behind him.

Chad turned to find a middle-aged Hispanic man in worn work clothes, his weathered hands wrapped around a cup of coffee, dark eyes holding the patient wariness of someone who'd learned to evaluate strangers carefully.

"You are looking for charter flights, yes?" the man continued in accented English. "I hear you asking questions at the computer."

Chad studied the man's face, reading genuine curiosity rather than threat. "Depends who's asking."

"My name is Carlos Hernandez. I drive taxi in this city for fifteen years. I see many things, remember some of them. But man asking about private flights to Caribbean? That one gets my attention."

Chad felt his pulse quicken but kept his expression neutral. "Why's that?"

"Because I know pilot who provides such services. Very discrete, cash only, no questions asked." Carlos sipped his coffee, his eyes never leaving Chad's face. "Two weeks ago, I drive Mexican man to his airfield. Expensive clothes, military bearing, cash fare to Homestead. No luggage, no conversation, just an address."

Chad's mind raced. Javier. Carlos had driven Javier to Ricardo's operation.

"This pilot, what's his name?"

"Ricardo Valdez. Former Navy pilot who lost his wings for smuggling cocaine out of Panama in the '90s. Now he runs charter flights for people who need to travel without paperwork." Carlos leaned closer. "Mexican man, he was very interested in flights to Cayman Islands."

Elena. Chad felt pieces clicking into place. Javier hadn't stayed in Miami—he'd used it as a waystation, connecting with a smuggling pilot who could take him to Elena Ramirez in the Caymans.

The woman behind the counter brought Chad his café cubano, setting it down with a knowing smile that made his skin crawl. But he was too focused on Carlos's intelligence to pay attention to her expression.

"Can you arrange a meeting with this Ricardo?" Chad asked, taking a sip of the strong, sweet coffee.

Carlos smiled, the expression of someone who'd found a profitable customer. "For the right price, yes. Ricardo is very careful about new clients, but I can vouch for serious customers."

Chad took a long sip of the strong, sweet coffee while processing this breakthrough. Finally, a direct connection to Elena's location.

At that moment, a younger man at a corner table suddenly looked up from his phone, his eyes widening as he stared at Chad. The man's gaze flicked between Chad's face and something on his phone screen—probably a news app with Chad's photo.

"¡Dios mío!" the young man shouted, standing abruptly and pointing at Chad. "¡Es él! The FBI man from the television! ¡El fugitivo! There's a fifty thousand dollar reward!"

The café went silent. Every head turned toward Chad as the young man continued shouting in rapid Spanish, his phone held high, clearly showing a news photo from Holmes' media campaign.

Chad started to stand, but suddenly felt dizzy. The café spun around him, and his legs felt like rubber. He reached for the counter to steady himself, but his hand wouldn't respond properly.

The café cubano. The woman behind the counter was watching him with calculating interest rather than surprise, her suspicious eyes now making perfect sense. She'd recognized him and drugged his coffee.

"FBI tip line? Yes, I want to report the fugitive agent Chad Lloyd," the young man was saying into his phone in accented English. "He is here in Miami, Little Havana, right now... and the lady put something in his coffee to keep him here for you!"

Chad tried to reach for his weapon, but his arms wouldn't obey. The world tilted sideways as he collapsed, his vision blurring as faces surrounded him. Carlos was still there, but his expression had changed from helpful concern to greedy satisfaction as he pocketed Chad's remaining cash and his weapon.

"Sorry, amigo," Carlos said, shrugging apologetically. "But FBI is offering fifty thousand dollars reward. That's more money than I make in two years driving taxi."

The woman behind the counter was already on another phone,

speaking rapidly in Spanish, probably coordinating with other customers to make sure Chad couldn't escape before federal agents arrived.

Chad's last conscious thought before the darkness took him was that he'd been brought down not by Elena's sophisticated planning, but by simple greed and the reward money Holmes had put on his head.

The manhunt was about to end not with Elena's elaborate trap, but with opportunistic Cuban immigrants who saw fifty thousand dollars walking into their café and decided to collect.

Chapter 61

PHOENIX Operations Center
FBI Headquarters

Agent Janet Holmes stood before the nearly empty operations center, watching the tactical displays with Agent Thornton as her phone buzzed with an incoming call from Miami Field Office. After the mass exodus of her task force the night before, only two agents remained to coordinate the largest manhunt in Bureau history.

"Agent Holmes, this is SAC Rodriguez in Miami," the voice announced. "We've got your fugitive."

Holmes felt a surge of vindication that made her momentarily dizzy. "Chad Lloyd is in custody?"

"Affirmative. Apprehended at an internet café in Little Havana approximately two hours ago. Subject was drugged by civilians attempting to claim the reward money and was unconscious when our agents arrived." Rodriguez's voice carried professional skepticism. "Agent Holmes, I need to ask—what's the official authorization for this arrest? My agents are requesting written orders from Director Huntington's office."

Holmes felt her stomach clench, but forced confidence into her voice. "SAC Rodriguez, Agent Lloyd is a federal fugitive who has made explicit threats against cartel organizations. The PHOENIX task force has broad discretionary authority to pursue threats to federal personnel."

"That's not what I asked. I need specific authorization for arresting a federal agent. This isn't standard procedure."

"SAC Rodriguez, time is critical. I need Lloyd transported to

Washington immediately for interrogation. Every hour he remains in Miami increases the risk of cartel retaliation or escape attempts." Holmes moved to the communications console. "I'm arranging federal transport. Have your agents bring Lloyd to Miami International within the hour."

A long pause. "Agent Holmes, I'm going to need documentation of this arrest authority before I release a federal agent to your custody."

"SAC Rodriguez, Agent Lloyd has been featured on national news as a dangerous fugitive. The Attorney General's office is monitoring this situation personally." Holmes played her strongest card, hoping Rodriguez wouldn't verify the claim. "Any delay in transport could compromise national security operations."

Another pause, then reluctant agreement. "Fine. But I want written confirmation of this authority within twenty-four hours, or I'm filing a complaint with OPR."

Holmes ended the call and immediately contacted federal aviation to arrange prisoner transport. But first, she had another call to make—one that would secure her financial future.

Holmes walked to her private office and closed the door, then dialed an encrypted number she'd memorized weeks ago.

"Elena, it's Janet. I have good news."

Elena Ramirez's voice came through the satellite connection with barely concealed satisfaction. "Tell me Chad Lloyd is no longer a problem."

"He's in federal custody as of two hours ago. Captured in Miami, currently being transported to Washington for interrogation." Holmes felt a surge of professional pride. "Your intelligence about his likely destinations was accurate."

"Excellent work, Agent Holmes. Chad Lloyd has been a persistent thorn in my operations. Having him neutralized by his own government is... poetic justice."

Holmes leaned back in her chair, savoring the moment of complete victory. "Elena, about our financial arrangement..."

"Of course. Twenty percent of our quarterly revenue, as agreed. Fifty million dollars will be transferred to your Cayman Islands account within the hour." Elena's voice carried the satisfaction of someone who'd just eliminated her most dangerous enemy. "Consider it a bonus for exceptional service."

Fifty million dollars. More money than Holmes could earn in twenty lifetimes of federal service, payment for ensuring that Elena's cartel operations could continue without interference from federal agents seeking justice for murdered families.

Holmes ended the call and immediately checked her offshore banking app, watching as fifty million dollars appeared in her account. The money Elena paid her to sabotage federal investigations into cartel terrorism was more than the entire annual budget of the PHOENIX task force.

She returned to the operations center where Agent Thornton was coordinating Chad's transport, knowing that she'd just been paid an enormous fortune for capturing the one federal agent who'd been successfully hunting Elena Ramirez.

Chad would arrive in Washington within four hours, and she would finally have the opportunity to prove that her aggressive manhunt had been necessary to prevent a rogue agent from destabilizing federal operations.

"Agent Thornton, I want a full media setup prepared for Lloyd's arrival," Holmes announced. "Press conference room, camera crews, the works. This arrest proves that the PHOENIX task force successfully prevented a potential federal catastrophe."

Thornton looked uncomfortable. "Ma'am, shouldn't we coordinate with Director Huntington's office before conducting media operations?"

"Agent Thornton, Director Huntington will want to see results. When we present Agent Lloyd in custody, along with evidence of his rogue operations and cartel threats, the Director will understand that our aggressive response was justified."

Holmes began drafting press releases while coordinating Lloyd's transport, envisioning the media coverage that would establish her as the federal agent who'd captured a dangerous rogue operative. The fact that she'd done it without authorization would be forgotten once the results proved her judgment had been correct.

Chad Lloyd would arrive in Washington as living proof that Agent

Janet Holmes had the tactical intelligence to prevent federal catastrophes before they occurred.

Even if she'd had to operate outside normal channels to achieve those results.

Chapter 62

C had's eyes opened slowly, his vision blurry and his head pounding from whatever drug they'd used to keep him unconscious. The steady drone of aircraft engines filled his ears, and he could feel the subtle vibration of high-altitude flight through the cabin floor.

He was handcuffed to an airline seat, wrists secured behind his back with federal restraints that cut into his skin with every movement. Two FBI agents sat across the aisle, their weapons visible but relaxed—they were transporting a drugged prisoner, not expecting resistance from someone barely conscious.

Chad tested his restraints carefully, finding them professionally applied with no hope of escape. His mouth felt like sandpaper, and every muscle in his body ached from the combination of drugs and awkward positioning during transport.

"Agent Lloyd's awake," one of the agents announced into his radio. "ETA to Reagan National in ninety minutes."

Chad's mind began clearing as the drugs wore off, allowing him to process his situation. He'd been captured in Miami through pure bad luck and greed, drugged by civilians seeking reward money rather than caught through superior federal tactics. Now he was being transported to Washington for whatever show trial Holmes had planned.

But Elena Ramirez was still free in the Cayman Islands, still planning whatever terrorist operations she'd been coordinating when Chad's hunt was interrupted. The real enemy remained untouched while the federal government congratulated itself on capturing one of its own agents.

"Where are we going?" Chad asked, his voice hoarse from the drugs.

"FBI Headquarters," one of the agents replied. "Agent Holmes wants to debrief you personally."

Chad almost laughed at the irony. Holmes had spent weeks hunting him instead of hunting the terrorists who'd actually murdered federal families, and now she wanted to interrogate him about his investigation into Elena Ramirez's operations.

What about Elena Ramirez?" Chad asked. "While you've been hunting me, she's been planning more attacks on federal personnel."

The agents exchanged glances, clearly uncomfortable with the political implications of their prisoner transport mission.

"Agent Lloyd, that's above our pay grade," the senior agent replied. "We're just following orders to transport you safely to Washington."

Chad leaned back in his seat, feeling the weight of complete failure. As the aircraft began its descent toward Washington, he realized his capture might actually serve Elena's purposes perfectly. With him in federal custody, painted as a dangerous rogue agent, Elena could continue her terrorist operations without interference from the one man who'd been successfully tracking her organization.

The system had actively protected the killers by eliminating their hunter.

Chad closed his eyes and tried to prepare himself for whatever media circus Holmes had planned. She would parade him as proof of her competence, evidence that the federal government could control its own personnel even when they sought justice outside legal boundaries.

All while the real terrorists laughed from their Caribbean safe haven, knowing that the American justice system was too broken to threaten them.

The aircraft banked toward Reagan National Airport, carrying a federal agent whose only crime had been loving his family enough to seek justice when his own government failed to provide it.

Below them, Washington D.C. sprawled in the afternoon sunlight, the seat of a government that had just captured one of its own heroes while allowing the real villains to escape unpunished.

Chad Lloyd was going home to face charges for hunting the people who'd murdered his wife and daughter.

And Elena Ramirez was probably toasting his capture with champagne served on her Caribbean terrace.

Chapter 63

Ramirez Compound
Grand Cayman

Elena Ramirez stood at the head of the mahogany conference table, champagne flute raised toward the most dangerous gathering of criminal minds in modern history. Around her sat the leaders of every major cartel in the hemisphere, alongside the operational commanders of Al-Qaeda, ISIS, and Taliban forces—fifty-three of the world's most wanted terrorists and drug lords united in her marble-floored conference room.

"Gentlemen," Elena announced in perfect English, her voice carrying the authority that had built a criminal empire, "I give you a toast to the elimination of our greatest threat. Chad Lloyd, the American federal agent who has been hunting our operations for months, is now in the custody of his own government."

The room erupted in appreciative laughter and applause. Miguel Treviño of Los Zetas raised his glass with a gold-toothed grin. "To the Americans who hunt their own heroes while protecting their enemies!"

"To Agent Janet Holmes," added Abu Hassan, the former ISIS logistics commander, "who has proven that American corruption runs deeper than we imagined."

Elena smiled as fifty-three glasses rose in salute to Chad Lloyd's capture. "My friends, what we accomplish in the next forty-eight hours will reshape the balance of power between criminal organizations and legitimate governments. For too long, we have operated independently, competing for territory and resources while law enforcement agencies coordinate against us."

She activated a wall-mounted display showing satellite imagery of major American cities—New York, Los Angeles, Chicago, Miami, Houston—each marked with operational targets that represented months of intelligence gathering.

"But Chad Lloyd's capture proves that the American government is more interested in politics than protection. While they hunt their own agents, we will demonstrate what coordinated criminal action can accomplish."

Carlos Montenegro, representing the Colombian cartels, leaned forward with predatory interest. "Elena, your intelligence network inside the FBI has been... impressive. Can we rely on continued protection from federal interference?"

"Agent Holmes will continue to misdirect federal investigations away from our operations. The PHOENIX task force has been neutralized as a threat, and Director Huntington remains unaware of our infiltration." Elena pulled up financial data showing cartel revenue streams. "In exchange for twenty percent of our combined quarterly profits, we have purchased immunity from the one federal agency capable of stopping us."

Rashid bin Omar, the Taliban explosives expert who'd killed three hundred American soldiers in Afghanistan, studied the tactical displays with professional appreciation. "Your plan for coordinated infrastructure attacks?"

Elena smiled, the expression of someone who'd spent months planning America's humiliation. "Simultaneous strikes on power grids, transportation hubs, and communication networks in twelve major cities. Your IED expertise combined with our logistical networks will create chaos that makes 9/11 look like a warm-up exercise."

"Casualties?" asked Dr. Hakim Al-Zawahiri, the Syrian chemical weapons specialist.

"Secondary consideration. Our primary objective is demonstrating that American homeland security is an illusion." Elena activated another display showing power grid vulnerabilities. "We're not trying to conquer America—we're trying to prove it can't protect itself."

Rosa Delgado, the ruthless leader of 18th Street, raised her hand. "What about retaliation? The Americans will respond to coordinated attacks."

"Against whom?" Elena's voice carried cold satisfaction. "We'll have plausible deniability through operational compartmentalization. Each attack will appear to be the work of different organizations with different motivations. The Americans will spend months trying to prove coordination while we prepare the next phase."

Javier Morales, recently escaped from federal custody, stood from his position near the window. "Elena, what if Chad Lloyd escapes federal custody? He's proven resourceful in the past."

Elena's expression showed the confidence of someone who'd eliminated every threat to her operations. "Javier, Chad Lloyd won't escape. I have people inside who will make sure Agent Lloyd doesn't live to see the sun rise once he's inside the prison awaiting trial."

She raised her champagne flute again. "My friends, Chad Lloyd sought justice for his murdered family. Instead, he'll die in federal custody while his family's killers reshape the criminal landscape of North America."

The room erupted in applause as Elena outlined the operational timeline for coordinated attacks that would demonstrate the impotence of American law enforcement.

"Phase One begins in two weeks. Simultaneous strikes on electrical infrastructure in six major cities, designed to create rolling blackouts that will paralyze emergency response systems."

Abu Hassan consulted his tablet, reviewing target packages his operatives had been developing for months. "My teams are positioned in New York, Los Angeles, and Miami. Two weeks gives us time to coordinate final positioning and communication protocols with your cartel networks."

"Phase Two follows within forty-eight hours of Phase One," Elena continued. "Transportation infrastructure—airports, train stations, major highways. We'll demonstrate that Americans can't travel safely within their own borders."

Bin Omar nodded approvingly. "Two weeks allows my IED

specialists to complete their final reconnaissance and coordinate timing with the other cells. This level of coordination requires careful preparation."

Elena activated a final display showing the scope of their coordinated operations—a map of the United States marked with dozens of target locations, each representing a carefully planned attack designed to overwhelm federal response capabilities.

"Phase Three is economic warfare. Financial institutions, stock exchanges, federal reserve banks. We'll prove that American economic power is as vulnerable as their physical infrastructure."

Al-Zawahiri's chemical weapons expertise would ensure that some attacks carried casualties designed to maximize psychological impact rather than body count—the kind of terror that changed how entire populations viewed their government's ability to protect them.

"Gentlemen, by this time next week, the United States will understand that designating cartels as terrorist organizations was the greatest strategic mistake in their history." Elena's voice carried the cold fury that had driven her since watching her father die on security footage. "They wanted to treat us as terrorists? We'll show them what real terrorism accomplishes."

The room filled with the excited chatter of criminal masterminds coordinating the largest terrorist operation in American history. Elena watched her guests networking, sharing intelligence, and finalizing operational details that would bring war to American soil.

As Elena moved through the room, accepting congratulations and finalizing attack timelines, she reflected on the beautiful irony of the situation. The man who'd killed her father was now in federal custody, painted as a terrorist by the same government that was unknowingly protecting the actual terrorists.

Tomorrow, the real war would begin. And America would learn that some enemies were too smart to be caught by a system more interested in hunting heroes than hunting villains.

Outside the conference room windows, the Caribbean sunset painted the sky blood red—a fitting omen for what Elena Ramirez and her allies were about to unleash on the country that had killed her father.

270

Chapter 64

Director Huntington's Office
FBI Headquarters

Director Brad Huntington looked up from surveillance reports covering his desk to find his outer office filled with federal agents he recognized as members of the PHOENIX task force. Agent Grey stood at the front of the group, his weathered face showing the grim determination of someone who'd reached the breaking point.

"Agent Grey, what brings the entire task force to my office?" Huntington asked, though the investigation files spread across his desk suggested he had suspicions.

Grey stepped forward, flanked by Agents Ruiz, Kim, Walsh, Martinez, and Sam Belle. "Director, we need to report that Agent Holmes has suspended Agent Belle and myself for questioning her unauthorized manhunt operations. The rest of us have walked out and are requesting immediate transfers out of PHOENIX."

Huntington's expression darkened. "She suspended you for questioning her authority?"

"Yes sir," Sam stepped forward. "Holmes has been conducting an unauthorized manhunt against Agent Chad Lloyd instead of hunting the terrorists who murdered his family. When we objected to hunting a victim instead of criminals, she relieved us of duty."

"This confirms what Deputy Director Walsh has been investigating," Huntington said grimly, gesturing to the files on his desk. "We've been documenting Holmes' unauthorized operations since her disastrous media interview, but I didn't realize she'd moved to suspending her own agents."

"Agent Lloyd isn't a fugitive," Grey added. "He's a federal agent seeking justice for murdered family members while his own task force wastes resources hunting him instead of his family's killers."

Huntington consulted Walsh's investigation reports. "Agents, your testimony confirms every detail of our investigation. Holmes has been operating completely outside her authority."

For the next ten minutes, the task force members outlined Holmes' unauthorized operations - confirming details that matched Walsh's investigation reports. Every unauthorized media appearance, every resource misallocation, every violation of federal procedure had been documented.

"And sir," Martinez added, "Holmes has been conducting unauthorized media interviews, claiming this manhunt has full FBI approval."

"I watched that interview," Huntington replied. "It's what triggered our investigation into her operations."

Huntington reached for his phone and dialed the PHOENIX operations center. "Let me speak with Agent Holmes."

Agent Thornton's voice came through the speaker. "Director, Agent Holmes is currently busy preparing for a press conference. We successfully captured Agent Lloyd in Miami, and she wants to announce it on national television."

The room went silent as Huntington processed what he'd just heard.

"Agent Thornton, when is Agent Lloyd due to arrive at Reagan National?"

"ETA is 1630 hours, sir. Agent Holmes wants the press conference timed for his arrival to maximize media impact."

Sam felt her legs go weak. Chad had been captured. "Director, is Chad injured?"

Huntington's face was turning red with fury. "Agent Thornton, by whose authority was Agent Lloyd arrested?"

"Uh... Agent Holmes said the PHOENIX task force has discretionary authority for threats to federal personnel."

Huntington hung up and immediately dialed another number. "Get me Attorney General Wells. Emergency priority."

Within minutes, AG Monica Wells' voice filled the office through the speakerphone. "Brad, what's the emergency?"

"Monica, I need to know if Agent Chad Lloyd is on any federal fugitive list. PHOENIX task force claims they arrested him under fugitive warrants."

A pause as Wells consulted her databases. "Brad, there's no Chad Lloyd on any federal fugitive list. No warrants, no BOLOs, no federal charges filed. Who told you he was a fugitive?"

"Agent Janet Holmes of my PHOENIX task force. Walsh's investigation shows she's been conducting an unauthorized manhunt for weeks, claiming Lloyd is a rogue agent threatening cartel operations."

Wells' voice grew sharp. "Brad, if Holmes arrested a federal agent without authorization, she's committed multiple federal crimes. False imprisonment, violation of civil rights under color of authority, conspiracy to deprive constitutional rights, unlawful detention, abuse of process..."

"Monica, what can we do about this?"

"We can arrest her for starters. Unauthorized arrest of federal personnel is a federal felony carrying twenty years minimum." Wells' voice carried prosecutorial fury. "Brad, I'm calling the U.S. Marshals Service right now."

Huntington put Wells on hold and addressed his agents. "Walsh's investigation confirms what you're telling me. Chad Lloyd is a victim, not a criminal."

Grey answered immediately. "Chad's a victim, sir. His wife and daughter were murdered by Elena Ramirez's cartel a month ago. He's been investigating their organization while Holmes wasted federal resources hunting him."

"And Holmes has been sabotaging his investigation," Sam added. "She's protected Elena Ramirez by eliminating the one agent successfully tracking her operations."

Huntington returned to Wells. "Monica, I want U.S. Marshals to arrest Holmes and her accomplices during their press conference. We're going to use their own media event to expose this corruption."

"Excellent idea. I'll coordinate with Marshal Jones. How many agents involved?"

"Holmes and Agent Thornton at minimum. Walsh's investigation may reveal others."

"Brad, I'll send four Deputy Marshals to arrest them during the press conference."

Wells paused. "Brad, I also want you to officially exonerate Agent Lloyd during this press conference. Make it clear that he's a victim of unauthorized federal persecution, not a criminal."

Huntington looked at Grey. "Agent Grey, I'm putting you in charge of the PHOENIX task force, effective immediately. Your mission is finding Elena Ramirez, not hunting federal agents."

Grey nodded. "Sir, I'll accept command on one condition. Chad Lloyd gets reinstated with full back pay and a formal apology from the Bureau."

"Done. Agent Lloyd will be fully reinstated the moment he lands at Reagan National."

Sam felt tears of relief streaming down her face. Chad would be free, vindicated, and back where he belonged—hunting the people who'd murdered his family instead of being hunted by his own government.

"Sir," Ruiz spoke up, "what about the media narrative? Holmes has spent weeks painting Chad as a dangerous rogue agent."

Huntington smiled grimly. "Agents, we're about to use Holmes' own press conference to reveal the truth. When those cameras are rolling and she's announcing Chad's capture, U.S. Marshals will arrest her for federal crimes."

"The media will see Holmes being arrested for corruption while we announce that Chad Lloyd is a hero who was wrongfully persecuted by his own government," Wells added through the speaker.

Grey smiled for the first time in weeks. "Sir, what about Elena Ramirez? While Holmes was hunting Chad, Elena's been planning more terrorist attacks."

"Agent Grey, once Chad is released and reinstated, I want him debriefed immediately. Whatever intelligence he's gathered about Elena's operations becomes our highest priority."

Huntington stood and walked to his window, looking out at the city where Chad was about to land as a federal prisoner rather than a federal hero.

"Agents, in thirty minutes we're going to watch Agent Holmes' career end on national television. And then we're going to give Chad Lloyd the resources he needs to find Elena Ramirez."

"Sir," Sam asked quietly, "what if Chad's been injured during transport?"

"Then Agent Holmes will face additional charges for assault on federal personnel." Huntington's voice carried the cold fury of someone who'd discovered massive corruption within his own agency. "Agent Belle, I promise you that Agent Lloyd will receive full medical attention and complete vindication."

As the task force members filed out to prepare for Holmes' downfall, Huntington remained at his window, calculating the scope of the disaster Holmes had created.

In twenty minutes, federal agents would arrest one of his task force leaders for kidnapping a federal agent. But more importantly, Chad Lloyd would finally be free to hunt the terrorists who'd murdered his family.

Justice was about to be served. But it was five weeks late and had required exposing federal corruption to achieve it.

Some victories, Huntington reflected, came at too high a price. But they were still victories.

Chapter 65

Press Conference Room
FBI Headquarters - 2nd Floor

Agent Janet Holmes stood before the mirror in the media preparation room, adjusting her jacket and checking her appearance one final time. In ten minutes, she would face the national media to announce the successful capture of Chad Lloyd, proving that her aggressive manhunt had been necessary to prevent a rogue federal agent from destabilizing counterterrorism operations.

"Agent Holmes," Agent Thornton appeared in the doorway, tablet in hand. "Transport confirms Agent Lloyd has landed at Reagan National. ETA to headquarters is twenty minutes."

Holmes felt a surge of vindication that made her almost giddy. "Perfect timing. The media will see Lloyd arriving in federal custody just as I'm explaining how the PHOENIX task force prevented a potential terrorist incident."

"Ma'am, there are twelve news crews set up in the press room. All the major networks and several independent journalists. This is going to be national coverage."

Holmes smiled, envisioning the career advancement that would follow from successfully capturing a rogue federal agent. "Agent Thornton, today we prove that the FBI can control its own personnel, even when they go off the reservation seeking vigilante justice."

She walked to the press room, noting the impressive array of cameras and reporters that had assembled to cover the capture. Holmes had spent the afternoon briefing key journalists about Chad's "terrorist threats" against cartel organizations, ensuring the narrative would frame his arrest as preventing federal catastrophe rather than federal persecution.

"Ladies and gentlemen," Holmes announced as she approached the podium, "thank you for joining us today. I'm Agent Janet Holmes, Director of the PHOENIX task force, and I'm here to announce the successful capture of federal fugitive, agent Chad Lloyd."

Camera flashes erupted as reporters leaned forward with interest. Holmes had successfully positioned this as a major national security story rather than an internal federal personnel matter.

"Agent Lloyd has been the subject of an intensive federal manhunt following explicit threats he made against the Ramirez cartel organization. Despite his grief over the tragic loss of his family, Agent Lloyd's actions threatened to destabilize years of careful intelligence operations against these criminal networks."

Holmes paused for effect, watching reporters scribble notes about her carefully crafted narrative.

"I want to be clear that while we sympathize with Agent Lloyd's personal tragedy, the federal government cannot allow individual agents to operate outside legal boundaries, regardless of their emotional state or personal motivations."

Her phone buzzed with an incoming call from Director Huntington's office, but Holmes ignored it, focusing on her moment of national prominence.

"Through coordinated federal effort involving multiple agencies, Agent Lloyd was apprehended this morning in Miami while attempting to make contact with illegal smuggling operators. He is currently being transported to Washington for interrogation and processing."

A reporter raised her hand. "Agent Holmes, what specific crimes is Agent Lloyd charged with?"

Holmes had prepared for this question. "Agent Lloyd will face federal charges related to threatening terrorist organizations, interfering with federal investigations, and attempting to conduct unauthorized operations against foreign criminal networks."

Another reporter stood. "Agent Holmes, some sources suggest that Agent Lloyd was investigating the same cartel organization that murdered his family. How do you respond to claims that he was seeking justice rather than revenge?"

"Agent Lloyd's personal motivations are understandable but irrelevant," Holmes replied smoothly. "The federal government has systematic procedures for investigating terrorist organizations. Individual agents cannot be allowed to circumvent those procedures, regardless of their personal stakes in the outcomes."

Holmes' phone continued buzzing with calls from Huntington's office, but she was too focused on her media triumph to answer.

"Agent Lloyd's capture demonstrates that the PHOENIX task force maintains operational control over federal personnel, even in cases involving extreme emotional distress. No agent is above the law, and no personal tragedy justifies operating outside federal authority."

Agent Thornton approached the podium and whispered urgently, "Ma'am, Director Huntington's office has called four times. He wants to speak with you immediately."

Holmes waved her away, not wanting to interrupt her national media moment.

"Ladies and gentlemen, Agent Lloyd's transport should arrive at FBI headquarters within minutes. You'll have the opportunity to see a rogue federal agent brought to justice through proper law enforcement channels."

Holmes felt supremely confident as she fielded questions from the media, unaware that seven floors above her, Director Huntington was coordinating with the Attorney General to ensure that her press conference would end with her own arrest for federal crimes.

"Agent Holmes," a reporter called out, "what's your response to suggestions that resources used to hunt Agent Lloyd could have been better deployed against the actual terrorists who murdered federal families?"

"I reject that characterization completely," Holmes replied firmly. "Agent Lloyd represented a clear and present danger to ongoing federal operations. Every resource deployed in his capture was justified by the threat he posed to national security interests."

As Holmes continued fielding questions, she remained oblivious to the U.S. Marshals gathering in the building's lobby, armed with federal warrants for her arrest on charges of kidnapping, false imprisonment, and violation of civil rights under color of authority.

Her phone buzzed with one final text message from Elena Ramirez: "Watching your press conference. Excellent work neutralizing our biggest threat. Your performance has exceeded all expectations."

Holmes smiled as she read Elena's praise, not realizing that in five minutes, her career would end on national television when federal marshals arrested her for treason.

The moment of glory she'd orchestrated was about to become the moment of her complete destruction.

But for now, Janet Holmes basked in the media attention, believing she'd successfully proven her competence by capturing the one federal agent who'd been effectively hunting America's enemies.

Outside the press room, Chad Lloyd was arriving at FBI headquarters in federal custody, unaware that his vindication was about to unfold on live television.

Justice was coming. But it was wearing a different uniform than Holmes expected.

Chapter 66

Press Conference Room
FBI Headquarters - 2nd Floor

Agent Janet Holmes was wrapping up her final question when the press room doors burst open with the authority of federal law enforcement. Four U.S. Deputy Marshals in tactical gear strode into the room, their badges visible and weapons holstered but ready.

"Agent Janet Holmes," announced Deputy Marshal Jones in a voice that carried to every corner of the room, "you are under arrest for violation of civil rights under color of authority, false imprisonment of a federal agent, kidnapping, and conspiracy to deprive constitutional rights."

The press room erupted in chaos. Camera operators swung their equipment toward the marshals while reporters shouted questions and Holmes stood frozen at the podium, her face cycling through confusion, shock, and dawning horror.

"There must be some mistake," Holmes stammered, but Marshal Jones was already approaching the podium with handcuffs.

"Agent Janet Holmes, you have the right to remain silent. Anything you say can and will be used against you in a court of law."

The second marshal moved toward Agent Thornton, who had gone pale as she realized the scope of the disaster unfolding on national television.

"Agent Thornton, you are also under arrest as an accessory to the unlawful detention of Agent Chad Lloyd."

"This is insane!" Holmes shouted as Marshal Jones secured handcuffs around her wrists. "I'm conducting authorized federal operations!"

"Agent Holmes," Marshal Jones replied loudly enough for the cameras to capture, "Agent Chad Lloyd was never a federal fugitive. You conducted an unauthorized manhunt against a federal agent whose only crime was investigating the terrorists who murdered his family."

The press room exploded with questions as reporters realized they were witnessing a complete reversal of the story they'd been covering.

"Are you saying Agent Lloyd is innocent?" shouted a correspondent.

"Agent Lloyd is a victim of unauthorized federal persecution," Marshal Jones announced to the cameras. "He will be fully exonerated and reinstated with back pay and a formal apology from the FBI."

Holmes struggled against the handcuffs as the enormity of her situation became clear. "You don't understand! Lloyd was threatening cartel operations! He was going to compromise federal intelligence!"

Director Huntington approached Holmes and held out his hand. "Agent Holmes, I'll need your phone and credentials."

"I don't have to give you anything!" Holmes protested, but Marshal Jones nodded to Huntington.

"Ma'am, Director Huntington has authority to confiscate evidence," the marshal explained as he retrieved Holmes' phone from her jacket pocket.

Huntington unlocked the device and immediately saw the text message that had arrived during the press conference: "Watching your press conference. Excellent work neutralizing our biggest threat. Your performance has exceeded all expectations. - E.R."

Huntington's face went white as he showed the message to Attorney General Wells. Wells read it twice, her expression shifting from professional anger to absolute fury.

"Elena Ramirez," Wells said quietly, then looked up at the cameras. "Agent Holmes has been receiving communications from the terrorist who murdered 284 federal family members."

She turned to Marshal Jones with prosecutorial fury. "Add treason to that list of charges. Agent Holmes has been collaborating with foreign terrorists while hunting the federal agents investigating them."

The press room erupted in chaos as reporters realized the story had just become even more explosive—a federal agent working for the very terrorists she was supposed to be hunting.

"Agent Holmes," Wells announced to the cameras, "you're now facing the death penalty for providing material support to terrorist organizations and conspiracy to commit treason against the United States."

"Agent Holmes, the only person who compromised federal operations was you," announced Director Huntington as he entered the press room, flanked by Attorney General Wells and Agent Grey.

The cameras swung toward Huntington as he approached the podium Holmes had just vacated.

"Ladies and gentlemen, I'm Director Brad Huntington of the FBI. I'm here to announce that Agent Janet Holmes has been conducting unauthorized operations for weeks without proper oversight or legal authority."

Wells stepped forward to address the media. "I'm Attorney General Monica Wells. Agent Holmes will face federal charges carrying a minimum of twenty years in prison for the unlawful arrest and detention of Agent Chad Lloyd."

"What about Agent Lloyd's status?" called a reporter.

"Agent Lloyd is a hero who was wrongfully persecuted by his own government," Huntington announced. "He will be immediately released, fully reinstated, and given every resource necessary to continue his investigation into the terrorist organization that murdered his family."

Holmes was being led away in handcuffs when she turned back toward the cameras, her composure completely shattered. "You're making a mistake! Lloyd is dangerous! He'll destabilize everything we've built!"

"The only thing Agent Lloyd will destabilize," Agent Grey announced as he took his position at the podium, "is the terrorist organization that murdered 284 federal family members while Agent Holmes protected them by hunting their victims."

The press room erupted with new questions as reporters realized the story had completely reversed—the supposed rogue agent was actually a hero, while the federal agent who'd captured him was the real criminal.

As Holmes and Thornton were escorted from the building in

handcuffs, their arrest broadcast live on every major news network, Director Huntington outlined the truth about Chad's investigation and Holmes' corruption.

"Agent Lloyd has been investigating Elena Ramirez's cartel organization—the same group that murdered his wife and daughter. While he was gathering intelligence on this terrorist network, Agent Holmes wasted federal resources hunting him instead of hunting his family's killers."

Wells added, "We have evidence suggesting that Agent Holmes may have been receiving payments from criminal organizations to sabotage federal investigations. The scope of her corruption is still being determined."

Outside FBI headquarters, Chad Lloyd's transport vehicle was pulling up to the main entrance, where instead of facing charges for terrorism, he would be greeted as a vindicated federal agent whose only crime had been seeking justice for his murdered family.

The press conference that was supposed to demonstrate Holmes' competence had instead exposed her as a corrupt agent who'd betrayed her oath to protect and serve. And Chad Lloyd, painted for weeks as a dangerous rogue operative, was about to be revealed as the hero the media coverage had tried to destroy.

Justice was being served live on national television. But it was wearing a different face than anyone had expected.

As Holmes disappeared into federal custody, Elena Ramirez's protection within the American government disappeared with her. The real hunt for the terrorists was about to begin in earnest.

And this time, Chad Lloyd would have the full resources of the federal government behind him instead of hunting him.

Chapter 67

FBI Headquarters
Main Entrance

The federal transport's engine ticked as it cooled in the humid Washington afternoon, its armored bulk casting a shadow across the limestone steps of the J. Edgar Hoover Building. Chad Lloyd sat in the rear compartment, steel cuffs biting into his wrists, the taste of whatever Mickey Finn they'd slipped him in Miami still coating his tongue like copper pennies and regret.

Through the bulletproof glass, he could see the building where he'd served for twelve years—first as a green agent fresh from Quantico, then as a seasoned investigator, finally as a counterterrorism specialist who knew the weight of classified secrets. Now he was returning in chains, branded a rogue agent by his own government.

But something was wrong with the picture.

Instead of the media circus he'd expected—news trucks, photographers with telephoto lenses, reporters shoving microphones at his face—Chad saw Agent Grey standing at the main entrance with what looked suspiciously like a smile. Sam Belle flanked him on the left, tears streaming down her face but her posture relaxed rather than tense. The other PHOENIX task force members formed a loose semicircle behind them, and not one of them looked like they were there to witness a perp walk.

"What the hell is this?" Chad muttered, his voice hoarse from the drugs and the dry recycled air of the transport.

The rear doors opened with a hydraulic hiss, and one of his escorts

—a young agent with kind eyes who'd been apologetic during the entire flight from Miami—stepped up to the vehicle.

"Chad Lloyd," the agent announced, but his tone carried respect rather than the cold authority of a federal arrest, "you're free to go. All charges have been dropped and you've been fully reinstated to active duty."

Chad blinked hard, wondering if the drugs were causing hallucinations. "Come again?"

"Agent Janet Holmes has been arrested on federal charges including treason, bribery, and conspiracy to commit terrorism." The agent's key turned in the handcuff locks with sharp metallic clicks. "Sir, on behalf of the Miami Field Office, I apologize for what you've been put through. We were following orders we now know were illegal."

The cuffs fell away, leaving red welts on Chad's wrists that felt like badges of vindication. He stepped out of the transport on legs that trembled—not from the drugs, but from the sudden rush of blood returning to extremities that had been bound for hours.

Sam was already running toward him, her composure finally breaking after weeks of maintaining her cover. She hit him like a linebacker, her arms wrapping around his chest with desperate strength, and Chad felt something inside him that had been frozen since Lana and Casey's murder finally begin to thaw.

"Chad, God, I'm so sorry," she whispered against his chest, her voice muffled by his shirt. "Holmes was working for Elena. She's been protecting the people who killed your family for fifty million dollars."

Chad held her tightly, breathing in the familiar scent of her shampoo —something normal in a world that had gone completely insane. "Holmes was on Elena's payroll?"

"The Attorney General found encrypted communications on her phone. Banking records showing wire transfers from shell companies Elena controls." Grey approached them with the measured pace of someone delivering news that would reshape everything. "Janet Holmes sold out the United States government to protect a narco-terrorist who murdered federal agents and their families."

Chad felt his knees go weak, and Sam's grip tightened to keep him steady. The weight of vindication hit him like a physical blow—all those weeks of being hunted, of having his own government treat him like a terrorist, of watching the media paint him as a rogue agent consumed by revenge. All of it because the person leading the investigation was being paid to ensure it failed.

His secure phone—returned with his personal effects by the apologetic Miami agents—began vibrating against his chest. The caller ID showed a number he recognized but had given up hope of seeing: Robert and Marie Thompson, Lana's parents.

He'd called them exactly once after the funeral, a conversation that had ended with them blaming him for not protecting their daughter and granddaughter. Every attempt since had gone straight to voicemail, his apologies and explanations echoing into the void of their grief and anger.

"Lloyd," he answered quietly, stepping slightly away from Sam but keeping one hand on her shoulder.

"Chad, we... we're watching the news." Marie Thompson's voice carried the weight of tears and something else—shame, maybe, or regret. "They're showing Agent Holmes being arrested. They're saying she was working for the people who killed Lana and Casey."

Chad closed his eyes, feeling twenty years of military training struggle to contain the emotion threatening to overwhelm him. "Marie—"

"No, Chad, please let us say this." Robert Thompson's voice came through the phone's speaker, heavy with the kind of regret that settles in a man's chest and never leaves. "We blamed you when you were the only one fighting for justice. We watched that FBI agent on television calling you dangerous, saying you were threatening the investigation, and we believed her instead of believing you."

"You were grieving," Chad said softly. "You needed someone to blame."

"That's no excuse." Marie's voice grew stronger, finding steel beneath the tears. "You were hunting the people who murdered our baby girl while we were condemning you for it. We want to apologize, and we want to support you while you finish what you started."

Chad had to lean against the transport vehicle, overwhelmed by the emotional whiplash of the last thirty minutes. From federal prisoner to vindicated agent, from condemned son-in-law to supported family member. The world had flipped upside down while he wasn't looking.

"Chad," Director Huntington approached with Attorney General Wells, their faces carrying the kind of gravity reserved for matters of national security. "I owe you a formal apology on behalf of the Federal Bureau of Investigation. You've been wrongfully persecuted by your own government while seeking justice for murdered federal agents."

"Sir, what matters now is stopping Elena before she can execute whatever she's been planning." Chad straightened, feeling operational focus return as the emotional storm settled into controlled determination.

Wells stepped forward, her hair catching the afternoon sunlight. "Agent Lloyd, you have unlimited resources and complete operational authority to pursue Elena Ramirez wherever that pursuit takes you. No bureaucratic obstacles, no jurisdictional limitations, no budget constraints."

"Including foreign territory?" Chad asked. "Because Elena's in the Cayman Islands."

"The CIA will provide full operational support," Wells replied without hesitation. "Elena Ramirez has committed acts of terrorism against United States citizens on American soil. Geography won't protect her."

Chad nodded, his mind already shifting into mission planning mode. "The next step is returning to Miami. I need to locate Ricardo, the pilot who flew Javier to the Caymans. He's the only lead we have to Elena's exact location and operational security."

"Full Miami Field Office support," Grey confirmed. "Plus I can have two FBI SWAT teams positioned in Nassau for rapid deployment if the situation requires tactical intervention."

"The problem is we're starting from behind," Chad said, the operational reality settling over him. "Elena's had weeks of freedom while I was being hunted. She could have moved locations, changed security protocols, coordinated with other organizations."

Grey nodded grimly. "Which is why the Ricardo lead is critical. If he flew Javier recently, his flight logs might be our only current intelligence on Elena's position."

"And if she's smart—which she is—she'll be expecting us to follow that lead." Chad's jaw tightened.

Sam squeezed his hand, her fingers intertwining with his in a gesture that felt like an anchor in the chaos. "This time you won't be alone."

Chad looked around at the faces surrounding him—his vindicated team, his apologetic in-laws driving south from Philadelphia, his reinstated authority backed by unlimited resources. For weeks, he'd been a man against the world, fighting shadows and ghosts while his own government hunted him like prey.

Now the tables had turned, and Elena Ramirez was about to face the full weight of American justice with Chad Lloyd as its instrument.

Chapter 68

PHOENIX Operations Center
FBI Headquarters

Chad had stood before the tactical displays in the PHOENIX operations center, but this time as the lead investigator rather than the hunted target. The room buzzed with legitimate activity—intelligence analysts tracking Elena Ramirez's financial networks, communication specialists monitoring cartel frequencies, and tactical planners coordinating with CIA assets in the Caribbean.

Agent Grey approached with a steaming cup of coffee and a briefing folder. "Chad, we've got everything arranged for Miami. SAC Rodriguez is personally coordinating support, and he's very apologetic about yesterday's arrest."

Chad accepted the coffee, noting how surreal it felt to be back in the operations center as a colleague rather than a fugitive. "What about Ricardo's location?"

"We've identified three private airfields in the Homestead area where he could be operating. Miami field office has surveillance teams positioned to avoid spooking him if he's still in the area."

Sam approached from the communications console, tablet in hand. "Chad, I've been tracking financial flows into the Cayman Islands over the past month. There's been massive movement of money from cartel organizations, terrorist groups, and several shell companies we can't identify yet."

"How massive?"

"Eighty-five million dollars in the past four weeks. That's not normal operational funding—that's coordination money for something big."

Chad studied the financial data, noting the pattern of payments from organizations that normally competed rather than cooperated. "Elena's paying for cooperation between groups that usually kill each other."

"Which suggests she's planning something that benefits everyone involved," Grey added. "Common enemy, shared objectives."

Chad's secure phone buzzed with an incoming call from Director Huntington.

"Agent Lloyd, I wanted to confirm your mission parameters before you deploy. You have unlimited operational authority, but I need to understand your tactical approach."

"Sir, the primary objective is intelligence gathering through Ricardo. We need Elena's exact location, the scope of her operation, and her timeline." Chad consulted his notes. "Secondary objective is assessing the threat level and determining what resources we'll need for interdiction."

"And if you encounter immediate threats to American security?"

"We neutralize them, sir. But I'd prefer to gather complete intelligence before taking action. Elena's operation appears to involve multiple terrorist organizations. I want to know what we're up against before we engage."

Huntington's voice carried approval. "Excellent approach. Agent Lloyd, you also have authorization to recruit local assets if necessary. Ricardo may require financial incentives to cooperate."

Chad smiled grimly. "Sir, I think Ricardo will be very motivated to cooperate once he understands his legal exposure for transporting terrorists."

"I'm deploying you, Agent Belle, and Agent Grey to the Caymans once you locate Elena's position. The rest of your team will establish operations in Miami to provide intelligence support and coordinate with our tactical assets."

Chad looked around the operations center at the analysts and specialists who would be supporting his mission from stateside. "I really wish we could deploy the entire team, sir, but I understand that some of them lack the tactical skills needed for this type of operation. We'll need to correct that for future missions."

"Agreed," Huntington replied. "But for now, your core team has the field experience necessary for reconnaissance in hostile territory. What's the status on those SWAT teams?"

"Two teams are deploying to Nassau this morning. HRT is on standby at Quantico. If you determine that Elena's operation requires immediate action, we can have tactical assets in the Caymans within four hours."

After ending the call, Chad gathered Grey and Sam near the main tactical display while the rest of the team continued their preparations. "Alright, it's going to be just the three of us going into the Caymans. The analysts and technical specialists will run support from Miami."

Sam checked her equipment bag, noting the difference between supporting Chad's mission and sabotaging Holmes' manhunt. "We'll have real-time communication with the Miami operations center, financial tracking through Treasury, and legal authority from Justice. This is how investigations should work."

"Let's hope Ricardo is feeling cooperative," Grey added. "Because if Elena's coordinating something involving eighty-five million dollars and multiple terrorist organizations, we need to know about it fast."

Chad turned to address the full team. "People, you'll be establishing our forward operations base in Miami. I need continuous intelligence analysis, communication intercepts, and tactical coordination with our assets in Nassau. When we go into the Caymans, you'll be our lifeline."

Agent Kim looked up from her workstation. "Chad, we'll have real-time satellite coverage and drone surveillance coordinated through Langley. You won't be going in blind."

"Financial tracking will continue from Miami," another analyst added. "If Elena moves money or resources while you're in country, we'll know immediately."

Chad's phone buzzed with a text message from Robert and Marie: "Chad, we're proud of you. Get the people who killed our daughter. We love you."

For the first time since Lana and Casey's murder, Chad felt like he had a family supporting his mission rather than condemning it. "Team, Elena Ramirez has had weeks to plan while the FBI was hunting the wrong person. Time to correct that mistake."

Grey and Sam gathered their gear while the rest of the team prepared for deployment to Miami. Chad paused at the tactical displays showing Elena's financial networks and terrorist connections.

"Three of us going into the Caymans," Sam said quietly. "Think that's enough?"

Chad looked at the data showing eighty-five million dollars in coordination money and connections to multiple terrorist organizations. "It'll have to be. We're not going in to fight an army—we're going in to gather intelligence so we can bring the right army to the fight."

Soon, those displays would show Elena's compound in the crosshairs of American justice. But first, they had to find Ricardo and learn exactly what they were up against.

Chapter 69

Federal Aviation Terminal
Miami International Airport

The FBI Gulfstream touched down at Miami International under crystal blue skies, carrying a six-person team with unlimited federal authority and complete intelligence support. Chad looked out the aircraft window at the city where he'd been captured just thirty-six hours earlier, noting how different everything felt with proper authorization and backup.

SAC Rodriguez met them on the tarmac with a convoy of federal vehicles and a briefing folder thick with overnight intelligence gathering.

"Agent Lloyd, I owe you a personal apology for yesterday's arrest," Rodriguez said as they walked toward the vehicles. "We had no idea Holmes was operating without authorization."

"SAC Rodriguez, what matters now is finding Ricardo and Elena. What's your intelligence on local aviation operations?"

"We've identified Ricardo Valdez operating out of Homestead Executive Airport. Small operation, cash transactions, minimal paperwork. Exactly the kind of service that would appeal to people avoiding federal oversight."

They climbed into the lead vehicle, where Rodriguez spread aerial photographs across the center console. "Ricardo's got a hangar at the south end of the field, away from commercial traffic. Our surveillance teams report he's been there since dawn, working on a twin-engine Cessna."

"Before we approach Ricardo, I need to make a stop," Chad

interrupted. "When I was captured yesterday, I secured some equipment at a 24-Hour Fitness in Little Havana. Off-the-books gear that might be useful if this operation escalates."

Rodriguez raised an eyebrow. "What kind of equipment?"

"Everything I'd need for independent operations." Chad met Rodriguez's stare. "Gear that's not traceable to federal sources if we need plausible deniability."

Sam leaned forward with interest. "Chad, you cached equipment before going to the café?"

"Basic operational security. Never walk into an unknown situation carrying everything you can't afford to lose." Chad pulled up GPS coordinates on his phone. "The gym is ten minutes from here. I can retrieve everything while your teams maintain surveillance on Ricardo."

Rodriguez nodded approvingly. "Smart thinking. If we're dealing with a terrorist summit, having these kind of assets could be valuable."

"What exactly are we talking about?" Grey asked.

"Everything Tony provided for independent operations." Chad's expression grew grim. "If Elena's compound is heavily defended, federal assets might not be enough."

Rodriguez redirected the convoy toward Little Havana. "Agent Lloyd, I'm impressed by your operational planning. Most agents would have carried everything into that café."

"Most agents haven't been hunted by their own government for weeks," Chad replied. "You learn to think several moves ahead when everyone's trying to arrest you."

Twenty minutes later, Chad emerged from the 24-Hour Fitness carrying a heavy duffel bag that contained enough firepower to assault a small fortress. He loaded it into the federal vehicle while Rodriguez and his team maintained discrete perimeters.

"Anything else we need to know about your independent operations?" Rodriguez asked as they drove toward Homestead.

"Just that Elena Ramirez is about to learn what happens when you murder federal families and think you can hide behind geography."

They climbed back into the lead vehicle, where Rodriguez spread aerial photographs across the center console. "Now, about Ricardo's hangar at the south end of the field..."

"Any indication he knows about yesterday's events?"

"Negative. He's been focused on aircraft maintenance, no unusual communications or movements." Rodriguez consulted his tablet. "We've got the airfield under discrete surveillance, but we haven't approached him yet per your instructions."

Chad studied the photographs, noting the isolated location and single access road that would make Ricardo's hangar perfect for discrete conversations. "What about his background?"

"Former Navy pilot, discharged in 1995 for smuggling cocaine out of Panama. Lost his commercial license, now operates under Part 91 regulations for private charters. Clean record since then, but specializes in Caribbean flights with minimal documentation."

Sam reviewed financial records on her laptop. "Chad, Ricardo's bank accounts show regular cash deposits over the past month. Someone's been paying him well for regular flights to the Caymans."

"How regular?"

"Twice weekly for the past four weeks. Always the same destination coordinates, always cash payment, always filed as recreational flying rather than charter operations."

Chad felt the familiar surge of operational focus. "Then Ricardo's our direct link to Elena's operation. And he's going to tell us everything he knows about her security arrangements, her timeline, and who else he's been transporting."

The convoy pulled away from the airport, heading toward Homestead and the pilot who held the keys to Elena Ramirez's Caribbean fortress.

Behind them, CIA satellite surveillance was already repositioning over the Cayman Islands, preparing to gather real-time intelligence on whatever terrorist summit Elena had been coordinating while Chad was being hunted by his own government.

The real investigation was finally beginning. And this time, Chad Lloyd had the full resources of the United States government backing his hunt for justice.

Chapter 70

Hangar 47
Homestead Executive Airport

The FBI convoy pulled up to the perimeter of Homestead Executive Airport, where Chad could see the isolated hangar at the south end of the field exactly as Rodriguez had described. A twin-engine Cessna Citation sat outside the building, its cowlings open while a middle-aged Hispanic man worked on the port engine.

"That's Ricardo Valdez," Rodriguez confirmed through binoculars. "Our surveillance teams report he's been here since dawn, performing routine maintenance."

Chad studied the hangar through his own optics, noting the single access road and clear sightlines that would make approach difficult without being detected. "What's the tactical setup?"

"We've got teams positioned at the north and east perimeters, but they're maintaining distance to avoid spooking him. If Ricardo runs, we can intercept, but I'd prefer a cooperative interview."

"He won't run," Chad said with certainty. "Ricardo's been flying criminals to the Caymans for weeks. He knows exactly how much legal trouble he's in."

Sam consulted her tablet, reviewing the financial intelligence they'd gathered. "Chad, Ricardo's been receiving fifty thousand dollars per flight, twice weekly. That's serious money for short-hop Caribbean charters."

"Serious enough that he won't want to lose it by fleeing," Grey added. "But also serious enough that he might be reluctant to cooperate."

Chad shouldered his equipment bag and checked his sidearm. "Let's find out. Rodriguez, I want your teams close enough to provide backup but not visible enough to make Ricardo think this is a takedown operation."

They approached the hangar in a single vehicle, Chad riding in the passenger seat while Grey and Sam flanked him in the back. Rodriguez had positioned his tactical teams for rapid response but kept them out of sight to maintain the impression of a routine federal inquiry.

Ricardo looked up from his engine work as the vehicle approached, his weathered face showing the instant recognition of law enforcement despite their unmarked car. He set down his tools but didn't run, watching the agents emerge with the careful wariness of someone who'd been expecting this conversation.

"Ricardo Valdez?" Chad announced as he approached the aircraft.

"Depends who's asking," Ricardo replied in accented English, wiping grease from his hands with a shop rag.

Chad produced his federal credentials. "Agent Chad Lloyd, FBI. We need to talk about your recent flights to the Cayman Islands."

Ricardo's expression shifted from wariness to resignation. "I run a legitimate charter service. All my flights are properly logged with the FAA."

"Mr. Valdez, we're not here to bust you for paperwork violations," Sam said, stepping forward with a non-threatening posture. "We need information about one of your passengers."

"I don't discuss my clients. Confidentiality is part of the service."

Chad moved closer, his voice carrying the quiet authority of someone who understood exactly what Ricardo was facing. "Mr. Valdez, how familiar are you with federal conspiracy laws?"

"I run a charter service—"

"You've been transporting members of terrorist organizations to foreign territories without reporting to federal authorities." Chad let that sink in before continuing. "That makes you an accessory to international terrorism under the Patriot Act."

Ricardo's face went pale as the scope of his legal exposure became clear.

"However," Chad continued, "we're more interested in the people you've been flying than in prosecuting charter pilots. Cooperation gets you immunity. Silence gets you twenty-five to life in federal prison."

Ricardo looked around the hangar as if considering flight, but Grey had positioned himself to block the exit while maintaining a casual stance.

"What do you want to know?" Ricardo asked quietly.

"Tell us about Elena Ramirez," Chad said. "Where exactly have you been taking her people?"

Ricardo's expression showed genuine fear. "Man, you don't understand what you're dealing with. Elena Ramirez isn't just some cartel boss. She's coordinating something that involves people I never thought I'd see working together."

"What kind of people?"

"Terrorists. Real ones. Not just drug dealers pretending to be dangerous—people who blow up buildings and kill government officials." Ricardo's voice dropped to a whisper. "I've been flying ISIS commanders, Taliban leaders, cartel bosses who normally kill each other on sight."

Sam and Grey exchanged glances as Chad felt pieces clicking into place.

"How many people have you transported?"

"Maybe fifty over the past week. All to the same compound on Grand Cayman. Elena pays cash, no questions asked, but some of these passengers..." Ricardo shuddered. "I've flown drug dealers before. These people are something else entirely."

Chad pulled out his tablet and showed Ricardo satellite imagery of the Cayman Islands. "Show us exactly where you've been landing."

Ricardo pointed to a location on the eastern shore of Grand Cayman, away from the main population centers. "Private airstrip, maybe two miles from Elena's compound. She's got security teams that meet every flight, transport passengers in armored vehicles."

"What kind of security?"

"Military-grade. Armed guards with automatic weapons, body armor, communications equipment. This isn't casual protection—it's professional security for a military operation."

Chad felt his pulse quicken. "Mr. Valdez, how many people are currently at Elena's compound?"

"I don't know exactly, but I've made twenty-six flights in the past 3 days. If they're all still there..." Ricardo calculated quickly. "Maybe fifty, sixty of the most dangerous criminals alive."

Grey leaned forward with professional interest. "What's the timeline? Are you scheduled for more flights?"

"Two more runs this week. Elena wants everyone in place by Friday." Ricardo's expression grew more nervous. "Agent, whatever Elena's planning, it's happening soon. She's been paying double rates for priority scheduling."

"Friday," Chad repeated. "That's three days from now."

Sam consulted her intelligence reports. "Chad, if Elena's gathering fifty-plus terrorist leaders for a coordinated operation..."

"Then we're looking at the largest terrorist summit in history," Chad finished. "Mr. Valdez, we need everything you know about Elena's compound. Security arrangements, personnel counts, operational schedules."

"I can do better than that," Ricardo said, his voice showing the relief of someone who'd finally found a way out of an impossible situation. "I can fly you there."

"Mr. Valdez, if you help us stop Elena Ramirez, the FBI will guarantee your safety and legal immunity. But if you're lying to us..."

"Agent, you don't understand. El Chapo's people killed my wife and children in 1996 because they thought I was working for the DEA." Ricardo's voice carried the weight of old grief. "I've been waiting twenty-eight years for someone to take these people down."

Chad felt a surge of recognition—another man whose family had been murdered by cartels, another victim seeking justice.

"I've been flying Elena's people because I know their routes, their methods, their security arrangements," Ricardo continued. "But I've also been waiting for the right federal agents to give this intelligence to."

"You've been gathering intelligence?" Sam asked.

"For almost thirty years. Every flight, every conversation, every detail about their operations." Ricardo's eyes hardened with long-suppressed fury. "Elena Ramirez thinks she hired a broken pilot who needs money. What she actually hired is someone who's been documenting everything for the day when the right agents would finally come."

Chad studied Ricardo's face, reading genuine determination mixed with decades of suppressed rage. "Ricardo, after you drop us off in the Caymans, would you be willing to sit down with the rest of my team in Miami and give them this intelligence? They'll have your immunity paperwork ready by that time as well."

Ricardo nodded slowly, the weight of three decades finally lifting from his shoulders. "Agent Lloyd, I've been waiting for this conversation my entire adult life. Yes, I'll tell your team everything I know. Every route, every safe house, every contact Elena has used. It's time these bastards paid for what they've done."

"Mr. Valdez, how long does it take to fly to Elena's compound?"

"Two hours and fifteen minutes in the Cessna. But Agent..." Ricardo's voice carried genuine concern. "That compound is a fortress. Elena's got enough security to fight off a small army."

"What's the response time for Elena's security after they hear the plane land?" Chad asked, his tactical mind already calculating operational variables.

Ricardo thought for a moment. "The airstrip is two miles from the main compound through jungle terrain. Security teams meet every flight within five minutes of touchdown—two armored SUVs with three men each. They escort passengers to the compound, but they also control who gets on and off that airstrip."

"So we'd have a five-minute window before armed response arrives?"

"Less than that if they're suspicious. Elena's people monitor radio frequencies, and they've got watchtowers overlooking the airstrip." Ricardo's expression grew more serious. "Agent, if Elena thinks you're federal agents instead of her expected passengers, those security teams will shoot first and identify bodies later."

Chad smiled grimly and patted his equipment bag. "Mr. Valdez, we brought a small army."

"Can you fly the three of us in tonight?" Chad asked, his mind already formulating the tactical approach. "Let us drop off the doors, don't completely stop, turn around and get the hell out of there in under five minutes?"

Ricardo considered the proposal carefully. "The airstrip is long enough for a rolling drop-off. I could touch down, slow to maybe forty knots, you bail out the doors, and I'm airborne again within two minutes."

"What about the security response?"

"If I maintain normal approach protocols and don't deviate from expected flight patterns, they might not realize anything's wrong until I'm already gone." Ricardo's expression showed professional assessment. "But once you're on the ground, you'll have maybe three minutes before those SUVs arrive."

Grey leaned forward. "Three minutes to cover two miles of jungle terrain?"

"No," Chad corrected. "Three minutes to disappear into the jungle and begin tactical approach to the compound. We're not racing them—we're avoiding them."

Sam consulted her tablet. "Chad, what about extraction? If Ricardo drops us off and leaves, how do we get out?"

"We don't," Chad replied simply. "This is a one-way mission until we neutralize Elena and her terrorist summit. Then we call in the cavalry."

Ricardo stepped forward, his voice carrying the determination of someone who'd waited 28 years for this moment. "If you need me, I will come back and extract you. But you have to make that runway secure first, or they will shoot us out of the sky on approach."

Chad studied Ricardo's face, reading genuine commitment mixed with tactical realism. "Mr. Valdez, that's asking you to fly into a combat zone."

"Agent Lloyd, Elena Ramirez and her people have been killing families for decades. If you can stop them, I'll fly through hell to get you out of there." Ricardo's voice hardened. "But I can't help you if those watchtowers are still manned when I come back."

"How would we signal you that the runway is secure?"

"Emergency radio frequency 121.5. Call sign 'Homestead' and I'll know it's you. I can be there within two hours of your call."

Grey nodded approvingly. "That gives us an extraction option if we can clear the immediate area around the airstrip."

Chad felt a surge of respect for the pilot who was willing to risk everything to help stop the people who'd murdered his family.

Chapter 71

Ricardo, what aircraft do you have available besides the Citation? Something with more... cargo capacity?"

Ricardo's eyes lit up with understanding. "I've got a Twin Otter in the next hangar. DHC-6, fully maintained and certified for Caribbean operations. She's what I use for the larger passenger runs."

"Service ceiling?"

"Twenty-five thousand feet, but she's most stable between fifteen and twenty thousand." Ricardo paused, studying Chad's expression. "Agent Lloyd, what kind of special cargo are we talking about?"

Chad turned to Grey and Sam, his tactical mind shifting into a different gear. "What if we don't land at all?"

"What do you mean?" Sam asked.

"HALO insertion. High altitude, low opening parachute jump." Chad looked back at Ricardo. "The Twin Otter has a cargo door, right?"

"Full cargo door, side exit. I've... handled some unusual cargo requirements before." Ricardo's expression showed he was connecting the dots. "Agent Lloyd, are you talking about a parachute insertion?"

"We jump at fifteen thousand feet, deploy chutes at two thousand. That puts us in Elena's compound area without ever touching that airstrip or alerting her security teams." Chad warmed to the idea. "No rolling landing, no three-minute window, no armored SUVs racing to intercept us."

Grey nodded slowly. "It's been a few years since my last jump, but I still remember how. Solo deployment shouldn't be a problem."

Sam's face went pale. "Chad, I... I'm not exactly comfortable with heights. Like, really not comfortable."

"That's why you'll be tandem jumping with me," Chad said, his voice carrying reassurance and authority. "You'll be strapped to my harness. All you have to do is enjoy the view - there's nothing for you to hold on to or worry about. I'll handle everything else."

"Enjoy the view?" Sam's voice cracked. "Chad, I get dizzy standing on a chair to change light bulbs. You want me to jump out of an airplane at fifteen thousand feet and enjoy the view?"

Sam began pacing in small circles, running her hands through her hair. "No. No, absolutely not. There has to be another way. What about the boat option? Or we could wait for backup? Or maybe we could—"

"Sam," Chad interrupted gently.

"—coordinate with the Coast Guard, or find another airstrip, or—"

"Sam."

"—maybe Elena's not even there, maybe Ricardo's wrong about the timeline—"

"Sam!" Chad's voice cut through her panic spiral. She stopped pacing and looked at him with wide, frightened eyes.

"I can't do this, Chad. I literally cannot jump out of an airplane. I've had nightmares about falling since I was a kid." Her voice was barely above a whisper. "What if the parachute doesn't open? What if you have a heart attack? What if I panic and somehow break free from the harness?"

"Sam, it's the safest insertion method we have," Chad explained patiently. "No exposure to Elena's security, no time constraints, complete tactical surprise. And you'll be with me the entire time."

Grey added his support. "Sam, tandem jumps are actually safer than solo deployments for inexperienced jumpers. Chad will control the chute, the landing, everything. You're just along for the ride."

"A fifteen thousand foot ride straight down," Sam muttered, but Chad could see her processing the tactical advantages.

Ricardo looked thoughtful. "Agent Lloyd, a night HALO insertion would work. I can climb to fifteen thousand feet over open water, you jump about two miles offshore at the airstrip, and I continue on without landing. Elena's security will think I'm just another charter flight passing through their airspace."

"What about the landing zone?" Grey asked. "Jungle canopy at night could be problematic."

"The airstrip itself," Chad said, studying Ricardo's description. "We land right on the runway, gather our chutes and gear, then disappear into the jungle before any security response arrives."

"There's a clearing about half a mile from Elena's compound," Ricardo replied. "Used to be a helicopter pad before she moved her operation to the main airstrip. It's overgrown now, but still open enough for parachute landing."

Chad turned back to Sam, who was staring at the ground and taking deep breaths. "Sam, I've done hundreds of jumps in the Army. Combat insertions, training exercises, everything. I'm not going to let anything happen to you."

Sam looked up at him, her eyes showing fear mixed with determination. "If I say yes to this insane plan, you promise you won't let go of me?"

"I promise. You'll be strapped to my harness with military-grade equipment. Even if I wanted to let go - which I don't - you physically couldn't fall."

"And you've really done this hundreds of times?"

"Hundreds," Chad confirmed. "Including tandem training jumps with new recruits who were just as scared as you are right now."

Sam closed her eyes, clearly fighting her phobia. "Okay. Okay, if it's the best tactical approach, then we do it. But Chad, if we survive this mission and I find out you exaggerated your experience..."

"You'll kill me yourself," Chad finished with a slight smile. "Understood."

Grey stepped forward, his voice carrying the authority of someone who'd worked with Chad for years. "Sam, Chad's been to jump master school. He's qualified to train other paratroopers. He knows what he's doing."

"Jump master school?" Sam looked between them. "What does that mean?"

"It means I'm certified to pack parachutes, conduct safety inspections, and train new jumpers," Chad explained. "I've supervised hundreds of first-time tandem jumps. You'll be safer with me than you would be driving to work."

Grey clapped Sam on the shoulder. "Welcome to the airborne club, Agent Belle. Most people pay thousands of dollars for this experience."

"Most people are insane," Sam replied, but there was acceptance in her voice along with the fear.

Chapter 72

Hangar 47
Homestead Executive Airport

Chad had studied satellite imagery of Elena's compound on Sam's tablet, noting the defensive positions and security arrangements that Ricardo had helped identify during their debriefing.

"Fifty-three terrorist leaders," Chad muttered, calculating the scope of what they were about to disrupt. "The largest criminal summit in history, and we're going in with three people."

"Three people with unlimited federal support and very personal motivations," Sam corrected. "Elena murdered your family, Chad. She murdered Ricardo's family. And she's been planning to murder thousands more American families."

Grey approached with a communication headset and tactical radio. "Chad, you'll have direct communication with the CIA operations center and drone surveillance. If those Reapers identify additional threats or security changes, you'll know immediately."

Chad accepted the radio gear, noting how different this mission felt compared to his weeks as a hunted fugitive. Instead of operating alone with improvised resources, he now had the full intelligence and military apparatus of the United States government backing his personal quest for justice.

"What's Elena's security routine?" Chad asked Ricardo.

"Guard changes every six hours—0600, 1200, 1800, and midnight. We're hitting them right after the evening change, so guards will be fresh but not yet settled into their positions." Ricardo consulted his watch. "If we take off at 1900 hours, we'll arrive just after 2100—perfect timing for maximum confusion."

Sam reviewed the tactical timeline on her tablet. "Chad, Ricardo says Elena wants all her people in place by Friday. That gives us two days before whatever she's planning reaches full operational status."

"Two days to stop the largest terrorist summit in history," Grey added. "We have no idea what they're coordinating, but with fifty-plus terrorist leaders involved, it's going to be massive."

"Then we stop them before they can finalize their plans." Chad walked to the hangar entrance and looked out at the darkening sky. "Elena Ramirez has spent weeks coordinating with America's enemies while hiding behind foreign borders. Time to bring the war to her doorstep."

Ricardo stopped his finished his pre-flight inspection and walked over to the team. "Agents, I want you to understand something. Elena's compound isn't just defended—it's designed to be a killing field for anyone who approaches without authorization. Watchtowers, motion sensors, overlapping fields of fire."

"What about the terrorist leaders inside? Are they armed?"

"Every one of them. These aren't businessmen attending a conference—they're military commanders who've been fighting wars for decades." Ricardo's expression grew grim. "You're not just assaulting a compound. You're attacking a military base filled with professional killers."

Chad smiled coldly, thinking about Lana and Casey and the 282 other federal family members who'd been murdered by Elena's organization. "Good. I'd hate for this to be easy."

Grey checked his equipment one final time—assault rifle, tactical gear, communications equipment, and enough ammunition for an extended firefight. "Chad, what's the primary objective? Capture Elena for interrogation, or neutralize the entire summit?"

"Both. Elena answers for murdering federal families, and her terrorist allies don't leave that island alive." Chad's voice carried the cold fury of someone who'd been denied justice for too long. "Those terrorist leaders killed friends of mine in Iraq and Afghanistan. I never thought I would have a chance to make it right with them, but we do. The world's most dangerous criminals are gathering in one location. We're going to make sure they never leave."

Sam approached with a secure satellite phone. "Chad, Director Huntington wants to speak with you before we depart."

Chad accepted the phone. "Director."

"Agent Lloyd, I want you to know that what you're about to attempt represents the highest form of federal service. You're risking everything to protect American lives."

"Sir, Elena Ramirez murdered my family and 282 other federal family members. She's planning to murder thousands more. This isn't just duty —it's personal."

"I understand. But Chad, if this mission goes badly, remember that you have extraction options. Don't let personal revenge override tactical judgment."

Chad looked around the hangar at Sam and Grey, who were risking their careers and lives to support his mission, and at Ricardo, who was risking everything to help strangers get justice for murdered families.

"Director, this mission succeeds or we don't come home. Elena Ramirez ends tonight."

"Good hunting, Agent Lloyd."

Chad ended the call and walked toward the aircraft, where Ricardo was completing final preparations for the most dangerous flight of his career.

Chapter 73

C had stood in Ricardo's hangar watching the pilot perform final pre-flight checks on the Twin Otter while Sam and Grey coordinated with FBI and CIA assets positioned throughout the Caribbean. The sun was setting over South Florida, painting the sky blood red—an appropriate omen for what they were about to attempt.

Three parachute rigs lay spread across workbenches—two solo rigs for Chad and Grey, and the specialized tandem harness system that would keep Sam securely attached to Chad during their fifteen-thousand-foot descent into hostile territory.

"Chad," Sam approached with her satellite phone, trying to mask her nervousness about the upcoming jump, "Director Huntington confirms we have two Reaper drones repositioned over Grand Cayman. They'll provide real-time surveillance and tactical support if needed."

"What's their loiter time?"

"Eight hours of continuous coverage. CIA is rotating shifts to maintain 24-hour surveillance once we're on the ground." Sam consulted her tablet, then glanced anxiously at the parachute equipment. "We also have the two FBI SWAT teams staged in Nassau, and HRT is on standby at Guantanamo Bay."

Chad moved to Grey's parachute rig, beginning the systematic inspection that could mean the difference between a successful insertion and a fatal equipment failure. "Response time for backup?"

"Four hours for SWAT teams, six hours for HRT," Grey reported while checking Chad's main chute deployment system. "But Chad, if this goes sideways, we could be fighting for survival long before help arrives."

"Then we make sure it doesn't go sideways." Chad examined Grey's altimeter and automatic activation device with the methodical precision of a jump master. "Your AAD is set for two thousand feet. Remember, we're deploying at two thousand, not the standard four thousand we used in training."

"Copy that. Low opening for maximum stealth." Grey tested Chad's harness buckles and checked the routing of his reserve ripcord. "Main chute looks good, reserve is properly packed and secured."

Chad turned his attention to the tandem rig that would carry both him and Sam to the target. The harness system was more complex, with multiple attachment points and backup safety systems designed to keep an inexperienced jumper secure during descent.

"Sam, come here. Time to get you fitted."

Sam approached the tandem harness with visible reluctance, her face pale despite her professional composure. "Chad, are you absolutely sure this thing won't come apart in mid-air?"

"Military-grade equipment, triple redundancy on all critical systems." Chad held up the student harness that Sam would wear. "Step into the leg straps. I'll adjust everything to fit properly."

Sam stepped into the harness while Chad made precise adjustments to the leg straps, chest strap, and back attachment points. His movements were confident and methodical, the result of hundreds of training sessions with nervous first-time jumpers.

"How does that feel? Too tight anywhere?"

"Like I'm wearing a straightjacket designed by someone who hates me," Sam replied, but she managed a weak smile. "But it doesn't hurt."

"Good. In the aircraft, I'll clip you to my harness with these attachment points." Chad showed her the heavy-duty carabiners and steel cables that would connect them. "Once we're connected, you can't fall even if you wanted to."

Grey finished inspecting his own gear and moved to the tactical equipment they'd be carrying. "Chad, Ricardo says Elena's compound has overlapping security zones. How are we handling equipment distribution?"

"You'll carry the explosives and detonators—your ruck is lighter for solo deployment." Chad shouldered his assault pack, noting the additional weight of the tandem rig. "Sam and I will carry communications gear, optics, and medical supplies."

"What about weapons?"

"All three of us carry assault rifles, sidearms and tactical knives. You'll have the sniper rifle since you're landing independently." Chad checked his equipment one final time. "Remember, we're going in for intelligence and interdiction. Avoid engagement unless absolutely necessary."

Ricardo looked up from the Otter's engine compartment. "Agents, I need to brief you on aircraft procedures. The cargo door opens to starboard, jump altitude is fifteen thousand feet, and I'll be flying at 120 knots when you exit."

Chad gathered Sam and Grey near a diagram of the aircraft that Ricardo had sketched on a whiteboard. "Exit sequence: Sam and I go first—we'll sit in the door and I'll push us out clean. Grey, you follow immediately after we clear the aircraft. Ricardo, what's our exit window?"

"Thirty seconds from first jumper to aircraft clear. I need to maintain course and speed to avoid suspicion from Elena's security." Ricardo's weathered face showed professional concern. "Once you're gone, I continue to Cuban airspace, then circle back to Miami. Elena's people will think I'm just another charter flight passing through."

Chad turned to Sam, who was staring at the aircraft door with undisguised anxiety. "Sam, we're going to sit in the door with our legs hanging out. You'll be basically sitting in my lap. I want you to focus on my voice, not the altitude. When I say go, I'll push us out—no hesitation, no stepping forward, just a clean exit. You don't have to do anything except stay attached to me."

"Sit on your lap with my feet dangling out into space fifteen thousand feet above the ground," Sam muttered. "Sure, no problem."

"You've done harder things," Chad said gently. "You've faced down cartel gunmen, survived federal manhunts, and outsmarted a corrupt FBI agent. This is just transportation."

Grey checked his altimeter one final time. "Chad, what's the rally point after landing?"

"Edge of the airstrip, south end. We'll have maybe three minutes to collect gear and move into the jungle before any security response." Chad consulted his tactical map. "From there, it's half a mile through jungle terrain to Elena's compound perimeter."

"Weather?"

Ricardo answered from the cockpit. "Clear skies, no precipitation forecast. New moon phase gives us maximum darkness. Surface winds are light and variable—perfect jumping conditions."

Chad helped Sam out of her training harness while keeping the adjustment settings marked for rapid re-fitting in the aircraft. "Sam, during descent, keep your legs slightly bent, arch your back against my chest, and keep your arms out to the sides with your hands cupped. Let me control everything else. The chute will deploy automatically, then it's just a gentle glide to the landing zone."

"Gentle glide while being shot at by terrorists," Sam added.

"They won't know we're there until we want them to know," Chad replied with confidence. "To Elena and her security, the plane will look like any other Caribbean tourist flight overflying the island, not delivering federal agents by parachute."

Grey shouldered his equipment and moved toward the aircraft. "Chad, what's the abort protocol if something goes wrong during insertion?"

"There isn't one. Once we jump, we're committed." Chad's voice carried the finality of someone who'd made peace with the risks. "Elena Ramirez murdered 282 federal family members and is planning to murder thousands more. We stop her tonight or die trying."

Sam took a deep breath and looked at the parachute equipment with new determination. "Then let's go stop her."

Ricardo completed his pre-flight inspection and walked over to the team. "Agents, fuel is topped off, aircraft systems are green, and flight plan is filed for a routine charter to Cuban airspace. We'll be at jump altitude in ninety minutes."

Chad looked around the hangar at Sam and Grey, who were risking their careers and lives to support his mission, and at Ricardo, who was risking everything to help strangers get justice for murdered families.

"People, Elena Ramirez has spent weeks coordinating with America's enemies while hiding behind foreign borders. Time to bring the war to her doorstep."

"Agents," Ricardo announced, "we're ready for departure. Two hours and fifteen minutes to target, and then you're on your own in hostile territory."

The team moved toward the Twin Otter, where Ricardo was starting the engines for the most dangerous flight of his career. Chad climbed aboard first, followed by Sam—who paused at the aircraft door and looked back at the solid ground with obvious longing—and finally Grey.

As the Otter's engines spun up and Ricardo taxied toward the runway, Chad felt something he hadn't experienced since Lana and Casey's murder: the possibility of justice.

Chapter 74

Twin Otter DHC-6
Airspace Over Caribbean Sea

The Twin Otter cut through the darkness at fifteen thousand feet, its twin turboprops the only sound in the vast Caribbean night. Chad checked his altimeter while helping Sam into her tandem harness, trying to keep his movements calm and methodical despite her obvious panic.

"Five minutes to target," Ricardo announced through the intercom, his voice steady despite the magnitude of what they were attempting. "I'm beginning approach to jump altitude."

Sam's breathing was becoming rapid and shallow as the reality of their situation hit her. "Chad, I can't do this. I literally cannot jump out of this airplane. My hands are shaking, I can't think straight, I—"

"Sam," Chad said gently, working to secure her harness connections. "Look at me."

"We're three miles above the ocean! This is insane! What if the parachute doesn't open? What if we hit the water? What if—"

Chad cupped her face in his hands and kissed her firmly on the lips. The unexpected contact shocked Sam into immediate silence, her panicked rambling cutting off mid-sentence.

"Now," Chad said softly, maintaining eye contact, "are you listening to me?"

Sam stared at him, still processing what had just happened. "I... yes."

"Good. Because I need you focused." Chad began clipping her harness to his with heavy-duty carabiners. "You're not jumping alone. You're attached to someone who's done this hundreds of times. I'm not going to let anything happen to you."

Grey finished checking his own gear and moved to the cargo door. "Chad, two minutes to target. We need to get positioned."

"Overwatch, this is Insertion Team," Grey spoke into his headset while Sam focused on Chad's voice. "Two minutes to target. Request final intelligence update."

The response crackled through their headphones: "Insertion Team, thermal imaging shows normal activity at target compound. Fifty-plus heat signatures in main building, guard rotations proceeding on schedule. No indication of increased security awareness."

Chad completed the final connection between their harnesses, double-checking each attachment point. "Sam, remember what I told you about body position?"

"Legs bent, back arched, arms out with hands cupped," Sam recited, her voice steadier but still showing fear.

"Perfect. And what do you do during freefall?"

"Nothing. You control everything."

"Right. I'll handle deployment, steering, landing—everything. All you have to do is enjoy the view." Chad tested their connection one final time. "We're literally tied together with equipment rated for ten times our weight."

Ricardo's voice came through the intercom: "One minute to target. Opening cargo door now."

The cargo door slid open with a mechanical grinding, and suddenly the aircraft interior filled with the roar of wind and engines. Sam looked at the rectangular opening showing nothing but black ocean three miles below and went rigid with terror.

"I can't, Chad. I can't do this."

Chad positioned them at the door, Sam sitting between his legs with both their feet hanging out into the darkness. "Sam, look at me, not down there."

She turned her face toward his, eyes wide with fear. "This is really happening, isn't it?"

"It's really happening. And in three minutes, we're going to be safely on the ground having just completed the most perfectly executed insertion of your career." Chad's voice carried absolute confidence. "Trust me."

"Thirty seconds!" Ricardo called out.

Grey gave Chad a thumbs up and positioned himself at the door edge. "See you on the ground, brother."

Chad wrapped his arms around Sam's chest, feeling her trembling against his tactical vest. "Sam, when I say go, we're just going to tip forward. No big movement, no drama. Like falling off a log."

"A log that's fifteen thousand feet in the air," Sam whispered.

"The best kind," Chad replied with a slight smile.

"Ten seconds!" Ricardo announced.

Chad felt Sam's breathing slow as she forced herself to focus on his instructions rather than the yawning void below them. Through the door, the dark waters of the Caribbean stretched endlessly in all directions.

"Go!" Chad said, and pushed them forward into the night.

For a terrifying instant, Sam felt the sensation of falling—no aircraft beneath them, no solid ground, nothing but empty air rushing past at terminal velocity. Then Chad's voice was in her ear through the intercom system.

"Sam, focus. Arch your back, bend your knees, extend your arms. That's it, you're doing great. Look around—you can see the lights of Grand Cayman ahead of us."

Despite her terror, Sam found herself looking at the island below, its scattered lights like jewels against the black ocean. The freefall was surprisingly smooth, almost peaceful, with Chad's steady presence behind her making the impossible seem manageable.

"Chute deployment in ten seconds," Chad announced calmly.

Sam felt the harness jerk as their parachute deployed, the violent deceleration followed immediately by gentle, controlled descent. The terrifying freefall transformed into a quiet glide through the warm Caribbean air.

"How are you doing?" Chad asked.

"I'm... I'm alive," Sam replied, surprising herself with a laugh. "And it's actually kind of beautiful up here."

Through their night vision optics, they could see Grey's parachute off

317

to their left, descending parallel to their course. Below them, the airstrip at Elena's compound was a thin line of minimal lighting in the jungle darkness.

"Landing in sixty seconds," Chad announced. "Remember—let me handle touchdown, keep your legs up, and we'll roll together."

As they approached the grass airstrip, Sam could see vehicle headlights approaching from the direction of Elena's compound. "Chad, they're coming to meet the plane."

"That's not right," Chad said, concern evident in his voice. "Ricardo's not supposed to land—this looks like a random security patrol." Chad pulled hard on the steering toggles, adjusting their approach angle toward the south end of the runway. "We need to land as far from those lights as possible."

"Why?"

"Because it takes time to get out of tandem harness, and I can't cut us loose while we're still attached." Chad steered aggressively away from the approaching vehicles. "If they spot us before I can get you disconnected, we're sitting ducks."

Through their night vision, they could see Grey adjusting his approach to match theirs, both parachutes now heading for the far end of the airstrip away from the security patrol. The vehicle headlights were sweeping back and forth across the runway as if conducting a routine perimeter check.

"Thirty seconds to landing," Chad announced quietly. "Soon as we touch down, stay low and don't move until I get these harnesses disconnected. We'll have maybe two minutes before they work their way down to our end of the runway."

Sam kept her feet up as Chad had instructed, feeling him expertly flare their parachute for landing. Chad's feet touched the grass runway first, absorbing the impact as they touched down softly on the far end of the airstrip.

"Okay, feet down," Chad whispered urgently as their parachute collapsed to the ground. "Stay low."

Sam put her feet down, feeling solid ground beneath her for the first time in what felt like hours. Within seconds, Chad was working frantically to disconnect their harnesses while Grey landed nearby and immediately began gathering his own chute.

"Welcome to the Cayman Islands," Chad whispered as they moved quickly toward the jungle tree line. "Now the real mission begins."

Behind them, the approaching vehicle headlights grew brighter as Elena's security patrol continued their sweep of the runway. They had likely detected Ricardo's aircraft on radar as it passed overhead and were conducting a routine check to ensure nothing had been dropped on the airstrip. What they would find instead was the beginning of their own destruction.

Chapter 75

G ear collection, now," Chad whispered urgently, working to stuff his and Sam's tandem parachute into its deployment bag. "Grey, get your chute packed. We've got maybe ninety seconds before that patrol reaches this end of the runway."

Grey was already compressing his parachute into its bag, moving with the efficiency of years of airborne training. Sam helped gather the suspension lines, trying to keep the nylon fabric from billowing in the Caribbean breeze.

"Where do we hide these?" Sam asked, looking around at the open grass airstrip with minimal cover.

Chad finished cramming the tandem rig into its bag and grabbed Grey's packed parachute. "You two head toward Elena's compound." He hefted the tandem gear and threw it deep into the overgrown vegetation at the runway's edge, where thick jungle growth would conceal it from casual search. "That won't be easily found. I've got an idea to buy us some time."

Chad shouldered Grey's parachute bag and harness. "This is what's going to save us."

"Chad, what are you planning?" Sam asked, concern evident in her voice.

Instead of answering, Chad sprinted toward the middle of the runway carrying Grey's parachute bag. When he reached the center of the airstrip, he pulled the nylon canopy partially out of its deployment bag and scattered it across the grass, letting the wind catch the fabric so it rippled and moved in the breeze like a signal flag.

Then he sprinted back toward the tree line where Sam and Grey were waiting with the hidden tandem gear.

"Now I'm going to delay the welcoming party," Chad explained quietly. "That chute will draw their attention to the middle of the runway. Give you time to get into position without them knowing there are three of us."

"Chad, that's suicide," Grey protested. "You'll be outnumbered six to one."

"I'll be fine. I've got cover, night vision, and the element of surprise. More importantly, you two need to get eyes on that terrorist summit." Chad checked his sidearm and grabbed extra magazines. "This is the mission, people. I draw fire, you gather intelligence."

Through the darkness, they could see the vehicle headlights approaching the airstrip, sweeping back and forth as the security patrol conducted their check. The scattered parachute fabric fluttered in the breeze exactly where Chad had positioned it—impossible to miss.

"There," Chad said with satisfaction as the vehicle headlights locked onto the billowing nylon. "Now they think there's one parachutist who landed in the middle of the runway and is hiding somewhere nearby."

Sam and Grey disappeared into dense vegetation just as the first security vehicle reached the parachute Chad had planted. Instead of moving directly toward the compound, they took defensive positions in the jungle and waited, watching Chad through night vision optics.

Two armored SUVs pulled up to the parachute, disgorging six heavily armed men who immediately began searching for the solo infiltrator. Chad could hear Spanish voices shouting questions, vehicle engines idling, the beginning of confusion that was rapidly becoming alarm.

Through his thermal scope, Chad watched the security team leader emerge from the lead vehicle. Even in the darkness, Chad recognized the military bearing and facial features from surveillance photos—Javier Santos, the man who had murdered Lana and Casey in their dining room two weeks ago.

"¡Busquen por todas partes!" the team leader shouted to his men.

"Someone parachuted onto our runway. Find tracks, equipment, anything!"

The sicarios spread out from the planted parachute, their tactical lights sweeping for signs of the infiltrator they believed had landed there. Chad remained motionless in the jungle undergrowth, controlling his breathing while watching them search in completely the wrong location.

"Overwatch, this is Grey," Grey whispered into his radio from their concealed position. "We're in position and have eyes on the situation. Advising immediate movement toward primary target."

"Negative," Sam replied quietly. "We wait for Chad."

Grey had seen Chad in situations like this before—especially that four-hour firefight in Afghanistan where Chad had been the only survivor against hundreds of Taliban fighters. Sam had never seen Chad in his tactical element and was curious about what he was planning.

"Sam, we need to move toward the compound now," Grey suggested urgently. "I know what Chad's going to do, and you don't need to see it."

"What do you mean?"

Through their optics, they watched Chad position himself behind cover near the runway, thermal scope tracking the security team as they realized the aircraft had been empty. Javier was barking orders in Spanish, his men spreading out to search the immediate area.

"Sam, Chad's about to engage six hostiles to give us time to reach the compound," Grey explained. "We need to use that time, not waste it watching."

But Sam remained fixed on Chad's position, watching as he prepared for what could be his final battle.

Chad's finger found the trigger of his suppressed rifle, the crosshairs settling on Javier's chest. One shot would end this personal war, but the other five sicarios would immediately know his position.

Patience. The sniper's greatest virtue.

"¡Busquen por todas partes!" Javier shouted to his men. "Someone landed here. Find tracks, equipment, anything!"

The sicarios spread out across the airstrip, their tactical lights sweeping for signs of Chad's passage. Chad remained motionless in the jungle undergrowth, controlling his breathing while watching Javier direct the search.

One of the sicarios approached Chad's position, following footprints where he'd entered the jungle. Chad waited until the searcher was within arm's reach, then struck with predatory precision. His hand clamped over the man's mouth while his combat knife drove into the base of the skull. The sicario died instantly.

"¡Carlos!" Javier called out. "¿Encontraste algo?"

Carlos would never answer again. Chad had already moved to a new position, using the jungle's dense canopy to mask his approach toward the remaining searchers.

The second man died at the edge of the airstrip, Chad's knife opening his throat from behind. The body dropped into tall grass, invisible to the other sicarios.

"¡Carlos! ¡Miguel!" Javier's voice carried irritation and the first hint of concern. "Report your positions!"

The third sicario turned toward Chad's location, weapon raised, instincts warning him something was wrong. Chad's suppressed rifle coughed once, the subsonic round taking the man in the head.

"¡Contacto!" Javier shouted, diving behind one of the SUVs as automatic weapons fire erupted from his remaining men. "¡Lloyd está aquí!"

Chad was already moving, using the jungle's natural cover to flank the surviving sicarios. The fourth man died when Chad appeared behind him like a ghost, the suppressed Glock coughing twice. The fifth tried to run but caught three rounds center mass.

That left Javier Santos alone behind the SUV, the monster who'd murdered Chad's family now facing the reckoning he'd earned.

From their concealed position, Sam watched in stunned silence as Chad systematically eliminated an entire security team. Grey grabbed her arm.

"Now we move," Grey whispered urgently. "While Chad has them distracted."

As they began moving toward the compound, Sam could hear Javier's voice calling out across the airstrip: "Chad Lloyd! I know you're out there. Your wife died beautifully! Such spirit, such defiance!"

"Don't listen," Grey warned as they pushed deeper into the jungle. "Chad's got this. We have a job to do."

Behind them, the personal war between Chad and his family's killer was about to reach its conclusion.

Chapter 76

Abandoned Control Tower
Grand Cayman Airstrip

Chad had appeared at the rear of the SUV like death incarnate, his suppressed Glock trained on Javier's center mass. The cartel enforcer spun around, bringing up his own weapon, but twenty years of combat experience had taught Chad to move faster than most men could think.

"Hello, Javier," Chad said quietly. "Remember me?"

Javier's eyes went wide with recognition and terror. The FBI agent whose family he'd murdered was standing behind him, very much alive and holding a smoking weapon.

But instead of firing immediately, Chad gestured with his rifle toward the abandoned control tower. "Walk."

"Agent Lloyd, perhaps we can—"

"Walk. Now. Or I put three rounds through your spine and drag you there myself."

Javier began moving toward the dilapidated building, understanding that his survival depended on whatever Chad had planned. Behind them, five bodies lay scattered across the airstrip, proof that the hunter had become the hunted.

"You know Elena is expecting you," Javier said as they approached the control tower. "She has fifty-three men waiting at the compound. Professional soldiers, international terrorists. You'll never reach her."

"That's my problem to solve." Chad forced Javier through the tower's broken doorway into a space that had been abandoned for decades.

"Right now, you have a different concern."

Chad zip-tied Javier's hands behind his back, securing him to a rusted support beam in the center of the room. The same flex cuffs Javier had used on Lana, the same helpless positioning that had made her torture possible.

"Two hours," Chad said, settling into a chair directly in front of his captive. "That's how long you spent destroying my wife while my daughter lay dead on our dining room floor."

Javier's breathing became shallow as he recognized the deliberate parallels Chad was drawing. "Agent Lloyd, I was following orders—"

Chad's fist connected with Javier's jaw, snapping his head to the side and splitting his lip. "Wrong answer. Let's try again. Why did Elena want my family tortured instead of simply killed?"

The interrogation that followed was methodical, precise, and absolutely merciless. For every detail of Lana's suffering, Chad extracted payment in kind. For every moment of Casey's terror, Javier paid with broken bones and internal damage.

"Tell me about the clown mask," Chad said, his voice never changing tone as he delivered another precise blow to Javier's ribs. "Why terrorize a six-year-old child in her final moments?"

"Elena's research showed the girl was afraid of clowns," Javier gasped through gritted teeth. "Maximum psychological impact."

Chad's kick caught Javier in the wounded shoulder, eliciting a scream that echoed through the abandoned tower. "Tell me about the plastic bag. Why suffocate her slowly instead of a quick death?"

"Elena wanted her to suffer like Salvador suffered watching your bullet—"

Chad's punch broke Javier's nose, blood streaming down his face as he fought to remain conscious.

For ninety minutes, Chad methodically worked through every detail of his family's murder. Each question about Lana's torture brought physical punishment when Javier tried to justify or minimize his actions. Each revelation about Casey's terror earned broken bones and internal damage.

"Tell me about Elena's operation," Chad demanded, his knuckles bloody from the systematic beating. "What's she planning with all those terrorist leaders?"

"Coordinated attacks," Javier gasped, his face swollen beyond recognition. "Infrastructure targets in twelve American cities. Power grids, transportation hubs, financial centers."

"When?"

"Friday night. Simultaneous strikes designed to overwhelm federal response capabilities."

Chad leaned back, processing the intelligence while studying Javier's broken form. "How many people will die?"

"Thousands in the initial attacks. Tens of thousands when emergency services fail and chaos spreads." Javier's voice was barely a whisper. "Elena wants America to understand what it means to cross the Ramirez family."

Chad stood and walked to his equipment bag, removing a clear plastic bag identical to the one Javier had used on Lana. "You gave me all the intelligence I need. Now it's time for justice."

Javier's eyes went wide with terror as Chad approached. "Agent Lloyd, please—"

"This is how my wife died," Chad said, his voice carrying that same emotionless calm. "Suffocating slowly while you walked away to report your success to Elena."

Chad pulled the plastic bag over Javier's head and sealed it tight around his neck, just as Javier had done to Lana. But unlike the cartel enforcer, Chad didn't walk away to pack his equipment and congratulate himself on a job well done.

Chad settled back into his chair and watched.

Javier's initial panic was immediate and intense—thrashing against the flex cuffs, trying to tear at the plastic with his bound hands, desperate attempts to tip the chair over that only resulted in more pain from his broken ribs. The bag fogged with his panicked breathing, obscuring his terrified features as he fought for air that would never come.

"My wife called my name during the worst of it," Chad said conversationally, as if discussing the weather. "She begged you to stop, offered you money, tried to bargain for Casey's life. What did you tell her?"

Javier couldn't answer, his consciousness fading as oxygen deprivation took hold. His struggles grew weaker, more uncoordinated, his body's survival instincts fighting a battle they couldn't win.

"You told her that her husband would watch this recording and understand what it meant to cross the Ramirez family," Chad continued, his voice never changing tone. "You told her that her daughter's death was my fault for doing my job."

Javier's movements became sporadic, then stopped altogether. But Chad remained in his chair, watching the man who'd murdered his family with the same patient intensity Javier had shown while torturing Lana.

Five minutes passed. Ten. Fifteen.

Only when Chad was absolutely certain that Javier Santos would never again hurt anyone's family did he finally stand and walk to the control tower's broken window.

Chad immediately keyed his radio to the CIA operations center. "Overwatch, this is Insertion Leader. Priority intelligence from interrogation of hostile KIA."

"Go ahead, Insertion Leader."

"Confirmed terrorist operation targeting American infrastructure. Coordinated attacks scheduled for Friday night, simultaneous strikes on twelve major cities. Targets include power grids, transportation hubs, and financial centers. Estimated casualties in the thousands initially, tens of thousands when emergency services fail."

The CIA operator's voice became urgent. "Insertion Leader, can you confirm the scope and timing?"

"Confirmed. Friday night coordinated strikes designed to overwhelm federal response capabilities. This is Elena Ramirez's retaliation for cartel terrorist designation." Chad consulted his watch. "We have approximately forty-eight hours to stop this operation."

"Copy all, Insertion Leader. Relaying to FBI Director, Attorney General, and Department of Homeland Security immediately. Do you have target specifics?"

"Negative on specific target locations. Source terminated during interrogation. Intel suggests the terrorist summit at primary target has operational details."

"Understood. Insertion Leader, you are authorized to take any action necessary to prevent these attacks. Repeat, any action necessary."

Chad felt the weight of federal authority behind his mission. "Roger, Overwatch. Moving to rejoin team at primary target."

Through his radio, he could hear Sam and Grey reporting their approach to Elena's compound. His family's killer was dead, but the war was far from over.

Chad checked his weapons and equipment, preparing to rejoin his team for the final assault on Elena's terrorist summit. Javier had given him the intelligence he needed—coordinated attacks on Friday night, infrastructure targets in twelve cities, thousands of casualties planned.

As Chad prepared to leave the airstrip, he noticed several coils of medium-gauge tow chains stored in the control tower—likely used for aircraft tie-downs during hurricane season. He grabbed all of them, about eighty feet of chain total, and distributed the weight across his gear. The chains weren't overly heavy, but they would be perfect for securing building entrances, blocking escape routes, or creating improvised barriers.

Two days to stop the largest terrorist operation in American history.

Chad keyed his radio. "Overwatch, this is Insertion Leader. Airstrip is secure. Moving to rejoin team at primary target."

"Copy, Insertion Leader. Team Two reports they're in position for surveillance of main compound."

Chad stepped over Javier's lifeless form and walked back into the Caribbean night. One debt paid in full. Two more to collect before the sun rose over Grand Cayman.

Chapter 77

Elena Ramirez Compound
Grand Cayman

Agent Belle pressed herself against the dense vegetation at the edge of Elena's compound, her thermal optics revealing a fortress that looked more like a military base than a criminal hideout. Through the night vision scope, she could see armed guards patrolling the perimeter, watchtowers with overlapping fields of fire, and enough defensive positions to repel a small army.

"Jesus Christ," Grey whispered beside her, studying the compound through his own optics. "This isn't a safe house—it's a command center."

The main building was a sprawling concrete structure built into the hillside, with multiple levels and reinforced walls that could withstand artillery strikes. Satellite dishes and communication arrays bristled from the roof, while armored vehicles sat parked in defensive positions around the perimeter.

"Overwatch, this is Team Two," Sam whispered into her radio. "We're in position and have visual on primary target. Requesting immediate analysis of defensive positions."

The CIA operator's voice crackled through their headsets: "Team Two, we're seeing your thermal signatures. Compound shows approximately thirty guards on patrol, plus additional personnel inside main structure."

"What about the meeting?" Grey asked. "Any indication of the terrorist summit?"

"Affirmative. Thermal imaging shows large gathering in main

conference room. Count approximately fifty-plus individuals in central location, consistent with terrorist leadership meeting."

Sam adjusted her long-range optics, focusing on the main building's windows. Through the reinforced glass, she could see silhouettes moving around what appeared to be a massive conference table, with displays and projection equipment visible in the background.

"Nolan, look at this," Sam indicated a section of the building where additional security was concentrated. "Three times as many guards around that wing. Whatever's happening in there, it's important."

Grey studied the guard positions, noting the professional spacing and overlapping coverage. "These aren't cartel soldiers. This is military-grade security."

"Overwatch, can you identify any of the individuals inside the conference room?"

"Negative on specific identification, but heat signatures match known patterns for high-value target meetings. These are leadership-level individuals, not operational personnel."

Sam's radio crackled with Chad's voice: "Team Two, this is Insertion Leader. I'm moving to your position. ETA fifteen minutes."

"Copy, Insertion Leader. We have eyes on primary target. Confirmed large meeting in progress."

"Roger. Maintain surveillance and prepare for coordinated assault. Intelligence suggests time-sensitive operation in progress."

Sam and Grey continued their observation, documenting guard rotations and defensive positions while the terrorist summit continued inside the fortified building. Through her thermal scope, Sam could see vehicles arriving periodically, delivering additional personnel who were escorted directly into the main conference area.

"Nolan, this is massive," Sam whispered. "We're looking at the largest gathering of international terrorists in history."

"And they're all in one building," Grey replied grimly. "If we can stop them here, we prevent whatever coordinated attack they're planning."

Sam's radio earpiece crackled with updates from the CIA operations center: "Team Two, be advised that Department of Homeland Security is raising threat levels nationwide based on your intelligence. Federal agencies are coordinating response to potential infrastructure attacks."

"Copy, Overwatch. What's our authorization for engagement?"

"You are cleared for any action necessary to prevent terrorist operations. Repeat, any action necessary. Federal response teams are positioning for support, but time factor requires immediate action on your part."

Grey checked his assault rifle and counted his ammunition. "Sam, when Chad gets here, we're going to hit that compound hard. Are you ready for this?"

Sam thought about the weeks of hunting Chad instead of hunting terrorists, about Holmes' corruption and Elena's payments to protect her operations. "Nolan, I've been ready since Holmes was getting paid fifty million dollars to hunt heroes instead of hunting villains."

Movement through the jungle behind them announced Chad's arrival. He materialized from the vegetation like a ghost, his tactical gear and weapons marking him as someone who'd just fought a personal war.

"Status report," Chad whispered as he took position beside them.

"Approximately fifty terrorist leaders in main conference room, thirty guards on perimeter patrol, reinforced defensive positions," Sam reported. "This is a military-grade fortress, Chad."

Chad studied the compound through his own optics, noting the guard positions and defensive arrangements. "Then we treat it like a military target. What's the meeting status?"

"Active terrorist summit. They're coordinating something major, probably the Friday night attacks you reported."

Chad's expression hardened as he calculated tactical options. "We have two choices. Wait for federal backup and risk them escaping when they realize we're here or hit them now while they're all gathered in one location."

"How many SWAT teams are on standby?" Grey asked.

"Two teams in Nassau, HRT at Guantanamo. Four to six hours response time." Chad checked his watch. "But what if they're finalizing operational plans tonight. If they scatter tomorrow, we lose the opportunity to stop coordinated attacks on American infrastructure."

Sam studied the compound's defensive positions, understanding the tactical challenge they faced. "Chad, it's three of us against fifty terrorists plus thirty guards. Even with our equipment, those aren't good odds."

"No," Chad replied, "they're not. But those fifty terrorists are planning to kill thousands of Americans in forty-eight hours. Sometimes you take the mission with the odds you have, not the odds you want."

Chad keyed his radio to the CIA operations center. "Overwatch, this is Insertion Leader. Request immediate coordination with federal response teams. We're going to hit this compound in thirty minutes."

"Copy, Insertion Leader. What support do you require?"

"Reaper drone coverage for real-time intelligence and precision strikes if needed. Federal teams on standby for extraction and cleanup." Chad's voice carried cold determination. "And tell Director Huntington that we're about to end the largest terrorist operation in American history."

Grey studied the compound's construction through his optics. "Chad, wait. Hellfire missiles won't penetrate that structure. Look at those walls—reinforced concrete, multiple levels built into the hillside. This is designed to survive air strikes."

Chad examined the building more carefully, noting the fortress-like construction. "How deep do you think that conference room is?"

"Based on the thermal signatures and building layout? Probably twenty feet underground, surrounded by steel-reinforced concrete. A Hellfire might damage the surface, but it won't reach the meeting."

Chad processed this tactical reality. "Overwatch, this is Insertion Leader. Stand by on previous request."

"Grey's right," Sam added, studying the compound's defensive design. "This place was built to survive military assault. They're not meeting in some surface-level conference room—they're in an underground bunker."

Grey keyed his radio to the CIA operations center. "Overwatch, this is Team Two tactical coordinator. Need immediate assessment of target structure penetration requirements."

"Go ahead, Team Two."

"Multi-level concrete structure built into hillside, estimated twenty-foot depth to primary target area. Hellfire missiles insufficient for target elimination. Request authorization for bunker-buster ordnance."

A pause as the CIA operator consulted with higher authority. "Team Two, what are you requesting specifically?"

"B-21 Raider with GBU-57 bunker busters. This facility requires deep-penetration ordnance to eliminate targets in underground conference room."

Another pause, longer this time. "Team Two, stand by for authorization from strategic command."

Chad looked at Grey with new respect. "You think they'll authorize a strategic bomber for this?"

"Chad, we've got fifty terrorist leaders planning coordinated attacks on American infrastructure. That's not a tactical problem—that's a strategic threat." Grey's expression was grim. "If we can eliminate them all in one strike, it's worth a B-21 mission."

The radio crackled with response: "Team Two, this is Strategic Command. Authorization approved for B-21 deployment with bunker-buster ordnance. Flight time from continental United States is four hours."

"Four hours," Sam repeated. "Can we keep them in that compound for four more hours?"

Chad checked his watch, calculating operational timelines. "We have to. If they scatter before the bomber arrives, we lose the opportunity to stop coordinated attacks on twelve American cities."

Chad turned to Sam and Grey, recalculating their mission parameters. "New plan. We're not assaulting the compound—we're containing it until the B-21 arrives. Our job is to make sure none of those fifty terrorists escape before the bunker busters turn that place into a crater."

"Containment operation," Grey nodded approvingly. "Much better odds than direct assault."

"How do we keep them locked down for four hours?" Sam asked.

Chad studied the compound layout, identifying key tactical points. "We eliminate the perimeter guards silently, take out the watchtowers, and secure all exit points. Nobody gets in or out until that bomber arrives."

"What about their helicopter?" Sam pointed to the aircraft parked near the main building. "If they try to evacuate by air..."

"I'll handle that," Chad replied, patting his equipment bag containing the C-4 explosives. "Plant charges under the seats and in the engine compartment. Anyone who tries to escape in that helicopter is going to have a very short flight."

Grey reviewed the guard positions through his optics. "Thirty guards on patrol, plus watchtower personnel. We can take them out systematically if we coordinate properly."

"Silent kills only," Chad emphasized. "We can't alert the leadership meeting that we're here. The moment they know they're under attack, they'll try to scatter."

Sam checked her suppressed sidearm. "What about sealing the exits?"

Chad shrugged the chains off his shoulders. "That's what these are for. We can chain the doors shut to keep them contained from the outside" Chad explained. "Then claymore mines positioned to face inward if they manage to breach the doors. We turn that compound into a tomb until the Air Force turns it into a crater."

"Claymores facing the occupants," Grey nodded approvingly. "Anyone who tries to force their way out gets shredded."

"How many exit points are we looking at?" Sam asked.

Chad studied the compound layout. "Main entrance, emergency exits on the east and west sides, plus the helicopter landing pad. Four choke points to secure."

"I've got enough chain and hardware to secure all the doors," Chad continued, checking his equipment bag. "Plus six claymores to cover the entrances. Anyone who tries to escape dies in the doorway."

"Four hours to eliminate thirty guards and secure a fortress without alerting fifty terrorist leaders inside," Grey summarized. "Challenging, but doable if we work smart."

Chad looked at his watch. "B-21 ETA is four hours. We start with the watchtowers—eliminate overwatch first, then work our way through the perimeter guards. Sam, can you coordinate with our team in Miami on communications jamming to prevent distress calls."

"What about the meeting itself?" Sam asked. "How do we know they won't finish early and try to leave?"

"According to intelligence from Javier's interrogation, they're finalizing attack plans for Friday night. That's a lot of coordination to accomplish." Chad's expression was grim. "Plus, Elena's got fifty egos in that room who all think they're the smartest terrorist alive. This meeting could last all night."

"And according to Ricardo, the last attendee isn't scheduled to arrive until Friday morning," Grey added. "They're not going anywhere until the summit is complete."

"Perfect," Sam said. "So we have them contained both physically and by their own schedule."

Grey smiled coldly. "And if it doesn't, we make sure the doors don't open until our bomber arrives."

Chad checked his equipment one final time—suppressed weapons, C-4 explosives, det cord, remote detonators. Everything he needed to turn Elena's fortress into an inescapable trap.

"Team, in thirty minutes we begin containment operations. Questions?"

Sam looked at the compound, thinking about the fifty terrorist leaders who were planning to kill thousands of Americans. "Just one, Chad. What happens if some of them try to surrender when they realize what's coming?"

Chad's smile was as cold as arctic wind. "There won't be any survivors."

The largest terrorist summit in history was about to discover what happened when you murdered federal families and planned to murder thousands more.

Justice was coming. And it was bringing enough firepower to level mountains.

Chapter 78

Elena Ramirez Compound Perimeter
Grand Cayman

C had checked his suppressed sidearm and combat knife, preparing for the systematic elimination of Elena's security forces. In the distance, the compound's main building glowed with lights from the terrorist summit, fifty of the world's most dangerous criminals finalizing plans to murder thousands of Americans.

"Sam," Chad said quietly, "I need you to maintain overwatch position here. Keep eyes on that conference room and make sure nobody inside gets alerted to what we're doing."

Sam looked between Chad and Grey, understanding the tactical logic but feeling the sting of being left behind. "Chad, I can handle myself in combat. I've been through the same training as you—"

"I know you can handle yourself. That's not what this is about."

"Then what? You think I'm going to freeze up? Get someone killed?" Sam's voice carried hurt and frustration. "I've been protecting you for weeks, risking my career—"

"Sam, you've never pulled the trigger to kill someone, and let's hope you never have to." Chad's voice softened. "It changes you. And I like you the way you are."

Chad stepped closer and pulled Sam into a brief but tight embrace, whispering so Grey couldn't hear: "Besides, I'm going to need someone to help me deal with this when it's all over. If you're messed up mentally, you can't do that."

Sam felt her resistance melting as she understood what Chad was really saying—not that she was incapable, but that he needed her to remain whole for what came after the violence.

"Okay," she whispered back. "But you come back to me, Chad. Both of you."

Chad pulled back and looked into her eyes. "I promise. We finish this tonight, and then we figure out what comes next."

Chad turned to Grey, his expression shifting to something Sam had never seen before—the look of two soldiers who'd fought together in hostile territory. "Just like old times?"

Grey smiled grimly, checking his own weapons. "Afghanistan was never this much fun. At least there we knew who the good guys were."

"Same principle applies," Chad replied. "We go in quiet, eliminate targets systematically, and get out without alerting the primary objective."

Sam positioned herself with optimal sightlines to both the compound and the surrounding terrain. "How do you want me to coordinate communications?"

"Radio silence unless you spot immediate threats," Chad instructed. "If someone inside that conference room looks like they're getting suspicious, you warn us immediately. If additional security arrives from off-site, you're our early warning system." Chad checked his equipment one final time. "You'll also need to coordinate with the Miami team to jam outgoing cell phone transmissions. Once Grey and I get those doors chained shut, have them expand the jamming to include all communications—internet, satellite, everything. We need those terrorist leaders completely cut off from their organizations."

"What if things go bad?" Sam asked.

Chad and Grey exchanged a look that spoke of shared experiences in places where things had gone very bad indeed.

"If this goes sideways, you call in the cavalry and get extraction," Chad said. "Don't try to rescue us. Complete the mission."

"The mission is stopping fifty terrorist leaders from killing Americans," Grey added. "Personal survival is secondary."

Chad pulled out his thermal optics and studied the guard rotations one final time. "Two watchtowers, eight roving patrols, fixed positions at the main entrance and helicopter pad. Thirty targets total."

"How long do you estimate?" Sam asked.

"Two hours if we're careful, thirty minutes if we're lucky." Chad shouldered his equipment pack. "Sam, if we're not back in three hours, assume we're compromised and call for immediate air strike."

"Don't assume anything," Grey corrected. "We'll be back. We've done this before."

Chad moved toward the perimeter, Grey following, both men shifting into the tactical mindset that had kept them alive through multiple combat deployments. Sam watched them disappear into the darkness like ghosts, professional killers moving to eliminate an entire security force without making a sound.

Through her thermal scope, Sam could see the terrorist leaders still gathered around their conference table, completely unaware that death was approaching their fortress with surgical precision.

She keyed her radio to the CIA operations center. "Overwatch, this is Team Two. Insertion Leader and Team Leader are beginning security elimination. Request continuous surveillance update."

"Copy, Team Two. Drone coverage shows normal patterns inside conference room. No indication of security awareness. You are clear to proceed."

Sam switched to the Miami operations frequency. "Miami Base, this is Team Two. I need Agents Kim, Walsh, and Ruiz to initiate communication jamming protocols. Start with cellular frequencies, standby for expansion to full spectrum jamming on my signal."

"Roger, Team Two," came the response from Agent Kim. "Cellular jamming initiating now. Walsh is coordinating with NSA for satellite communication disruption, Ruiz has internet backbone access standing by. All systems ready for your go signal."

Sam settled into her overwatch position, watching Chad and Grey begin their systematic approach to the first watchtower. In the compound below, Elena Ramirez was coordinating the largest terrorist operation in American history, completely unaware that Chad Lloyd had finally come to collect the debt she owed for murdering his family.

Chapter 79

Elena Ramirez Compound
Perimeter Security Zone

Chad and Grey moved through the darkness like predators, their years of shared combat experience evident in every calculated step. The first watchtower loomed ahead—a concrete structure with open firing positions designed to repel conventional assault.

But Chad and Grey weren't conducting a conventional assault.

"Two guards in the tower," Chad whispered into his throat mic, studying the target through thermal optics. "Open positions, clear shots."

"I've got the left target," Grey replied, settling into a prone shooting position with his suppressed rifle.

"Right target is mine," Chad confirmed, finding his own firing position with clear sightlines to the tower.

Through her overwatch position, Sam monitored both the compound's conference room and her teammates' preparation. The terrorist summit continued undisturbed, fifty silhouettes still gathered around the massive table where America's destruction was being planned.

"Overwatch to Insertion Team," Sam whispered. "Conference room stable, no security alerts. You're clear to engage."

Chad and Grey synchronized their breathing, both rifles trained on their respective targets. The guards were casually positioned, confident in their fortress's defenses, completely unaware that two expert marksmen had them in their crosshairs.

"On my mark," Chad whispered. "Three, two, one, mark."

Both suppressed rifles coughed simultaneously. The guards dropped instantly, killed before they could even register the threat.

"Tower One neutralized," Chad reported. "Two down, twenty-eight to go."

"Moving to Tower Two," Grey confirmed, already repositioning for the next target.

Sam watched through her thermal scope as Chad and Grey approached the second watchtower, "Overwatch to Insertion Team. Second tower has two guards in position, one patrol at ground level."

"Copy. Grey takes the patrol, I'll handle the tower guards."

Grey moved silently through the jungle undergrowth, positioning himself behind the patrolling guard. His knife ended the man's life before he could make a sound, the body dragged into concealment.

"Ground patrol eliminated," Grey whispered.

Chad found his shooting position with clear sightlines to both tower guards. Two quick shots from his suppressed rifle, and Tower Two went silent.

"Tower Two neutralized. Five down, twenty-five remaining."

"Copy. Moving to perimeter patrol intercept."

Sam maintained her surveillance of both the tactical situation and the terrorist summit, noting that the conference room activity had actually increased—more animated discussions, additional displays being activated, the urgent energy of people finalizing complex plans.

"Overwatch to Insertion Team. Conference room activity is intensifying. They're definitely coordinating something major."

"Understood. How long until B-21 arrival?"

Sam checked her watch. "Three hours, fifteen minutes."

"Roger. Continuing elimination operations."

Chad and Grey began the systematic hunting of roving patrols, using the compound's own defensive terrain against Elena's security forces. Each guard died silently, professionally, without alerting his companions that the fortress was being infiltrated by two ghosts who'd learned their craft in the mountains of Afghanistan.

The terrorist summit continued in the underground conference room, completely unaware that their protection was evaporating one guard at a time.

In three hours, a B-21 Raider would arrive with bunker-busting ordnance that would turn Elena's fortress into a crater. But first, Chad and Grey had twenty-five more targets to eliminate, ensuring that no terrorist would escape the justice that was coming.

Chapter 80

Elena Ramirez Compound
Perimeter Security Zone

With both watchtowers neutralized, Chad and Grey began the systematic hunting of the remaining security forces. The compound's roving patrols continued their routes, unaware that their overwatch was gone and death was stalking them through the Caribbean darkness.

"Overwatch, give me patrol positions," Chad whispered into his throat mic.

Sam studied the compound through her thermal scope, tracking heat signatures moving in predictable patterns around Elena's fortress. "Four-man patrol approaching your position from the east. Single guards at main entrance and helicopter pad. Two-man teams covering north and south perimeters."

"Copy. Grey, we'll take the four-man patrol together. Coordinated takedown, no survivors."

"Roger. Moving to intercept as a team."

Chad and Grey positioned themselves on opposite sides of the patrol route, using hand signals to coordinate their timing. Years of shared combat experience had taught them to work as a seamless unit, each man understanding the other's capabilities and limitations.

The four-man patrol approached in tactical formation, weapons ready but unaware they were walking into a perfectly coordinated ambush. Chad counted down silently with his fingers - three, two, one.

Both agents struck simultaneously. Chad's suppressed rifle took the lead man while Grey eliminated the rear guard. The two middle guards turned toward the threats but found themselves caught in a crossfire with nowhere to run. Within seconds, all four were down without having fired a shot.

"Four down," Chad whispered into his radio.

The main entrance guards were professionals—former military by their posture and equipment, positioned to cover each other's blind spots while maintaining communication with the roving patrols. But they were defending against conventional assault, not elimination by covert operators.

Chad approached from the compound's blind side, using landscaping and architectural features to mask his movement. The guards were focused outward, watching for threats approaching from the jungle rather than from within their own defensive perimeter.

The first guard died with Chad's knife between his ribs, the blade finding the gap in his body armor with surgical precision. Chad caught the body as it fell, lowering it silently behind decorative stonework.

The second guard turned to check on his partner's position, finding Chad's suppressed sidearm instead. One shot to the head, and the main entrance was clear.

"Main entrance secured," Chad reported. "Seven down."

Chad immediately moved to secure the entrance while he was in position. He wrapped the heavy tow chains from the tower around the massive steel doors, using the hooks on each end to create multiple securing points. He pulled the chains as tight as possible, threading them through the door handles and frame in overlapping patterns that would prevent the doors from opening even an inch. Next came the claymore mine—an M18A1 directional anti-personnel weapon positioned to face inward toward the entrance. Anyone who managed to break the chains would walk into a kill zone designed to shred human targets with 700 steel balls moving at 4,000 feet per second.

"Main entrance chained and mined," Chad reported.

Through the radio came Grey's voice: "Eleven down, nineteen to go."

The helicopter sat on its landing pad like a mechanical vulture,

Elena's potential escape route gleaming under security lighting. Chad approached the aircraft with C-4 explosives and remote detonators, planting charges under the passenger seats and in the engine compartment.

Anyone who tried to escape in Elena's helicopter would have a very short flight.

"Helicopter rigged for destruction," Chad confirmed. "Moving to secure emergency exits."

Grey had moved to the compound's north perimeter, where two guards maintained positions near an emergency exit that provided alternate escape routes from the underground conference room. Both men died within seconds of each other, Grey's knife work eliminating threats before they could raise an alarm.

"North exit cleared. Thirteen down, seventeen remaining."

Chad reached the east emergency exit, where a single guard maintained watch over a reinforced door that connected to the compound's lower levels. The man never saw the suppressed bullet that killed him instantly.

Chad chained and secured the east exit, then positioned another claymore mine facing inward. Anyone trying to escape through this route would trigger an explosion designed to turn the doorway into a charnel house.

"East exit secured and mined."

Sam watched the systematic elimination continue, noting that the terrorist summit showed no signs of security awareness. The conference room thermal signatures remained stable, fifty terrorist leaders completely absorbed in coordinating what would be the largest attack on American soil since 9/11.

"Overwatch to Insertion Team. No security alerts detected. Targets remain contained."

"Copy. Grey, status on south perimeter?"

"Three guards eliminated, south exit secured and mined. Fourteen down, sixteen remaining."

Chad moved toward the western section of the compound, where the remaining guards continued their patrols without realizing that half their force had been silently eliminated. The systematic hunting continued—professional soldiers reduced to prey by two ghosts who understood that sometimes justice required operating outside conventional rules.

"West exit secured," Chad reported twenty minutes later. "All primary escape routes chained and mined. Eighteen down, twelve remaining."

"Final sweep for remaining security," Grey confirmed. "Then we wait for the bomber."

Sam maintained her overwatch position, watching Chad and Grey complete the systematic elimination of Elena's protection while the terrorist summit continued planning coordinated attacks on American infrastructure.

In two hours and fifteen minutes, a B-21 Raider would arrive with bunker-busting ordnance powerful enough to penetrate twenty feet of reinforced concrete. The terrorist leaders planning America's destruction would never know what hit them.

Elena Ramirez's fortress had become her tomb. She just didn't know it yet.

Chapter 81

Elena Ramirez Compound
Grand Cayman

C had and Grey completed their systematic elimination of Elena's remaining security forces with the clinical efficiency of professional soldiers who'd spent years perfecting the art of silent warfare. The final guard died without ever knowing that death had come for Elena's fortress, his body joining twenty-nine others scattered around a compound that had become a tomb.

"All security eliminated," Chad reported to Sam. "Thirty down, zero remaining. Compound is secured."

"Copy that," Sam replied from her overwatch position, watching the terrorist summit continue through her thermal scope. "Conference room still shows fifty heat signatures. No indication they know what's happened."

Chad and Grey regrouped at the helicopter pad, where Chad performed final checks on the C-4 charges he'd planted in Elena's escape aircraft. Remote detonators armed, charges positioned for maximum destruction, enough explosive to turn the helicopter into shrapnel if anyone tried to use it for evacuation.

"Overwatch, this is Insertion Leader," Chad spoke into his radio. "Request status update on B-21 arrival."

The CIA operator's voice crackled through their headsets: "Insertion Leader, bomber is one hour fifteen minutes from target. Bunker-buster ordnance confirmed, flight path cleared for precision strike."

"Copy. All exits secured, all security eliminated, targets contained.

Ready for air strike."

Grey settled into a defensive position overlooking the compound's main building, his rifle trained on the reinforced structure where fifty terrorist leaders continued planning coordinated attacks on American infrastructure, completely unaware that their fortress had been turned into an execution chamber.

"Chad," Grey said quietly, "in all our deployments, we never took down anything this significant."

Chad studied the compound through his night vision, thinking about the scope of what they'd accomplished. "Fifty terrorist leaders, representatives from every major cartel and terrorist organization in the Western Hemisphere. When that bomber arrives, we're going to decapitate international terrorism in one strike."

Sam monitored the thermal signatures inside the conference room, noting that the meeting showed no signs of concluding. "They're still actively coordinating. Lots of movement, animated discussions, additional displays being activated."

"What do you think they're planning?" Grey asked.

Chad recalled the intelligence he'd extracted from Javier during the interrogation. "Coordinated infrastructure attacks on twelve American cities. Power grids, transportation hubs, financial centers. Designed to overwhelm federal response capabilities and create maximum casualties."

"And we're about to stop all of it," Sam said with grim satisfaction.

Chad's radio crackled with an incoming transmission from the Miami operations center: "Insertion Leader, this is Miami Base. Bomber is inbound, ETA one hour twelve minutes. Confirm all targets are contained and accounted for."

"Miami Base, this is Insertion Leader. All entrances secured, terrorist leaders confirmed inside main conference room. No indication of security awareness or escape attempts."

"Copy that. Overwatch confirms thermal signatures match expected count. You are cleared to maintain containment until air strike arrival."

Chad checked his watch, calculating the timeline. "Understood, Miami Base. Will maintain overwatch and report any changes in target status."

"Roger. Good work out there, Lloyd."

Sam maintained her surveillance of the terrorist summit, watching thermal signatures move around the conference table where Elena was probably presenting operational timelines and target assignments. Fifty terrorist leaders coordinating the largest attack on American soil since 9/11, never suspecting that their safe haven had become their tomb.

"Chad," Sam said quietly, "do you think Elena knows? About her security being eliminated?"

Chad considered the question, studying the compound's main building where lights continued to burn in the conference room. "Elena's smart enough to know something's wrong if her guards stop reporting. But she's also arrogant enough to believe her fortress is impregnable."

"What if they try to evacuate before the bomber arrives?"

"They can't," Grey replied. "Every exit is chained and mined. Anyone who tries to leave dies in the doorway."

Chad keyed his radio. "Sam, have Miami step up the jamming to 100% communications blackout. I want complete electronic isolation— no cell phones, no internet, no satellite communications. If Elena suspects something, I don't want her able to contact anyone outside that compound."

Sam switched to the Miami frequency. "Miami Base, this is Team Two. Need Agent Kim to initiate full spectrum communications blackout immediately. Complete electronic isolation of the target compound."

"Copy, Team Two," Kim's voice came through clearly. "Walsh, execute full jamming protocols now. Ruiz, kill all internet backbone access to the island. I want zero electronic communications in or out of that compound."

"Initiating full spectrum jamming," Kim reported back to Sam. "Estimate five to ten minutes for complete communications blackout. Cellular is down now, working on satellite and internet backbone."

"Roger, Miami Base. Target will be completely isolated in ten minutes."

Chad checked his watch: one hour and eight minutes until the B-21 arrived with enough explosive power to penetrate twenty feet of reinforced concrete and eliminate every terrorist in the underground bunker.

"Team, now we wait," Chad announced. "Maintain overwatch, monitor for any escape attempts, and prepare for extraction after the air strike."

Sam continued monitoring the thermal signatures inside the conference room, watching Elena coordinate with the world's most dangerous criminals. The terrorist summit showed no signs of concluding, which meant the targets would still be contained when the bomber arrived.

"Overwatch, this is CIA Operations," the voice crackled through their headsets with sudden urgency. "Be advised, thermal shows two heat signatures approaching Team Two's position from the southeast. Range fifty meters and closing."

Sam's blood went cold as she realized they'd missed a patrol. She began to turn toward the approaching threat when a strong hand clamped over her mouth and the cold steel of a knife blade pressed against her throat.

"¡No te muevas!" a voice hissed in Spanish. "FBI puta."

Sam felt her rifle being yanked away as a second figure emerged from the jungle, both guards having approached her overwatch position with the stealth of professionals who'd realized something was wrong when their comrades stopped responding to radio checks.

"Overwatch to Insertion Team," the CIA operator's voice carried alarm. "Team Two has been compromised. Repeat, Agent Belle is in hostile hands."

Through her earpiece, Sam could hear Chad's voice, tight with controlled fury: "Status on Team Two. Immediate response required."

The guard holding the knife to Sam's throat spoke into his radio in rapid Spanish, alerting the compound that they'd captured one of the infiltrators. In the distance, Sam could see lights beginning to activate throughout Elena's fortress as the terrorist summit learned they were under attack.

"Chad," Sam whispered as quietly as possible, "they know. The summit knows."

The knife pressed deeper against her throat, drawing blood.

In the compound below, Elena Ramirez was about to discover that Chad Lloyd had found her fortress. And Sam Belle was about to pay the price for their success.

Chapter 82

Elena Ramirez Compound
Grand Cayman

Chad's world narrowed to a single point of focus as the CIA operator's words echoed through his earpiece: "Agent Belle is in hostile hands." Through his thermal scope, he could see Sam's heat signature surrounded by two guards approximately 200 meters from his position, one figure clearly holding a weapon to her throat.

"Nolan, do you have visual on Team Two?" Chad whispered, his voice carrying the deadly calm of someone shifting into combat mode.

"Affirmative. Two hostiles, one has blade to Sam's neck. Range is 220 meters, partially obscured by vegetation." Grey's sniper training was evident in his clinical assessment. "I can take the shot, but there's risk to Sam if the blade hand spasms."

Chad studied the tactical situation through his own optics, calculating angles and probabilities while lights began flickering on throughout Elena's compound. The terrorist summit was awakening to the reality that their fortress had been infiltrated.

"Negative on the long shot," Chad decided. "Too much risk. I'm going to get closer."

Through the compound's main building, Chad could see increased activity—thermal signatures moving with urgent purpose as Elena's people realized their security network had gone silent. Emergency lighting systems activated, casting harsh illumination across the defensive positions where thirty dead guards would never respond to radio calls.

"Overwatch, this is Insertion Leader," Chad spoke into his radio while beginning his movement toward Sam's position. "What's the status inside the target building?"

"Insertion Leader, thermal shows significant activity increase. Conference room meeting is breaking up, multiple signatures moving toward what appear to be communications areas." The CIA operator's voice carried concern. "Target compound is transitioning to high alert status."

Chad moved through the jungle with predatory silence, closing the distance to Sam's captors while Grey maintained overwatch. Two hundred meters. One hundred fifty. One hundred.

Through his earpiece, Chad could hear Spanish voices as Sam's captors communicated with the compound. The guards had realized that their prisoner was part of a larger infiltration, and they were reporting their discovery to Elena's command structure.

"Chad," Sam's voice came through the radio, barely a whisper. "They're moving me toward the compound. Elena wants to see who's been hunting her."

Chad's jaw tightened as he realized Elena was about to get exactly what she'd wanted since murdering his family—a face-to-face confrontation with the federal agent who'd been tracking her organization.

"Sam, can you create separation from the knife?"

"Negative. Blade is against my carotid artery. Any sudden movement..." Sam's voice trailed off as one of her captors barked orders in Spanish.

Chad reached a position seventy-five meters from Sam's location, close enough to see the tactical situation clearly. Two professional guards, one holding a combat knife to Sam's throat while the other maintained security. Both men positioned to use Sam as a human shield against any rescue attempt.

"Nolan, new plan," Chad whispered into his throat mic. "When I engage the guards, you put precision fire on any armed personnel who emerge from the compound."

"Copy. But Chad, if Elena gets Sam inside that building..."

Chad understood the implication. Once Sam was inside Elena's fortress, rescue would become impossible, especially with a bomber approaching in fifty-eight minutes that would turn the entire compound into a crater.

Through the compound's loudspeaker system, Chad could hear Elena's voice amplified by speakers—speaking in English now, addressing her captive audience of fifty terrorist leaders. With all other communications jammed, the internal PA system was the only way left for her to coordinate with her people.

"My friends, it appears that the American government has finally found our summit. But they have sent only a few agents to stop the largest terrorist operation in history."

Chad felt cold fury building in his chest as Elena's voice continued.

"We have captured one of their infiltrators—a female FBI agent who will tell us exactly how many others are hiding in our jungle. And then we will demonstrate what happens to Americans who interfere with our operations."

The guards began moving Sam toward the compound, using her as a shield while advancing toward the main building where Elena waited. Chad paralleled their movement, staying in the jungle shadows while calculating increasingly desperate rescue options.

"Overwatch, this is Insertion Leader. What's the bomber ETA?"

"Fifty-six minutes to target. Bunker-buster ordnance will eliminate the compound regardless of personnel location."

Chad processed this tactical reality. In fifty-six minutes, Sam would die along with everyone else in Elena's fortress when the B-21's ordnance turned twenty feet of reinforced concrete into rubble. Unless he could extract her before then.

"Chad," Sam's voice came through the radio, tight with pain as the knife pressed deeper. "Don't compromise the mission. Fifty terrorist leaders are more important than one agent."

"Sam, shut up," Chad replied, his voice carrying lethal promise. "You're coming home."

Chad began his final approach toward the compound, knowing that he was about to face Elena Ramirez in the confrontation she'd orchestrated by murdering his family. But first, he had to save the woman that had fallen in love with him from the monster who'd destroyed his life.

Chapter 83

Elena Ramirez Compound
Main Courtyard

C had crept through the jungle undergrowth, closing the distance to Sam's captors as they approached the compound's main entrance. Through his night vision, he could see the chains and claymore mine he'd positioned earlier—deadly obstacles that would kill anyone trying to escape, but also blocking his potential rescue route.

"Fifty meters to the entrance," Chad whispered into his throat mic. "Nolan, do you have clean shots if I create a distraction?"

"Negative. They're using Sam as perfect cover. Any shot risks hitting her."

Chad watched the guards force Sam toward the chained entrance, where they would encounter the claymore mine he'd positioned to face outward. But one of the guards stopped suddenly, his tactical training recognizing the telltale shape of an anti-personnel mine positioned near the entrance. He began shouting warnings in Spanish, pulling Sam backward from the lethal device.

"They've spotted the claymore," Chad whispered. "Moving to secondary position."

Through the compound's speakers, Elena's voice cut through the chaos: "All personnel to defensive positions. We have multiple hostiles on the compound. Secure the conference room and prepare our guests for emergency evacuation."

Chad realized with growing horror that Elena intended to torture Sam in front of fifty terrorist leaders, using her suffering to demonstrate cartel power before coordinating the Friday night attacks on American cities.

"Overwatch, this is Insertion Leader. Request immediate tactical options."

"Insertion Leader, recommend maintaining distance until bomber arrival. Risk to Agent Belle is acceptable compared to mission success."

Chad's jaw tightened at the cold calculation. The CIA was right from a strategic perspective—fifty terrorist leaders were worth more than one federal agent. But Chad wasn't operating from strategic logic anymore.

"Negative, Overwatch. I'm going in."

The guards studied the mine for several moments, then one of them carefully approached from the side, staying out of the kill zone while attempting to disarm or bypass the explosive device. His movements were professional, methodical—someone with combat engineer training.

Chad made his decision. Rising from the jungle undergrowth, he activated the remote detonator for Elena's helicopter, turning the aircraft into a fireball that lit up the night sky and drew every eye toward the explosion.

In the moment of distraction, Chad sprinted toward Sam's position, covering thirty meters of open ground while the guards turned toward the burning wreckage of Elena's escape route.

Chad's knife found the first guard's kidney before the man could react, the blade severing vital organs while his other hand clamped over the terrorist's mouth. The second guard spun toward the threat, but Chad was already moving, his suppressed sidearm coughing twice into center mass.

Sam rolled away from her dead captors, blood streaming from the knife cut on her throat but alive and mobile.

"Are you hit?" Chad demanded, checking her for wounds.

"Surface cut, I'm fine," Sam gasped, retrieving her rifle from where the guards had dropped it. "Chad, they know something's wrong. Elena's been trying to reach her security teams for the past hour, and when nobody responded, she started preparing evacuation protocols."

Chad felt his stomach tighten. If Elena suspected a major threat, she'd try to evacuate her terrorist allies as a precaution, even without knowing about the incoming air strike.

"How much do they know?"

"They know their entire security force is gone and that professional operators are on the island. Elena's assuming worst-case scenario and trying to get everyone out through emergency tunnels."

Chad's mind processed this new intelligence. Elena's compound wasn't just a fortress—it was connected to underground escape routes that would allow the terrorist leaders to scatter before the bombing.

"Overwatch, this is Insertion Leader. Targets may be attempting evacuation through unknown tunnel systems."

"Copy, Insertion Leader. Thermal shows significant movement in lower levels of compound. Multiple signatures moving toward what appear to be subsurface areas."

Chad stared at the compound where fifty terrorist leaders were potentially escaping through routes he'd never identified, carrying plans to kill thousands of Americans in coordinated attacks.

"Sam, can you move?"

"I'm fine. What's the plan?"

Chad looked at the chained entrance, the claymore mine he'd positioned, and the burning helicopter that had eliminated Elena's air escape option. "We go in. Stop them from reaching those tunnels."

"Chad, that's suicide. There are fifty armed terrorists in there, plus however many guards they have left."

"Then we make sure none of them leave alive." Chad checked his weapons and equipment, calculating ammunition and explosives against the number of targets he needed to eliminate. "Nolan, what's your position?"

"Overwatch with clear sightlines to compound. I can provide covering fire."

Chad approached the compound entrance, unwrapping the heavy tow chains he had secured around the steel doors and carefully disarming the claymore mine. The main doors swung open, revealing a corridor that led deeper into Elena's fortress.

"Overwatch, this is Insertion Leader. We're going in to prevent terrorist evacuation. Maintain surveillance and coordinate with bomber."

"Insertion Leader, you are walking into a fortress full of armed hostiles. Recommend waiting for air strike."

"Negative. If they escape through those tunnels, they'll coordinate Friday night attacks from other locations." Chad looked at Sam, seeing determination rather than fear in her eyes. "Time to finish what Elena started when she murdered my family."

Chad and Sam entered Elena's compound, moving deeper into the fortress where the world's most dangerous criminals were preparing to escape justice. Ahead of them lay a maze of corridors, heavily armed terrorists, and the woman who'd orchestrated this entire confrontation by murdering Lana and Casey.

Behind them, a B-21 Raider approached with enough explosive power to level mountains.

But first, Chad Lloyd was going to ensure that Elena Ramirez and her terrorist allies never left Grand Cayman alive.

Chapter 84

Elena Ramirez Compound
Main Corridor

Chad and Sam moved through Elena's fortress like ghosts, their suppressed weapons ready as they navigated corridors designed to confuse and channel intruders into kill zones. Emergency lighting cast harsh shadows across marble floors that had probably cost more than most federal agents made in a lifetime.

"Forty-five minutes until bomber arrival," Sam whispered, checking her watch while they approached a junction that led deeper into the compound.

Chad studied the architectural layout, noting multiple levels descending into the hillside where Elena's conference room was located. Somewhere below them, fifty terrorist leaders were being evacuated through tunnel systems he'd never identified during reconnaissance.

"Movement ahead," Chad reported, hearing voices echoing from a stairwell that descended toward the lower levels. "Multiple contacts, heading downward."

They reached the stairwell to find chaos—terrorist leaders and their security personnel moving in urgent columns toward what appeared to be emergency evacuation routes. Chad recognized faces from federal wanted posters: cartel bosses, ISIS commanders, Taliban leaders, all the criminals he'd spent years hunting now gathered in one location.

"Jesus," Sam breathed, studying the targets through her thermal scope. "It's like a convention of America's most wanted."

Chad counted approximately thirty figures still moving through the evacuation route, which meant twenty others had already reached the tunnel systems. Time was running out to prevent their escape.

Chad pulled a fragmentation grenade from his tactical vest, calculating the throw into the crowded stairwell below. "Sam, cover your ears."

The grenade bounced off the concrete walls and detonated among the terrorist column, the explosion echoing through the compound like thunder. Screams and shouts in multiple languages filled the stairwell as shrapnel tore through the packed evacuation route.

"Frag out worked," Chad reported grimly, watching thermal signatures disappear from his scope. "Estimate twelve to fifteen targets eliminated."

"Jesus," Sam breathed, studying the carnage through her thermal scope. "That's half the remaining evacuation."

But the explosion had also alerted everyone in the compound to their presence. Emergency lighting began flashing as Elena's remaining security forces converged on their location.

"This is Insertion Leader," Chad spoke into his throat mic. "We have visual on terrorist evacuation in progress. Request immediate support."

"Copy, Insertion Leader. I'm moving to compound perimeter. Can provide overwatch on exit points if you can identify tunnel locations."

Chad and Sam began their descent into Elena's fortress, following the terrorist column while staying out of sight. The architecture became more utilitarian as they moved deeper—reinforced concrete walls, steel blast doors, the kind of construction designed to survive military assault.

"This place is built like a bunker," Sam observed. "Elena was planning for this kind of scenario."

They reached the lower level to find themselves in a maze of corridors that connected to multiple exit points. Chad could hear Spanish and Arabic voices echoing from different directions as terrorist groups moved toward separate escape routes.

"They're splitting up," Chad realized. "Multiple tunnel systems, different exit points. Even if we stop some of them, others will escape."

Sam studied the corridor layout, noting directional signs in multiple languages that indicated emergency evacuation procedures. "Chad, if we can reach the central control room, we might be able to seal the tunnels electronically."

"Where?"

Sam pointed to a heavily reinforced door marked with warning signs in Spanish and English: "AUTHORIZED PERSONNEL ONLY - EMERGENCY SYSTEMS."

Chad approached the control room, noting the electronic lock and security cameras that monitored access. Through the reinforced window, he could see multiple screens showing tunnel layouts and evacuation status.

"That's our target. If we can lock down those tunnels—"

A voice behind them spoke in perfect English: "Agent Chad Lloyd. The man who murdered my father."

Chad spun to find Elena Ramirez standing at the far end of the corridor, flanked by six heavily armed guards. She was smaller than he'd expected but carried herself with the authority of someone who'd built a criminal empire through intelligence and ruthlessness.

"Elena," Chad said quietly, his weapon trained on the woman who'd murdered his family.

"You've caused me considerable inconvenience, Agent Lloyd. Thirty dead guards, a destroyed helicopter, and now my carefully planned summit interrupted by two federal agents who should have died weeks ago."

Sam positioned herself to cover the guards while keeping her rifle trained on Elena. "Chad, we need to reach that control room."

"Oh, you won't be reaching anything," Elena replied with cold satisfaction. "My friends are already safely in the tunnels, and you're about to join your wife and daughter."

Chad felt fury building in his chest, but his voice remained steady. "Elena, you murdered 284 federal family members to draw me into hunting you. Congratulations. You found me."

"I found you, and I'm going to kill you the same way I killed them. Slowly, painfully, while recording every moment for the world to see."

Elena gestured to her guards, who began advancing with weapons raised. "But first, your partner dies. I want you to watch another woman you care about suffer because of your arrogance."

Chad calculated the tactical situation—six guards with automatic weapons, Elena positioned behind cover, approximately forty feet of corridor between them. The control room was twenty feet to his left, but reaching it would require exposing himself to concentrated fire.

"Sam," Chad whispered, "when I move, get to that control room. Lock down the tunnels."

"Chad, there are six of them—"

"I've got this. Stop the evacuation."

Chad stepped forward, his weapon steady despite the overwhelming odds. "Elena, you want me? Here I am. Let's finish what you started in my dining room."

Elena smiled with predatory satisfaction. "Kill the woman first. I want Lloyd to watch."

The guards raised their weapons toward Sam as Chad made his choice. Twenty years of military training, two years of hunting Elena's organization, and two weeks of being hunted by his own government had led to this moment.

Time to end it.

Chapter 85

Elena Ramirez Compound
Lower Level Corridor

The corridor erupted in gunfire as Elena's guards opened up with automatic weapons, their muzzle flashes strobing in the emergency lighting while concrete chips exploded from the walls around Chad and Sam. Chad dove behind a marble pillar, dragging Sam with him as bullets chewed chunks from their cover.

"Suppressive fire!" Chad shouted over the din. "Keep them pinned while I move to the control room!"

Sam's rifle began its steady rhythm, her suppressed shots forcing Elena's guards to take cover while Chad sprinted toward the reinforced door marked "EMERGENCY SYSTEMS." Twenty feet of open corridor under direct fire, but the only way to stop the remaining terrorists from escaping through the tunnel network.

Chad's shoulder slammed into the electronic lock, his combat knife jamming into the mechanism while bullets sparked off the steel door frame. The lock shattered under his assault, and Chad rolled into the control room as automatic weapons fire chewed the doorway behind him.

The room was a maze of monitors and control panels showing tunnel layouts, evacuation status, and security systems throughout Elena's compound. Chad could see thermal signatures moving through multiple escape routes—the remaining terrorists were less than ten minutes from reaching exit points that would scatter them across the Caribbean.

"Sam, status!" Chad called out while studying the tunnel control systems.

"Six hostiles still active! Elena's behind cover directing fire!"

Chad found the tunnel control panel and began systematically shutting down escape routes. Steel blast doors slammed closed throughout the underground network, trapping the remaining terrorists in corridors that would become tombs when the B-21's bunker-busters arrived.

"Tunnels sealed!" Chad reported. "All remaining targets contained!"

Through the control room's reinforced window, Chad could see Elena screaming orders at her guards, her carefully planned evacuation collapsing as her terrorist allies found themselves trapped in her own fortress.

Chad emerged from the control room with a fresh magazine, his assault rifle tracking toward Elena's position. "Elena! It's over! Your people are trapped, your compound is surrounded, and a bomber is thirty minutes out!"

Elena's voice carried across the corridor with cold fury: "Agent Lloyd! You think killing my guards and sealing my tunnels ends this? I have backup plans you can't imagine!"

"Then you better start imagining a coffin!" Chad replied, moving to flank Elena's position while Sam maintained suppressive fire.

Elena's remaining guards were professionals, but they were defending a fixed position against two federal agents who'd spent the night systematically eliminating superior forces. Chad's grenade had shaken their confidence, and Sam's precision shooting was reducing their numbers one shot at a time.

"Four hostiles remaining!" Sam called out. "Elena's trying to reach another corridor!"

Chad saw Elena moving toward what appeared to be a private elevator—probably her personal escape route to a different tunnel system he hadn't identified. If she reached it, she could still escape before the bombing.

"Not happening," Chad muttered, pulling his last fragmentation grenade.

The explosion in Elena's corridor eliminated two more guards and collapsed part of the ceiling, blocking Elena's access to her private elevator. She was trapped in the lower level with Chad and Sam, exactly where Chad had wanted her since the night she murdered his family.

"Two guards left!" Sam reported. "Elena's pinned behind that pillar!"

Chad moved through the smoke and debris, his rifle ready as he approached Elena's position. "Elena Ramirez!" Chad called out. "You murdered my wife and daughter! You murdered 282 other federal family members! Time to pay the bill!"

Elena's voice came from behind her marble cover, no longer commanding but defiant: "You want me, Lloyd? Come and take me!"

The last two guards emerged from cover with weapons blazing, choosing to die fighting rather than surrender to federal agents. Chad and Sam's coordinated fire cut them down before they could advance five feet.

That left Elena alone, trapped in her own fortress while a B-21 Raider approached with enough explosive power to turn twenty feet of reinforced concrete into dust.

"It's over, Elena," Chad announced, moving toward her position with his rifle trained on her cover. "Your guards are dead, your terrorists are trapped, and in twenty-eight minutes this entire compound becomes a crater."

Elena emerged from behind the pillar with her hands raised, but Chad could see the small device in her right palm—probably a dead man's switch connected to explosives throughout the compound.

"Agent Lloyd," Elena said with cold satisfaction, "if I die, this entire complex detonates immediately. Your partner dies with us, and my terrorist allies have already escaped through routes you'll never find."

Chad studied Elena's face, reading the desperate gambit of someone who'd finally run out of options. "You're lying. I sealed all the tunnels."

"You sealed the tunnels I wanted you to find. Did you really think I'd build only one escape route?" Elena's smile was predatory. "Half my people are already free, and they're carrying attack plans that will kill thousands of Americans."

Sam maintained her position, rifle trained on Elena while monitoring the tactical situation. "Chad, we need to get out of here before that bomber arrives."

"No," Chad replied, his weapon steady despite the dead man's switch. "Elena dies here. Tonight. For Lana and Casey and all the other families she murdered."

Elena laughed, the sound echoing off the concrete walls. "Then we all die together, Agent Lloyd. Just like I planned from the beginning."

The final confrontation had arrived. Chad Lloyd was face-to-face with the woman who'd murdered his family, and only one of them would survive Elena's fortress.

But first, he had to decide if justice was worth dying for.

Chapter 86

Elena Ramirez Compound
Lower Level Corridor

Chad had stared at Elena across twenty feet of smoke-filled corridor, his rifle trained on the woman who'd murdered his family while she held a dead man's switch that could kill them all. The mathematics of justice had never been more brutal—Elena's death in exchange for Sam's life, with twenty-six minutes until a bomber turned the entire compound into rubble.

"Chad," Sam whispered, her voice steady despite the tactical situation. "Take the shot. Don't let her escape because of me."

"How touching," Elena said with cold satisfaction. "Agent Lloyd has found another woman to love, just in time to watch her die for his mistakes."

Chad's finger tightened on the trigger as fury built in his chest. "Elena, you murdered my wife and daughter because I was doing my job. You turned fifty terrorist leaders into targets by gathering them in one location. The only mistake here was thinking you were smart enough to outplay the United States government."

Elena's laugh echoed off the concrete walls. "Outplay? Agent Lloyd, I've been playing you since the moment my father died. Every step of your investigation, every piece of intelligence you discovered, every path that led you to this island—all of it orchestrated to bring you here."

"To what end?" Chad demanded, his weapon unwavering.

"To prove that American justice is an illusion. To show the world that your government will sacrifice its own agents to protect political interests." Elena's voice carried vindictive satisfaction. "You spent weeks being hunted by the FBI while I coordinated the largest terrorist operation in history. Even now, your bomber is approaching to kill American agents along with terrorists."

Chad felt pieces clicking into place—Elena's real strategy had never been to escape, but to create a scenario where the U.S. government would be forced to kill its own people to stop her operation.

"You wanted me to find this compound," Chad realized. "You wanted federal agents inside when the bombing happened."

"I wanted to demonstrate that America will murder its heroes to stop its enemies. That your precious justice system is willing to sacrifice anyone for political convenience." Elena's smile was predatory. "When that bomber arrives, it will kill two federal agents along with the terrorists. The headlines will write themselves."

Sam maintained her position, understanding the psychological warfare Elena was conducting. "Chad, she's trying to manipulate you into questioning the mission."

"The mission is right," Chad replied, his voice carrying cold certainty. "Fifty terrorist leaders die tonight, even if we die with them. Sometimes justice requires sacrifice."

Elena's expression shifted from satisfaction to surprise. She'd expected Chad to prioritize Sam's life over the mission, to prove her point about American moral weakness.

"You would sacrifice your partner for revenge?"

"I would sacrifice myself for justice," Chad corrected. "There's a difference."

Chad's radio crackled with Grey's voice: "Insertion Leader, I have movement at the compound's north perimeter. Multiple figures emerging from concealed tunnel exits. Elena was right—some targets have escaped."

Chad felt his jaw tighten. Elena had been telling the truth about backup escape routes. Some of the terrorist leaders were already free.

"How many?" Chad asked.

"Approximately fifteen individuals, moving toward what appears to be a concealed boat dock on the north shore. They're trying to escape by water." Grey paused. "Chad, I can confirm Hector Ramirez is leading the group. Elena's brother is trying to get the leadership off the island."

Elena's smile returned. "Agent Lloyd, even if you kill me, Hector has half my allies with him. They have fast boats waiting, and once they reach international waters, your jurisdiction ends. My brother will continue our work."

Chad studied Elena's face, reading the satisfaction of someone who believed she'd won regardless of the outcome. But Elena had made one crucial miscalculation—she'd assumed Chad was operating alone.

"Elena, you're forgetting something important," Chad said, his voice carrying quiet confidence.

"What's that?"

"I'm not the only one hunting your people."

Chad keyed his radio. "Overwatch, this is Insertion Leader. Request immediate engagement of escaping targets at north shore boat dock."

The CIA operator's response was immediate: "Copy, Insertion Leader. Reaper drone has visual on fifteen targets approaching dock. Coast Guard cutters are moving to intercept, and Hellfire missiles are armed and ready."

Elena's expression shifted to alarm as she realized the scope of the trap that had been prepared. "You can't—"

"Overwatch, you are cleared hot. Eliminate all escaping targets before they reach the water."

Through the compound's reinforced walls, Chad could hear the distant explosions as Hellfire missiles turned Elena's boat dock into smoking wreckage. Fifteen of the world's most dangerous criminals, eliminated before they could escape Grand Cayman.

"Targets eliminated," the CIA operator reported. "All fifteen hostiles confirmed KIA, including Hector Ramirez. No survivors detected."

Elena stared at Chad with dawning horror. "You murdered them all. You murdered my brother."

"I stopped them from murdering thousands of Americans," Chad replied. "Just like I'm about to stop you."

Elena's hand tightened on the dead man's switch. "If I die, this compound explodes. Your partner dies with us."

Chad looked at Sam, seeing determination rather than fear in her eyes. She nodded slightly, giving him permission to take the shot that would end Elena's life and potentially theirs.

"Elena," Chad said quietly, "you murdered my wife and daughter. You planned to murder thousands more Americans." Chad's voice carried the weight of absolute judgment. "Justice doesn't negotiate with terrorists."

Chad's rifle coughed once. The suppressed round took Elena right between the eyes—exactly where he'd shot her father two years ago in that Colombian warehouse. The ironic precision wasn't lost on Chad as Elena's body crumpled backward against the marble pillar. The dead man's switch fell from her nerveless fingers, clattering on the floor without detonating.

Elena's body crumpled to the floor, killed instantly by Chad's precise shot. There would be no dying speeches, no final threats, no dramatic last words. Just the sudden, final silence of justice delivered with military precision.

Chad approached his family's killer, looking down at the woman who had ordered Lana and Casey's torture. After weeks of hunting, after losing everything he'd cared about, Elena Ramirez was finally dead.

Justice had been served with a single, well-placed bullet.

"Overwatch, this is Insertion Leader," Chad spoke into his radio, his voice steady despite the magnitude of what he'd accomplished. "Primary target eliminated. Elena and Hector Ramirez confirmed KIA. All terrorist leaders confirmed dead or contained. Mission complete."

"Copy, Insertion Leader. Outstanding work. Bomber is fifteen minutes out—recommend immediate extraction."

Chad looked at Sam, who was checking Elena's body to confirm the kill. "How do you feel about getting out of here before twenty thousand pounds of explosives turn this place into a parking lot?"

Sam smiled, the first genuine expression of joy Chad had seen from her in weeks. "I thought you'd never ask."

They moved toward the compound's exit, leaving Elena Ramirez's body in the fortress she'd built to coordinate America's destruction. Behind them, thirty-five terrorist leaders remained trapped in the sealed tunnel systems, waiting for twenty thousand pounds of bunker-busting ordnance to end their plans for American destruction.

Ahead of them lay whatever future Chad and Sam could build together, free from the shadows of murdered families and government corruption.

Chapter 87

Elena Ramirez Compound
Jungle Perimeter

Chad and Sam emerged from Elena's fortress into the humid Caribbean night, moving quickly through the compound's courtyard while emergency lighting cast eerie shadows across the bodies of thirty guards who would never again protect terrorist operations. Behind them, the sealed blast doors held thirty-five of the world's most dangerous criminals in underground tunnels that would become their tombs in ten minutes.

"This is Insertion Leader," Chad spoke into his radio as they reached the jungle tree line. "Package is complete. Elena Ramirez is KIA, all terrorist targets contained. Moving to extraction point."

"Copy, Insertion Leader. I'm falling back to the airstrip to wait for the ERT teams and federal backup. We can take shelter in the control tower structure to stay clear of the blast radius."

Chad checked his watch—eight minutes until the B-21's bunker-busters turned Elena's compound into a crater that would be visible from orbit. They'd covered two miles of jungle terrain during their infiltration, but extraction meant following the same route in reverse while racing against incoming ordnance.

Two miles in eight minutes through jungle terrain," Chad muttered, calculating the impossible timeline. "We need transportation."

"Over here," Sam called out, spotting something at the compound's perimeter. "Two dirt bikes from the security patrol."

Chad saw the Honda motorcycles parked near where they'd

eliminated the outer guards. Keys still in the ignitions, fuel tanks full.

"That'll get us to the airstrip in four minutes," Chad said, swinging his leg over one bike. "Follow my route, stay close."

The engines roared to life as they raced through jungle paths toward the extraction point.

"How's your throat?" Chad asked Sam as they began racing through the dense vegetation.

Sam touched the knife wound on her neck, feeling dried blood but no active bleeding. "I'll live. How does it feel to finally get justice for Lana and Casey?"

Chad considered the question as they navigated through jungle undergrowth, following GPS coordinates toward the airstrip. "Empty. I thought killing Elena would bring them back somehow, but they're still gone."

"But the people who murdered them are dead," Sam pointed out. "And thousands of Americans who would have died in Friday's attacks are going to live."

They pushed deeper into the jungle, using night vision to avoid obstacles while maintaining tactical spacing. In the distance, Chad could hear voices echoing from the compound—the trapped terrorists calling for help that would never arrive.

"Overwatch, this is Insertion Leader," Chad radioed. "What's the bomber's ETA?"

"Six minutes to target, Insertion Leader. Recommend you clear the immediate area. Bunker-buster ordnance will create significant blast radius."

Chad and Sam increased their pace, knowing that GBU-57 bombs carried enough explosive power to level city blocks. Elena's reinforced compound would absorb most of the energy, but the shock wave would still be dangerous within a mile radius.

"There," Sam pointed ahead, where they could see lights from the airstrip cutting through the jungle darkness. "Half a mile to extraction."

Chad gunned the dirt bike's engine, weaving between trees as they raced through the jungle paths toward the control tower. Behind them, the compound's emergency lighting continued to strobe, marking the location where Elena Ramirez had planned America's destruction and found her own death instead.

"Insertion Team, this is Grey," came the voice through their radio. "I'm at the control tower. Area is secure and I have eyes on the bomber's approach vector."

"Four minutes out," Chad replied, the motorcycle's engine roaring as they covered the final distance. "We're almost to you."

"Copy. Tower provides good blast protection - we should be safe from the shock wave in here."

Chad and Sam roared into the airstrip clearing, their dirt bikes kicking up clouds of dust as they skidded to a stop near the control tower structure. Grey was positioned at an upper window, his sniper rifle providing overwatch of the surrounding area.

"Three minutes!" Chad called out as they abandoned the motorcycles and sprinted toward the tower. "Everyone inside now!"

They reached the concrete structure just as Chad's radio crackled with an incoming transmission.

"Overwatch, this is Insertion Leader. We are clear of the target area and in protective cover. Execute bombing mission."

"Copy, Insertion Leader. B-21 is on final approach. Weapons hot."

The bomber was invisible in the darkness above Grand Cayman, but Chad could imagine the pilot's final preparations—target confirmation, weapons systems check, the moment when twenty thousand pounds of bunker-busting ordnance would fall toward Elena's fortress.

"There," Grey pointed through the tower window. "Twelve o'clock."

Chad watched two streaks of light descend toward Elena's compound like falling stars, the GBU-57 bombs approaching their target with mathematical precision. For a moment, the night was silent except for the distant hum of insects.

Then the island exploded.

The bunker-busters penetrated twenty feet of reinforced concrete before detonating, the explosions creating a fireball that lit up the Caribbean sky like a miniature sun. Elena's fortress simply ceased to exist, vaporized along with every terrorist leader who'd been planning coordinated attacks on American cities.

The shock wave hit the control tower moments later, the concrete structure shuddering as atmospheric pressure waves rolled across the island. The windows rattled violently, but the solid construction protected them from the devastating blast effects.

"Jesus," Sam breathed, watching the mushroom cloud rise above where Elena's compound had been. "It's like a nuclear explosion."

"Bunker-busters aren't subtle," Chad replied, studying the destruction below. "But they're effective."

"Overwatch, this is Insertion Leader," Chad spoke into his radio. "Confirm target destruction."

"Target eliminated, Insertion Leader. Thermal imaging shows complete destruction of compound and all subsurface structures. No survivors detected."

Chad felt a weight lifting from his shoulders as he realized the magnitude of what they'd accomplished. Elena Ramirez was dead. Javier Santos was dead. Fifty terrorist leaders who'd been planning coordinated attacks on American infrastructure were dead. The largest terrorist threat in American history had been eliminated in one night.

"ERT teams are inbound," Grey reported, monitoring his radio. "Twenty minutes out for cleanup and evidence collection."

"Sam," Chad said quietly, "what happens now?"

Sam looked at the man who'd been through hell to get justice for his murdered family, then chose to save her life instead of pursuing personal revenge. "Now we wait for extraction. And we figure out how to live with being the good guys again."

Chad settled against the tower wall, watching the glow on the horizon fade as emergency response teams prepared to secure the area. Elena Ramirez's war against American families was over. The debt for Lana and Casey's murder had been paid in full.

For the first time in weeks, Chad Lloyd could rest knowing justice had been served. The mission was complete.

Chapter 88

C had Lloyd stood before the floor-to-ceiling windows of Director Brad Huntington's office, watching the morning sun illuminate the nation's capital while reflecting on how much his world had changed since Elena Ramirez murdered his family. The man who'd spent weeks as a hunted fugitive was now being honored as the agent who'd prevented the largest terrorist attack in American history.

Around the conference table sat the entire PHOENIX task force— Agents Ruiz, Kim, Walsh, Martinez, Grey, and Sam—all the federal agents who'd risked their careers to support Chad's mission when Janet Holmes was hunting him instead of hunting terrorists.

"Team," Huntington said from behind his desk, "the President wants to personally thank all of you for your service. The coordinated attacks Elena planned would have killed thousands of Americans and crippled our infrastructure for months."

Chad turned from the window, noting the stack of commendation letters and award recommendations that covered Huntington's desk. "Sir, we were just doing our jobs. Elena made it personal when she murdered federal families."

"You eliminated fifty-three terrorist leaders in one operation. ISIS, Taliban, Al-Qaeda, and every major cartel in the hemisphere." Huntington's voice carried genuine respect. "Agent Grey, Agent Lloyd, Agent Belle—your on-site actions deserve the highest recognition. But this mission succeeded because the entire team supported it, even when that support meant defying corrupt leadership."

Huntington looked at each team member individually. "Agents Ruiz, Kim, Walsh, and Martinez—your refusal to participate in Holmes' unauthorized manhunt, your intelligence support during the mission, and your courage in exposing corruption within federal law enforcement exemplifies the highest standards of the FBI."

Sam Belle sat in one of the leather chairs facing Huntington's desk, her throat wound healed but leaving a thin scar that would forever remind her of their mission together. She'd spent the past two weeks debriefing intelligence analysts about Elena's network and testifying before congressional committees about Janet Holmes' corruption.

"What's the status on Holmes' prosecution?" Sam asked.

"Treason, conspiracy, accepting bribes from terrorist organizations, and about a dozen other federal charges," Huntington replied with satisfaction. "She'll spend the rest of her life in federal prison, assuming she survives that long. Turns out other inmates don't appreciate federal agents who work for terrorists."

Chad felt a grim satisfaction at Holmes' fate. The woman who'd hunted him while protecting his family's killers was now facing the justice she'd tried to deny others.

"Director, what about the families?" Chad asked. "The other victims of Elena's attacks?"

"Full federal support for all survivors. Counseling, financial assistance, whatever they need." Huntington's expression grew serious, then shifted to satisfaction. "Chad, we also seized the fifty million dollars Elena paid Holmes for her corruption. That money is being used to establish a victim support fund and educational scholarships in the names of all 284 family members who were murdered."

Chad felt a surge of poetic justice. "Elena's blood money supporting the families she destroyed."

"The Lana and Casey Lloyd Memorial Scholarship will provide full college funding for children who've lost parents to terrorist attacks," Huntington continued. "Elena thought she could buy our system. Instead, her money will educate the next generation of Americans who'll stand against terrorism."

Sam wiped tears from her eyes. "That's... that's perfect. Lana would have loved knowing her death helped other children get an education."

"We failed those families when we didn't move fast enough against Elena's organization," Huntington acknowledged. "But Elena's own money will ensure we never forget them, and that their sacrifice leads to something positive."

Agent Grey knocked on the office door and entered, carrying a tablet with intelligence updates. He'd been promoted to Deputy Director of Counterterrorism Operations, a position that would let him ensure the FBI actually hunted terrorists instead of hunting heroes.

"Chad, Sam," Grey nodded to his former teammates. "Thought you'd want to know—Ricardo Valdez has been officially cleared of all charges and hired as a CIA contractor. Turns out the Agency values pilots who've been gathering intelligence on cartel operations for thirty years."

Chad smiled, thinking about the man who'd waited twenty-eight years for justice and finally helped deliver it. "He earned it. What about Tony Kowalski?"

"All charges dropped, public apology from the Bureau, and a medal for providing material support to federal counterterrorism operations." Grey's weathered face showed satisfaction.

Huntington stood and walked to a wall safe, removing two small boxes that contained the kind of recognition reserved for the highest levels of federal service.

"Agent Lloyd, Agent Belle, the President has authorized the Presidential Medal of Freedom for your actions on Grand Cayman. You prevented coordinated attacks that would have killed thousands of Americans and eliminated the leadership structure of international terrorism."

Chad accepted the medal box, feeling the weight of recognition he'd never expected to receive. two months ago, he'd been a grieving father planning his family's funeral. Now he was being honored for preventing a national catastrophe.

"Sir, there's something I need to discuss," Chad said, his voice carrying the weight of a decision he'd been considering for weeks.

"What's that?"

"Sam and I would like to accept positions under Grey's new counterterrorism division. The PHOENIX task force has proven that when used properly we can prevent attacks like Elena's."

Huntington smiled with obvious relief. "Chad, you're the most effective counterterrorism agent in Bureau history. I was hoping you'd stay."

"The country still has enemies," Chad replied. "And now we have a team that knows how to find them and stop them before they can hurt American families."

Sam leaned forward. "Director, we'd like to continue the PHOENIX mission. Hunt the next threat to the United States before it becomes the next Elena Ramirez."

Grey nodded approvingly. "I can't think of two better agents to lead field operations for the new division."

As the meeting began to wind down, Chad caught Sam's eye and nodded toward the hallway. They stepped outside the Director's office, finding a quiet corner away from the bustle of FBI headquarters.

"Sam," Chad began, his voice quiet but steady, "I need to say something before we go back in there."

Sam looked at him with those intelligent eyes that had seen him at his worst and somehow still believed in his capacity for good. "What is it?"

"I know there's... something between us. I felt it during the mission, and I think you did too." Chad ran a hand through his hair, struggling to find the right words. "But I'm not in the right headspace to even think about a relationship right now. It's only been a couple of months since I buried my wife and daughter, and I spent that whole time consumed with revenge instead of grief."

Sam's expression softened with understanding. "Chad, you don't have to explain—"

"Yes, I do. Because you deserve honesty." Chad met her gaze directly. "You kept your promise to Lana. You've been making sure I see the good in life, not just the darkness. And maybe... maybe someday I'll be ready to build something new. But right now, I need time to properly mourn my family and figure out who I am when I'm not hunting killers."

Sam nodded slowly. "I understand. And I'll wait, Chad. However long you need."

"That's not fair to ask of you."

"You're not asking. I'm choosing." Sam's voice carried quiet conviction. "Lana was my best friend, and she'd want me to make sure you heal properly. And when you're ready—if you're ready—I'll still be here."

Chad felt a weight lift from his shoulders, grateful for her understanding. "Thank you. For everything. For keeping your promise to her."

They returned to the Director's office, where Chad made his next request.

"However," Chad continued, "I am requesting thirty days of administrative leave first."

"Any particular reason?" Huntington asked.

Chad was quiet for a moment, choosing his words carefully. "Sir, I need time to properly grieve my family. It's only been a few months since I buried Lana and Casey, and I've spent that entire time hunting their killers instead of processing their loss."

Sam nodded understandingly. "Chad needs space to heal. This mission consumed everything—there was no time to actually mourn."

"I need to find a house of my own, somewhere I can remember them without the constant pressure of federal operations," Chad continued. "Maybe try writing fiction based on my experiences. Just... normal things that help me figure out who Chad Lloyd is when he's not hunting terrorists."

Huntington's expression softened. "Of course. Take all the time you need, Chad. Grief doesn't follow operational timelines."

"And after that?" Grey asked.

Chad's expression grew serious. "After that, I come back and make sure no one else has to bury their family because we weren't fast enough to stop the bad guys."

Chad stood to leave, but Huntington called out one final question.

"Chad, do you think Elena won? She wanted to prove that American justice was an illusion, that our system would sacrifice heroes to stop villains."

Chad considered the question, thinking about the weeks he'd spent hunted by his own government while Elena coordinated terrorist attacks. But he also thought about Huntington firing Holmes, Grey taking command of counterterrorism operations, and the fifty-three terrorist leaders who'd died in Elena's compound.

"No, sir. Elena lost because she misunderstood what American justice actually means. It's not about perfect systems or flawless institutions. It's about good people who refuse to give up, even when their own government hunts them for doing the right thing."

Chad paused at the door, looking back at the Director who'd finally chosen to support justice over politics.

"Elena thought she could break our system by corrupting individual agents. But the system isn't the buildings or the bureaucracy—it's the people who believe in protecting innocent lives. And those people can't be bought, corrupted, or broken."

Epilogue

Chad had walked alone through Oak Hill's perfectly maintained grounds, following a path that led to the section where America's heroes were laid to rest. The autumn air was crisp and clean, carrying the scent of fallen leaves and the promise of winter.

He stopped at two graves marked with granite headstones that made his chest tighten with gratitude: "Lana Marie Lloyd, Beloved Wife and Mother" and "Casey Elizabeth Lloyd, Beloved Daughter and Joy of Our Lives." Below Lana's name, the inscription read "Loving Husband and Father" - the Thompsons had understood what Chad was trying to do and ensured the final headstones reflected his love.

Chad knelt between the graves, placing fresh flowers on each. The cemetery was silent except for the distant sound of traffic from the city where he had spent six weeks being hunted for seeking justice.

"I got them," Chad said quietly to the headstones. "Elena, Javier, Hector, all of them. The people who hurt you are dead, and they'll never hurt anyone else's family."

He sat back on his heels, feeling the weight of everything that had happened since that terrible night when his world had ended.

"Sam kept her promise to you, Lana. She's been making sure I see the good in life, not just the bad. She risked everything to help me find justice, and now she's trying to help me find peace." Chad's voice grew softer. "She won't let me disappear into the darkness. Just like you never would have."

The wind rustled through the trees, and for a moment Chad could almost hear Casey's laughter, almost feel Lana's hand on his shoulder.

"I don't know what comes next. I don't know how to live without you both. But I'm going to try to figure it out. I'm going to take some time. Write about what happened, maybe. Try to make sense of it all. Try to remember who I was before I became someone who hunts killers."

Chad stood slowly, his knees stiff from kneeling on the cold ground. He looked at his family's graves one final time.

"I love you both. And I'm going to try to live the kind of life you'd be proud of."

He walked away from the cemetery alone, leaving behind the graves of the family he'd lost and moving toward whatever future he could build from the pieces Elena Ramirez had left behind.

Chad Lloyd was going home. Not to an empty house filled with memories of the dead, but to a life filled with possibilities for the living.

The war was over. The debt was paid. And for the first time in weeks, Chad Lloyd was truly free to grieve.

About the Author

C.E. O'Neil is a storyteller at heart who believes the best books are the ones you can't put down. Crimson Phoenix is his debut novel - a dream years in the making. He writes to create moments that keep readers turning pages late into the night and characters who stay with you long after the story ends.

He lives in Wyoming with his wife and three cats.